MW00929947

Lost Treasures of the Heart

To Patti

Thanks for sharing
the life of our heroin
Kate. Our dreams our
often actually our
ancestors past. Enjoy the
moment. *[signature]*

A Red Sky Presents Book/published by arrangement with the authors

Copyright © 2016 - Charlie Most and Charlene Keel
All rights reserved. No portion of this book may be reproduced, stored in a retrieval system or transmitted in any form or by any means, mechanical, electronic, photocopying, recording or otherwise, without written permission from the publisher.

Red Sky Presents © 2016
Published by Red Sky Presents
A division of Red Sky Entertainment, Inc.

Lost Treasures of the Heart

BY
CHARLIE MOST
&
CHARLENE KEEL

RED SKY PRESENTS
NEW YORK

Dedication

To my dearest brother, Christopher Most, who struggled with many demons on this earth.

May he now be at rest.

—Charlie Most

Special thanks to gentleman pirate Stede Bonnet.

Acknowledgements

Daniel Vovak, "The Wig Man," who instilled in me the power of writing and guided me through the early days of outlining and composing this manuscript.

Dr. Bradley Rodgers of East North Carolina University, for his help with the research.

The city library of Charleston, South Carolina, for providing a wealth of historical information.

Assistant Chief Jeff Foster of Corolla Fire and Rescue for providing an account of the salvage operation of the oldest known shipwreck on the Outer Banks coast.

Gentlemen pirate, Stede Bonnet, who inspired the story.

Jim Gately, who shared the ghost ship sighting with me one night. My life was never the same.

Gifted photographer, Alana Beall, who contributed the image of pirate Kate to the cover. See her work at www.vanitysedge.com

And the free spirits of those who dare to be adventurous.

Dedication

To my beautiful daughter, Rachel Giordano:

May you find all the treasures of your heart!

—Charlene Keel

Other books by Charlene Keel:

The Congressman's Wife
Dark Territory
Ghost Crown
Shadow Train
The Lodestone
Seventh Dawn of Destiny
Rituals
Come Slowly, Eden
Living Single: How to Live Single and Like It
The Sky's The Limit

Acknowledgements

A Change Is Gonna Come

Words and Music by Sam Cooke, copyright © 1964

Yo Ho Ho and A Bottle of Rum

Robert Louis Stevenson, *Treasure Island, 1883*

Graveyard of the Atlantic Museum in Hatteras, North Carolina

Table of Contents

Chapter One

Early Summer, 2015
Baltimore, Maryland

Loaded down with a slew of architectural renderings he'd scooped up in his arms Jonathan left his office, heading out to a meeting with a new client. Although his older daughter Christiana and some of his wife's friends assured him he looked younger than fifty-three, his daily work load made him feel every minute of each year.

He was chief architect and owner of a small firm that had made its reputation on projects of notoriety, like the new NFL stadium he'd designed and constructed. Now he was working in the field of green architecture, using sustainable design with renewable energy sources. It was a slowly developing area of work, largely untested, and he had only a handful of clients who were willing to invest in it. His wife thought it too risky after all the years he'd spent building his business, but it was important to Jonathan—just as important as making money. Concerned about nature, future generations, the harmony of structure and how they could coexist, he wanted to use green options in all his work.

"Hey, Jonathan!" Jim stuck his head out the window of his pickup as Jonathan struggled to open the back door of his blue Jeep Cherokee. "You interested in a fishing trip to the Outer Banks? Just had a client cancel on us, so I got room."

Jonathan nodded a greeting. Jim sold commercial solar

panels, and they'd done several projects together. "I'm tempted, man," he answered. Jonathan loved sport fishing, and he loved being out on the open ocean. "But you know how busy I am."

"Yeah, okay," Jim said. "I also know you're the type who'll work yourself to death if somebody doesn't stop you." He fidgeted with his watch a moment and then went on. "We're set for Thursday, back on Sunday. You're lucky getting the bite, Jonathan, and that'll be lucky for all of us. Come on—don't keep me hanging."

"Sorry, timing's bad. I'm heading down there in a couple of weeks anyway. We're buying that new vacation place Patrice has her heart set on."

"Real estate," Jim scoffed. "That's not relaxing. Man, you've got to see this place! A massive beachfront house with a Jacuzzi and wrap-around deck. We have it for the whole week—our own fisherman's retreat. This time tomorrow you could be on that deck looking out at the endless Atlantic."

"I don't know." Jonathan wanted to go—he just didn't see how it was possible. He finally got the car door open and put his prints in the back seat. Closing the door he added, "Anyway, I have no desire to drive over three hundred miles to North Carolina twice in the same month."

"But dude," Jim countered. "You never take time to chill. I've got a good group going down. It'll be awesome! You should get away and kick back a little. It'll keep you on top of your game. Come on—take a break for a couple of days."

"Why don't you take some time off?" Patrice asked a few hours later, as Jonathan paced in the kitchen. She was chopping carrots slowly, precisely, carefully making all the pieces the same size. "You work all the time. All you do is work." She tried to sound concerned but he felt the undercurrent of her old resentment stirring beneath her calm. She dumped the carrots into the salad and started tossing it.

Jonathan stopped pacing and braced himself for an argument. "I have to work if I don't want to lose accounts," he said patiently. He couldn't get past the feeling that she was trying to set him up so she could play martyr. It was one of her favorite games.

The phone rang. He reached for it and drew it to his ear. "Hello? Oh—hey, Jim." He went silent a moment and then, "Really? Yeah—unbelievable. Let me see what I can do." He put the phone on mute.

Patrice stopped working on the salad. "What's so unbelievable?" she asked. Small, tight lines formed around her mouth.

"Jim had two more cancellations. He wants to know if I have anyone who can fill in. If Mike and Tim are available, maybe I'll go." He took the phone off mute. "Jim, let me call a couple of my buddies. I'll get back to you."

Patrice put down her big spoon and fork and glared at him. "So . . . if those two crazy bastards are in, you are too? Is that the verdict?"

"Come on, Patrice—it's only a couple of days. You just said I need to take a break."

"And you just said you're too busy." She arched her eyebrows and cocked her head slightly, as she always did when she was angry. "I should have known. Let the animals loose in the Carolinas and you can't wait to join them. I said you needed a break, not an excuse to guzzle beer and go carousing the Outer Banks with your drinking buddies."

"I promise not to guzzle," he joked, trying to soften her up a little. "It would be a good day on the water—fishing with the guys and seeing Dave and Captain Harv again. Look, when we go down to finalize the house, I'll make it up to you." He reached for her hand but she turned away. "It would give me a chance to check out the wind turbine," he said. "They've got it fully operational now—"

"Right!" she snapped sarcastically, cutting him off. "You'll drive by and look at it for a few minutes—and then you'll all be knocking them back at the Brew Station."

That was probably true, even though he wasn't ready to admit it to his wife. He really did want to see the progress the restaurant had made in moving away from using fossil fuels, especially in so serene a location. It was a first step, anyway. If other businesses followed, it would preserve the area for generations to come. But relaxing at the Brew Station with the guys also had its appeal.

"My car will be in the shop," she reminded him. "You said I could use yours."

"I'll take a rental," he countered.

"So go then." Her voice was a resigned monotone. As she took the salad to the table she added dourly, "Just go."

Quickly, before she could change her mind—and before he could get into a debate with her about how much time they didn't spend together—Jonathan called Jim. He could use a break, especially if it meant he could breathe in some fresh sea air. Getting out on the ocean again might help him gain a new perspective.

"Yeah," he said when Jim answered. "I'm in."

‡‡

Early Spring, 1717
Queen Anne's Creek, Carolina

Several times a day I gaze through my telescope, looking for Jacob's ship bobbing between the dips and swells of the unpredictable Atlantic waters. A general malaise has

*developed within me during these weeks I have waited for
him, gaining such a foothold that it grows into a maddening
obsession and threatens to consume me. I awaken every
morning in my cold, lonely bed and spring to my feet, praying
I have not missed his return in the night. And then I go
immediately to my telescope and peer through it again, as I did
the previous day, scanning the battered, wooden docks for any
trace of his vessel. And every day, it is the same.*

In those endless days of torment, I often stood on my
balcony, dressed only in my nightgown and the fine cotton robe
I wore when last he held me in his arms. Had my cousin Shelly
not burst into the room the last night we were together, to warn
me of Papa's early return, who knows where our passion would
have taken us?

That day, as always, I adjusted the telescope lens and
scanned the horizon until I had covered every wave I could see
beyond the barrier islands. Still there was no sign of Jacob's
brigantine. After an hour's passage, I repeated the same
sequence. Despite my anguish, I remained always confident I
would be the first to know when he had come back for me.

In anticipation of his arrival I had planned everything
to the finest detail and accordingly, I would be at the landing
when he arrived. My new yellow dress hung on a brass hook
behind the door, and already I knew how long it would take to
throw off my nightshift, don camisole and pantalets (foregoing
corset and stockings), slip into my dress and matching shoes,
take up my cloak, and run down the stairs. I added a few
minutes in case there were carriages crossing the cobbled
streets. It was about the same amount of time it would take for
the brigantine to get through the narrow strait and come around
to the dock at Queen Anne's Creek, the little village downriver
from our plantation. That's where all the ships came into port
with passengers and cargo, and where Papa built a cottage so
we would have a place to stay when in town.

That day, Shelly sat in a large, comfortable chair near the door leading to the balcony just off my bedroom. Enjoying the luxury of goose-down cushions she toyed with a long tendril of her hair, already bored with my sea watch. It was chilly but the breeze coming off the ocean was gentle. Truth be told, I was almost as bored as she. I left my perch near the railing and went inside.

Shelly was the daughter of my late mother's sister, who died when Shelly was but a child of nine years—old enough to remember the poverty of her beginnings and young enough for my father to indulge, as he had always indulged me. He had raised Shelly as his second daughter and we were almost the same age, both twenty, with but three months between us. I loved her dearly. She was the only person in the world to whom I could reveal the secret desires of my heart. How many friends can a woman really trust with intimate words and thoughts? Not even in prayer could I share so much, or reveal my hopes for the future or reveal the few disappointments I had known in my young life—but I shared everything with Shelly.

Bertha, who had been my governess and now served as ladies' maid and chaperone to us both, and who had come into town to stay with us in the cottage, often whispered to me that I was prettier—although there was such a resemblance between Shelly and me that we could have passed for sisters, even twins, except that her hair was brown and mine a deep shade of auburn.

"He's not going to marry you," Shelly announced. "Even if your father would consent—which he will not."

It wasn't the first time she'd said it and I could hear the old resentment in her voice, a resentment I had seen often in our childhood when she had compared every gift she got from my father to whatever he had given me, when she carefully measured any benefits we received, even to the food on our plates, to make sure I got no more than she. Papa told me years ago that it was only because she had endured such poverty and hardship in her young life before she came to us. He told me to try to be patient with her. I had always hoped her jealousy would ease with time but at any moment, I knew, it could crop up again.

"He *will* marry me," I insisted. "As for Papa withholding his approval, that's why we are not asking his permission. But once it is done, he will accept it."

Shelly shifted in the chair. "You must put that thought away, Kate," she warned. "Jacob is a pirate—"

"So was my father, once," I reminded her. "Before the king engaged him as a privateer. And if a pirate was good enough for my mother, why would it not be for me? In time, Papa will see that. He is a reasonable man."

"You can dress a cat in an elegant cloak and fancy boots but it is still a cat," she retorted. "Whatever you want to call it, Jacob is an adventurer, a *pirate*. And he likely has a woman in every port."

I was getting more distressed by the moment. I had doubts enough of my own and didn't need my cousin to confirm them. "Bertha will be up with our tea soon," I said. "So kindly make your point and be done with it."

"All I am saying," she returned stubbornly, "is that you should not fancy yourself in love with Jacob simply because he has traveled the world over and has pretty stories to tell you about places you will never see. It's all very romantic, Kate, but he is not going to marry you."

I felt the sudden sting of tears but quickly blinked them away. "I will tell you this," I said. "As sure as I am standing here before you, Jacob will be my husband."

"What if he doesn't want that?" she asked, relentless, as she rose from the chair. I put down my telescope and watched as she walked to the mirror and preened in front of it, turning for a better view of her figure. "What if you were to learn that he prefers another? What if he tells you he does not love you?"

"I would never love again," I declared softly. "I would throw myself off my balcony to my death. If I found he loved another I could not bear to live."

Shelly laughed gaily. "Listen to yourself, Kate! Throw yourself off the balcony indeed! We're on the second floor—at best you would have a broken leg. And even if Jacob does love you, do you really believe he will settle down, become a gentleman farmer and try to involve himself in the settlement of Carolina, as your father does? Surely you do not expect him to give up his adventures for such a placid life? That would be like asking him to sever a limb."

I began to pace. I couldn't deny there was some truth in what she said, and I marveled that she was so perceptive about my beloved. With such a restless nature Jacob would be bored with a life on land. Unlike Jacob—who was indeed an adventurer—my father had become a privateer not by choice or greed, but by necessity, responding to the needs of brave men and women who were trying to make a life in this wild, untamed country. While the British crown does not tax supplies brought in by ships from other countries, it forbids them all from trading in the colonies. Thus, privateers are necessary. Settlers venturing inland require supplies, and weapons, more often than British ships can deliver, else they starve or be carried away by Indians as befell those poor souls in Roanoke. Even then, I knew, Papa was moving goods up Chowan River to the new settlement, and was not due back for two or three more days. Although I missed him, I wasn't worried he would return in time to interfere with my plan to elope with Jacob.

In the meantime, I would not let Shelly's words discourage me. I knew she was envious. In spite of her outrageous flirting with the men Papa had set to guard us out at the plantation house—and those who worked for the notorious Blackbeard who often did business with my father—she had yet to find one who would claim her as his own.

But I had no doubt Jacob loved me and I *would* marry him and he *would* settle down with me and raise a family—and he would become the sort of husband my father wanted for me. I understood why Papa did not want me with a man like Jacob—or like himself. Pirates—and privateers—were more than willing to race the devil even when the prize was only a tankard of rum. They were dangerous, not only in the lives they chose but also the company they kept. But, I told myself, Jacob was different. All he needed to steady him was a good wife and loving children. What an innocent I was!

It had been an exhausting day. After my morning watch at the telescope, Bertha took Shelly and me to the dressmaker to be fitted for new frocks—two to see us through the spring and summer, and one for the harvest ball we would host at the plantation at season's end. Then we made calls on Miss Penelope Golland, Governor Eden's stepdaughter, and Mrs. Mary Arnold, the wife of a gentleman who was important to Papa's political aspirations. I thought again that it was impossible not to admire my father. He had such great hopes for the colonies, and for himself. He was determined to advance his position in society enough to excuse his questionable beginnings.

As soon as we returned from our outing, I resumed my watch for Jacob's ship, and then had this impotent verbal sparring with my cousin. But my mood was soon to lift. Not long after Bertha took our tea tray away, I spotted a ship, still some distance out, its sails outlined starkly against the horizon. It was a brigantine and it looked like Jacob's, I told myself, although I knew I could not trust my eyes—especially at such a distance.

Already I had endured false sightings and dashed hopes and each time I ran through my preordained pattern, rehearsing in my mind how I would quickly dress and hurry to the docks while Shelly distracted our chaperone. I told myself the disappointments only made me better prepared for the day he would finally arrive and I would again be in his arms.

His kiss, so many months ago, had been my first. I had no doubt he would be my love for life—my first and last and only love. I was so naïve. Whatever I knew of love came from Jacob and his whispered promises, each of which I shared with Shelly, my sister, my friend, my confidante. Talking about it, she told me, would help me view it with more clarity. If only I had known then the extent of her duplicity.

She always wanted details—as many as I would provide—never chiding me for talking about him too much or becoming bored with my endless conversations late into the night, when the last candle dripped and sputtered to its death. She knew my most intimate secrets and I was glad I had someone to tell.

I cannot be sure for my cousin was not as forthcoming with me, but I suspected she had been intimate with one of the men who worked for Papa, or one of Blackbeard's men, during the month they lodged with us at the plantation. Although I asked her about it on more than one occasion, she always changed the subject, refusing to confide in me.

Turning my attention back to the ship on the horizon, I saw it was closer. At last I got a clear look at it.

"He's come," I said softly.

"Are you sure?" Shelly asked. "You've thought that before."

"He is here," I assured her. "You must distract Bertha as you promised, so she will not question where I have gone."

"Of course." She laughed and her delight was remarkable. Even with all her doubts and questions, I thought, Shelly was happy for me. I removed the blue dress in which I'd dutifully made calls that day and then reached for my pretty yellow dress with the lace cuffs. Goose bumps raced up my arms and danced down my back, and I couldn't be sure if it was the chilly air on my skin or my anticipation. Already I could feel Jacob's kiss and his body pressing close to mine. How I longed for his embrace.

After Shelly fastened up my buttons, I went out onto the balcony to raise my father's flag so Jacob could be sure of my presence in town. I knew he would be looking through his own telescope, watching for my sign.

As we had planned, Shelly went to Bertha and asked to learn a new embroidery stitch. I wasted no time in rushing down the stairs, my feet almost gliding over each step as I descended. I lifted my skirt as I went out onto the street, so as not to catch the hem on the cobblestones. I would let nothing deter me from my march to the sea.

In my haste I tripped and almost fell, righting myself just in time to avoid catastrophe. Forcing myself to walk at a ladylike pace I resolved to steady my nerves, and I recalled how Jacob came into my life.

It was late in the previous spring, when a man named Edward Teach arrived at our plantation house, saying he had urgent business with my father. His dress was most distinctive and quite unique—a naval officer's jacket mismatched with black and white striped pantaloons and heavy, rough boots. His beard was long and black and he had red ribbons tying his hair back from his face, and scattered throughout his beard. A young man, clean-shaven and more handsome than any I had ever seen, was with him.

Jacob.

I was in the library of our house with my father when they arrived. I was not surprised that Papa knew the man with the black beard, even though I could tell he was not a gentleman and not someone whose company my father relished.

"Go into the parlor with Bertha and your cousin," Papa told me as soon as he had introduced me to his guest.

"But you have not given me your answer," I protested. "*Will* you permit me, Papa—*please*?" I had been pestering him for days to be allowed to take lessons from the new fencing master who was newly come to Queen Anne's Creek.

"We will continue our discussion after I have concluded my business here," Papa said gently. "Go now, my dear."

"Oh, leave her be, Steadman," Mr. Teach intervened. "My business is simple enough and I know you cannot refuse me, old friend. Let there be no secrets here."

I could see that Papa was annoyed with Mr. Teach's interference but he did his best to hide it. "Very well," he agreed. "What is it you require of me, Edward?"

"Safe harbor," Teach promptly replied. "For a few weeks, no more. I have recently . . . ah . . . acquired a new ship, which is presently in Martinique undergoing some necessary improvements." He went on to say he'd left his brigantine, which was under Jacob's command, at the landing in Queen Anne's and he and Jacob and a handful of his men had rowed upriver to our plantation. "My men and I need rest," he concluded quietly, looking my father in the eye. "And the peace and quiet of the country."

"You need to stay out of sight," Papa surmised shrewdly and I gasped before I could stop myself.

"You're a pirate!" I exclaimed.

Mr. Teach laughed heartily at that, and Jacob, his eyes fastened on mine, laughed with him. I think that is the moment I fell in love with him.

"You are very direct, young miss," said Teach. "That is a desirable trait in a woman—is it not, Jacob?"

"Indeed it is," Jacob said. "I've never met any so direct."

Teach turned back to my father then. "What say you, Steadman? You are in my debt, you know."

After but a moment's hesitation, Papa said, "Of course. You are welcome here, Edward. But mind—we live quietly

and I have two young women in my care. I trust you will keep
your men in check."

"Oh, aye—no worry there," the pirate replied. "We'll
be no trouble at all and we'll show the young ladies their
due respect. Now tell me," he concluded, his great dark eyes
twinkling with amusement, "What is it the lovely Kate was
trying to wheedle out of you when we arrived? Forgive me but
I cannot contain my curiosity."

"Fencing lessons, of all things!" Papa announced. "Not
the most ladylike skill I would wish her to improve upon."

"But you are the one who first instructed me when I was
scarcely big enough to hold a sword," I argued. I did not need
to remind him it was my mother's death during an Indian raid
on our home that inspired him to teach me how to defend
myself. For my fifteenth birthday, he had presented me with a
rapier he'd had made expressly for my hand. It was perfectly
balanced to my strength and stature, and I had become quite
proficient with it. "I learned a lot from you, Papa—and now I
want to improve on what I know. This teacher is rumored to be
the best in France. Say you will allow it, Papa. Say you will
allow me to gain the skill that will save my life if we are set
upon by savages."

He looked at Mr. Teach and shrugged. "I seem unable to
refuse my daughter anything," he said. And then to me, "Very
well—but it will have to wait until our guests have departed.
And you will have to stay in town, which Bertha will not like.
I cannot spare the men to row you down there and back again
every day, and to safeguard you at the cottage."

Jacob spoke up, surprising all of us. "I can instruct
her," he said and bowed slightly to my father. "With your
permission, sir."

"I wager my man is better than your Frenchman," Teach
put in. "Jacob is the best swordsman I've ever seen. And he
can throw a knife to hit a target dead on."

That was the beginning. Jacob and Mr. Teach, who I soon came to know was the infamous Blackbeard, stayed with us at the plantation house for over a month, and during all that time Jacob and I were scarcely parted from each other. He was, as Teach had said, an expert swordsman and he taught me all the skill and tricks he knew, working me without mercy and never giving me an advantage simply because I am a woman. He also taught me how to throw a knife to hit a target, and he boasted to his men that I was almost as good as he.

I was delighted to learn he could read and write. We often took books with us on our walks into the countryside, with Shelly and two of my father's men to act as chaperone and guards. When Bertha could be spared from household duties, she went with us. When we stopped to rest in a clearing or beside a stream, we took turns reading to each other. In the evenings, after dinner, Bertha played for us on the pianoforte with one of Blackbeard's men accompanying her on his guitar.

Jacob and I stole away often to the barn, or to any quiet corner where we could be alone, and I returned the kisses he bestowed upon me without, as he said, the false modesty of a maiden. All too soon, Mr. Teach's ship arrived from Martinique and Jacob had to go—but he declared his love for me and told me he would leave Blackbeard's employ when he had a ship of his own. We made our plans to marry as soon as he could return.

Early Summer, 2015
Baltimore, Maryland

Jonathan awoke earlier than he'd intended. He never slept well after a clash with his wife. At least the latest one had not developed into a full-blown battle.

The house where he and the other guys were staying was incredible, as Jim had promised. From his window Jonathan had a magnificent view of the ocean, which he could enjoy while lying in bed. It was calm—a favorable sign for a good bite. A veteran of these off-shore fishing expeditions, he had often entertained clients this way, but this trip was about relaxing.

This morning wasn't much different from those that had gone before, he thought as he waited in the predawn gloom, watching waves caress the shore. Soon everyone else would be awake. They would start their day with hot, black coffee, changing later to beer, which might induce them to reminisce about old times and past lovers. Jonathan's thoughts drifted back to Patrice. He wondered—and not for the first time—exactly when she had stopped loving him. Truth be told, it had to be long before she cheated on him. Probably about the same time he'd fallen out of love with her. The cheating simply made it a stark reality instead of something in the back of his mind that he might have to deal with some day.

When Jonathan had learned of his wife's affair with Garrett Paulson, he was right in the middle of building Baltimore's new NFL stadium. It was the biggest project of his career and he couldn't afford to take his focus off the job for a second. Garrett had been Jonathan's right hand man then—two years before—and he'd had no reason to doubt Garrett's loyalty. He didn't know when or how it had started and he didn't want to know, even though Patrice had wanted to tell him. The more she tried to explain, the more he refused to listen.

Patrice would never leave him for Garrett, Jonathan knew—simply because Garrett would never make as much money as Jonathan. Garrett would never be able to provide her with the luxurious lifestyle she currently enjoyed—especially now. After Jonathan fired him without a reference, the only job he'd been able to get was salesman in a used car lot. The real question, Jonathan realized, was if he wanted to leave Patrice.

He wondered if Patrice really loved Garrett. Or if Garrett had simply been a new toy. Something to distract her from her general dissatisfaction with life. Still, it didn't make it hurt any less, or any easier to process.

When Jonathan had first confronted her, she hadn't tried to deny she'd cheated on him—but even her unfaithfulness she had managed to make his fault. She had cried and told him it was only because she was so lonely. He put in too many hours at work, she'd said, and they never did anything together and she had felt so unappreciated. She'd never had the decency to apologize for the affair, insisting that he'd brought it on himself. It had meant nothing to her, she'd told him, and she didn't want a divorce. All she wanted was a husband who would pay attention to her.

Before marriage, she had been sweet and compliant, supportive of everything Jonathan did, including his work. After the wedding, she had dominated the relationship, and had made all decisions concerning the house and the girls. He had never minded that; he was glad to leave those things to Patrice so he could concentrate on building his business—the business she now resented. She had, for years, ruled Elaine and Christiana, which she found increasingly difficult as they approached their teens. She kept busy with her clubs and committees but as her daughters grew older and less malleable, she developed an insatiable need to be the center of her husband's universe.

There was no explosion when Jonathan found out about Garrett—there hadn't been time. Jonathan couldn't take his focus off the stadium project and it was a relief to immerse himself in it. He had never said what he wanted to do about the marriage. He hadn't said because he didn't know—he wouldn't know, until he could figure out what to do with his anger. After he'd recovered from the initial shock, they had just stopped talking about it.

He wondered for maybe the hundredth time what it would do to his girls if he did leave their mother. If he moved out, where would he go and how would he accomplish it? His work schedule left him no time for apartment hunting—and going home every night to a strange, empty place wasn't something he'd ever wanted to do. In fact, the thought was overwhelming. So, instead of leaving, instead of asking for a divorce, he'd agreed to buy the vacation house that, a few months ago, Patrice had announced she wanted. It was good he'd decided to come along on this fishing trip, he thought. He needed time away so he could figure it all out.

By now, he should have gotten over the fact that his wife had slept with another man. He'd gotten past it but he didn't think he would ever get over it. It had happened almost two years before, and if what she said was true, it had only been "a couple of times." If he split from Patrice now, he knew, that wouldn't be the reason. It would be the deeper sense of discontent that had started even before he knew she'd been unfaithful.

Maybe he was in some kind of mid-life crisis, he considered. He was the right age for it. He had everything he'd ever wanted, had accomplished every goal he'd set for himself back when he was a young, naïve college sophomore. He had a successful career and he loved his work. He had a beautiful home and cars that were paid for. He had Chrissie and Lanie—two healthy, gorgeous daughters (one only a year away from going off to college herself). He had an attractive wife that other men desired and other women envied. But something was missing—had been missing even before Patrice's affair. Something important. Something he wondered if he could go on without.

If only he could figure out what it was.

He stared, almost hypnotized, at the rotating blades of the ceiling fan, transfixed by their movement as if he could find some hidden wisdom inside the whirling pattern. Sighing deeply, he looked out the window again and let the waves take him away, into some alternate reality, some fugue state, for a few moments. Then he got out of bed, intent on finding the kitchen and getting coffee started.

Good old Jim had set the timer on the coffeemaker the night before. Jonathan poured himself a cup and took it out onto the deck overlooking the ocean. He stayed there, sucking in deep breaths of fresh sea air, until shouts and laughter inside told him the others were awake. It was time to load up the truck with a couple of coolers full of beer and another one with the spicy foods all the men loved. Then they'd be off to Pirate's Fishing Center to hook up with Captain Harv and his first mate Dave.

Tim Conners and Mike Dahl (who Jonathan had christened Masterbaiter Mike because of his skill with the hooks) rode in front with Jim. The rest of the party crowded into the back seat of Jim's truck for the forty-five minute trip, and Jonathan was squashed between two big guys. He tried to focus on the animated conversation about the catch they were anticipating.

"Think we'll meet up with Lady Luck this time out?" the bigger one—Lou—asked.

"Luck's got nothing to do with it," the less large one replied. Jonathan thought his name was Al. He took a laptop out of his backpack and balanced it on his knees so he could scan the previous day's fishing reports, looking for the spot where they'd be likely to find the biggest haul.

Jonathan leaned back and closed his eyes, determined to enjoy the ride.

‡‡

Early Spring, 1717
Queen Anne's Creek, North Carolina

Breathless from my run, I stood on the dock where four
men were tying up Jacob's ship. The anticipation of being
again in his arms was almost more than I could bear.

"Ahoy!" I called out cheerfully. "Where is your captain?"

They looked at me, annoyed at the interruption. "Cap'n
is in his cabin, miss," growled the one with a torn black patch
over his eye, but I would not let his scowl deter me. As soon
as the gangway was in place I rushed aboard. From our last
interlude—for Papa had allowed Shelly and me to accompany
Mr. Teach and his crew to the brigantine when it was time
for them to sail—I knew my way to Jacob's cabin. I walked
confidently along the deck. His crew did not try to stop me or
question what I was doing there.

Another man who was rolling a barrel toward the ship's
railing greeted me. "I see ye've come to welcome the cap'n
back, lass!" he sang out. I recognized him as one of the sailors
who had been with Blackbeard when he'd stayed with us the
previous spring. "Jacob'll be glad of that, 'e will!"

I smiled and waved to him as I continued on my way. His
men obviously knew about me so, I reasoned, they knew he
loved me. Perhaps Jacob had even told them we were to be
married. I felt treasured—indeed, I was the gold he'd been
seeking. No more would he have to plunder foreign ports and
King George's fleet to find it. In my innocence and hope, I had
no doubt my father would grant us a sizeable tract of land and
workers to farm it, as soon as he learned we were wed—and I
had often assured my beloved of that.

I descended a ladder and then walked down a dim passage
until I passed beneath a skull atop a doorway, and through what
I had thought on my previous visit was a beaded curtain. Jacob
had laughed heartily at my shock when he'd told me what I had

named as beads were actually bones taken from the fingers of Blackbeard's enemies. They clattered eerily against each other when I pushed the strings aside and entered Jacob's cabin. He sat at his desk, making an entry in the ship's log. At my sudden intrusion he stood, wielding a long knife with a shimmering blade.

"Kate!" he cried. He looked as if he had not expected me. Seeing my surprise at his reaction, he softened and added, "Never burst without warning into the cabin of a dangerous pirate." He grinned and tossed the knife aside. It landed on his desk with a clatter. "I thought you were some savage come to murder me."

Joyfully, I hurried to him but instead of embracing me, he sat down again, picked up a quill pen and made an entry.

I was puzzled. This was not the reception I had envisioned. "Jacob—I have missed you terribly," I said. "Won't you come and kiss me?"

"Indeed, I will," he returned, not even looking at me, "when I have completed my duties." He dipped the pen in the inkwell and continued to write. "Your father," he said absently as he sprinkled fine sand on the words he'd written and gently blew it off the page. "Is he in town with you?"

"No," I replied. "He has gone upriver with supplies for some new settlers. We needn't worry he will interfere."

Finally, he came to stand before me. As he looked down at me I felt myself melting into the depths of his dark brown eyes. It took a moment for me to realize that he was regarding me more with amusement than passion.

"You *are* the eager little one, are you not?" he asked, smiling at me the way he had when last we were together.

"And you are teasing me," I scolded softly. "Now kiss me, please, or I fear I shall go mad with wanting you."

He laughed and the rich timbre of his voice sent a thrill of expectation racing through me. What pleasure it gave me to hear him! At last, he placed his strong, broad hands at my waist and drew me to him and then, very gently, his lips came down upon my own. Another thrill assaulted me as the tip of his tongue invaded my mouth, probing softly until it engaged mine.

Unashamed, I pressed closer to him and when I felt the evidence of his arousal firm against my belly, it incited my desire as I had never thought possible. I had no doubt that I loved him as I would never love another, and that he would soon be my husband—but I didn't want to wait. My every thought—as if my sanity depended upon it—was having him completely.

"Jacob," I whispered frantically, as if a fever raged in my soul. "Can you not bolt your door and put your ledger aside—and take me now? I can wait no longer for you!"

His breathing grew rapid and his voice was husky. "Is that what you want, little one? Truly—is that what you want?"

"Yes! With all my heart and soul, my dearest! Take me—here and now."

His lips captured mine once more and tortured me with the deepest, the sweetest, of kisses. I was lost in it until a harsh voice intruded upon my paradise.

"Isn't *this* a pretty picture?"

Startled, we parted and turned to find the owner of that voice. To my surprise, it was Shelly standing in the doorway, staring at me as if she hated me. I was so astonished I could not speak.

"What the hell are you doing here?" Jacob demanded.

"At the moment, I am waiting to see if you will accept her invitation," Shelly said, her voice full of contempt. "Are you going to take her—here and now? I do not recall that being part of the plan."

"What—plan?" I finally managed, looking from one to the other and back again, my gaze finally resting on Jacob. "What is she saying?" I asked. "What plan?"

"Pay no heed to the words of a foolish maiden," he told me and then he looked at Shelly with contempt. "You must go—" he began but she cut him off.

"I will not!" she declared. "Not until my poor, besotted cousin learns the truth. I followed her to assure myself of your fidelity. But despite your promises as we lay together in my bed when you were last in port, it is clear that you do, indeed, desire her."

"Jacob?" My heart was beating so fast I was not surprised that it was also breaking. It was *me* he loved, I thought. Why would he be in her bed? "What does this mean? Of what plan does she speak?" He released me and moved to the wide aft window in his quarter gallery that gave him a view of the barrier islands, and the ocean beyond. As he stared out to sea, silent, I turned back to my cousin, the friend to whom I had entrusted my most intimate secrets. "Shelly?"

"You poor, misguided fool. It is not you he loves, dear Kate. Jacob loves me."

He whirled about, his eyes flashing with rage. "Be silent!" he roared at her. "Not another word!"

Shelly walked to him, swaying her hips seductively, glancing at me as if I were no more important than a mosquito.

"If you won't tell her, Jacob, I will," she said. "Did you think I would stand patiently by and see you put your hands on another—and see you kiss and whisper endearments to another?" Still looking at him, defiant, she addressed her next words to me. Until that moment, I had no idea how truly she disliked me—and how consumed with jealousy and resentment she was. "You see, dear cousin—Jacob was not going to marry you for love. He was only after the land your father would give him and a ship of his own. The land he would have sold to buy his way out of Blackbeard's service. The ship he would have used to sail away with *me*, after he had accomplished his goal. He told me you were a ridiculous little prude and he would not even have to consummate the marriage to get his way. But now I have to wonder which of us is the fool. You or I—or our mutual beloved, if he believed I would stand by quietly while he *takes* you as you have so ardently demanded." She turned back to Jacob. "So now, my darling—you will have nothing. Not the land, and not the ship—and certainly not Kate."

Before I knew what he intended, before I could intervene, he grabbed Shelly by the throat and shook her, his face red with his anger. "I told you to be silent!" He shook her again as she clutched desperately at his iron grip. "You stupid cow—you have ruined everything!"

She struggled in his grasp and her complexion turned blue as he used both hands to squeeze, lifting her so that her feet barely touched the floor. It was all a dreadful mistake, I thought. It was some kind of terrible misunderstanding and we would find a way to sort it out—but I couldn't let him kill Shelly. I grabbed the first thing at hand to throw at him, just to surprise him, to make him release her.

It was the knife with the long, shimmering blade he had tossed so casually aside. I was as surprised as he when it struck him in the neck, instantly causing a profusion of blood. I had seen the way my father's slaves killed hogs at harvest time, cutting the large vein beneath their chins. I knew instantly there was no saving Jacob.

He let go of Shelly. His eyes on me, full of shock and disbelief, he slipped to the floor. His gaze held mine until every bit of life had drained from him.

Chapter Two

Late Summer, 2015
Corolla, North Carolina

"Hey, Jim—it's almost five," said Lou, and Chad closed his laptop. "Better hustle. Captain Harv is not a patient man."

"I know," Jim agreed. "And he'll expect us to pay even if he shoves off without us."

"Check it out," put in Masterbaiter Mike. "That's the Hog Wild docked next to Outer Limits. You think it's carrying Deadskins this time out?"

The Hog Wild catered to Redskins fans and Mike and Tim enjoyed harassing them at any opportunity. No one would give Mike a hard time unless they had back up. He was a former NFL offensive lineman with the Kansas City Chiefs and he could hold his own in a fight. Tim, who was Mike's best friend, wing man and sidekick, was the size of a front lineman.

"Hey, guys," the Outer Limits first mate greeted them as they boarded.

"Hey, Dave. Where's the bite today?" asked Jim.

"According to yesterday's reports, Norfolk Canyon's the best place to get what you're lookin' for. Heard tell there's bait fish hangin' out there. Only problem you'll have is reelin' 'em in 'fore the sharks get 'em," Dave said as they boarded. "Okay, boys—settle down, now," he added. "Let me make mahself clear. When I say, 'fish on—you bettah be in that chair! We unnerstan' each othah?" Jonathan got a kick out of Dave's southern accent. Everyone nodded and Dave went on. "All right, then. Now—as I have *nevah* lost a fish at the boat, I will take it personally if *any* of y'all screw up my perfect record."

It took them half an hour to get out of the inlet, and another hour and a half to Norfolk Canyon where they would put out the tuna teasers and spread bars. The fair weather promised a good journey and fair chances for the bite. This was a rare treat for Jonathan—to get away from phones and meetings and all the pressure at the office, not to mention Patrice's complaints and maneuvering. Out here, he didn't have to make any decisions. He didn't have to think about anything except the wonder of nature.

By the time they reached their destination, Dave had every rod and hook ready and baited. He started letting out the lines and Jonathan knew he was calculating in his head how much each would take to reach the desired depth. Dave was a man of few words. No bite meant no returning clients. He lived on tips and if he couldn't deliver the bite, he couldn't eat. He took his job seriously—so seriously that he had won a title and a fifty-foot, wide-body, smooth-action Shimano Tiagra reel and a star rod. The side of the reel was engraved with the inscription, *To Dave, best First Mate in the Hamptons and Carolina Region.*

Captain Harv leaned back in his seat on the bridge and scanned the horizon for any sight of tuna rolling on the surface. A seasoned captain with ten years' experience, his clients seldom returned empty-handed. Jonathan relaxed, enjoying the colorful sunrise over the Atlantic, the gentle ocean breeze, and the salty tang of sea air mingled with their breakfast of glazed donuts and coffee.

For three hours, they cast and trolled but nothing disturbed the surface. Without a single tug on any line, Dave was getting antsy. Intermittently, Captain Harv dabbed at the sweat on his brow, which was heavier than usual. Finally,

Dave broke the silence.

"That's it!" he proclaimed. "Time for drastic measures." He went below for a moment and returned with a shark jaw about the size of a man's head. It was yawning wide, as if about to swallow prey. Dave was also clutching a gaffing hook, decorated at one end with a colorful array of yarn, feathers and shells.

Jim, Mike and Jonathan, who had all witnessed this ritual in the past, exchanged looks. Jonathan couldn't suppress a chuckle as the mouths of the other men fell open in surprise when Dave clamped the shark jaw over his face like a mask.

"Let the appeasement to the tuna gods begin!" he bellowed. Then he grabbed the gaffing hook and beat it on the deck as he started chanting.

"What the hell . . ?" mumbled Chad.

"Don't laugh," Jim said. "It works. You'll see."

"Bring us tuna!" Dave sang out, entreating the fish gods. "Bring us tuna! Bring us tuna!" As he chanted, he stomped and pounded on the deck so that the sound could permeate through the boat and into the sea. After a few minutes he stopped and put the shark mask and ceremonial hook down near the railing.

The sea remained calm. They continued trolling, slugging back beers and talking quietly, as Dave stared intently out at the water.

Suddenly, he shouted. "Look!" He was pointing at a flock of gulls that came out of nowhere and started diving. "They're after bait fish!" Captain Harv turned the wheel and headed for the birds. Within seconds, Dave was yelling, "Fish on!"

Jonathan saw a big tuna roll in and grab the bait, and the line disengaged from the snap hooks. They got one.

"Two on!" Dave shouted. "Anglers, get to the back of the boat!"

Jonathan took turns with Jim and Mike working the

first line. The pull on it told him the tuna had to be over two hundred pounds. It took an hour and forty-five minutes of sweat, struggle and determination to reel it in. As soon as it was on the boat, Dave hurled himself onto it. With a filet knife, he savagely pierced its side and extracted its pulsing, throbbing heart.

"Here," he said, pressing it to Jonathan's lips. "You gotta eat it while it's still beating, to pay homage to the tuna gods."

This part of the ritual Jonathan had never seen. He wondered what had gotten into Dave. But the others were watching and if he didn't want to come off as a wuss he was going to have to put the tuna heart in his mouth. *It's just sushi, after all*, he told himself—and he liked sushi. He took the heart between his teeth and bit down on it, chewing and swallowing as fast as he could.

"Would have been better with some soy sauce," he quipped, and the others cheered and laughed.

Dave ignored the joke. "Jonathan," he continued soberly. "Once you've eaten a beating tuna heart, your life on the sea will never be the same. Spirits old and young will accept you and Neptune himself will protect you. You have earned the privilege of wearing this." He crowned Jonathan with the shark-jaw headdress and firmly placed the gaffing hook in his hand. "Now go get 'em, brother—you gaff the next one," he ordered.

Suddenly, they heard the snap of the line from the outrigger clip, and Chad quickly put on his waist belt. He reached for the reel but the line was going out far and fast, and all they could see at the surface, in the distance, was a blue fin. Then Chad slipped and the rod and reel went over the side. Jonathan saw it grabbed up by one of the lines.

"What the hell?" Dave yelled. "You know what it'll cost me to replace that rig? In fact—it can't be replaced! I had it for five years and now it's gone!"

"Maybe not!" Jonathan yelled as he jumped into action. The line was rapidly spooling out, and he could see a blue fin at the surface. He tossed the headdress and hook to Dave and grabbed the rig from Chad. Strapping himself into a fighting chair, he prepared for battle. The fish broke water and then dove again and for a few seconds, Jonathan lost sight of it. Then suddenly, it broke the surface on the port side and Jonathan had more of a fight on his hands than he expected. When he finally subdued the creature, Dave stepped in and yelled at Chad and Lou.

"Okay, boys—clear the way so I can gaff this one."

When they got the fish onboard, they found Dave's prize rod and reel caught in the tangle of lines. Dave cleared them away and recovered his treasure, hugging it to him like a long-lost child. Jonathan and the other guys cheered.

The sun was getting higher and the winds subsided. The seas calmed and the bite disappeared. It became just another lazy, warm summer afternoon. But it wasn't long before things got busy again, as if the sea gods were rewarding them for Jonathan's heroics. The starboard outrigger line snapped. Lou picked up the rig and strapped himself into the fighting chair.

"You lose that fish and you're going in after it," Dave grumbled, still not mollified after the close call with his rig. The fish turned and crossed the bow of the boat, and then took off for the bottom. They lost sight of it for a few seconds. Suddenly, it broke the water off the port side. Lou said later it was the fight of his life but he brought it in. They didn't get a break in the action for the rest of the afternoon. Their haul included two large blue fin tuna, two yellow fin and some Mahi Mahi.

Satisfied that his customers were happy, Dave called to Captain Harv, "Let's head it back and get 'em weighed and filleted!"

Lex, the man at the weigh station, divided the catch into

separate portions and bagged everything for them, and the tired fishermen headed for the beach house. A sense of contentment Jonathan hadn't felt for a while crept in as they drove through the Village of Wanchese and turned north onto Highway 12. The ocean had always done that for him, ever since he was a kid. One of his first memories was standing on a beach in Miami, looking out at the enormous Atlantic, while his mother sat reading in a chair nearby. He was about five or six but even then, he'd felt a connection—such a strong connection that he'd started walking into the surf, reaching out as if embracing it. His mother pulled him back just as a wave came bearing down on him, and the next day she enrolled him in swimming classes at the Y. The pool had been nice but it had never called to him like the sea.

By the time they got back to the house, another crew of six was in residence, preparing for fishing the next day. Butch, a big ol' southern boy, was wearing a Barbeque Pit Stop apron over Bermuda shorts. He had prepared a feast for twelve— spare ribs, filet mignon, shrimp, asparagus and a gigantic salad. Everyone gathered around when he announced it was ready.

"Gentlemen," he said seriously. "The tradition at my table is to give thanks to the Man above who provided the food for tonight and the bounty of fish we'll catch tomorrow. Now join hands and bow your heads."

Jonathan got a little misty-eyed at the sight of twelve big men holding hands, their eyes reverently closed. For a moment, it reminded him of going to Sunday school when he was a little boy, and he thought of Jesus sitting with his twelve disciples, many of them also fishermen. He blinked away the unexpected emotion before anyone could see.

After dinner, he showered and went back to his room but he wasn't ready to sleep. The sounds of waves crashing onto the shore drew him out onto the deck where he looked up and noticed a handful of clouds passing in front of the full moon. It was one of those storybook moments—a picture perfect scene. It started a restless stirring in his soul.

The cloud formations were eerie, like some kind of ghostly mist he'd seen on a TV show about the paranormal, and like those his mom had described to him when he was growing up. He tried to shake it off. If Patrice were there she would already be making fun of him, asking him how many beers he'd consumed that day. His mother had been a true clairvoyant, and in his teen years some of those traits had briefly manifested in Jonathan. Early in their marriage he'd tried to share that with his wife but she hadn't believed him. She didn't believe in any of that so-called paranormal stuff, she'd told him. Anyway, with all the years of hard work and the pressures of business, the proclivity had faded. Jonathan had forgotten about it, until tonight.

But something was happening—something he didn't understand. He could feel it as he stood alone with his thoughts, gazing out at the powerful, beckoning sea.

‡‡

Early Spring, 1717
Queen Anne's Creek, Carolina

Shelly looked at me for a moment in stunned disbelief, and then she moved quickly to Jacob. He was lying on the floor of the cabin, his eyes open and empty, staring at eternity.

"Jacob?" Her voice was a hoarse whisper. "Jacob?" She knelt before him a moment and took his hand. "Jacob . . . my love?" Still kneeling beside him, she turned to me. "You've killed him," she said softly and then she screamed. "Murderer! You've killed him, Kate! You've killed him!" She got to her feet and ran to the doorway, trembling as if a demon from Hell was after her.

Crying out for help, she ran through the door and down the passageway. I knew I had only moments to save myself, for Jacob's crew would surely make me pay for what I had done. I had to get off the ship before Shelly returned with them, and there was only one way I could go.

I was still in shock, I suppose, for I felt nothing except a primitive instinct for survival. I ran to where Jacob lay motionless and pulled the knife from his neck. Unmindful of the blood that streaked my dress, I put the blade through the fabric at the bodice and cut it enough so that I could rip it open, down to my waist. I yanked it off and stepped out of my slippers.

I was going into the water and I knew better than to let my garments weigh me down.

Clad only in my camisole and pantalets I clambered up on Jacob's desk and tried to open the porthole window, which was beautiful, clear glass edged with a circle of tinted blue. It wouldn't budge. There was a lantern hooked on the wall next to it. I could hear footsteps thundering down the stairs from the deck. Grabbing the lantern, I mustered all my strength and threw it at the window, which broke into long shards and fell into the creek. There was no time to think about it—this was my only means of escape.

At our plantation, I had often practiced diving into a large lake Papa said had a natural spring as its source. I was quite good at it. My father had taught me to swim at a very early age. This was no different, I told myself, aside from the fact that I would now be swimming for my life. I dove in and seconds later, broke the surface to the sound of men shouting.

"She's gone overboard!" a deep voice called. "She's done for!"

"No!" Shelly exclaimed. "She can swim! She will escape!"

The water was cold but a bit warmer than the air. I

took a big gulp and dove deep, swimming well past the two other ships docked there. The afternoon was late and I knew nightfall would soon be upon us. I had to keep out of sight until then. Hiding among the dinghies, skiffs and canoes crowded around the docks, I managed to avoid Jacob's men.

After a while, I heard one of them say, "Avast, mates— we're wasting good drinking time. She's not surfaced again. Mayhap she's drowned by now."

"Aye," one of the others agreed. "Better for her if she is. Teach will put such a price on her head there'll be no escape but death. But one thing is sure—we'll not find her in the dark. We need draw lots now, to see who will deliver the news. I wouldn't want to be the one 'at tells 'im the man 'e loved like a brother is dead at the 'and of a treacherous woman."

Even though it seemed they had given up looking for me, I couldn't take any chances. I remained motionless, shivering in water up to my neck, until I could be sure they had gone back to their duties securing the ship. Soon I saw Shelly disembark and head back toward our town house. She would no doubt tell Bertha what I had done, as well as King George's soldiers and the sheriff. My only hope, I knew, was to get to my father before she could report it to him.

Still I waited, hidden among the small boats until the last rays of sun had faded and I knew I could count on the cover of darkness, relieved that there was but a sliver of moon that night. I had to get out of the water, for my teeth were chattering so with the cold I thought the sound would surely give me away.

I could only hope Papa had returned to the plantation early, even though his men were not scheduled to escort Shelly, Bertha and me back home for two more days. If he had not returned, I resolved, I would go and find him. I knew where the settlement was, where he had gone to take supplies. All I had to do was make my way upriver. But first, I would stop at home.

With great stealth I untied one of the canoes from its mooring and found good fortune. It appeared to be a trapper's vessel and it had a rough, woven blanket and a cured deer hide bundled at one end of it, next to two roughly hewn paddles. I was thankful that Papa had taught me to row and swim, arguing with my nanny that those were talents the daughter of a sea captain should not be without. Thinking of how he had always indulged me, from the time I could walk and talk, taking me all over his ships and teaching me the names and functions of every part of them, I threw the blanket around my shoulders and placed the hide across my lap so that it covered my legs and feet. At last, I found warmth and was able to think more clearly. I had to find my father. He would know what to do.

The tide was going out so I had to row quickly before it carried me back to Jacob's ship, and again I was grateful for the darkness.

Jacob. My beloved.

He was dead—and I had killed him. I had to face what I had done. The love of my life was gone, except that he had not been the love of my life. He had betrayed me with the woman whom I had always thought closer to me than sister. *They* had betrayed me.

I was devastated and sorely grieved, yet no tears came, and Shelly's cruel taunts still rang in my ears. She and Jacob had planned to use me and then run away together. He had not even bothered to deny it, and yet I wouldn't, for any price, have condemned him to death. I had killed him trying to save her— but most likely neither Blackbeard nor the British crown would take that into account. I was a murderer and I could hang for it—or worse, if Blackbeard's men caught up with me. I refused to dwell on the punishment God would mete out.

My every thought focused on getting to my father, I stayed as close to the shore as I could without running aground. If need be, I knew I could hide in the trees and foliage that grew along the banks of the Chowan River.

My luck held. I don't know how long it took to reach our dock at the plantation but even in the dim moonlight, I could see his skiff tethered there. Silently, I made my way to the house, clutching at the woolen blanket for warmth and security. Papa would know what to do. He would not condemn me too much when he learned what had happened. He would help me.

The only lamp burning was in the library, which meant the house servants had gone to bed and Papa was up reading or working in his ledgers. It was the latter, and when I crossed the patio and slipped silently through the door he looked up, startled—as he had every right to be. His eyes were lit with happiness—until he realized my state. He had never seen me in such a condition. My feet were muddy and my hair was a tangled mess. I was wrapped in a dirty Indian blanket with only my undergarments beneath it.

"Papa?" I ventured softly.

"Kate—good lord, girl! What has happened to you?" He stood and reached for the bell to summon a servant. "First, let Phoebe see to you and then you will tell me."

"No, Papa!" I rushed to his side and stayed his hand. "No one can know I am here. I have done something terrible and I need your help. You must tell me what to do."

"Calm yourself, my dear," he said. "Nothing can be as bad as all that—"

"It is!" I interrupted him. "Of course it is—look at me!" My tears, so long delayed, began to flow. I collapsed against him and sobbed like a child, but only briefly. I forced my emotions down and told him everything.

He stared at me for a moment. "You really killed him?"

"I did," I whispered in agony, and the tears started again. "I didn't mean to do it, but yes! He was going to kill Shelly!"

"One of Blackbeard's captains. Nay—one of Blackbeard's

favorites. He will have your head for this. Do you know what Edward Teach did to his wife?" I shook my head, miserable, not wanting to hear the answer. "He gave her to his crew for their pleasure," my father continued gravely. "Simply because he grew tired of her nagging. No one knows exactly what happened after that. Some say he hung her from a tree in back of his house—or she hung herself. He left her corpse there for a month. You can expect no mercy from him. The English courts would be more merciful but if Teach finds you first . . ." his voice trailed off. He could not finish the thought.

"What should I do?"

"Get yourself cleaned up, quickly. Dress for a hard ride through the forest. Pack only what you need for a short journey—and bring your sword. Meet me in the stable. I must get you to the docks, to the Royal Thomas. It's fully stocked and you'll need only eight men to sail it, though twenty-eight would be better. I will deed the ship to you, and you will sail south, to Charles Town. When you arrive, go to the Pink House Tavern on Chalmers Street and ask for Marcus Garrity. He is an excellent quartermaster and he will find a crew for you. I'll give you a letter for him. Tell him everything, as you have told me. You can trust him, as I trust him, with your life." He took a deep breath as if to fend off his sorrow, and his voice broke a little when next he spoke. "You will sail as soon as all is ready, and go as fast as the winds allow. Somehow, we must manage your departure unnoticed."

"What about Shelly?" I asked.

"I shall see to her," he said quietly. "I shall settle a sum of money on her—on the condition that she not report this to the British authorities."

"But what if she has already done so?" I demanded, determined not to give in to the tears that threatened.

"Not likely." Papa tried to reassure me. "Blackbeard's men would not turn to the crown for justice and they would have ordered Shelly not to do so. Once you are safely away, Kate, I'll send her to a new settlement in the west, with a dowry, where wives are sorely needed. 'Tis far enough away that no one will listen to her tall tales, or care what you have done."

My heart felt frozen inside my chest. I was to leave my home that I loved so dearly, never to see it again. In all likelihood, this would be the last time I would see my father. I would not be able to stay in this dear place, where I'd hoped to marry and raise my children, and when I died to be buried on my father's land.

"And from Charles Town?" I asked. "Where will I go from there?"

"I wish I knew, lass," he said. "I know only that you must steer clear of any waters Edward Teach is prone to frequent. Head for England, perhaps—or Scotland." -

Instead of returning to the docks by boat, we took two of my father's strongest horses, staying hard and fast to the trail he knew so well. The only travelers we might chance to meet in the middle of the night would be Indians. Papa had established a peaceful relationship with them since the Tuscarora War, so they were of little concern. As it was, we saw no one and we arrived at the landing well before dawn, when Papa thought Jacob's men would be drunk or sleeping.

He woke the crew of the Royal Thomas, men who had sailed with him for years and who had watched me grow up, and gave them strict instructions. I was his emissary, Papa told them, and I was going to Charles Town on important business for him. I had full authority on board, acting as captain in his stead, and they were to obey me accordingly or answer to him. And, he finished, if any man among them had a problem sailing under a woman's command, they were to gather their belongings and clear off the ship, as it now belonged entirely and solely to me, his one and only heir. I don't think I'd ever loved Papa more than at that moment.

Before he disembarked he took me to his cabin—now mine—and embraced me, holding me close to his heart for a moment. Then he kissed my forehead and pulled a leather bag from his pocket. From it he took several gold coins and a letter. I opened it to see that it was a bank note:

> *I promise to pay Miss Katherine Russell*
> *or Bearer of this Letter,*
> *On Demand, the Sum of*
> *Five Hundred Pounds*
> *London, the 5th day of March, 1717*
> *500 pd. St. For the Govr. and Compy.*
> *Of the Bank of England*

"Put these away," he said as he gave me the coins. "When you dock in London go immediately to the office of Henry Goldsmith, in St. James Street, and give him the bank note. He is my banking agent and will be of great help to you. When you have cashed in the note, you'll have the money with which to pay the balance owed to your crew."

"And what then, Papa?" I asked. "Am I to make my life in England?"

He hesitated a moment, his lips set in a tight, thin line, before he said, "Yes, if it seems safe. I believe it will be, if we can silence Shelly. Once Mr. Goldsmith has helped you secure a residence, you must turn your attention to trade. From London you can sail to Italy and Spain and import goods to England." I looked puzzled for a moment and he added, "Soaps and perfumes, ribbons, fabrics and laces—items that will turn a pretty penny."

"Papa—I am so sorry I brought this trouble to our doorstep," I offered but he waved my words aside.

"We have no time for impotent regret, my dear. We must

hurry." Taking something else from the bag he placed it carefully around my neck, clasping it securely.

"My mother's necklace," I said softly. "Are you sure?"

"I am," he said. "It belongs with you. You know its history. All my ships fly the flag with heart and sabers. It was to be yours on your wedding day." His voice broke once more and for a moment, he could not speak. He simply hugged me again. Gently, I placed my hand on the necklace. It was in gold settings, surrounded by rubies and emeralds, and at the center was a large ruby cut in the shape of a heart, with two gold sabers crossed before it. The emeralds, Papa had always told me, were the exact color of my eyes. It had belonged to his father and his father's father, passed on to him to give to his bride. Papa had shown me many times how the clasps that held it together on two sides could be undone, dividing it into two smaller pieces. Until Mama had died, she wore one around her neck and he used one as the chain for his pocket watch. I always wished I could remember her more clearly. Last, Papa gave me the miniature portrait he'd always kept beside his bed. It showed the three of us—Papa, Mama and me when I was a small child. I would treasure it always, especially knowing how much it meant to him.

We cast off at first light, moving silently past Jacob's ship, where I could see that all was quiet. I surmised that the few sailors who had returned from the pub or the brothel were overcome with the grog they had consumed. Our passing through the barrier islands strait was uneventful and once our sails were fully unfurled, we headed due south for Charles Town.

This ship—now mine—was not quite a decade old. Constructed of sturdy oak by one of the finest shipbuilders in Boston, it had two masts, twelve guns and plenty of room for a crew of thirty. Although a merchant vessel with a proven track record, it was not the crown jewel in my father's fleet of four ships but it was certainly worthy of any sailor's high regard.

Somehow I had the strength to behave as a true sea captain's daughter, remaining at the helm until we were well out to sea before turning it over to Mr. Bridges, my first mate. Then I sought refuge in my cabin.

I closed the door and sat down at the desk. Paper is precious and scarce but a luxury Papa could not do without, and for that I was grateful. I had a need to put my thoughts in order and somehow try to understand what I had done and the direction my life now must take. Perhaps, also, I simply needed to confess. I found a new journal he had left in his desk, with most of the pages blank. Dipping the pen in ink I then put it to paper and began keeping this journal, not knowing if another soul would ever read my words.

I am captain now, I wrote. *And the seas I must call my home. Wherever the winds take me, there shall I be, perhaps forevermore. After Charles Town, I shall set my course for England and if they will not accept me there, I will sail on. I am neither pirate nor fiend but I have killed a man—a man who was my first, my only love—and I am consumed with a pain I fear will never let me go. I am alone, for the first time in my life.*

I have lost my love and I have lost my home. I will never walk in my garden or see my animals again. How am I to function without my father near, or my best friend who betrayed me so cruelly? My life has changed forever because I loved the wrong man, and trusted a woman I loved like my own sister.

After committing my thoughts to paper, and every detail of my love and how I had murdered him, I got into my bunk, trying not to think of Jacob. Perhaps it was foolish to confess my crime in writing but I was desperate for a way to come to terms with what I had done. I wondered if I would ever find anyone I could love as I had loved him. Someone who would be able to love me and make me whole again.

Chapter Three

Early Spring, 1717
Charles Town, Carolina

Entering the bustling port of Charles Town would have been an occasion of happy anticipation had I not been distracted by my grief for Jacob and my worry about what would become of me, both my person and my soul.

It was a walled city, strongly fortified against potential raids from France and Spain who disputed England's claim to this part of the new world, and from the Indians who might resent the intrusion into their native land. I had never been to this amazing place but thanks to Papa's stories I recognized many sights as we coasted in and made our way to the dock. Those I didn't know, Mr. Bridges was quick to point out.

"There, Miss—I beg your pardon—*Captain* Russell," he said, gesturing to a row of houses on an island as we sailed past. "They be pest houses. That's Sullivan Island. They keep the new slaves there for a month or so before bringing them onto the mainland, in case they have some kind of exotic disease."

"I see."

Papa had told me a little about the pest houses. Although he had explained to me more than once why it was necessary, and why slavery was necessary, in order to build this new country, I did not approve of the practice. It seemed wrong to me that one man should own another and that children should be so heartlessly separated from their mothers on the auction block. Evidently the city fathers of Charles Town had no such misgivings. I could see, even before I disembarked from the Royal Thomas, that African servants far outnumbered their English masters.

Mr. Bridges, as he had promised my father, insisted on accompanying me to the Pink House Tavern. As we left the ship I could not help but appreciate the ingenuity of the settlers who had come here from all over Europe—Germany, Scotland, Ireland and France as well as England. The marketplace along the docks seemed to be thriving. Brightly colored calicos, cottons and silks were on display, and beneath a canopy of hides many products made of deerskin were available for purchase—gloves, boots for men, ladies' shoes, coats and greatcoats, breeches and pantaloons. There were even books bound in deerskin. I also saw barrels of rice and all kinds of tea and straw baskets full of herbs and spices. I was astonished at the activity and I greatly admired the enterprise. It made Queen Anne's Creek seem even more like a sleepy little village, where nothing much happens—until young ladies kill their sweethearts and must then make a run for their lives.

Mr. Bridges interrupted my thoughts. "I want to beg pardon, miss, ahead of time," he ventured.

"Whatever for, Mr. Bridges? You have been nothing but kind."

"The part of town I must take you into," he explained. "'Tis a bit . . . unsavory, especially for a gently raised young lady such as yourself. I am surprised your father did not think to send me on whatever this business is."

"You must not worry," I assured him. "I am not as sheltered as you might think. It is my father's wish that I deliver a letter into Mr. Garrity's hands."

"Then it is not for me to question. Still . . ." his voice trailed off as if he didn't want to finish.

"What is so unsavory about that location?" I asked.

"Well, miss . . . aside from the fact that the Pink House is a gathering place for the roughest kind of sailors and scoundrels from every corner of the world, it's right in the middle of Mulatto Alley."

"Oh."

I knew about Mulatto Alley—Jacob had told me. There were bordellos up and down the street with ladies of every color and flavor (as Jacob had said, laughing in the way I had so loved), all there for a man's pleasure if he had the price. My heart did a funny little lurch. Would I always see his face, stunned and pale, that last time he had looked at me?

"Please have no fear for my delicate sensitivities, Mr. Bridges," I said, forcing back my tears. "We shall stay no longer than it takes us to find Marcus Garrity."

We turned a corner and we were there. The Pink House was impossible to miss. Perhaps to ward off his own discomfort, my first mate launched into an explanation of how it came to be so pink.

"Built of Bermuda stone," he said. "Ships brought it from the West Indies, using it for ballast, as they did the cobblestones of the very street we are walking on."

"How fascinating," I replied as he held the door open for me and ushered me inside. "Thank you, Mr. Bridges."

The wide, square room that comprised the entire first floor of the grogerie had low ceilings and at one end of it, a large fireplace where a pig was roasting on a spit. A group of men were gathered around it, some staring into the flames, a few eating heartily some kind of stew in a bowl made of hard bread, and one or two bantering with the stout and cheerful cook who was turning the pig. The walls were paneled in swamp cypress and at the other end of the room, I saw a narrow staircase. Several trestle tables were set about and Mr. Bridges escorted me to one of them and signaled the serving maid to come to us.

"Bring me a tankard of ale," he told her. "And for the lady, a glass of sherry or brandy, if you have it."

"Lady, is it?" the girl replied with a derisive snort. "If she be a lady you wouldna be bringin' 'er in 'ere."

"Mind your tongue, wench," Bridges commanded harshly. "Do you have the brandy or not?"

"Never mind," I spoke softly to the maid as I reached into my reticule and took out a silver coin. "Bring me a tankard as well. What is your name? I am Kate."

This, as I knew it would, completely disarmed her.

"Molly," she said quickly. "Beg pardon, miss. I meant no 'arm."

"None taken, Molly," I assured her as I pressed the shilling into her hand. "I am looking for Mr. Marcus Garrity. Do you know him?"

Surprised, she looked at the coin a moment before securing it in her blouse, hiding it in the generous swell of her bosom. "Indeed yes, miss. 'E be upstairs now, engaged wi' one o' the—I mean," she paused and glanced at Mr. Bridges. "'E's likely engaged in a game o' cribbage or some 'at."

"Go and fetch our drinks, then," said Bridges, his face turning as pink as the house. "And be quick about it. Then go and fetch Mr. Garrity. Tell him someone's come with a message from Captain Russell."

Our tankards were but half-finished when Mr. Garrity joined us, a scowl clouding his visage. He came directly to our table and sat down across from me, and his frown changed to a wide smile.

"I'd know ye anywhere, miss," he said. "You be the image of your dear mother. Mr. Bridges—it's been an age since I've laid me eyes on you."

"Indeed it has," Bridges returned his greeting. "Good to see you, Marcus."

Relief flooded over me; there would be no need to entreat

and persuade to gain his loyalty. "I am so happy to meet you, Mr. Garrity," I said. "I bring tidings from my father and a letter he instructed me to give to none other than yourself."

Molly brought us another round of ale and set a full tankard before Marcus Garrity. I noted his Scotsman's brogue, his thick neck and muscular frame, and eyes that could go in an instant from hard as flint to soft and kind. He took a sip of his drink before he broke the seal on Papa's letter and unfolded it. He read it, looked at me for a moment and read it again. And then he walked to the fireplace, threw it into the flames and watched as it burned down to ashes before he returned to our table.

"It will be an honor to serve you, Captain Russell," he said, giving me the respect my father's missive commanded. "I knew your grandfather as well," he continued. "I was an orphan and he took me on when I were but twelve year old, to serve as cabin boy on his ship. Taught me to read and write, he did. I owe me life to him and I would lay me neck on the chopping block for him or his kin."

"I wish I had known him," I replied softly. "Thank you for that, Mr. Garrity. And it makes no difference to you that I am a woman?"

"None at all," he assured me. "For your father to have such faith in your abilities lets me know he has trained you well, and I know from experience that a seafaring man—or woman—could have no better training than what he gets from Steadman Russell. Your father's missive said ye'll be needing a crew."

"Yes," I said. Feeling I could trust him completely, I added, "And a plan. Papa thinks I should set sail immediately for—"

He held up a hand to silence me. "Not here," he said. "Too many ears." He signaled Molly and ordered ale and vittles to be taken up to the third floor for us. To Mr. Bridges, he said, "Best you start putting the word about. Molly will bring you paper and pen so you can make a handbill to post. Hang it on the wall next to the fireplace yonder and the news will spread quick enough. What crew have ye now?"

"Eight good and able-bodied men," Bridges told him. "She'll also need a first mate and quartermaster. My instructions are to find passage back to Queen Anne's Creek after seeing Cap'n Steadman's daughter safely out of port here, with a complete crew and fully stocked vessel."

"Put on the handbill that sailors be needed for a brigantine, with half wages paid on signing aboard and the balance at the end of service." Marcus turned to me. "You'll need at least thirty," he said. "I be an excellent quartermaster. You need look no further for that. Come now—follow me."

The third floor was, like the first, one large square room. There were fewer tables and in each corner sat a comfortable sofa, three of them behind screens where, I surmised, a gentleman could take his pleasure with one of the women the establishment kept for that purpose. The walls slanted in from a gambrel roof. Marcus seated me at one of the tables and then, standing before me, he said, "You know that as long as Blackbeard is alive you can never return home?"

"Yes. I am resigned to that fact." By his statement, I knew that my father's letter had told him everything. I could not repress a sigh. "I believe I shall never see my father again," I said. "After what I have done, I suppose even that fate is too kind for me."

"If it helps, Captain Russell—"

"Please—you must call me Kate."

He grinned. "Cap'n Kate it is," he said. "Well, if it helps you to know it, Jacob was a scoundrel—a cheat at cards and a rogue with the ladies. He woulda robbed the farthings off a dead man's eyes."

"Thank you," I replied. "I appreciate your kind intent

but it doesn't help. You see, I was in love with him and while it is true he betrayed me, I did not mean to kill him. It was a terrible, tragic accident."

"That may be, but Teach will never believe it—and he will not care. He will put such a price on your head that it will be tempting for many a man to earn it, be he friend or foe. Blackbeard will have his revenge if he finds you. So we must make sure he does not."

‡‡

Early Summer, 2015
Corolla, North Carolina

Jonathan woke early the next morning, just as dawn broke in an explosion of pink and gold and red, reflecting off the blue water like splashes of paint on canvas. Lying in bed, he enjoyed the view out his window for a few minutes before he stirred. He'd had a restless night, which was no surprise considering Patrice's phone call. He should have expected it. He should have known she would find some way to ruin his trip.

He'd planned to spend another day on the boat fishing with the guys but that was out of the question now. According to his wife, there was a problem with the beach house she wanted and he had to meet with the realtor—and maybe the mortgage broker—to straighten it out.

"So what problems are we talking about?" he'd asked Patrice. The night before, after dinner, he'd been back in his room for only a few minutes when his cell phone started ringing.

"I don't know," Patrice had told him. "Rich said it was minor but I need you to take care of it, Jonathan. I don't want anything to mess this up. That house is the perfect summer place. You know how much I love it."

"Yeah, I do," he'd said. "So I'm meeting with Rich? What time?"

"No—Rich is out of town. You're meeting with someone named Mattie. She works with him and she'll meet you at nine in the morning at Duck's. Don't keep her waiting." Duck's Coffee, News and Books Cottage was a local hangout, popular with residents, fishermen and tourists alike.

"No problem," he'd said, when he'd really wanted to protest her invasion into the closest thing he'd had to a vacation in ages. Jim had two more days reserved with Captain Harv and this would cost Jonathan one of them. But he didn't argue with his wife anymore; he'd lost all interest in that. He had pretty much lost interest in doing anything with her—even sex, which he'd once enjoyed immensely.

It had gotten better, a little, since he'd come to believe she had cheated on him only briefly, and that such an aberration was over and done. But it wasn't as good as it had been. He didn't believe it would ever be good with Patrice again, and he hadn't been able to get past resenting that.

Lying now in an unfamiliar bed, he thought about packing his things and heading home after he saw the realtor. The old bitterness, the resentment over his wife's affair, started building in him again, but he refused to give in to it. He decided to stay. Even if today turned out to be a wash, he'd still have tomorrow. Today he'd take care of business with the new house, kick around the islands for a while, stop by the Brew Station and check out the wind turbine and be back in time for dinner with the guys. Then he'd have one more day on the boat. One more day of drinking in sunshine and sea air and the kind of male camaraderie that didn't require any heavy thinking. He deserved that, and he'd be damned if he was going to let Patrice take it away from him.

That decided, he got up, showered and dressed, explaining his change of plans to Jim and Mike on his way out. He took their good-natured taunts about being whipped in the spirit in which they were dumped on him.

He set the navigation system in his rental car and followed it to Ducks, his mind wandering to the previous day's events—especially Dave offering him the still-beating tuna heart. His gorge rose slightly but, as he had on the boat, he fought off the urge to vomit. The heart had been warm and rubbery and he hadn't wanted to put it in his mouth. It had been a matter of pride, with his buddies watching, amused—but more than that, it was the look in Dave's eyes that convinced him. He'd chewed it quickly, getting it just pliable enough to swallow.

The bite had started not long after that, and had kept up most of the day.

As he passed the mushroom-shaped water tower, one of the local landmarks, Jonathan tried to relax. If he spent the day doing what he wanted to do, it wouldn't be so bad—as long as the problem with the house really was minor. He pulled into the crushed oyster-shell parking lot at Duck's and got out of the car, pausing a moment to enjoy the view.

The place had started out as an old hunting lodge some New York duck hunters had built back in the 1920s. It had been converted just a few years ago to a chic coffee bar. The old cottage, rustic on the outside, had a wide inviting porch across the front, and a white picket fence encircling it. Because of erosion along the shore, the new owners had moved it about a hundred yards from its original location but they'd had the good sense not to upgrade its weathered cedar shake exterior. Inside, everything was new. The lighting was good enough to enjoy the books in the cedar shelves lining the walls but dim enough to give the place a cozy ambiance.

The books were a mix of current bestsellers and old favorites, with a corner shelf full of books for kids. There were a few tables inside and more tables and chairs on the porch. A gentle breeze was blowing, providing some relief from the heat of early summer. At least this realtor—this Mattie—had picked a good place to meet.

Jonathan went inside, browsed the shelves for a few minutes and then got in line to get coffee. It annoyed him that the books were not organized in any logical order—not alphabetically, not by author or type, fiction or nonfiction. Rich had told him it had been tried, but with all the customers taking them out, leafing through them while having coffee and then putting them back randomly, there was no point.

He asked for straight, hot and black—none of those fancy flavored blends for him—and took it out on the porch to wait for Mattie. He hadn't thought to ask Patrice if she knew what kind of car the woman drove, but he was sure it would look pretty much like most realtor's cars. They all had a little flash to them.

It didn't take long for him to get bored. He slugged back his coffee, which had cooled considerably, and walked down the rickety wooden steps to the parking lot. As if that's exactly what she'd been waiting for, an attractive blond wheeled quickly in, going just a touch too fast in a new white Ford Explorer. Her license plate read PIRATE GIRL. She parked and got out of the car, all long legs, long blond hair, self-assurance and a full bosom that accentuated her small waist. She looked to be in her mid to late thirties, with a radiant complexion and makeup that was subdued and perfect. He knew it was rude to stare but he couldn't help it.

"You got a problem with something, Yankee?" she asked when she looked up and caught him at it.

"Not at all," he said. "Just enjoying the view."

She gave him a big flash of a smile and he wondered why he'd said it. It wasn't like him to flirt. Not like him at all.

"Are you Mattie?" he asked.

"Sure am, sugah," she answered and he noted that her accent was just as deep and southern as Dave's, but much more charming. Her voice had a pleasant, soft lilt to it that was kind of sexy. "You Jonathan?" He nodded and returned her smile. "It's easy to see you're not a local boy," she concluded.

"How can you tell?" He was beginning to relax. He moved closer to her car.

"Oh, you got a different way of walkin' and talkin'. Not like the beer-guzzlin' rednecks around here." She paused and looked him up and down, head to toe and back again. "You are one tall drinka water."

"You're almost as tall as I am," he observed.

"Yeah," she replied with a grin. "Almost."

"Can I get you a cup of coffee?"

"Thanks—but none of that flavored stuff," she said. "Just low-fat milk and some Sweet an' Low, okay?"

He liked her. Patrice would have ordered the Coconut Crunch with a shot of vanilla—and she would have hated Mattie simply for being younger and prettier with a bright personality to match. He got Mattie her coffee and another cup for himself and went back to the porch where she was waiting.

"So what happened to Rich?" he asked as he passed her cup and sat down in one of the oversized wooden deck chairs across from her.

"He went up to New Jersey to see his daughter's new baby," Mattie said. "He sends his regrets. He told me how much he enjoyed working with you when you bought that property in Pirate's Cove a few years ago. What made you sell?"

"Oh, you know—the family kind of outgrew it," he lied. He'd actually sold it right after he'd learned about Patrice's affair, when he'd planned to leave her. "It was small and my kids had to share a room, which neither of them liked."

"You got boys or girls?" she asked. It sounded like she

was really interested and not just making conversation. He thought that probably made her good at selling real estate.

"Girls," he said. "Two. Both teenagers now, which makes it even more important for them not to share a room—not even for five minutes."

She stirred her coffee and sipped it. He liked the way she licked her lower lip as she put her cup down and gazed out at the sea for a moment. Then she asked, "You get down here often? You and the family?"

"Not as often as I'd like," he said. "This time it's a last-minute fishing trip, nothing I planned. So I guess it's good I came down. Patrice—that's my wife—she said there's some kind of problem with the loan?"

"Oh, no—not the loan." Mattie took another swig of her coffee. "Your credit is impeccable. Nothing to worry about there. The owner has decided he doesn't want to sell after all."

"I see," he said. "That's too bad. Patrice is really in love with the place. She's going to be pretty upset."

"We sure wouldn't want that," Mattie said softly, looking right into his eyes as if she had something else on her mind.

He wondered if she was flirting with him. It had been so long since a woman had done that he didn't know if he'd be able to pick up on the signals. Or what he would do about it.

"Don't worry," she continued after a moment. "I've got some beautiful properties to show you—even better than that one. Let's stop by my office so I can pick up the listings and we'll make a day of it. I'll show you some amazing places and buy you lunch. I'm sure we have something you'll like. We can leave your car here and pick it up later. How 'bout it, Yankee?"

She tossed her hair, releasing a light whiff of her perfume—just enough to be tantalizing. It smelled clean and crisp and citrusy.

"All right," he agreed.

It was ideal beach weather—hot but not brutal—and he liked the expert way she handled her car, even if she did drive a little too fast. Soon they were walking into her office. Outside it had a white stucco façade and tall, modern windows. Inside it was all rich leather and antique oak. Plants of all sizes and varieties were set artistically about and there was a big philodendron with vines that stretched from the table where it sat to half way around the room.

"That's some plant," he said, pointing to it.

"Oh, that's my baby," she said. "Had it for years, and I take very good care of it." She added softly, "I take care of everything that's important to me."

She maintained eye contact with him as she delicately touched the diamond pendant that hung from a gold chain around her neck. It fell right in the valley between her breasts. There was no question about it, he thought. She was definitely flirting. He was aroused, and he decided not to feel guilty about it.

"Good to know," he said.

"Well, let's do this and get out of here," she told him, reaching into a desk drawer and pulling out a list of oceanfront properties. She opened another drawer and extracted a coffee cup with her business card in it. "Here," she said. "This is for you. My cell number's on the back of the card, so you can always reach me."

"Thanks," he said. The cup was white and had a beautiful old brigantine engraved on the side of it, in a pencil-like gold etching. He turned it around and read the inscription on the back: *The Royal Thomas, flying the heart and daggers, lost at sea in 1721, off the coast of the Carolinas.* "Where'd it come from?"

"I'm not really sure," she replied. "Some vendor must have left it here. Rich likes to have little goodies on hand to give to clients, after he has them stamped with our logo and phone number. I think that's a sample."

They had a full morning, looking at properties in North Corolla's Whalebone Beach, and then moving south to Ocean Sands. After lunch they drove down to Southern Shores, and then back to Kill Devil's Hill, where he saw the only place that really impressed him. It was different than the other beach homes, darker somehow, but something about it called to him. It had space around it instead of neighbors encroaching on all sides, which he liked; it gave the place a sense of isolation. He hoped Patrice would go for it—although he didn't think much about Patrice as he drove all over the Outer Banks with Mattie. She seemed interested in his work and she really listened to his ideas about green energy. She was even happy to stop by the wind turbine, where he explained what his company was trying to do for the environment and for future generations.

They ended the day with a walk on the beach, both holding their shoes as they strolled (and he resisted the urge to take Mattie's hand). Then they had dinner at Ocean Boulevard Bistro. He couldn't remember the last time he'd felt so relaxed.

"So, Yankee—when you gonna get down this way again?" she asked as she finished her rum and Diet Coke.

"I'm not sure. My wife has to see the house. She'll be coming back with me—probably in three or four weeks."

"That long, huh?"

"I won't be able to catch a break from work before then. In the meantime, we can speed up the process. You have my application on file and we already know my credit is good. Let's go ahead and make an offer on the place."

"If you're sure," she said. "I mean, before your wife sees it?"

"I'm sure."

Both of them were silent, caught up in their own private thoughts, as Mattie drove Jonathan back to his car. "Well, I'm glad you found something you liked," she said as she parked next to his rental. She was looking into his eyes again and he had a feeling she wasn't talking about houses.

"Yeah," he told her. "I did. Thanks for putting up with me. I didn't mean to take up your whole day."

"It was my pleasure," she said, and again he wondered if she was talking about houses.

He wasn't going to address it, though—he wouldn't even know how. She was definitely putting out signals, which surprised him. He'd never been one to inspire that kind of interest in women—or if he had, he certainly hadn't realized it.

"Thanks again, Mattie," he said, enjoying the sweet scent of her and the remote possibility that she could be his if he decided to pursue the subject.

Back at the fisherman's retreat, Jim told him the weather forecast had reported a storm moving in. Captain Harv had called to let them know the next day's outing now depended on the weather. "But," Jim added, "I convinced him that if we get out early enough we can get in a couple of hours before it hits—so get to bed, sailor. We gotta get up around five to beat the storm."

Chapter Four

Early Spring, 1717
Charles Town, Carolina

Within an hour of Mr. Bridges posting the handbill he had made, sailors were lining up to talk to him. After Mr. Garrity and I enjoyed a leisurely meal of stew, bread, potatoes and roast pig, he escorted me back downstairs. I was relieved to see so many there.

"I am not surprised," he told me. "The Pink House is frequented by good men wantin' to sign on a voyage that promises good fortune. We will find a worthy crew—as long as you are not bothered by a reputation that can be called into question. Some of 'em mayhap served on pirate ships but that don't make 'em less of a sailor. Makes 'em better, in fact, is my opinion."

"I am happy to trust your judgment, Mr. Garrity," I said. "I know you and Mr. Bridges will not steer me wrong."

"Indeed not—but we must do this quickly, Kate. It would not be good to linger in port."

"Yes, I agree." I glanced at the first man in the line. He was bald and missing the better part of an ear and he was cleaning his broken nails with the tip of a knife.

"Step up, mate," Marcus said, and I noticed that sometimes his smile didn't quite reach his eyes.

"Please order more ale for yourself and Mr. Garrity," I told Bridges as Marcus began the interview. "And see if there's a pot of tea or coffee to be had in this place."

The second man in line, also bald, was tall and muscular and he had a wicked looking scar on the back of his head. Engaged in conversation with the sailor behind him he had his back to Marcus.

"Next up!" Marcus said and when the man didn't turn around, Marcus hit his head, dead on the jagged scar, with the flat of his hand. The man yelped and pulling a dagger from his belt, he turned viciously on Marcus.

"Who the blasted dickens do ye think ye are!" he bellowed, sounding like a snarling hound after a jack rabbit. Then his disposition instantly changed. "Marcus!" he exclaimed joyfully, a big grin spreading across his pockmarked face as he put his knife away. "Where the bloody 'ell have ye been?"

"As far away from you as I could get, you bilge-suckin' blackguard" Marcus retorted, and this time I noted that his smile did indeed reach into his eyes. The two big men hugged like long-lost brothers and slapped each other on the back. "How have you been, Oliver?"

"Drunk as oft as I could be, and lying atop a pretty little wench when I couldn't," Oliver replied, and they both laughed. "So 'tis you doin' the hiring here?"

"Aye," Marcus told him. "Let me introduce you to my new captain." He turned and nodded in my direction. "Captain Kate Russell, this here's Oliver Biddle and a better first mate there never was."

Oliver stared at me. "Captain?" he scoffed. "Don't be tellin' me you're serving under a woman's command!"

"Indeed I am," Marcus returned. "Or I will be, come high tide two days hence, as quartermaster. But she's not just any woman. She be the daughter of Steadman Russell who never had any sons—and he's trained her himself. I'm as proud to serve her as I was him."

"But—a woman?" Oliver seemed to be having trouble with the concept. I extended my hand to him.

"I'm very glad to make your acquaintance, Mr. Biddle," I said politely, as if we were at high tea. "The Royal Thomas is a fine ship in need of an excellent crew. I hope you will join us."

He looked at me, surprised, and then he threw back his head and laughed uproariously. "Thank 'e, mum," he said, taking my hand, engulfed in his huge fist. "Sign me up, then." He slapped Marcus on the back again and added, "I wouldn't miss it for the world! A wench fer a captain—this'll be rich!"

At this, Marcus climbed up on a chair to better address the crowd of applicants. "Here now, you laggards! Listen up!" he shouted. "The ship is sturdy, the wages are good and the work is true. But if any man jack of you will be draggin' his feet on taking orders from a woman, best be on your way. Cap'n Kate comes from a long line of hardy seamen. I served with her grandfather and her father, who taught her everything she needs to know—and she's under my protection by his decree. The Royal Thomas is hers and hers alone and she be needing a loyal crew. So—are ye in or are ye out?"

It was no surprise to me that some of them swore and walked away. The bigger surprise was that most of them stayed. Bridges brought me a pot of strong coffee with a generous helping of milk and sugar, as well as a plate of biscuits that were surprisingly tasty. I shared them with him and Mr. Garrity.

Before long, we had found a cook in Andrew Potts who brought two galley assistants and a fine array of cooking utensils with him. We also took on a second mate, two sail makers and a carpenter. Among the many seamen who remained in the line, Marcus found three waisters, two holders, a couple of after-gangers and a very able anchor man. Seeing that I could, without worry, leave the hiring of the crew in his hands, I asked Bridges to take me back to the ship.

I was exhausted—mentally, physically and spiritually—and I needed a good night's rest as I intended to be up at first light. Mr. Potts had agreed to meet me in the marketplace so we could select fresh vegetables, rice, smoked meats, salted fish and other provisions for our journey to England. I told Marcus to meet me at the market as well; there we could breakfast and map out our destination.

✠✠

Early Summer, 2015
Outer Banks, North Carolina

Jonathan saw dark clouds in the distance, and the swell of the sea and the rolling waves were on the rise. They'd gotten out on the boat early that morning and the weather had seemed fine, with the predicted storm holding far out at sea. The bite was good and he had all but forgotten the warnings. Jim had made salad and sandwiches from the previous night's leftovers and they'd had a hearty lunch. When the clouds started building, Captain Harv turned the boat around, heading back to port. Some of the waves were cresting almost level with the boat.

Dave pulled in all the lines and ordered everyone to put on their life jackets, adding gruffly, "Do it now!"

"Pretty exciting, huh?" Jim shouted.

"Terrifying, if you ask me!" Jonathan yelled back as a wave crashed over the bow of the ship, sending a spray of sea foam right in his face. The truth was, he had never felt so alive in his life. He had a quick flash of himself being swept overboard. In his mind he heard Patrice, agonized, demanding to know how he could be so inconsiderate—how he could get himself killed when his wife and children needed him. And somehow that made the wild beauty of nature even more enjoyable.

"Want to go inside with the others?" Jim asked. Captain Harv's cabin was roomier than most of the other charter boats Jonathan had been on.

"Shouldn't we help Dave batten down the hatches or something?" Jonathan was stalling but he didn't know why, except that he wanted to be out in the storm.

The wind was stronger now and Jim had to shout again. "Nah—we'd just be in the way. Something else for him to worry about."

"Okay—yeah. Right behind you," Jonathan said, still peering out at the crashing waves. After a moment, he followed Jim inside. The ride was rough but they made it back to port without incident. A little shaken, Jim remarked that he was glad to be on solid ground again.

The storm continued for hours, lashing the Outer Banks without mercy. Their host kept the weather channel on all afternoon and they watched anxiously, certain they would hear hurricane warnings, but it was just heavy rain, rough seas and strong winds. Jonathan spent the afternoon reading and thinking about Mattie. He was tempted to call her but resisted the urge. He didn't know what could come of it—especially if he'd misread what he thought were overtures. Anyway, he'd see her again soon, when he brought Patrice down to look at the house.

There was something about the place that connected with him the moment he stepped inside. He couldn't have described it, certainly not to Patrice. He just . . . *liked* it. It felt right. It was the right house. The house he wanted. The house that wanted him. As soon as the thought occurred to him, he realized how bizarre it was.

Dinner was delicious—steak, shrimp and some of the fish they'd caught the day before, all grilled to perfection.

The men laughed and joked and told tall tales about previous experiences out at sea, trying to ignore the fury of the storm. Finally, the weather settled down a bit. Jonathan decided to turn in.

After he'd brushed his teeth and packed his bags, he went out on the deck for one more lung full of ocean air. The rain had become a gentle mist, although dark clouds still roiled in the sky above. Jim, Mike and Tim were on the deck too, smoking cigars and sipping bourbon. After exchanging a few words, each man drifted into his own private thoughts, looking out at the tempestuous sea.

Suddenly thunder boomed louder than Jonathan had ever heard it. There was a bright flash of lightning and a volley of huge raindrops pounded the deck and the men standing there. They took shelter beneath the big umbrella so they could watch the storm. Rain poured from the sky like a waterfall for a minute or so and then, as suddenly as it had started, it stopped. The moon came out, full and bright, and as it dipped through the departing clouds it rendered some of the most beautiful colors Jonathan had ever seen—silver, white, violet and dark navy blue with touches of pink at the edges. The three men went to the railing and gazed out at the eerie stillness.

As the moon climbed in an inky sky, a mist rose from the sea and for a moment Jonathan felt an almost transcendent calm steal over him. Stars were beginning to dot the night canopy and he stared into the distance, out at the horizon.

And what he saw there made him draw in his breath and hold it for a moment.

Patches of mist and fog drifted, separated, came together and separated again. The moon reflected off the surface of the water and shone through the mist, making it sparkle like diamonds. Then it separated once more, for just a few seconds, and in the distance he saw a dark shadow drifting slowly, gliding across the surface of the water. It entered a patch of moonlight and he could see it clearly, sharply outlined in the glow. It was a ship—and he saw a woman standing on the bow. Like the ship, she was from another era—one long since passed. Her vessel was old and square-rigged, and its sails were unfurled to capture the wind. There was something about it—and about the woman—that was achingly familiar. As if he should know it. As if he should know *her*.

She turned then, and he got a glimpse of her pale face and long red hair.

And her eyes.

She looked directly into his, her eyes glinting in the moonlight with unshed tears. Her gaze was full of sorrow. He had never seen eyes so full of pleading. It hit him like a sucker punch to the gut.

She wanted something from him.

"What the hell?" Jim said under his breath.

"You see it too?" Jonathan asked, still staring at her, feeling like he was in a dream.

"Yeah," Tim said, also staring. "It's a ship—like, one of those old-timey ships you see in pirate movies." Mike also seemed mesmerized. He didn't speak.

The ship was about a hundred feet long and traveling at twelve or thirteen knots, the best Jonathan could tell. The biggest sail was in the center and it had two or three smaller sails in front. They all watched in a silence that was almost reverent, for maybe five seconds, until it drifted into another patch of fog.

Then the fog lifted. The ship was gone.

"What the hell was that?" Mike asked.

After a moment, Jim spoke. "Ghost ship," he said quietly. "Never seen one before now and wish I hadn't seen this one. I didn't think they really existed but they sure as hell do."

Jonathan didn't know how to react and he didn't trust his voice. As ridiculous as he knew it was, he thought if he tried to talk he would start crying. The experience was that deep, that profound. Even when the ship was gone, the image of it remained burned into his brain, engraved into his consciousness.

He'd seen a ghost ship—and seeing it *meant* something. It was important.

He would never forget it. After a moment, when he could be sure he wouldn't give way to the emotion that was trying to take over, he asked, "Did you see—was there anyone on board?"

Tim shook his head and Mike said, "No—it was just an old sailing ship. It was there, though. We all saw it. And then it just disappeared."

Jonathan walked along the deck, still searching the horizon for any sign of the mysterious ship, wondering what he had just witnessed. Something new was pulling at him, something powerful and strange—a yearning he couldn't name, one that would consume him if he didn't satisfy it. It took a minute for him to realize that Mike was right behind him. Jonathan stopped, still looking out at the waves.

"That was weird," Mike said.

"Yeah."

"Maybe that's why they call this area the graveyard of the Atlantic."

"For real?" asked Jonathan.

"Yeah," Mike told him. "There are ships all over the place down there, under the waves. Thousands of them."

"Seriously?" returned Jonathan. "Thousands?"

"Yep," said Mike. "There's a stretch that goes along the Outer Banks of North Carolina and Virginia, outside the mouth of the Chesapeake Bay. It's where the undercurrent of waters from Greenland collide with the warm waters of the Gulf Stream from the Caribbean Sea."

"There's even a museum about it in Hatteras Village, with

lots of cool shit in it," said Tim. "Even some Nazi torpedo boats. Hell, if they could drain the Atlantic, they'd find a ton of ships down there, some of them worth a fortune. They'd find gold coins and jewels and treasure chests, to boot. Pieces of old wrecks wash ashore all the time around here—and sometimes old coins and stuff."

"Really?" Jonathan couldn't be sure he wasn't kidding. "Along the Outer Banks?"

"Yeah," said Mike. "You can keep what you find, too. They even find pieces of old ships on the beach. Most people think it's just ordinary driftwood. If Captain Harv isn't careful, that could be his fate someday. All it takes is one tuna too many—well, that or a nor'easter."

"You mean a hurricane?" asked Jonathan.

"No," Tim interjected. "It's the nor'easters that do the most damage. The winds whip down the east coast and kick the shit out of the Outer Banks. They feed off the warm southern waters. With hurricanes, the water gets into everything and the wind blows out summer houses and spews sand all over the place. But with the nor'easters, we lose a ton of sand from the beaches. Dead bodies wash ashore, too."

"Maybe that's what we saw," said Mike. "The ocean giving up her dead." He laughed and Jim tried to, but it came out sounding hollow.

Then Tim said, "Don't listen to him, Jonathan. He's just messing with you. There's no bodies. The sharks and crabs eat all the bodies. And the boats disintegrate over the years. Only the treasure remains." He added nervously, "But we shouldn't be treating it like a joke. Maybe we shouldn't be talking about it at all. It gives me the willies."

"Before, you said you wish you hadn't seen it," said Jonathan. "Why?"

Tim took a long drag on his cigar and then put it out. "Nothing good comes of a ghost ship sighting," he said. "Like my grandpa always told me, you don't want to see one and you shouldn't go looking for 'em. A ghost ship is not a harbinger of good things to come. Only sadness follows a sighting like we had tonight. Yeah—I wish to hell I hadn't seen it."

That's what he felt, Jonathan realized. Sadness. Such a sadness that it was almost overwhelming.

They stayed out on the deck a while longer. The night had turned clear and beautiful, as if the storm had never happened. Morning would come all too soon, Jonathan thought, and he needed to get some sleep—but he was starting to hate the idea of going home. He wanted to stay. He wanted to see the ghost ship again and he wanted a closer look at the woman he was sure he'd seen standing at its bow. Even after Tim and Mike went inside, he remained where he was, scanning the horizon, hoping to catch another glimpse of it.

Of her.

At last, he went to bed and fell into a fitful sleep. He was awake at first light, still restless and uneasy. He stared at the rotating ceiling fan, somehow finding comfort in its gentle murmur and hypnotic rhythm as he thought about the woman on the boat. Who was she? Why had he seen her, when no one else had?

Realizing there would be no more sleep for him, he got up, took a shower and got dressed. He threw his toothbrush and shaving stuff into his bag but it wasn't until he started to close it that he remembered the cup Mattie had given him. He picked it up and glanced at the engraving on its side. The words jumped out at him.

The Royal Thomas, lost at sea in 1721, off the coast of the Carolinas.

It looked exactly like the ship he had seen. The ghost ship. He couldn't have imagined it. Tim and Mike had seen it too.

Chapter Five

On the drive home, Jonathan stopped in Virginia Beach for a late lunch with a friend and sometimes client. Bruce was head of a construction firm he had worked with a couple of years before, to move the old Seven Foot Knoll Lighthouse from Chesapeake Bay to a property near Pier Five. It had been a delicate operation—structurally and emotionally. The lighthouse was a historical landmark, a century and a half old and made out of iron. It was one of the oldest in Maryland and had a unique screw-pile design. Jonathan had thought at the time it was just a hunk of junk but Baltimore city government and some citizen volunteers were determined to preserve it. After lunch, he and Bruce drove out to the lighthouse and looked around. Jonathan enjoyed seeing it again, but he knew he was stalling. He didn't want his little getaway to end.

Four hours later he was back in Baltimore, turning into his cul de sac in an exclusive section of Long Green Valley. It had been a long drive and the closer he'd gotten to home the less he'd wanted to go there. His mind kept drifting back to the Outer Banks, to Mattie's ready smile and long, trim legs—and to the strange sighting of the ghost ship and the apparition he'd seen standing at its bow.

It was after nine and the house was dark. When Alex heard Jonathan put his key in the door, he emitted a happy little yelp and was there in the foyer to greet him, wagging his tail. Absently, Jonathan gave him a quick pat on the head and then, switching lights on as he went, he headed for the kitchen. He grabbed a cheese stick and a beer, which would be his dinner, and took them into the den. Alex jumped up on the sofa beside him for a snuggle. The energetic little rat terrier had started out as a pet for Elaine and Christiana but soon formed an attachment to Jonathan, who fed him in the mornings while he had his coffee. For a few minutes Jonathan gave him the attention he demanded, trying to get his mind off the sighting of the ghost woman and her ethereal ship. It didn't work. He couldn't shake the sense of some presence reaching out to him, whispering in his ear.

It was an unusual sensation—warm and gentle—almost like he was asleep. Whatever it was, it had changed him. Somehow, everything in his life seemed different. He knew it.

He also knew it was the ghost ship that had done it.

It had looked like the pirate ships from the books and movies of his boyhood—of that he was certain, even though he'd seen it for only a few seconds. It was like the ship on the cup Mattie had given him, so it had to be from some time in the eighteenth century, when pirates had roamed the seas.

He knew he wasn't delusional. If he was, then so were Mike and Tim. While Jonathan didn't understand how the sighting could influence him so strongly, he had no doubt that it had. Whatever was different, whatever had changed, he knew he would never be able to change it back. He didn't even want to.

The image of that ship, and the woman on board, tugged at his heart, like a deep longing for something he hadn't even known he wanted. Or mourning the loss of something he'd had no idea he possessed. It was almost like love, like the romantic love he'd once had for Patrice, but not exactly. Somehow it went even deeper than that.

Two hours later, Jonathan woke up on the couch. Alex was nuzzling his shoulder and whimpering, wanting to be let out.

"Okay, okay," Jonathan mumbled, half asleep. "Let's go."

He stood up on shaky legs, like a man on land after having

been too long at sea. Passing through the kitchen, he noticed that the microwave door was slightly ajar, which meant that Patrice had left dinner in there for him. After he let Alex out, he saw her note, scribbled on a Post-It, stuck to the refrigerator door.

"Gone with the girls to the art show opening at Mount Vernon. There's a reception after, for the artist (who we're sponsoring, in case you forgot). We'll be late. Don't wait up."

Suddenly he was starving. He quickly nuked the leftover pot roast, green beans and mashed potatoes his wife had made earlier and waited a few seconds for it to cool. After he wolfed it down he turned on the back porch light and went out into the yard to get Alex.

"Alex! Come here, boy," he called out, but he didn't see the dog. He walked a few feet toward the fence, until he got to the small kiddie pool Patrice had bought for Alex to use as a doggie pool. "Alex—come on!" Jonathan called again and the terrier came running around the corner of the house. He went straight to the pool and greedily lapped up water, then he started scratching at an image imprinted on the bottom of the pool. It was something Jonathan had seen many times but had never really thought about—a pirate, holding up a sword with that brazen, confident air only a pirate has.

Again, Jonathan thought of the ghost ship.

✝✝

Early Spring, 1717
Charles Town, Carolina

The port was filled with sailing vessels of all types, and I was excited to see their flags and banners fluttering festively in the morning breeze. In spite of my troubles I felt a little better. The sea air had given me an appetite and I devoured the porridge the serving wench placed before me, along with two Dutch sweetcakes, a chunk of toasted bread and cheese and a mug of cider.

Marcus and our cook, Andrew Potts, had met me at the row of vendor stalls near the docks. After we'd purchased rice, dried beans, coffee, tea, salt, flour and corn meal, Mr. Potts went looking for new kettles and pans while Marcus and I took our breakfast. It was our plan to spend the day hiring more sailors while Mr. Bridges stayed aboard the Royal Thomas to oversee loading provisions. Marcus believed that with scores of men hanging around the wharf looking for work we would be able to complete our crew by nightfall. We would leave the following day.

We had discussed sailing up the coast to Boston to lay in materials for ship repairs and then make our way via the northern route to England, but as we finished our second pot of tea, Mr. Bridges came running up faster than I thought a man of his age could move.

"Captain Kate!" he exclaimed. "There is a problem." He had to pause to catch his breath, and then he sat down with us and lowered his voice. "I've had news of Mr. Teach."

Trying to ignore the sinking feeling in my stomach, I asked, "What news—and what is the source?"

"One of his own men," said Bridges. "He jumped ship at Beaufort Inlet and traveled by land until he got here. He was drinking and whor—uh, I mean gambling—in the Pink House last night. One of our men heard him tell how he'd made fun of the ribbons Teach ties in his beard. When he learned there was a chance Teach had heard of it, he got scared and ran."

"That's all?" asked Marcus. "Nothing newsworthy in that."

"No," said Bridges. "But he also said Blackbeard is after a young woman who killed one of his best men, and he believes she's traveling north. He bypassed Charles Town not to lose

time in gaining on the murderess. Ye'd best not make for
Boston, mum."

"Indeed, no," Marcus agreed. "Better we head straight
for England. We can take the southern route, around Jamaica.
The king's navy's looking for Teach there, so I wager he won't
show his face in the islands, at least not for a while. We can
lay in anything else we need when we reach Nassau."

I nodded. "Of course," I said. "Thank you, Mr. Bridges.
I am grateful my father entrusted me to your care. We should
get these interviews underway, Marcus, so we can be off at
dawn."

"No," he said. "We need to go now, mum—as soon as we
can make ready. With the men we took on last night and the
crew you arrived with, we'll have enough to get to Old Fort.
We'll find able-bodied men there, eager for a wage. Best you
go back to the ship with Mr. Bridges and stay out of sight. I'll
round up Mr. Potts and spread the word—discreetly—to the
new men that we be sailing earlier than planned."

As we rose from our chairs to leave I spotted the tiniest
dog I'd ever seen. I recognized the breed from paintings my
father had brought home from his travels. He was white, with
large dark eyes that looked deeply into mine as if begging
me to help him. His little black nose twitched in the air as he
sniffed the remains of our morning meal. I dipped a crust of
bread into the cream pitcher and tossed it to the small creature.
He gobbled it up.

"He's starving," I said, noting how thin he was. It looked
as if his skin had been stretched over his skeleton and his ribs
might poke through at any moment.

"We must go, Kate," said Marcus. "Leave the dog and
come away."

"I'll not leave it," I replied firmly. I approached the little
thing and leaned down to give it a pat, but it quivered as if
expecting abuse instead of affection. Then it backed up into a

pile of shredded ropes. Gently, I picked it up and held it close to me.

"Cap'n Kate," Marcus tried again. "Most of the men believe it's bad luck to have a woman on board—but two females? We'll lose half the crew we've got now."

I held the dog up and inspected its underbelly. "There, see?" I said. "It's a boy. I'm keeping him."

Beads of sweat appeared on Marcus's forehead. "Please understand me, Captain. Loyal to the bone I am and I'll gladly serve you as I did your grandfather and your father. But a dog on a boat is something I have never encountered."

"Well, there's going to be one on the Royal Thomas," I said.

Marcus made one more attempt to dissuade me. "The high winds we'll encounter will blow him right overboard."

"Don't worry—I'll watch out for him." I stroked the dog's head and he licked my hand. "I am determined to have him, Marcus." The pup looked as lost and desperate as I felt. I knew if I abandoned him I would die as surely as he would. I signaled to the serving wench and told her to bring a bowl of stewed meat, which I put down on the ground for him. He started to eat as soon as I placed it before him. Then he looked up at me, his eyes lit with hope. He wagged his tail and went back to his meat.

As we watched him, Marcus said, "I confess I've never seen a dog such as that."

"He's a Chihuahua," I explained. "They possess a fearless nature. They come from Mexico and are a royal breed. Spanish explorers found them when they conquered the Mayans. Mayan kings kept them as guard dogs because they are so alert."

Marcus chuckled. "I believe that, considering those big ears."

By now the dog had finished what I knew was his first

meal in days and he had licked the bowl clean. "I shall call him Stewie," I said as I picked him up again. "Before we go back to the ship, I must make one more stop."

On my way to the docks I had seen a haberdashery shop and I wasted no time in going there. From the goods the tailor had hanging in the store, I selected my new wardrobe. I knew I couldn't perform the duties of captain in petticoats, corsets and dresses. Clothing made for boys would be ever so much more practical and comfortable for a long sea voyage. Marcus shook his head as I selected trousers, shirts, a heavy jacket and two fine-knit tunics as well as thick woolen socks. To save him further embarrassment, I told the tailor's wife, who helped me, that I was shopping for my nephew, who was about my same size. From the tailor I went next door to the cobbler for some heavy boots.

‡‡

Early Summer, 2015
Baltimore, Maryland

The only thing worse than his work overload, Jonathan thought, was playing catch-up while trying to meet a massive deadline, all in the week after a spontaneous vacation. With a major project due for presentation to the owners of the Green Arbor Restaurant the next day, he was feeling a little stressed, which was strange. Deadlines usually inspired the adrenalin he needed to get him to his goal.

This meeting was particularly important. The clients were bringing a check for over a hundred thousand dollars—a little more than the down payment Jonathan needed for the Outer Banks house. He knew Patrice would be pissed that he'd made an offer on something she hadn't seen, but he had to have it. It was a beautiful place and its forbidding exterior gave way inside to a design that was open and airy, beautiful and bright. The thing he loved most about it was the panoramic view of the ocean.

His eyes strayed for a moment from the prints he was studying to the cup on his desk, the cup with the old sailing ship—the Royal Thomas—etched on its side. His new house (already he thought of it as his) would be the perfect place to keep lookout for the ghost ship and its beautiful, lonely passenger.

The sighting still haunted him. He hadn't been able to get her out of his mind, waking or sleeping. He longed to see her again—and the ship. It was like . . . he was homesick for them. That's the only way he could describe it, and it was affecting his work. Since he'd returned to his office on Monday morning after the fishing trip, his productivity had diminished. Not so much anyone noticed—but he knew. That wasn't good. That was the way you made mistakes. He tried to stay focused on his work but she kept creeping in, like she was looking over his shoulder.

He forced his attention back to the blueprints. They had consumed most of his time today, and he hadn't seen anything with the restaurant's design that would cause construction problems. Again and again he checked his calculations. Everything seemed fine.

But then his assistant's voice came over the intercom. "Jonathan, phone call for you on line one."

"From?"

"Banisters International."

"Thanks, Angie. Send it through." He put the phone on speaker. Hello, Keith."

"Hey, Jonathan—I'm afraid I have some bad news."

"Don't tell me you don't have the chrome banisters."

"Oh, no—we have them," Keith assured him.

"So what's the problem?"

"The company we get them from—in Germany—well, now they make them only in eighteen-foot lengths."

"You're kidding, right?"

Keith Murphy's basso profundo deepened even more. "Wish I was. Seems it converts more easily from metric that way. Plus, it costs a lot to manufacture them in Germany and then ship them here. One uniform size is more cost effective for them. We can only get them in that length."

"Crap."

"But they still have the same curve in them."

"But with an extra two feet."

"It's that or nothing," said Keith. "They won't even discuss a special order."

"That's crazy."

"It makes 'em cheaper," said Keith. "If that's any consolation."

"Not much." Jonathan was silent for a moment. "Okay," he said at last. "I'll get back to you." He hung up and headed down the hall to see his senior project manager. "Nigel," he said as he walked through the door. "We're fucked. Our supplier for Green Arbor just changed their specs. Eighteen feet per banister—two feet longer than we want. They won't make any other size."

"You're screwing with me!" Nigel exclaimed. "How are we going to get them inside? I don't think anything above like, sixteen feet will fit—seventeen at the most."

"I know." Jonathan started pacing. "There's no way we can get anything that long into the building."

"Unless we cut them before we take 'em in."

"Can't," said Jonathan. "The material warps when you cut it. It's something funky in the metal."

"We'll have to cut a hole in the exterior wall to get them to the second floor," said Nigel. "Then maybe we can make it around the bend in the stairwell."

Jonathan shook his head. "I don't think that's going to work. We can't let the builder or the client know, not yet—or we'll be dead."

He walked back to his office and closed the door. He couldn't believe he'd made the whole project dependent on a specific material, and that he'd confirmed the order the day before without checking one last time with Keith. It wasn't like him. Frustrated, he leaned against the door and looked up at the ceiling. He didn't make that kind of mistake. That wasn't how he did business. His schedule was demanding, sure, but that was nothing new. The problem was, he couldn't stay focused.

His success as an architect was based on how much of himself he put into each project, and his clients liked the attention they received. Jonathan's touch was on each design, and every design was a statement of his talent. His good reputation had grown to the point where neither new nor old clients wanted to bother shopping around for better prices. It was the architect that mattered, and they were willing to pay his price.

He had less than twenty-four hours to fix the banister problem before meeting with Fong Lee and Eddie Wong, partners in the Arbor Restaurant, who were to look over the plans and deliver a check. Jonathan would have to completely redesign the staircase. His only hope was to stay late and get it done. Patrice would be angry—he'd promised to try and get home early and take her to dinner at some new place that had just opened. Angry was an understatement, he knew. She would be livid but there was no other way.

He'd been working at his desk for three hours after everyone else had left when his cell phone rang. He looked at the caller i.d. *Patrice*. He'd meant to call her but time had gotten away from him.

"Where are you?" she asked brusquely as soon as he answered.

"At the office." Dead silence on the line. "Patrice?"

"What?" she snapped.

"You tell me," he retorted, his voice sharper than he'd intended. "Look—I'm sorry," he went on more gently when she said nothing. "There's a big problem with one of the jobs. I have to fix it before tomorrow."

"It would have been nice if you'd shared that information," she said. "I had a chance to go with Jill and Beverly." Two old friends from her college days, also married to busy, successful men. He wondered if they felt as neglected as she claimed to feel.

"Again, I'm sorry. Maybe you can still catch up to them—"

"Not likely," she interrupted. "That was two hours ago, Jonathan." After a brief pause she added, "Why the hell do I even bother?"

He tried again to mollify her. "When I get caught up, we'll make some time."

"You've said that before."

"It is what it is, Patrice." He was losing patience with her but he tried not to lose his temper. He didn't have time for a full-out battle, not tonight. "Please try to understand," he went on. "We're at a crucial point with this job. When we go down to see the house in a couple of weeks I'll take an extra day."

"I'll believe that when it happens," she retorted with a hint of the old resentment. "You'd rather work until all hours instead of come home and be with your family."

Not my family, he thought but didn't say. *Not my daughters—just you. I can hardly look at you since I found out you got into bed with another man.*

"Well," she demanded. "You're not even going to deny it?"

"Patrice, for godssakes!" he exclaimed. "Did it ever occur to you that if I didn't work until all hours you wouldn't enjoy the kind of life you have?"

But they had been through it all before. There was no point in rehashing it tonight. He had provided Patrice with a life of peace and plenty. She never had to worry about money or housing or food or clothes or a new car to drive every couple of years. She had everything a woman could possibly want, except his undivided attention. With a small shock, he realized that he no longer cared if she found *other outlets*, as she'd called it when he'd caught her cheating. Again, he thought of the ghost ship and its lonely passenger.

"When will you be home?" Patrice asked.

"I'm almost done," he said, lying to her because it was easier than the truth.

"Of course you are," she said, and he felt more than heard the bitterness in her tone. He walked over to the large work table where two sets of prints were spread out and started leafing through them. "Are you even listening to me?" she asked.

"I'm under a tight deadline here," he said. "I need to get back to work."

"Fine. Before you go, tell me—how many properties will we see next weekend?"

"One."

"Only one? So, you've already decided?" Without waiting for him to answer, she added quickly, "Never mind. We'll be lucky if we get down there more than four times a year, anyway."

He sighed. "It's a beautiful house, Patrice. It's got a spectacular view of the ocean. It's perfect. Believe me, we couldn't do any better."

There was another moment of silence and then she asked, "Will you be home at all tonight?"

"I doubt it."

"Whatever." With that, she ended the call.

Jonathan went back to his desk. Suddenly, he was

exhausted. He folded his arms in front of him, put his head down on them and closed his eyes for a moment. When he opened them, his gaze rested briefly on the coffee cup Mattie had given him. He'd brought it to the office intending to drink coffee out of it but instead decided to put his pens and pencils in it. He liked looking at the etching of the Royal Thomas and he didn't want it in the kitchen where anyone could use it. He looked at his watch. It was just after three-thirty in the morning.

"Damn!" he said, jumping to his feet. He smelled fresh coffee and when he went into the kitchen he saw that the coffee maker was running and the pot was filling with the fragrant brew. He didn't remember setting it and he knew there was no one else there. He grabbed a cup and poured it full, and the image of the woman he'd seen on the ghost ship suddenly flashed through his mind.

It was ridiculous, he knew, but he couldn't stop thinking about her. He finished his coffee, filled his cup again and went back to his desk. With renewed vigor he attacked the problem of the banister length. Getting the banister through on the first floor wouldn't be a problem. It was the turn it would have to make to get up the second flight of stairs. Then it hit him.

How about a window in the stairwell?

He moved his mouse over the computer screen and clicked on the project folder, and then clicked again on the contract. He quickly scanned its contents. His client had set strict parameters on the design of the building—but the contract made no mention of windows.

All he had to do was place a window in the stairwell and make it visually appealing—a stained glass design of an arbor, with flowers in full bloom. The banister for the second landing could go in through the window before they installed the glass. The client might complain about the change but it would be a small hit to take and one Jonathan could handle.

Chapter Six

"I love those guys," said Nigel as he and Jonathan entered the Bahama Breezes. A two-man band, both on guitars, was playing on a sandy area in the middle of the restaurant. Their position, next to the bamboo bar, created an instant tropical ambiance that made Jonathan think of summer afternoons in his childhood, on the beach in Florida, with his mother.

The Breezes was a Caribbean-themed restaurant—although the music had more of a Mexican flare, which no one seemed to mind. There were live palm trees rooted in big planters full of sand spread throughout, and a wooden boardwalk stretched from the entrance to the dining area.

"Nobody even knows their names," said Jonathan. "Just *The Two Amigos*. I hope Fong Lee and Eddie like this place as much as we do."

They were early—Jonathan had made a practice of being early. He had always believed it was important.

"Don't worry—we'll be fine," Nigel assured him as they walked to the bar. "Except for that stained glass window you threw in at the last minute—which was brilliant, by the way—I don't foresee any surprises."

The bartender greeted them like old friends. "Hey, Jonathan—Nigel. What can I get you?" He was in his early thirties and had a shaved head, a gold loop earring in one ear and a small palm tree tattooed on his neck. He made Jonathan think of a pirate. His look was perfect for the place.

"Hey, Doug," Jonathan replied easily. "You have any Chinese beer?"

"Oh, sorry," Doug said. "It's on order along with some

wine from Antarctica."

"Smart ass," Jonathan shot back with a grin. "I guess we'll have two Margaritas then—unless you can think of something more exciting."

"You're in luck, dude," Doug told him, sounding like a throwback to the seventies. "Been working on a new cocktail. You know—something to draw in the young upwardly mobiles. They used to call 'em yuppies."

Jonathan laughed. "Not like tonight's crowd," he said and glanced around. It was a mix—a slew of businessmen in suits and ties, and some locals wearing everything from Ravens and Orioles jerseys to tee shirts, jeans and expensive loafers.

Doug was already busy with the martini shaker. He poured the cocktail over crushed ice. Most of the liquid was clear but there were swirls of blue and green running through it and blending together, reminding Jonathan of the ocean.

"I call it Elusive Ghost," Doug said, hanging a slice of lime on the rim of each glass. "Taste it and tell me what you think."

Jonathan's mind took him back instantly to the night he'd seen the ghost ship and its passenger. Logic told him it couldn't have been real, but Mike and Tim had seen the ship too, even if they hadn't seen the woman. *It's like she's talking to me*, Jonathan thought. *Even now. Who would name a cocktail Elusive Ghost?*

Already he had formed a bond with her, whoever she was—or had been.

"What's in it?" he asked the bartender, trying to shake off the thought that if he didn't get a grip on reality it was going to affect his life in a way that wouldn't be good for business.

"It's pretty simple," Doug said. "Vodka, some Blue Curacao, a splash of Midori and a squeeze of lime juice. What do you think?"

Jonathan took a tentative sip. It was actually delicious.

"It's good. Nice and crisp. A little sweet but the lime balances that out. I like it." He paused for a moment but he had to ask. "How did you come up with the name?"

"I don't know," Doug admitted. "It just came to me. Sunday night, when I was here alone, just before I closed up the place. I was playing around with some new recipes and it came to me, just like that."

Sunday night. The night Jonathan had seen her. A coincidence, he thought. It had to be. "And you call it Elusive Ghost," he said. "You ever hear that name before?"

"Don't think so," Doug replied, distracted as he got busy with another customer.

Nigel looked at his watch. "We still have . . . like, fifteen minutes before Eddie and Fong Lee get here. We should go lay out the plans while we're waiting."

"Right." Jonathan took a longer pull on his drink. Then they went to the private dining room he had reserved, with Nigel carrying the prints and Jonathan carrying the cocktails.

"You look kinda tired," Nigel said. "How late did you work last night?"

"Beats me," Jonathan answered. "I never left the office." He'd had his morning shower in his executive wash room and he always kept a change of clothes at the office, just in case.

"Yeah," Nigel said. "You did what you always do. You stayed up all night and fell asleep at your desk until the smell of Angie's coffee woke you up this morning, right?"

"Who are you—my mother?" Jonathan joked. "Come on—you know how it is when we're on a tight deadline."

"You think they'll come through? Fong Lee and Eddie?"

"Oh, yeah," Jonathan said. His energy suddenly returned. He took another sip of his drink. "We'll get a check today. I'm sure of it." He needed a check for the deal to go through, and he needed the deal to buy the beach house.

They entered the private dining room and Jonathan

was surprised to see that it had been redecorated. Even the paintings hanging on the walls were new. One was a scene with three people—two women (one thin and one buxom) and a man in a straw hat—in a small rowboat. The man was holding a pistol and chewing on a piece of straw. He seemed to be contemplating which woman he would shoot. One of the women was looking in a hand mirror and seemed to be primping. For some reason, each woman's face was blurred.

Another painting, a little larger, was the stern of a small vessel showing its flag—the Jolly Roger. *Like the flag you'd see on a pirate ship*, Jonathan thought. The perspective of the third painting was from a ship's deck looking out at the scenic Caribbean Sea, with several palm trees on an island in mid-ground.

At that moment, Jonathan realized he wasn't going to wait two weeks to go back to the Outer Banks. He wanted to see the house again. He wanted to see *her* again. Patrice would be pissed at the short notice but she always seemed to be pissed about something. It might as well be something that was important to him. She could go with him or not—but he was going, and soon.

☩☩

Late Spring, 1717
Off the Coast of Nassau

The voyage from Carolina to Nassau was uneventful, except for my recurring dreams of Jacob. In those nocturnal wanderings, we are together and all is well. He is alive and he has not betrayed me with my heartless cousin Shelly—and we are happily planning to wed, with my father's blessing. And then I awaken in my bunk, longing to feel Jacob's arms around me once more, and I am bereft anew. He was my one, my only, love—and he died by my hand.

As the days wore on I found my grief for Jacob slowly turning to anger. If he had not lied to me and plotted with Shelly to use me as a means of getting property from my father, if he hadn't lain with Shelly in her bed when he had pledged his heart to me—if he hadn't grabbed Shelly by the throat in a fit of rage when she revealed his true nature—none of this would be happening.

Perhaps my own guilt over his death, I realize, has prevented me from rational thought. I have come to understand that what led to my predicament were Jacob's cruel lies and his proclivity for violence. Even if Shelly had tempted him, if he had loved me as he had sworn, he wouldn't have betrayed me.

So it was his fault—all of it—and I was furious with him. But somehow, I recognized my mercurial emotions as part of the process of healing. The fresh sea air, the congenial company of my crew and the marvelous food Mr. Potts serves me has helped to do the rest.

Little Stewie, sleeping curled against my side, always wakes within seconds of my first stirring and his delight at seeing my eyes open never fails to cheer me. My tiny, adorable pup is the only thing saving my sanity. Daily I draw great comfort from feeding him and cuddling him and watching his antics as he grows accustomed to life on board the Royal Thomas. It has not taken him long to win the heart of even the roughest seaman. Oliver, Marcus's gigantic friend and my first mate now that Bridges has gone back to my father's service, was especially taken with him and soon became his special protector.

When I am not playing with Stewie, I look through the ship's logbooks. There are three of them, beginning with the one started by my grandfather, who had the Royal Thomas built. His entries filled one and about a third of another, until my father took over as captain and made the entries. It gives me such a longing for home to see Papa's bold, familiar hand on the page. He had made the remainder of the entries in the second logbook and had then gone on and filled about a third of the last one, the most recent one—the one that I will be keeping from now on.

The most intriguing thing about my grandfather's entries is his reference to a secret place in Nassau where he hid something, and I wondered if it could be some kind of treasure—perhaps a fortune in gold and jewels. I remember my grandfather only vaguely but my dear papa always said he never divulged to a soul the location of this mysterious place, or what he had secreted there. As the years passed, the legend of my grandfather's lost treasure grew, until it became fodder for speculation among many a seagoing man.

There was a reference to a concealed grotto in Grandfather's log. It was, he wrote, to remind him that this was the first marker to look for in locating the right spot, when he returned to the island. He'd evidently had to make a quick escape from someone and had to leave it—whatever *it* was—behind. He'd made himself some kind of map and years later, when I was an infant, he had gone back to find his treasure—a journey from which he never returned. My father never learned what became of him.

There were references to other markers that only my grandfather or someone close to him would recognize, and I wondered idly if it would be possible to discover the location. I mentioned the legend to Marcus and asked if he thought there really was a treasure hidden away somewhere. He told me that even if it were so, it was unlikely anyone would find it for my clever ancestor would have concealed it well. Still, 'tis the thing legends are made of, and I remained curious over the years I had heard of it.

After many days on the ocean, I heard the lookout's robust call from his post atop the mast.

"Land ahoy!" Hans yelled, and I saw him move the telescope away from his eye for a moment. He waved down at me where I stood on the bridge. "Captain Kate—I see the entry!"

From his place beside me Marcus, my quartermaster, said, "Have no worry, Kate. The harbor has a deep enough draft to allow us in—but just barely. We must take care. This is the safe harbor where your grandfather hid from the British navy. That's how we know 'tis deep enough here."

"How did you discover it?" I asked. My curiosity about Papa's father had never been truly satisfied. All I knew about him was that he was a fearless and much feared pirate, a brigand who would do whatever it took to increase his fortune.

"We were thrown here during a storm," Marcus explained. "The only thing we need worry about is the coral reef, but I can navigate us around that easily enough."

"And you don't think Blackbeard will look for me here?"

"Nay—he's avoiding these parts out of fear for his own neck. By the time he realizes you did not sail north to New York or Boston, we'll be away from here. We'll take a day or two to rest, collect supplies and recruit some more men."

"And go to the pubs and find us some whores, as well!" exclaimed Hans, a handsome young sailor. I gave him a stern look and he added quickly, "Beg pardon, Captain. I mean no offence."

In spite of my shock, I laughed. "And I have taken none," I assured him. "Feel free to amuse yourself in any way you choose as long as you do not neglect your duties."

As much as I feared for my life—and how Captain Teach would torture me before he put an end to my misery—I knew it would not be easy to spend the rest of my days among these coarse men. I turned the wheel over to Marcus then, intending to watch carefully how he steered us clear of the coral reef. It was my intention to be the best captain I could be, and to learn everything Marcus could teach me.

As soon as we got past the reef and dropped anchor, six of us boarded the dingy and headed for shore. With me, I took Marcus, Hans, Oliver, Jamie and an old sailor called One-Eye. The waves were gentle and low and I could easily see into the clear water. I was in awe of the plentiful marine life below us. There were two large schools of fish swimming alongside our small craft, one populated with narrow, thin fish about the length of a man's hand, and extremely fast. There were also bigger fish with red stripes on their backs. I was thrilled at the vivid colors and the variety as I noticed even more species. They instilled within me a sense of peace. I loved watching them.

As Jamie and Hans rowed, I glanced from time to time toward the shore, feeling as if I was on a leisurely holiday. I wished my life could be again the way it was before I had met—and loved—Jacob.

Already I missed my father and our plantation with its beautiful grounds, gardens and fruit orchards. I missed my little waterfront cottage in Queen Anne's Creek, from whence I used to look out at the ocean and daydream about the wonderful future I would have with the man I loved. But what's done is done, I know; and I must now turn my life in a different direction.

Reasoning that I have less to fear from the king's navy than from Blackbeard I have decided Marcus is right. It is best to make for England while the path is clear, while Blackbeard thinks I am bound for New York. I must reach my father's banker so I can pay my crew what is due them before we go on to Spain and Italy to pick up shipments of fine goods to sell back in London. I remain in hopes that Papa's banker will be able to advise me as to where I can live without attracting too much attention.

If Papa was able to convince Shelly to say nothing of my

crime to the British authorities, perhaps I can settle into a new, anonymous life. I can create a new identity for myself, and if I invest wisely in cargo that turns over quickly, I believe I can be successful. If Papa has not been able to silence Shelly and I have reason to believe her account of my crime will follow me, I will take my ship and my crew and sail for another destination, until I find a place where neither Blackbeard nor the king's justice can reach me.

In spite of my father's assurances that he would prevail upon my cousin, I've had to accept Shelly's hatred for me, and I know I must always be careful, wherever I might travel. Still, I have the false hope of youth, I suppose, that if I can make it to my father's homeland, I will be safe. Perhaps one day I will find a love that is good and true—even if that kind of joy is something a murderer such as I does not deserve.

"Here we are," said Hans, interrupting my reverie as he pulled his oar out of the water and wiped the sweat from his brow.

"Step lively, now!" Marcus ordered the men. "We'll hide the boat in the bushes and head to the pub where we can post our notice."

Soon we were standing in a cobbled street before a busy saloon just inside the entrance to the fort, which had been built in the shape of a four-pointed star. A sign in front identified the pub as Mr. Proud's Tavern. Although it was but mid-morning, a drunken old man sat outside the establishment.

"Do 'e 'ave ought for a poor, tired sailor?" he entreated, holding his dirty, worn cap out to us. "A copper or two—just a widow's mite to buy a bit o' grub."

Marcus tossed a coin into his hat. "We be looking to take on sailors," he said. "Where's the best place to post a handbill to that end?"

The old drunk pointed to a spot behind us. "That pole yonder's good enough for daylight," he said. "Them 'at cannot read'll find out what it says from them 'at can. Hang one inside, too, if the proprietor will allow."

"Is that where you spent your fortune, mate?" Hans asked the old man with a chuckle.

The ancient mariner raised a gnarled fist to him. "Part of it, aye," he said. "And I 'ad one, too. Spent it all on 'ores and grog—and you will, too, you mewlin' fool. If I was younger by a day I'd thrash you good and proper for 'at insult!" He croaked out a harsh but good-natured laugh, revealing that he had not a tooth in his head.

Marcus ignored them as he secured a handbill onto the thick wooden post, pushing the paper into the nails that were already there, to keep it in place. Oliver and I stood next to him and surveyed the pole, which was the communication center for Old Fort, where citizens could be informed about employment opportunities and other important issues, including sea routes. I read Marcus's handbill and was satisfied it would do the trick:

> *All gentleman volunteers: Seamen and able bodied Landsmen, who wish to acquire RICHES and HONOR are invited to repair on board the ROYAL THOMAS, now laying in PLACE; mounting thirty carriage guns with cannonades, swivels and more, bound on a voyage to England and Spain for four months. All volunteers will be received on board said ship or by Marcus Garrity, Quartermaster, at his rendezvous point, at Mr. Proud's Tavern, where they will be met with all due encouragement, and the best treatment. Proper advance will be given. Leaving port two days hence.*

We'd not been inside Mr. Proud's place for an hour when it was clear the word was already spreading round the town.

There were half a dozen men waiting to talk to Marcus, with more coming in and lining up every few minutes, eager to be interviewed. What followed for the rest of that day was a repetition of our stay in Charles Town, except that in this instance, I had decided to dress like a boy. I wore my trousers, a light linen shirt and a brocade jacket and I secured my long hair beneath a knitted cap. I had discussed it with Marcus and he thought it wise to conceal my true identity whenever we were in port. He will inform the new crew members that I am a woman, he says, shortly before we sail, thus giving them an opportunity to refuse employment under my command, if they wish.

I could have gone with Mr. Potts on what would be his last expedition to purchase supplies before reaching England, but I realized it would be best for me to stay with my quartermaster and first mate. At some point, I knew, my crew would have to judge the mettle of their new captain and I meant to be ready for the challenge. I didn't realize how soon it would come.

With the midday meal I had a draft of cold ale. The proprietor, Mr. Proud, kept the casks in a spring of fresh water that bubbled up in back of his tavern, and it was so refreshing in the tropical heat that I had another.

Many sailors followed the example of the natives and took siesta in the afternoon, during the hottest part of the day. Those of us who did not were enjoying a brief respite from the barrage of men wanting to be hired. Marcus pointed out three bewigged, well-dressed men sitting together at a table in a dim corner and whispered to me that they were officers of the British Royal Navy, whose ship was in port. I tensed for a moment, until he added, "You've naught to fear. Word about is they be looking for Spanish pirates who be getting in the way of the king's privateers."

I relaxed, secure in my masculine disguise. Oliver was playing a game of darts with a man who was dressed like a member of French nobility. He introduced himself to Marcus as Girard Fournier, a merchant trader and captain of the Elizabeth Rose, and he was careful to boast to any who would listen that she was the sixth largest boat in all of France.

"What do you trade?" I interjected. From the moment I saw him, I judged him to be a vain braggart. Granted, he was handsome—but he was far too self-assured for my liking.

"Many fine things that a lad such as yourself, just starting out, cannot afford," he answered with a broad smile. "Furs, silks, spices and the like." I did not trouble to correct him as to my sex. I realized I would be quite comfortable traveling incognito.

I had to admit he cut a fine figure in a waistcoat made of the same fabric as his long coat, which he'd thrown carelessly over the back of a chair. It was of a green color and the waistcoat was fashioned low in front to better display his embroidered linen shirt with its frill of lace spilling down his chest. His breeches were fitted to his form and his silk stockings were impeccable, as were his polished leather, red-heeled shoes. A dark mustache was set artfully above his full, perfect lips and his beard was close-cut and neatly trimmed. I wondered if it was as soft as it looked. His long dark hair was tied at the nape of his neck with a green ribbon. He'd also removed his hat, which he'd tossed onto a nearby table. It was quite a handsome one, elaborately adorned with peacock feathers. I had to stifle a laugh as I thought it quite suitable to its owner.

He and Oliver were standing at a soot mark on the floor, taking turns throwing daggers at a target made from the cross-section of a tree, aiming at the center and the spaces between the rings. Between turns, the Frenchman ate bites of an apple he had sliced into neat sections.

"That is three out of three," he told Oliver, and I must admit his voice had a deep, rich timbre I found singularly attractive. "The game goes to me. Perhaps you want to try again?"

"I don't know," Oliver mused. "I've lost too much to you already."

"Come now," Fournier insisted. "Another game?" When Oliver shook his head, Fournier turned to survey the room. "Anyone?" he inquired. "I promise to make it interesting."

"And how would you do that?" Marcus asked with a chuckle.

Fournier signaled the serving wench and when, with much swaying of her generous hips she strolled near, he grabbed her and pulled her close.

"'Ere now!" she warned with a throaty laugh. I could tell she enjoyed his attention. "That'll cost ye extra, Fournier."

He gazed longingly at the swell of her bosom and took a gold sovereign from his pocket. "Will this buy your services for an hour?" he enquired.

"Oh, indeed sir," she said, reaching for the money. He held it just out of her reach as he took another apple from the bowl on the table. Then he placed her against the wall at the end of the long bar and put the apple atop her head.

"Who will take the odds that I can hit the apple in three throws?" he asked, and the wager was in place. The British officers were watching with amusement. They made no move to interfere with the sport. Marcus whispered to me that, as they were vastly outnumbered by the pirates in residence, they were careful to avoid conflict while in port.

"Wait, Fournier!" the maid protested, her voice trembling. "I didn't agree to be yer target!"

He flashed her a charming smile. "Have faith, my beauty," he said. "Keep very still and we shall both be the richer for it." Looking around at the excited crowd, he added, "And who will take my challenge to do better, in but two throws?"

I could see she was terrified but hesitant to refuse him,

and I reminded myself that I was not among gentlemen at a tea party. These were hard, brutal men, many of them criminals who would stop at nothing to get what they wanted. Some of them were also handsome, silver-tongued devils—like Girard Fournier—who were accustomed to persuading women to give them everything, including their hearts. It was clear that, in spite of the maid's desire to trust in his ability with the dagger, her fear was mounting. It was also clear she had an intimate relationship with the handsome sea captain.

The envy I felt at her good fortune took me by surprise. The thought of being in such raw, honest company excited me. I wondered if the need for adventure was in my blood, passed down from my grandfather to my father and then to me.

Holding the serving wench against the wall with one hand, Girard used the other to hoist a tankard of ale to his lips. He gulped the whole thing down. Then laughing drunkenly, he said, "Ah . . . I feel perhaps the odds have changed a bit."

Instantly more money went down, with Mr. Proud holding it, and the odds were now against Fournier. Grinning broadly, he walked a few feet away from the frightened maid and raised his dagger, preparing to throw. Already tipsy by the time he'd finished his game with Oliver, he was now swaying on his feet, fully inebriated. But with all confidence he cocked his arm back, took aim and hurled his knife at the target. It whizzed through the air and stuck in the wall, in a hair's breadth of the wench's ear. With a small yelp that reminded me of Stewie, she tried to move away from the wall.

"Stay where you are!" roared the Frenchman as he took a full tankard from the tray of another maid. "I've two more tries."

"No more, Girard—please!" she whimpered. "Keep yer sovereign and I'll keep me life!"

I could see she was as worried as Fournier was drunk, and I was sure the game would not end well. I made an involuntary move in her direction but Marcus grabbed my shoulder, looked at me and frowned, shaking his head slightly. I took his meaning and kept silent. It would be better if I did nothing to call attention to myself.

None too steadily, Girard raised his dagger again, took aim and let it fly. This time it landed between the frightened woman's earlobe and her collarbone, in the curve of her neck. I could sit in silence no longer. As a young sailor pulled the dagger out of the wall and returned it to Fournier, I called out to him.

"I will take your challenge, Captain!"

All heads turned to where I stood, and Fournier studied me with interest. There was something about his lips and the sparkle in his eyes that made me warm inside. It was at once disturbing and exceedingly pleasant, and I realized with a small shock that not even Jacob had ever made me feel like this. Fournier emitted a low chuckle.

"And what wager do you put on it, lad?" he asked. "For three chances to hit the target?"

"Your hat, sir," I said. "I rather fancy it. I can hit the apple with one try so I shall take your last turn. Those are the terms of *my* wager."

His smile broadened. "One try?" he asked. "And you want me to put up my hat against—what? What are you putting up?"

"What do you want?"

He studied me for a moment and then he said, "You look to be a sturdy lad—small but sturdy. I find I am sorely missing the services of my cabin boy here in port. I could do with a valet for a few days."

"A valet?" I questioned, trying to deepen my voice a little. "With what duties? What would I have to do?"

"Oh, the usual. Prepare my bath. Lay out my clothes. Scrub my back. Help me dress. Scratch me arse if I tell you."

"Agreed," I replied. A quick glance at Marcus told me he was worried; he'd never seen my prowess with the blade. "With one condition," I added.

"You're a bit arrogant for one so young," said the Frenchman. "But—very well. I find I am amused. What is your condition, lad?"

"If I am able to hit the apple on yon maid's head with one try, you will then take her place against the wall and allow me three tries at that same target she wears now."

There arose such laughter from all the customers in the pub that even those taking siesta stirred into wakefulness.

"Indeed?" said Fournier. He turned and called out to the other patrons, "Is there any man here who objects to the terms of the new wager?"

"Nay!" A chorus of cries went up, along with shouts of, "Let it stand! The new wager stands!" Immediately the pub was in an uproar and coins were flying from every direction onto the bar.

I smiled at Fournier. "Unless, of course, you are afraid," I said.

"Nonsense!" he protested. "I am not afraid of anything! I accept your terms. I suppose if you can do it once you can do it again."

By now the men who'd been sleeping were fully roused and gathered round, watching with interest. I took my position a few feet away from the maid and Fournier brought the dagger to me. As he placed it in my hand his flesh pressed into mine and I grew instantly warm from the sensation. He bowed quickly and moved out of the way, and I turned to the serving wench.

"Please," she said with a little sob. "I do not want to die today—"

"And you will not," I assured her. "What is your name?"

"Annabelle," she said uncertainly. "My friends call me Nell."

"Then I shall call you Nell," I said, capturing her gaze in mine and holding it, trying to project a sense of calm. "Hold steady now and all will be well. I know what I'm about. Unless, of course, you'd prefer to take a chance with Captain Fournier in his current state of inebriation?"

We glanced in his direction. He was gulping down another draft of ale.

"No," she whispered. "Guess I'll take me chances wi' you, lad. At least you be sober." Her breathing steadied and she stopped shaking.

"Close your eyes," I told her gently, and she obeyed. Aiming with the skill I had learned at my father's side and refined at Jacob's, I threw the knife. A gasp went up from the crowd as it hit its mark—and then a cheer arose.

"All right, Fournier!" Mr. Proud called out over the heads of the excited gamblers who were all clamoring for their winnings. "Put yer back against the wall and let the lad have a go at you!"

The stunned look on Fournier's face gave me a deep satisfaction. I walked to the wall and pulled the dagger out. Nell had already retreated, running upstairs to the private rooms as soon as the apple split and fell off her head. Slowly I turned back to the Frenchman.

"If you are having second thoughts, you can forfeit the game and give your hat to me now," I offered.

The crowd erupted in objections. "No—a forfeit is the coward's way!" and, "A wager set is a wager done! No forfeit!"

Fournier looked down at me curiously for a moment, as if he could see through my masquerade, and then he gave a little shrug. "It seems that is not an option," he said, quickly downing a glass of whiskey. "Very well, young man. Lead me to my fate."

When I took his hand to do as he bade, he held my own

tightly. I looked quickly into his eyes and his brows arched slightly, as if a question had occurred to him. In standing him against the wall I realized how very tall he was and wondered if I could adjust my throw to take that into account. I decided not to take any chances.

"Because there is such a difference in our height," I said, "I will have you seated in a chair."

"I accept, sir, but only because I am too drunk to stand."

Mr. Proud signaled one of the serving maids who hastened to drag a chair over and place it against the wall. Fournier staggered to it and sat. I followed him there, watching closely. Making a mental note of how he was sitting and his precise height, I patted his head and placed an apple on it.

"It looks good on you, Fournier," I said. "Much better than your hat, which will soon be mine." I walked back to the soot mark, trying to appear nonchalant. I was actually paying attention to each step I took, carefully measuring my walk. When I had reached my place, I took out my handkerchief. "Marcus," I said. "Please tie this so that it covers my eyes."

"Blindfolded!" exclaimed Oliver.

"Preposterous!" bellowed Fournier, catching the apple as it toppled from his head. "That was not part of the deal."

"It is now," I said complacently. "Unless you admit you are afraid and agree to forfeit."

"Never!" he declared and put the apple back in place.

I was surprised that one as well traveled as Girard Fournier seemed to be didn't know the trick of this—as I held the kerchief for Marcus to tie it, I carefully maneuvered it so that I could see enough to do what I needed to do.

"Turn me once around," I told Marcus when his task was done.

This created another uproar in the crowd. When it quieted, I drew my arm back and heaved the dagger. It hit the apple, which split—and some of its juice splashed onto Fournier's neck.

"I'm hit!" he exclaimed loudly. "I am wounded!" An image of Jacob, blood streaming from his throat, suddenly flashed into my mind. I ran to Fournier and pulled his hand away so I could examine him.

"Don't be ridiculous," I told him. "'Tis only a few drops of juice—" but my explanation was interrupted when his flailing hands became entangled in my cap and pulled it from my head, releasing a mass of curls that fell down around my shoulders. Fournier was stunned and the crowd was delighted.

"'Tis a woman!" someone shouted. "A woman has bested Fournier!"

Rising from the chair, the Frenchman protested. "Nay— the wager was made under false pretenses. Had I known I would never have made the bet. You must forfeit."

"Indeed not," I said. "You never raised the question of my sex, sir. It was not an issue then nor is it now. I'll have the hat, Fournier, if you please."

The spectators and Mr. Proud were all cheering in my favor so Fournier had no choice but to hand over the prized chapeau.

My own crew surrounded me then, and Jamie and Hans hoisted me onto their shoulders and carried me to the bar where they sat me down. The rest of the afternoon Fournier's hat remained on my head and my tankard stayed full of ale as one after the other, spectators insisted on buying me a drink. It was with some satisfaction that I noticed my opponent studying me, and ignoring the efforts Nell was making to get back in his good graces.

Berta, my old governess and companion, had told me many times when I was a little girl that the young are resilient, and the younger you are the faster you heal. It must be true, I thought. I had been convinced that I would never stop thinking about Jacob or missing him or grieving for him or being angry with him for trying so despicably to use me, yet here I was, suddenly consumed with the notion that perhaps the handsome Captain Fournier was as attracted to me as I was to him.

From the corner of my eye I saw the British officers conferring with each other, and then one of them left their table and hurried out of the pub. I paid it no mind. Exhausted by my journey and the exciting afternoon—and warmed by the ale and the new, intriguing thoughts of passion and romance that were suddenly invading my mind—I had Marcus go to Mr. Proud and hire a room for me. Exhausted, I made my way up to it, intending to get a good night's sleep on solid ground.

I had also ordered a bath brought up and it was waiting in my room. After soaking for a few minutes I scrubbed myself clean, put on a cotton nightgown and got into bed where I soon fell into a fast sleep. It seemed only moments had passed when a light knock on the door awakened me. Reluctantly I rose from my comfortable nest and went to answer it.

"Who is it?"

"Open the door."

"By whose orders?" I demanded.

"By the orders of the true owner of the most distinguished hat in all the world."

"Fournier?" Scarcely believing the audacity of the man, I pulled the door open to find him standing there. Without invitation he strode into the room.

"You did win it under false pretenses," he said.

"I did not," I retorted, and I noticed that he didn't seem so drunk after all. For some reason I didn't understand, I was glad to see him. "What do you want?"

"Only to give you the opportunity to do the right thing so your conscience will not suffer."

I could not contain my laughter. "Oh, I do assure you sir," I told him. "My conscience will not suffer in the least. I won the hat, fair and square. You'll not be getting it back."

"Then you must grant me something else."

"Very well. If it is not too complicated a request and it will finish this discourse and allow me to get some sleep, pray tell me what you want."

"Only this."

He caught me in his arms and before I quite knew what was to happen, his mouth covered mine in a searing kiss. Even as I struggled against him, he pulled me closer. I stopped struggling and gave myself fully to the kiss, just to see what would happen next.

Chapter Seven

Early Summer, 2015
Outer Banks, North Carolina

It promised to be a weekend of ideal weather and if he were completely honest with himself, Jonathan would have to admit he wasn't looking forward to spending it with Patrice. He had told her Mattie would be showing them the house and then they would swing by the mortgage broker's office and get the ball rolling.

"Whether I like it or not?" Patrice had asked caustically. When he'd stared at her, clearly puzzled, she'd added, "The house. Whether or not I like the house? She's only showing us the one."

Jonathan had sighed and weighed his words carefully. If his wife had to come along, he thought, he didn't want to spend the whole weekend fighting.

"I wish you'd trust me on this," he'd told her. "None of the others I looked at were anywhere near as nice. And like you said, we'll be lucky to get down there four or five times a year anyway."

"Then why are we bothering?" she'd shot back, still packing her overnight case. "Why don't we just stay in a hotel whenever we do go down?"

He'd tried to keep the impatience out of his voice when he replied. She was the one who'd wanted a vacation house in the Outer Banks in the first place, and who complained the most about outgrowing the one they'd sold not long after he'd learned of her affair, but he didn't remind her of that.

"It's a good investment," he said. He also didn't remind her that they'd made a healthy profit on the Pirate's Cove house.

What he hadn't wanted to say, but was thinking about more and more, was that it would be the ideal place for him to live, at least half the week, especially if tensions continued between them at home. He was already thinking about how he would set up his office at the beach house, and with his competent staff and Nigel to run interference up in Baltimore, he'd be able to work from there with no problem.

The drive had taken them five hours since Patrice wanted to stop for breakfast. After the meal, they were mostly silent. Patrice had her earphones on, listening to an audiobook while she browsed through a new art catalogue. Jonathan was happy to have the time to himself.

They got to the motel by one in the afternoon and Mattie was right on time. When he heard a car horn beep outside he knew she had arrived. "Time to go!" he called out to Patrice, who was in the bathroom checking her makeup.

He didn't respond quickly enough to Mattie's summons and the next thing he knew there was a loud banging on the door. He opened it to find her standing there, smiling up at him in a way his wife hadn't smiled at him in years.

"Come in," he said softly, and he couldn't help searching her eyes for the expression of warmth he had seen in them when they were last together. He wasn't disappointed. "Would you like a cold drink?"

"No thanks," she said. "I'm good."

Patrice came in before he could tell Mattie how truly good she was. She didn't wait for Jonathan to introduce her.

"Hi, Mattie," she said, holding her hand out to the realtor. "I'm Patrice. Thanks for coming, but I was hoping Rich would be able to make it."

Jonathan recognized the subtle put-down. He hoped
Mattie didn't notice. If she did, she didn't seem to mind.

She shook Patrice's hand. "On weekends we can't tear
him away from that new grandbaby," she said in her delicious
southern accent. "I'm so pleased to meet you, Mrs. West."

"Call me Patrice," was his wife's response, her tone
all honey and butter. Jonathan went on instant alert as she
continued. "You know, we dealt with Rich when we purchased
the Pirate's Cove House. We became friends after that. The
kids—we have two daughters—have always loved having
dinner with him at Tale of the Whale. Please give him our
regards."

"I sure will," Mattie returned politely. "Now, I think
it'll be better if we all go in one car, so let's take mine. I hope
you'll like the house as much as your husband seems to."

"And if I don't, I assume you have others you can show us?"

"Well . . . sure. Of course," Mattie responded. "But I
thought you guys were pretty sold on—"

Jonathan held up a hand to stop her. "It's okay," he said.
"We won't need to see anything else."

Patrice took his hand and beamed up at him. "I'm sure my
husband is right." Then she looked at Mattie and said brightly,
"All right, Mattie. Show me what you've got."

It was a not-so-subtle challenge and Jonathan was relieved
when Mattie didn't take the bait. So often in the past, when
it was the furthest thing from his mind, Patrice had accused
him of flirting with other women, of giving them the idea
that he was interested in them, and making them think he was
available. Now, after she'd been the one to break the trust
between them, she was still at it and obviously willing to make
a scene.

"You know, I'm famished," she said as they walked
outside. "Why don't we take Mattie out for a nice lunch and

then go see the house?"

After her late breakfast on the way down Jonathan knew she couldn't be hungry, but he didn't argue. Mattie spoke up quickly.

"Thanks, you guys—but I won't hear of it. It's customary for the realtor to take the client to lunch, so this one's on me. Hurricane Mo's is on our way to the property. That sound okay?"

"That sounds lovely," said Patrice. "They have a great menu." And over appetizers, she grilled Mattie about everything except the new house.

"You have a charming accent," was how she began the interrogation. "Where are you from, Mattie?"

"Edenton," Mattie responded pleasantly, unsuspecting. "It's a small town—really just a bump in the road—not too far from here. I'm a North Carolina girl, born and bred."

"How nice." Patrice toyed with her salad. "And you like it so much you never wanted to go off to the big city and do something wonderful?"

"Well—you know—life happens," Mattie said, a little hesitant and obviously puzzled at the line of questioning.

"Indeed, it does," Patrice quipped. "But you seem so bright and you're so pretty. There can't be much opportunity around here for a girl with your . . . attributes. Where did you go to college?"

By now, Jonathan could see, Mattie had caught on to what Patrice was up to, which was trying to make Mattie feel small and inadequate. He intervened, changing the subject.

"We need to get a move on," he said. "Why don't we take the main course to go, and eat at the house so we can really get a feel for the place?" He looked at Mattie. "If you think that would be all right?"

"Of course."

He signaled the waiter and asked for take-out boxes for the salads. "And you can pack up the rest of the order," he added.

"Is there a problem sir?" the waiter asked, looking around

the table. Jonathan thought he couldn't be more than nineteen or twenty.

"Not at all." Jonathan glanced at Patrice. "We're just in a hurry. Sorry for the inconvenience."

Patrice studied Mattie as the waiter rushed off. "I went to Notre Dame," she said. "Majored in art history, with a minor in philosophy. That's where I met Jonathan. We've been together ever since." She placed one hand possessively on Jonathan's arm.

Yep, he thought. *Staking her claim.* But Mattie was nobody's fool. She was too polite to say what Jonathan was thinking. Patrice's college education, of which she was so proud, had prepared her for nothing except being a socialite. It was clear that Mattie was making her own way in life and appeared to be doing okay.

"Well, believe it or not, Mrs. West—I mean, Patrice," she said, "a girl like me has plenty of opportunities right here. I started working for Rich a week after I graduated high school. First as a receptionist and then as his administrative assistant. Over the years, he encouraged me to study for the test and get my realtor's license. I'm exactly where I want to be, doing exactly what I want to do. How many people can say that?"

Surprised, Patrice shrugged. "Not many, I guess," she admitted. But Mattie wasn't done with her and it was all Jonathan could do not to laugh.

"And how many people can say they get to have Sunday dinner surrounded by brothers and sisters and nieces and nephews, grandparents and great-grandparents, laughing and talking and sharing all the crazy events of the week?"

Patrice did laugh, and she tried another put-down. "My goodness! How many people would want to?"

But Mattie ignored the jibe. "We usually have three or four generations crowded around my granny's dining table every Sunday. We bring pot luck and we have ourselves a ball.

My ancestors settled our land and we've lived here for as long as anyone can remember. I love it here. I'm sure you will, too."

And at that moment, Jonathan loved her. He'd never seen anyone squelch Patrice's sarcastic barbs more effectively. Their boxed-up food arrived and Jonathan paid the waiter in cash, along with a generous tip.

"Okay," he said cheerfully. "Let's go see the new house."

Patrice didn't care for it much. "It's so dark," she said as they pulled into the driveway. She stared up at the weathered cedar exterior. "Nothing like the other houses in the area. It's like something out of a Stephen King novel. It seems kind of desolate."

"That's one of the things I like most about it," Jonathan told her. "It's quiet. Surrounded by nature instead of people. I don't want neighbors so close I can hear them fighting or flushing the toilet."

The house was built on stilts and had (including the mud room adjacent to the parking area) three stories. The only road that gave access to it was unpaved and it veered off from a two-lane blacktop miles away from the Croatan Highway—the road that would get them to State Road 158 and eventually to the North Carolina border. A wrap-around deck went three-quarters of the way around the house and looked out on a wide expanse of ocean. At the rear of the structure, dense grasses and prickly cactus filled the landscape.

"It's really sturdy," said Mattie. "It was built in 1987 and has withstood every hurricane that's hit here since. I think you'll love the interior. It's light and airy and spacious." She opened the lock box, retrieved the house key and opened the door for them. Jonathan gave Mattie the bags from the restaurant.

"Would you mind setting this out for us while I give Patrice the tour?" he asked. He suddenly wanted to protect Mattie from his wife's disdain.

"No problem," she said, giving him a reassuring grin before turning to Patrice. "If you have any questions, just give me a holler and I'll come a-runnin'."

Jonathan realized she was putting on her southern, country-bumpkin accent for Patrice's benefit and again, he wanted to laugh—but he knew better. He led Patrice up the stairs and into the living room and it hit him again how much he loved the place.

"What did I tell you?" he asked enthusiastically. "Check out the view. You can see for miles." Patrice gave a little sigh and walked over to one of the panoramic windows.

"At least the beach is nice," she said, ignoring the rippling blue waves of the ocean. "But I still don't like it. It seems so exposed to the elements. One good wind or a big storm surge would sweep it away."

"You heard what Mattie said," he responded mildly, still enjoying his view of the seascape playing before them. "About withstanding hurricanes."

"Oh, I certainly did," Patrice said, lowering her voice a little as if she didn't want Mattie to hear. "If I didn't know better, Jonathan, I'd swear you've got something going on with her."

He turned away from the window and frowned at her. "Don't start that nonsense again," he said. "I'm not the one who—"

But she cut him off. "Don't *you* start—it was a joke. You should be flattered." She gave him a brilliant smile and he could tell she was happy she'd gotten to him, that she'd been able to remind him that other men found her attractive. "Come on," she said. "Show me the rest."

There were four bedrooms and three baths, a breakfast room just off the spacious kitchen, a den (which he would make into his office) that overlooked the beach and the ocean, a formal dining room and a media and game room. "Well," he said when they'd circled back to the large kitchen. "What do you think?"

"It's pretty big," she said. "What's the list price again? Did you ever tell me?"

"That's big, too—six hundred forty-five thousand. We could offer six and go from there." When she didn't say anything, he added, "I thought big is what we wanted. The girls will have their own rooms, which still leaves a guest room. There's plenty of space for Franco and Beatrice when they come down with their brood." He knew that was an argument she couldn't counter. Her pothead brother-in-law was always glad of a free vacation. Jonathan didn't see how Patrice's sister Bea put up with him but they seemed happy— much happier than he and Patrice.

"I guess," she said. "They'd enjoy spending some time here during the summer, and maybe over Christmas. And we could have them down for a housewarming party. At least the inside is more cheerful than the outside. I guess we could paint. Well—I suppose you've made up your mind. This is really what you want?"

"It is," he assured her. He hadn't yet explained that he planned on spending a lot of time down here, away from her. He needed time to think about what he wanted to do about their marriage, and whether or not he could stick it out until his daughters went off to college. But that wasn't the only consideration.

He also needed time to think about the ghost ship, and the strange, unearthly woman he'd seen on board. The desperate plea in her eyes haunted him, every day and every night. He wanted to see her again. He *had* to see her again. Part of his mind insisted that he was being silly and gullible like those people who claimed to see UFOs and swore that it changed their lives—but it was true. The sighting had changed his life—or at least, his priorities.

After Mattie set their lunch out in the breakfast room she

made an excuse about checking on something outside and left them alone.

"She *is* pretty," Patrice ventured again. "But kind of young, don't you think?"

"That would depend on what you have in mind," Jonathan replied with more patience than he felt. "Planning to fix her up with that artist you're sponsoring?"

"Now there's a thought," she said. "Any objections? I mean—she seems quite taken with you. Do you really want me to set her up with someone else?"

"Let it go, Patrice." Although tempted, he didn't add, *if I thought you really cared I might find your accusations amusing.* Then again, maybe she wanted him to cheat in order to salve her own conscience, or to justify what she had done—maybe make them even or something. He wondered. If he cheated on Patrice would that really help him get over her infidelity?

But he wouldn't do that to Mattie. To use her like that, just to see if it would change anything in his screwed-up marriage, would be reprehensible.

During the drive over to the mortgage broker, Patrice decided to behave herself. She was actually pleasant, pointing out interesting sights or asking Mattie some question or other about local customs. But she insisted on sitting in the back and Jonathan knew it was so that she could watch the two of them together, to see how Mattie responded to her husband, and he to her.

Coastal Mortgages was, like Mattie's office, in a small, commercial strip mall with a stucco façade. A skinny blond woman in her twenties was sitting behind the reception desk, texting rapidly on her iPhone.

"Hi, Dario," Mattie greeted her like an old friend. Then she introduced Jonathan and Patrice and told Dario that they were making an offer on the Gulfstream property. Dario stopped texting and pressed the intercom button.

"Ms. Miller," she said, "Mattie's here with Mr. and Mrs. West, about that beach house he wants."

In less than a minute, Margo Miller came out to greet them. She was an older woman—in her early sixties, Jonathan thought—and it was easy to see that in her youth she had been a great beauty. She wore a simple, tailored sundress and jacket, perfect for the spring, and expensive-looking sandals. Mattie and Dario were more casual in crisp cotton slacks and sleeveless white cotton sweaters. They looked ready to hit the beach as soon as they got off work.

Margo shook hands with him and Patrice and then led them back into her office. Although she looked as if she had just stepped out of the special spring edition of *My Outer Banks Home*, her southern drawl was even more pronounced than Mattie's.

"You've chosen a wonderful place," she said, gesturing to the elegant chairs in her little sitting room area. "I know y'all will be very happy there. Go on an' set down, now." She took a stack of papers off her desk and joined them. "All I need is for you to sign the disclosure form." She slid it across the coffee table to Jonathan. He quickly scanned the document, signed it and slid it back to her. "Mattie has already made your offer to the owner," Margo added. "So we're good to go."

Patrice looked at him, surprised. In all truth, he didn't know why he hadn't told her. Maybe it was because he was already starting to think of the place as his, and his alone.

Margo was speaking again. "If everything checks out, we should have an answer for you by Monday afternoon—Tuesday at the latest. You folks staying down here this weekend?"

"Yes, we are," Patrice said and took Jonathan's hand. "My husband has promised me a long overdue romantic weekend and I fully intend to hold him to it."

"Oh, that's sweet," said Margo. "You better hang on to

him. A romantic man doesn't come along very often."

"So true," agreed Patrice. "Can you suggest a good place for dinner?"

"If it's romance you're after, you better go to The Meridian 42—you know where it is? Just as you enter Southern Shores? The view from the dining room is spectacular. You can go for a nice walk on the beach afterwards."

It was the last thing Jonathan wanted to do. He'd rather go back to the beach house, eat pork and beans out of a can and walk on the beach with Mattie. He didn't dare look at her now, for fear it would give him away. Instead, he said to Margo, "Thanks. We'll be sure and check it out."

"Well, if you don't need me anymore, I'm off and running," Mattie put in. "Patrice, it was so good to meet you. If you need anything else, you've got my number."

Patrice looked at her smugly. "I sure do," she purred. "I can't tell you how *much* I appreciate your help—but we'll be fine."

For the rest of the weekend Jonathan did his best to be a dutiful husband but it wasn't easy. He couldn't really relax until after dinner; he was waiting for Patrice to give him hell about making an offer before she'd seen the place. Strangely, she didn't mention it.

Instead of going back to the motel after they left Margo, they drove around like tourists enjoying the sights, including a spectacular sunset over the water. All the while, Jonathan found himself scanning the horizon, gazing out over the ocean as if the ghost ship might appear at any moment. He scarcely listened to Patrice's commentary about the house, and how they could redecorate. They had cocktails at the Ocean Boulevard Bistro, and then went to the restaurant Margo had suggested for a wonderful dinner of scallops and Swiss chard.

"So," Jonathan asked over coffee and dessert. "Do you want to go for that walk on the beach?"

"Not really," Patrice told him, giving him what he knew she thought was her best seductive look and caressing his calf under the table with the foot she had slipped out of her shoe. Her voice had just the right amount of huskiness as she added, "I'd rather go to bed."

Before she'd been unfaithful to him, Jonathan had enjoyed making love to his wife. Now, at least, he was able to perform again but that was about it. He wanted to make love to her tonight—or at least, he wanted to want to, if only he could get past the fact that, with one careless act of betrayal, the woman he'd slept beside for years had become a stranger.

Still, he didn't want to fight with her and when she dimmed the lights and undressed in front of him as he sat on the edge of the bed, he resolved that one way or the other, he would give her pleasure. When she was completely naked, she stood before him, letting him look at her, letting him run his hands over her curves, before she went on her knees before him and helped him out of his trousers.

She clearly wanted to please him. He went through the motions, letting her arouse him, then skillfully bringing her to orgasm before he allowed himself release. But it wasn't his wife he was thinking about. It was the way Mattie's eyes sparkled when she looked up at him.

And he didn't feel any guilt about it, whatsoever.

Chapter Eight

Late Spring, 1717
Old Fort, Nassau

"What do you think you're doing?" I demanded. With great reluctance I ended the kiss and moved away from Captain Fournier. "Think you I am some simple serving wench you can hire by the hour?"

He gave me a wicked grin. "Can I?"

"Indeed not! And if that's what you are seeking from me, you are a devil and a scoundrel and I would never—" I could not finish the thought for I found that it intrigued me.

"You misunderstand, mademoiselle," he said softly and his deep voice warmed me anew. "I have learned you are the captain of your own vessel and in port to take on more crew before sailing for England."

"You have been asking questions about me," I observed.

"Indeed I have."

"Why?"

He gave a great sigh. "I find you fascinating. And when I find a woman fascinating I want to keep her around for a while. It has often been my undoing."

"Then how sad it is we shall never see each other again," I quipped. "Unless you also plan to be in England."

A shadow briefly crossed his countenance. Then he said, "No, I do not. So . . . let us not waste a single moment."

He bent to kiss me again but I quickly stepped aside.

"Why are you turning away from such profound pleasure, mademoiselle?" he asked. "You enjoyed that kiss as much as I did."

I was not at all sure how to respond to this French stranger with his probing brown eyes and perfect lips. He was so handsome, so engaging and so free. He was strong and able and a captain himself. What was it about those lips that heated my blood with such unexpected passion? My attraction to another man, so soon after losing Jacob, surprised me. If I had not led so sheltered a life, I wondered, would I have been so vulnerable to Jacob's manipulation?

And, with Jacob cold and dead but these few weeks, was I ready to have Fournier's lips on mine again . . . and again?

There was no denying it. With all my soul, I was ready. At last I spoke—but I knew he could see through my lie.

"I certainly did not enjoy it," I protested, trying for my own protection to create some distance between us. "Now state your business, Captain Fournier. I need my rest."

He smiled and his dark eyes looked deeply into mine, so deeply it made me catch my breath. That seemed to satisfy him for the moment.

"I may need passage to Paris," he told me. "It will depend upon the outcome of a card game I am about to join."

"Indeed? But I heard you boasting about your fine ship— the sixth largest in France, I believe?"

He nodded. "Yes . . . and it is my great misfortune to have lost her in a previous card game. If I do not win tonight I must get to France, to my banker in Paris, to raise the funds to get her back."

"It is also your misfortune, sir, that I am not going to France."

He reached out one broad, strong hand and gently stroked my arm. "I would make it worth your trouble," he said. "I will pay you handsomely." He leaned closer and whispered the rest: "And I will provide you with memories to last a lifetime."

"In spite of Mr. Stanhope's treaty and the alliance between our countries, Fournier, I have no wish to go to France," I replied. "If I get you as close as London, then you can find your own way across the channel."

"You'll take me on then?" he asked. I didn't miss the double meaning in his words—but I pretended I did.

"I will take it under consideration," I said, although the idea of being in close proximity to him during a lengthy ocean voyage had some appeal. "We sail two days hence. Come aboard if the cards do not bring you luck, and I will give you my answer then."

I slept fitfully that night, my dreams invaded alternately by Jacob and Girard Fournier, and I woke before dawn, eager to get back to the ship and my sweet little Stewie.

Marcus had been able to complete the crew and Mr. Potts reported that his galley was bursting with provisions that included fresh fruit and dried fish. There were even two live pigs in the hold to ensure our access to fresh meat. Previous generations of pirates had thought to seed the islands with cattle, goats and pigs that now proliferated, running wild for anyone to hunt. Mr. Potts had bought our pigs from the cook at Proud's Tavern, and he told me we would likely reach journey's end with supplies to spare.

I had sworn to myself not to give it another thought, but as we prepared to sail my gaze wandered across the landscape. I didn't want to admit it but I was actually hoping Fournier would appear. If he found me fascinating, I found him intriguing—but when it was time to cast off he still had not arrived. I could only assume the card game had gone in his favor.

We were just three hours out of Nassau when we caught sight of it—a ship flying the king's flag—and it was heading straight for us. I had already enjoyed a leisurely breakfast and conferred with Marcus and Oliver about navigation and wind speed. Dressed again in my masculine garb, I was taking a stroll along the deck with my little dog when I looked up, over the starboard bow, and saw them. At the same time, Hans called down from the crow's nest.

"Ship ahoy, Cap'n Kate! And it's showin' the king's colors!"

Quickly I put Stewie in my cabin and rushed up to the bridge, where I waited with my quartermaster. "Marcus," I spoke quietly, trying to stay the panic from my voice. "What could they want? The Royal Thomas flies the flag of a merchant vessel. Surely a report of my crime could not have reached them so soon—"

"Easy now, lass," he said. "They'll likely want to come aboard and ask some questions, is all. Their main concern is patrolling these waters for Spanish pirates. Stay calm, Cap'n Kate. There's naught to worry about yet. We've done nothing illegal and we're carryin' no contraband. Do 'e want to go to your cabin and let me attend to this?"

I did—oh, I most certainly did—but I knew that would be the coward's way out. If I was to gain the respect of my crew, I had to show even the royal navy that I was in charge.

"No," I said. "I'll not hide from them. But you answer their questions. I'll not speak unless it is necessary."

He nodded, satisfied, and I knew I'd made the right decision. By now the *HMS Royal Dragon* was pulling alongside us.

"First rate ship of the fleet," Marcus said, his voice low in my ear. "She's got a hundred cannon aboard."

Then I heard the Dragon's quartermaster shouting through the megaphone and a signal flag went up, announcing their intention.

"By decree of His Majesty King George, prepare to be boarded! Stand by, Royal Thomas!"

Marcus looked at me, waiting for my order. I nodded, and he bellowed: "Come aboard! Royal Thomas standing by!"

With neat, military precision the Dragon's crew tossed grappling hooks onto my ship and pulled close. As soon as the lines were secure, they placed an elegant gangway from one vessel to another, bridging the gap between. Moments later, they were on board—and it took every ounce of self-control I could muster not to laugh aloud.

The leader of the group stepped forward and the quartermaster announced him as if he was about to enter a grand ball. "Sir David Chatham, in service of King George, in command of His Majesty's Ship, The Royal Dragon!"

He was wearing a well-made suit of brown velvet trousers, fine stockings, high-heeled slippers with bright buckles, a brown and gold brocade jacket, and an elaborately embroidered vest over a linen shirt with a heavily ruffled ascot at the neck. Beneath his cocked hat, which was adorned with an elaborate ostrich plume, was a wig that had to be the eighth wonder of the world, with generous waves and a multitude of curls. I was sure it gave fits to his valet.

I knew the Royal Navy had no uniform as such but it was easy to tell which men were officers for they dressed similarly to their captain, although not quite as extravagantly. With him besides his quartermaster were his first mate and a dozen sailors, three with muskets and the rest armed with cutlasses and daggers.

"State your business and who it is commands you," the quartermaster said.

"The Royal Thomas, a merchant ship out of Charles Town in the colonies, enroute to London and then on to Spain to purchase goods," said Marcus.

The impeccably dressed captain raised one eyebrow as he stared up at Marcus. "And who commands you?" he asked again. His voice was quiet, calm, but I could tell from the set of his mouth that he was a man used to getting his way without question. He was also tall and powerfully built but not particularly handsome with his large nose and stern, thin lips.

"I do," I said, stepping forward. "Captain Russell, at your service, sir."

He gave me an odd look and raised his other eyebrow. "A boy? As young and slight as you?" he asked. "I didn't catch your Christian name, sir—if you please."

I took off my cap and let my long hair tumble down around my shoulders. "I beg your pardon, Sir David," I said. "I am not a boy, and I am in command. Kate Russell. My father is Steadman Russell."

The captain of the Royal Dragon paced before me, his gaze raking over me from my head to my toes, and not troubling to hide his interest as it came to rest on my bosom.

"Indeed?" he said at last. "I know of Steadman Russell— but something is quite *off*, here. Quite off, to be sure. I trust you have your ship's papers in order, Captain . . . *Russell*?"

"I do," I replied and turned to my first mate. "Oliver, please go and get the ship's logbook from my cabin. You will find it on my desk. Bring it at once, for Sir David's edification."

As we waited, Sir David continued his rude perusal of my person, looking me over from my head to my toes. "Steadman Russell has a good reputation—as privateers go," he said. "He has found his majesty's favor since settling in the New World, although I have heard he is recently in danger of losing it. I have also heard he has a daughter, whom he has raised as a proper gentlewoman."

Oliver returned then with the logbook, which he handed to the Dragon's captain. Sir David examined it carelessly, flipping a few pages before turning it all the way to the front to read the ship's registration.

"There is a letter there as well," I said. "From my father,

deeding the ship to me on my departure for England. You will
see that everything is in order."

"Is it?" Sir David shook his head. "No . . . it is *quite* off.
If Steadman Russell decided to send his daughter abroad, it
would be with a companion and a lady's maid. He would not
dress her as a boy and consign her, unchaperoned, with the
crew! Where is she?" he demanded. "What have you done
with her?"

"Forgive me, Sir David," I replied. "I do not know what
you mean."

"You know very well," he said gravely. "What have
you done with Kate Russell—the *real* Kate Russell? Are you
holding her on this ship, or have you consigned her already to
the deep?"

"I am the real Kate Russell," I insisted. "I dress as a boy
because it is more efficient in seeing to my duties—and I am
captain of this ship, which my father has given to me. You
have the papers there before you."

"And indeed, you would have them if you had pirated this
vessel and done away with its captain. Come now—the game
is up. I know who you are."

"I've told you who I am, sir." I was alarmed but tried to
stand firm. "I am Kate Russell. My father is—"

"Yes, yes, yes," he cut me off impatiently. "I do not
believe a word of it. Kindly surrender yourself and there will
be no trouble. I am placing you under arrest."

"For what?"

"For piracy," he replied. "I recognized you last night in
Mr. Proud's establishment, you see, the moment your cap fell
off. You're Anne Bonny and I am taking you back to England
where you will spend the rest of your life in a prison cell—
unless the court choose to hang you."

I had heard of the infamous female pirate, of course, and it
seemed ridiculous that anyone would mistake me for her. "You

are in error, Sir David," I said. "If I am that same criminal you seek, would I not have stolen treasure aboard? You will find none on this ship."

He called forth four of his men and told them to search the ship. "Confiscate any of their supplies that will be of use in service of the king," he added. Then he gestured to two of the others and nodded at me. "Take her!" he ordered.

As they stepped forward to do his bidding, so did my crew—with swords drawn and muskets raised. Sir David's men did likewise.

"Wait!" I cried. I could not allow my men to die on my behalf, especially for something as silly as mistaken identity. Besides, I had a sudden inspiration. I ordered my men to stand down and then I told Sir David, "I will go with you quietly if you will leave my crew in peace."

"No, lass!" said Marcus. "You cannot!"

"Have no worry," I said. "All will be well." Again I directed my attention to Sir David. "In London, my father's banker, Mr. Goldsmith, will speak for me. He knew my mother and it is said I look much like her. He will vouch for me."

"But captain," again Marcus tried to intervene. "I don't like the feel of it, 'aving you go off alone with this gentleman." He turned to Sir David. "Meanin' no offense, sir."

"Indeed," Sir David returned. "You are right to be concerned, of course. Or would be, were she an innocent, sheltered maiden instead of a disreputable hoyden of a female pirate. Now stand away from the prisoner."

I saw Marcus's hand tighten on his sword and Sir David's marksmen raise their guns. "Wait," I said. "There's no reason for bloodshed here, or the loss of lives or vessels. Sir David, if I can secure your promise to treat me as a guest instead of a prisoner, I am sure my quartermaster will be satisfied."

"I could arrest your crew—all of them—for interfering," replied Sir David. "But since I have no room for additional prisoners, I am willing to accept your bargain, even with the stipulation you attach." He looked over my head to address Marcus and my crew. "Put away your weapons!" he ordered. "This is your chance to avoid arrest—or execution—on this very spot. You have my word as gentleman and officer that the prisoner will be treated with all respect due the woman she claims to be—until I am satisfied she is not."

"Do it, Marcus," I said. "Don't you see? This is the best way for me to get to London. Give me two days head start, then make for England straightaway. Mr. Goldsmith, in St. James Street, will know my whereabouts. In the meantime, I will be safe on one of his majesty's ships."

Indeed, I thought. *Blackbeard will not be able to get to me there.*

✠✠

Early Summer, 2015
Baltimore, Maryland

Jonathan was eating pancakes and sausages at the kitchen table and playing with his cell phone, trying to change the ring tone. Using Google, he'd searched the Internet with the word, *shipwreck,* and had come upon a website that offered free ringtones, including the pirate ditty, *Yo Ho Ho and a Bottle of Rum.* He clicked on the play button next to the title.

> *Fifteen men on the dead man's chest,*
> *Yo-ho-ho, and a bottle of rum!*
> *Drink and the devil and done for the rest!*
> *Yo-ho-ho and a bottle of rum!*

He was delighted with the results and played it again— and again.

"Jonathan, seriously—must you?" Patrice cut into her pancakes as if she wished it was her husband she'd skewered with her fork and decimated with her knife. Her sudden harshness after a relatively pleasant weekend in the Outer Banks was a complete reversal of her attitude, but not surprising. Jonathan sighed. Things were back to normal.

"Aye-aye, matey!" he sang out, doing his best imitation of a pirate, trying to lighten the mood. "I like it. Arrrgghh!"

"Give me a break," she said, her lips pressed together in a tight, annoyed line. "I've got a newsflash for you. It doesn't sound any better the fourth time than it did the first."

Jonathan clicked the download button, sending it to his mobile phone. Then he reached for their kitchen wall phone and called his cell. He laughed aloud when the new ringtone played. Patrice gave him a curious look, as if he'd lost his mind.

Maybe he had, he considered. Since seeing the beach house again, he'd felt strangely uplifted. From its deck, and its huge picture window with its panoramic view, he was going to see the ghost ship again, and its lonely passenger. He knew it. And somehow he also knew that if he could see them again, everything would be all right. This strange, new sensation of being unsettled (no, he realized; *untethered* was more like it) would disappear and all would be well.

As he finished his last bite of pancakes and sausage his phone rang again, the familiar pirate anthem pealing out loud and clear.

"Cool!" he exclaimed. Ignoring him, Patrice poured herself another cup of coffee. She picked up the remote, turned on the TV and put on the news as Jonathan looked at the identity of the caller. "It's Mattie," he said, and answered. "Hello?"

"Hello yourself, Yankee. The deal went through. The house is yours!"

"That's wonderful," he replied. "That's terrific!"

"The lights, TV and Internet are still on from the winter tenant, so all you have to do is switch everything over to your name."

"Great," he said as his wife watched him closely. "Thanks for all your help."

"My pleasure," she said. "Why don't you come down right away and get the show on the road. I know you're eager to take possession."

"Right. I'm not sure about today, though. I've got to check in at the office and take care of a couple of things."

"Okay then, Yankee," she said, and Jonathan thought her voice lowered seductively. He wondered if it was on purpose. "Just so you know—I'm ready when you are."

He almost dropped the phone. She *was* being seductive and it was on purpose. He was not accustomed to any woman, not even Patrice, paying that kind of attention to him. The fact that his wife was sitting right there somehow made it more arousing, and he sensed that Mattie knew it. He cleared his throat and Patrice looked at him.

"How's the weather?" he asked into the phone.

"Oh, it's always breezy along the Atlantic coast," Mattie told him. "We don't worry about every little gust of wind."

"All right then," he said. "I'll see what I can do. Thanks for letting me know." He ended the call and turned to Patrice. "We got the house."

She uttered a short, derisive laugh. "So I assumed."

"Mattie says we can pick up the keys anytime."

"Don't tell me," she said. "You want to go back today, right?"

"Yeah," Jonathan admitted. "I was thinking about it."

"Whatever." Patrice picked up her cup and stared out the kitchen window into the backyard.

"You're welcome to come along," he said. *Not really*, he

thought. But he didn't want to start a fight.

"You know I can't be ready on such short notice," she said. "And besides, there's a hurricane brewing."

He didn't respond to that. Instead, he went upstairs to their bedroom and started packing. A few minutes later, she was standing in the doorframe, watching him. He had the TV on, tuned to the Weather Channel.

"Did you hear me?" she asked. "There's a hurricane brewing." She crossed her arms and stared at him. "They just said on CNN. It's heading right for North Carolina."

"Did they say when it'll hit?"

"Not until tomorrow sometime," she said. "But it's still not a good idea—"

"I can beat it," he interrupted. "I can make it there, grab the keys, take another look around the house and head back before it gets there."

In the background the TV weatherman was standing next to a map, pointing to the Caribbean islands. "Hurricane Charlotte is now a Category One," he said. "It developed from a tropical storm near the Windward Island and quickly moved across the Caribbean, officially becoming a hurricane just before it hit Jamaica. That land mass didn't do much to weaken it. It's picking up steam again as it hugs the coast of the U.S. and heads north."

"There," said Jonathan. "It's only a Category One." He threw socks and underwear into his suitcase.

"For now," Patrice said caustically. "You know how fast that can change."

"Yeah. It could just as easily head back out to sea. There's plenty of time. You sure you don't want to come along?" That was the last thing he wanted. He'd already started to think of the house as his, and he didn't want to share it with anyone—at least, not at first. Not until he'd had some time alone there.

Patrice turned from the window as a light breeze moved the leaves on the trees outside. "No," she said. "I can't. The girls have school. I think you're crazy to head down there when everyone else will be trying to leave."

On top of a couple of tee shirts and a pair of jeans that were already in his suitcase, Jonathan placed a worn Baltimore Ravens football jersey, along with a pair of brown shorts that had seen better days. It was his favorite outfit for construction work or home repairs. Storm or no storm, he was going to make a thorough inspection of the place, from top to bottom, inside and out.

"Don't worry—I'll be fine," he told her.

"You're not coming back tomorrow," she said flatly. He stopped packing and turned to face her as she continued, "You're *hoping* you'll get trapped by the storm. You're counting on it." Her voice was full of accusation, but he didn't take the bait.

"I'll see you in a couple of days," he said as he closed his bag. On his way out, he leaned in to kiss her cheek but she turned away. He let it go. It no longer bothered him.

Eager to get back to the beach house, he was tempted to head straight for the Outer Banks—but that would be inviting disaster at the office. He had to make sure his staff stayed on top of everything in his absence if he was going to spend any quality time at the new place. His secretary would coordinate everything, but he still had to go over a few things with Nigel, including putting him in charge for a few days.

Before he did any of that, he called Mattie and made arrangements to meet her.

Chapter Nine

Stuck in traffic on I-495 near Washington, D.C. (also known as the Capital Beltway), Jonathan glanced at the clock on his dashboard, then turned his gaze out the window again. Vehicles of all shapes and sizes were crawling along in a stop-and-go ballet, but since he was always in his car or the company truck, meeting with new clients to look over designs or finalize blueprints, running his crews, sometimes even showing up at a site to help pound nails, he decided not to stress about the traffic. He was used to it.

Instead, he would enjoy the solitude of being alone on the road. The sense of unrest that had been haunting him seemed to abate as he got closer to the Outer Banks. With every mile he covered, he felt a new sense of peace.

Getting that particular house on that particular stretch of beach meant something. Jonathan knew it. For some reason he couldn't identify, he *knew*. It wasn't just his love for the sea, although that surely was part of it. It was more than that.

It was seeing the ghost ship. It was the possibility of seeing *her* again.

It was making a sharp, poignant connection to something otherworldly, something spiritual and deep, something long gone from this earth. Something *important*. Something beyond the banal daily routine into which he'd escaped, in which he'd cocooned himself these last couple of years. The eerie sighting had been instantly addictive. He needed the experience again, like a junkie needs a fix.

He hardly noticed, at first, when the traffic finally started moving at the posted speed limit. In his mind he was already at the beach, even if he still had a few more hours of highway to go. Mile by mile, little by little, his worries faded. He let himself get lost in laying out his plan. It had started out as a mental diversion from the disappointment his marriage had become but with the purchase of the beach house, it had started to take on more solid form. With the realization that he now had a real means of escape, Jonathan felt suddenly liberated. The rest of the drive was a blur until he turned onto the bridge that crossed over Albemarle Sound and he had to look for markers.

He would start making the transition to the new property with long weekends, going down every Friday. Then, little by little, he'd extend his stay to include Monday and Tuesday. First, he had to get his staff used to the idea that he'd be working remotely part of the week. The timing for that was perfect, since he still had a lot to do on designs for two new projects. And he preferred working on new designs in peace, quiet and isolation, something he hadn't been able to do for years.

As for Patrice's adjustment to the new living arrangements, he knew that would take time. He would have to be patient until the charm of the new place wore off, as he knew it would. Once she'd had a couple of parties—and after she'd had the house written up in the lifestyle section of one of the local papers and *My Outer Banks Home*—she would become bored with it all, and with the drive down from Baltimore. She would be annoyed with wet swimsuits and beach sand, fishing gear and fishing stories and most of all, with him. Then, when she got used to the fact that Jonathan was spending more time in the Outer Banks than at home, he would tell her he wanted to try a separation.

He wasn't sure when that part of the plan had first formed

in his mind but it seemed right. He and Patrice needed some time apart in order to figure out how to be together. At least, he needed to get away from her, and from the anger and sense of betrayal he always felt when he was with her. As soon as he thought he'd gotten past it, it would start eating away at him again, and the old bitterness and resentment would rise up.

When he'd learned about his wife's affair Jonathan's first instinct had been to leave her, but after the initial shock wore off, he'd given in to her pleas to stay and try to work things out. Gradually he came to believe her assurance that it had only happened a couple of times (or maybe that's what he wanted to believe) and that it was over. She'd suggested marriage counseling but he'd been too furious to attempt it. His anger had gradually faded. Now it was mostly background noise—always there and always digging at him, somewhere in the back of his mind—but he'd found a way to live with it. After a while he had even resumed having sex with his wife. True, it was with less frequency and much less satisfaction than before, and it was mostly to stop her from complaining that he didn't. But it was better than nothing. At least that's what he'd been telling himself.

He'd also been telling himself he was sticking around for his girls, until both of them went away to college, but that was just an excuse. He knew that now. His daughters were already young women, already had lives of their own, and they were well on their way to adulthood and independence. They could survive quite well on weekly or even monthly visits with their dad. Patrice had no need of him, really, besides financial support, and that wouldn't be a problem. He would always provide for her and the girls.

It could be managed. Nothing would change initially, of course, but when the time came for the ultimate, final separation, it could be managed.

And so his mind drifted, lost in thoughts of the adventure

that lay before him, and he wondered why he was even having such thoughts. Was he in his second adolescence, or was he having some kind of midlife crisis? He didn't know—but a change was coming, and he was ready for it. The lyrics to an old Sam Cooke song suddenly came to mind.

It's been too hard living but I'm afraid to die
'Cause I don't know what's up there beyond the sky.
It's been a long, a long time coming
But I know a change gonna come, oh yes it will."

"Oh, yeah," he muttered under his breath. "A change gonna come. Oh yes, it is." *Yes, indeed.* He didn't know what it was or when it would happen but he knew it would be good. Because *he* was the one who was changing.

Before he realized how much time had gone by, the sun was going down and he was turning into the parking lot of the restaurant Mattie had suggested. The place was right on the beach and the wind was blowing, stirring the waves up to a gentle froth and moving dark clouds off, out over the sea. He parked and headed inside.

She was waiting for him at the bar. He didn't realize how much he'd wanted to see her again until she was standing there before him.

"It's official," she said brightly as he approached. "It's all yours."

He had also forgotten how beautiful she was, how young and fresh and eager she looked. Her sandy-blond hair was pulled back and secured behind one ear with a clip embellished with seashells, rhinestones and tiny, fake seed pearls. Her short skirt revealed long, lean, tan legs and she was wearing pink, spike-heel sandals that showed off a perfect pedicure. The sight left him momentarily speechless.

"Welcome to Rebel country, Yank," she continued warmly.

"Let's have a drink to celebrate and then—you want to have dinner with me?"

"Sure," he said.

A plump hostess with a tattoo on her wrist hurried over to them. "Hey, Mattie," she said. "That table in the corner you wanted just opened up. Better grab it now or it'll be gone. I'll get your drink order in." She looked at Jonathan. "Whatcha havin', honey?"

"Beer," he said. "Corona's fine."

Mattie gulped down the last of her rum and Diet Coke and grabbed Jonathan's hand. The hostess led them to a table in a quiet corner, between a big potted plant and two huge windows that looked out on the churning surf, providing a splendid view of the Atlantic. It was exactly what he needed, he thought.

"Okay, now Yankee—you better watch out," Mattie told him as they settled into their seats and took menus from the hostess. "Once you get a taste of our southern hospitality down here you'll never go back up north."

"It's already pretty tempting," he said. "What's the latest on the hurricane?"

She gave a nonchalant wave of her hand. "Oh, it's turned around and headed back out to sea. Looks like we may luck out this time. You hungry?"

"Starving." And he was. On the road, he'd fallen into some kind of somnambulant driver trance but now he was wide awake, energized and famished. "What do you recommend?"

"Everything's good here," she told him. "Seafood's all fresh, too."

A waitress came with their drinks, poured his beer into a tall glass and took their orders. When she left they sat back and looked at each other. After a moment, he raised his glass. "To my new house," he said. "And the awesome realtor who helped me find it."

They touched glasses with a soft clink and then drank.

"Now, seriously," she asked. "What are you planning to do with the place when you can't get down? Interested in renting it out by the week or month? Some of our part-time people do that and—"

"Oh, no," he interrupted. "No—I'll be spending a lot of time here. I plan to work from here at least a couple of days a week. And maybe . . . make the transition complete after a while."

"You mean live here full time?"

"I think so," he said. Something odd flickered in her eyes for a moment, something like hope. She brushed away a lock of her hair that had fallen forward onto her cheek but she didn't say anything. It was marvelous, he thought, that she seemed so comfortable with the brief silences between them, exhibiting no need to fill the empty spaces with meaningless words. "So you've got to clue me in on the local customs," he added.

She sat up straighter and leaned toward him just enough that he could appreciate the generous swell of her breasts. Smiling a lazy, leaned-back kind of smile she said, "But you're no stranger to these parts, Jonathan. You and your wife have owned places here before."

"Place," he told her. "As in, one. We bought it a few years ago when the girls were small. We just outgrew it. But Patrice is right—after the first year or so we didn't get down here much—just a couple of times a year."

"Why not?" she asked. "What happened?" And he thought again how easy she was to talk to. And she smelled like surf and rain and bright, golden days in the sun.

"Oh, you know," he said. "My business took off, the girls became teenagers—more interested in hanging out with their friends than going on weekend getaways with their folks." He took a long pull on his drink. "My wife was involved in taking care of them, and she had her clubs and community projects. You know—life happens."

The waitress came back with their food—Mattie's filet mignon and Jonathan's lobster, shrimp and crab combo, with a big platter of oysters on the half shell as an appetizer for both of them. They dug in and after another comfortable silence, Mattie picked up the conversation again.

"So y'all used to come down here to chill," she surmised, and he found her soft, southern lilt charming and a bit seductive. "To get away from that dog-eat-dog corporate world and spend some quality time with your kids—and each other?"

"It was like that at first," he admitted, feeling a twinge of nostalgia as he remembered. "At any rate, we weren't actual residents. More like tourists here for the beaches, good restaurants, and great bars—and for me, the fishing. We didn't even go to the grocery store. We mostly ate out or ordered in. That's why you're going to have to clue me in on where to go and who to know. Also good restaurants and great bars—the ones the tourists don't know anything about. You have to tell me where the locals go."

"Sure, be happy to," she said as she finished another rum and Diet Coke. "I'll give you a guided tour and take you around and introduce you. But I'll need to know a little more. I mean—like, besides fishing—what do you like to do?"

"Well, the first thing I have to do is get my home office set up," he told her. "So fishing's enough for me right now— that and beachcombing. I hear that sometimes pieces of old shipwrecks wash up around here."

"Yeah," she admitted slowly, and he wondered why she seemed reluctant. "After a big storm, people find some interesting things, I guess. What about your wife?" she asked. "What are her interests? You mentioned clubs and community projects. We have a couple of women's clubs and theater groups, and there are loads of art galleries—"

He raised a hand to stop her. For some reason, he wanted to tell her everything. He wanted to unburden himself, to spew out the bitterness that had been festering in his soul since he'd learned about his wife's infidelity. He wanted to vent his anger at Patrice with a sympathetic listener and he sensed Mattie would be exactly that.

But he resisted the urge. He didn't know Mattie that well. He wondered if he knew anyone that well, trusted anyone that much. He didn't think so—and he'd been sublimating his anger and holding on to his self-control for so long he didn't think he could take a chance and let go. If he started laughing, or crying, or screaming, he wasn't sure he would be able to stop.

Instead he said simply, "After the first couple of months I doubt Patrice will be spending much time here. She has a pretty full life back in Baltimore."

"I see," said Mattie. And for some reason, it was important to him that she did.

"Truth is, we've been having some tough times lately," he said, swirling the beer in his mug and then draining it. "We need some time apart, so finding the house—well, it's perfect timing."

"Hey," she said softly. "Is that supposed to be some kind of line? You know. 'My wife doesn't understand me, but oh you kid'?"

"Not at all," he assured her. "I'm afraid I don't have a line."

She studied him a moment and then shrugged, and he noted how firm and well-shaped her shoulders were and how well they supported her curvaceous bosom. "Well, just so you know, you need to be careful who you say it to, line or no line," she warned.

"Why is that?"

"Because a lot of women around these parts are looking for a big, rich northern whale to land as their very own sugar daddy."

He chuckled. "You're kidding."

She shook her head. "No I'm not, Yankee. I'm serious as a heart attack. A lot of northerners with a lot of money come down here, and catching one is the fulfillment of every redneck girl's dream. At least around here, it is."

They'd finished eating by then and he signaled the waitress. Instead of coffee, they both ordered another drink. Outside, a strong wind blew, pelting the window with grains of sand.

"Is that your dream?" he asked.

She smiled. "Uh-uh," she said. "Not me. I've had my share of those, thank you very much." Gently, she toyed with the diamond pendant hanging from the thin gold chain between her breasts and he wondered if it had been a gift from one of them. He also wondered if she had a tan line, and where it stopped, and he felt himself go hard for a moment, under the table.

"What's your dream, Mattie?" he asked to distract himself from his need. "Tell me about yourself."

"There's not much to tell. I've pretty much got my dream. Like I told you and your wife, I started working for Rich the week after I graduated from high school. The only advice my mama ever gave me before she ran off with the Amway man was, 'Whatever you do, girl, you better be learnin' you some sec-a-tarial skills.'"

A soft chuckle escaped Jonathan as she let her accent lapse briefly into real, down-home redneck.

"It was the best advice she ever gave me," Mattie continued in her own slow, enticing drawl. "It got me the job with Rich. He trained me right, helped me get my realtor license, and I've done well for myself. I've got a great place on the beach, a new car every few years, and just about anything else I want."

"But you don't want a sugar daddy?"

Her brow furrowed almost imperceptibly but he saw in her eyes the sudden flash of pain she was quick to hide.

"No," she said. "Been there, done that. No future in it. I've never been one to hold on to empty promises. I live my life the way I want and I take my pleasure where I find it—with no remorse. Some people call it irresponsible, just living for the moment. I call it living for myself."

"Is that why people call you Pirate Girl?" he asked. "I saw it on your plates."

"Some folks," she said.

He smiled. "I think it suits you."

She turned her attention out the window, watching as tumultuous waves painted a beautiful seascape, and they finished their drinks in companionable silence. The waitress brought their check and Jonathan announced he had to get to the beach house while he could still drive.

"As soon as you hand over my keys," he finished with a smile.

"Well—about that," she said. "It's the strangest thing. I could have sworn we had another set in the office but I absolutely could not find them." She held up her key chain. "But I've got a key to the lock box, where I know there's a house key. I mean, I could give you my key to the lock box and stop by tomorrow to pick it up, but it can be kind of tricky. Besides, it's on my way."

"You sure you don't mind?"

"I'm sure," she said softly, her voice full of promise. "I don't mind at all." Jonathan reached for the bill but she quickly put her hand over his. "I've got this," she told him.

"No," he said, placing his other hand over hers. "It's on me this time." *And the next time,* he thought. *And the time after that.* As he signed the credit card slip, the wind blew against the window again, startling them both. "That was pretty strong," he said. "Guess Hurricane Charlotte's coming back this way."

"Maybe," Mattie said. "Maybe not—but you'll get used to the eccentricities of our weather down here."

Her honeyed hint of southern accent was incredibly sexy, he thought. He smiled, enjoying the sight of her, the smell of her perfume mingled with Captain Morgan and Diet Coke. "You sure the weatherman said it's heading out to sea?" he asked. "Couldn't it have turned around?"

She shrugged. "Sure—it could. But we're safe here, at least for now. This place was built with storms in mind. It's withstood some of the worst. Know what that means?"

"What?"

She grinned. "It means it's pretty much the last place to close when a hurricane hits, and the best place to hole up and wait for one. We can stay here if you're nervous about driving."

Jonathan glanced around to see that most of the customers looked like rugged locals instead of tourists—and none of them seemed the least concerned about the coming storm. "No," he said, "I think I should get over to the new house and batten down the hatches."

"You got it, Yankee," she said, slugging back the rest of her drink. He was impressed by how much alcohol she could put away with no apparent effect. She didn't seem even the slightest bit tipsy.

✝✝

8 Hours out of Old Fort, Nassau
Late Spring, 1717

There was no reason, initially, to think that Sir David Chatham, captain on the HMS Royal Dragon, was acting with anything other than honor in arresting me. His conviction that

I was the notorious lady pirate, Anne Bonny, remained firm and while such a notion seemed preposterous to me, I had to admit it was also intriguing. I almost envied Miss Bonny the freedom from the constraints of society she must surely enjoy.

Marcus and Oliver were none too happy about letting me go off with Sir David, but after I had secured Oliver's promise to take care of little Stewie, I assured them once again that this was a blessing in disguise. While Sir David would not allow me to take my little dog, he did let me take a few articles of clothing and the documents I would need in order to prove the Royal Thomas was mine. I knew Mr. Goldsmith would be able to confirm my identity, along with some of my father's other friends whom I would contact, or have Marcus contact for me, when he and the rest of my crew arrived in London.

As soon as he had me on board the Royal Dragon, Sir David signaled to a young officer who stood nearby. "Lieutenant Preston, show this young woman to my quarters," he ordered. "And be quick about it."

The young man saluted smartly and took my elbow, but I resisted. "That is most kind, Sir David," I said. "But entirely unnecessary. I'll not have you give up your comfortable room on my account. I would be happy with any small cabin or berth you have available."

He looked at me oddly for a moment. "I would not have it any other way, I assure you," he said with a tight little bow, then he nodded at the officer. "Take her now, Mr. Preston." And to me he added, "I shall have a bath sent to you and after you have thus refreshed yourself you must try to rest until dinner."

He was absolutely charming so I did not think anything amiss. I enjoyed the bath and then selected a simple day dress to wear for the voyage. Already I was missing the comfort and freedom of my boy clothes. I thought, and not for the first time, that whoever dictated women's fashion was part of a cruel conspiracy.

It wasn't long before two sailors came to take away the bathtub. As the sun was going down, creating a rosy display on one wall of the cabin, they came back to arrange an elaborate dining table, which they set for two. Still, in my naiveté, I thought only about how kindly disposed my host seemed to be and saw no reason to be concerned. Thinking, after the two sailors departed again, that I might have time before dinner for a stroll around the deck, I went to the door and tried to open it.

To my surprise, it was locked.

At that moment I knew exactly what my captor intended. Before I had time to form a plan or even look for a means of escape, I heard a key rattle in the lock. The door opened and Sir David entered the room. I had never before seen a look as lascivious as the one he turned on me before he closed the door. He twisted the key in the lock, then put it in the pocket of his coat.

"My dear Miss Bonny," he said. "How fresh and sweet you look. I trust you enjoyed your bath."

"Immensely," I said. "But that is not my name. I am—"

"Silence!" he roared and I started with surprise. "It is for me to say who you are until a court undertakes that task. Until I can ascertain your true identity I can only assume you are indeed that infamous girl and treat you as such."

I backed away from him. "Then you are not the honorable gentleman you claimed to be," I observed. "What is your intention, sir? Are you going to lock me in the brig and give me bread and water for the duration of our journey?"

"Don't be silly, my girl." With one hand, he gestured gracefully around the cabin. "As you can see, there is no need for you to suffer any discomfort. As long as you cooperate this will be a very pleasant voyage—for us both."

"I said I would," I reminded him.

"Excellent!" he retorted with a broad smile. "Now—I've

had my cook prepare a special feast for us. After we have dined, I will put a few questions to you. I promise you, Miss Bonny—if you are a good girl and do as you are told, there will be no difficulties for you on board my ship."

There came a knock on the door and Sir David unlocked it to admit two sailors bearing trays overflowing with food— soup, bread, cheese, fruit and some kind of roasted meat— along with a flagon of wine. After they placed it on the table they departed and Sir David closed and locked the door behind them. Like the gentleman I had believed him to be, he escorted me to my chair and held it for me as I took a seat. I began to relax—but not enough to drink all the wine he tried to give me. I noticed that each time I took a sip, he refilled my glass, and I realized he was trying to get me intoxicated.

When we had finished eating, I looked up at him. "I believe you have some questions for me," I said.

He stood, took off his jacket and hung it over the back of a chair near his bunk. Then he loosened his cravat and came back to the table. "Only one," he said. "Where is your lover? Where is Calico Jack?"

"Since I am not Miss Bonny, I would have no way of knowing that."

"Things will go better for you, my girl, if you give me what I want."

"That would depend, sir, on what you want. I cannot tell you what I do not know."

"Very well. Since you refuse to answer my questions, I have no choice but to treat you like the common criminal you are."

"And what does that mean?" I asked, although I was sure of his thought on the subject.

"Perhaps I *should* throw you in the brig. Perhaps a few hours chained up below, with the rats, will soften your resistance."

Another knock sounded on the door. He threw it open to find the same two sailors who had served our meal. "What do you want?" he demanded brusquely. From their timid demeanor and anxious expressions, I could see they feared to displease their captain.

"Beggin' yer pardon, Captain," one of them explained timorously. "We be here only to clear away. At yer convenience, sir."

"Then do it and begone!" Chatham ordered. Agitated, he turned back to me. His gaze traveled from my face, down my neck and along the curve of my bosom. He seemed so entranced with the sight that he failed to secure the door behind his men after they had grabbed up our dishes and the remains of our feast and scurried out. He came back to the table to stand before me.

I saw my chance and took it. In a move that surprised him I pushed past him and ran for the door. He put out one arm and caught me easily about my waist.

"Remove your hands from my person this instant!" I commanded.

"Or what, my fancy piece?" he wanted to know. "What match are you against my strength—and where did you think you were going? If you had managed to get out of this room, my men would return you here immediately. There is nowhere else for you to go except into the ocean." He pulled me away from the door, locked it and put the key in the pocket of his breeches.

"What will you do with me, then?" I asked. "You promised to treat me with respect—"

He cut me off. "With the respect you *deserve*," he corrected, then added darkly, "You will only deserve it if you cooperate."

"I've told you, sir," I insisted. "I cannot give you information I do not possess."

"There are other ways of cooperating." His tone was full of lewd suggestion. Leaning closer, he whispered, "It is a long way to England, my girl. You entertain me properly and it will be a *most* pleasant voyage."

His breath was hot on my cheek and I struggled to get away, but his grip was like iron. Still holding me about the waist with one hand, he moved his other hand upward.

"No!" I protested. I thrashed against him, thinking all the while how curious it was. While Fournier's touch had excited me beyond belief, I found Sir David's quite reprehensible. Placing my hands against his chest I pushed with all my might. He stumbled backwards and almost fell.

"You vile little strumpet," he hissed at me, righting himself and coming at me again. Grabbing my arms, he pulled me close once more. "If you can give yourself to a wharf rat like Calico Jack, you can damned well give yourself to me!"

With that declaration, he grasped my face and pulled it toward his in an attempt to kiss me. Again I fought him off until he drew back his fist and hit me, knocking me down at his feet. Momentarily stunned I tried to sit up, but he grabbed me by my hair and dragged me toward his bunk. He threw me down on the mattress, next to a silk robe that was lying there. I struggled to remain conscious in spite of the blow.

Then, mercifully, I heard a series of shrill whistles. Captain Chatham abruptly ceased his assault.

"I am needed on deck," he said huskily. He straightened his clothes and threw on his coat. "When I return, Miss Bonny—or whoever you are—I shall expect your full compliance. You will do exactly as I say for as long as I say, and then you will do it again, whenever and wherever I want you to do it."

"If I refuse?"

"You will never see London," he said. "Nor anywhere else."

He left me then. At first I simply lay there, determined to resist the tears that threatened. If I gave in to feminine histrionics, all would be lost. I would never find a means of escape.

Slowly, I sat up and looked around. There had to be something I could do, some way I could overpower him when he returned. But it would have to be later, when most of the crew would be sleeping. If I could gain the advantage and knock him out, I could take the key from his pocket. Once out of that horrid room, I could creep on deck and make my way to one of the lifeboats.

I searched his desk and found a letter opener almost as sharp as a dagger. Then I looked about for something heavy. I spied the empty wine bottle left from our dinner. There was nothing else so it would have to do. If I could conceal it so I could take him unawares, I might have a chance.

Chapter Ten

Early Summer, 2015
Outer Banks, NC

A gale force wind was blowing as Jonathan and Mattie left the restaurant, and they stepped right into it. "Follow me—I'll pull around and get in front of you!" she yelled. "Stay close!" she finished as the rain came down harder. "It might not be so easy to see where you're goin'." He got quickly into his car and watched her sprint to hers, appreciating the way her hips moved in time with her stride.

They drove slowly, hyper-vigilant as they approached each intersection. Traffic lights, swinging precariously above the road, were all out. As they drove further south on Croatian Highway, he saw, on his left, that the wind had ripped the canopy over the gas pumps at the Shell station off its supports. It was now lying upside down in the middle of the entrance. Keeping his eyes on Mattie's tail lights, Jonathan reached over and turned on the radio. A reporter was warning that the ocean could once again cut through Hatteras, as it had during Hurricane Isabel a few years before.

Hurricane Charlotte had, indeed, turned back toward the Carolinas and it was already carving a path of destruction through the Outer Banks. Jonathan wondered what it would take to worry Mattie. She hadn't seemed concerned, even though the weather had rapidly gone to hell while they were in the restaurant. Now water was spilling over the roadway and he saw a sign with blinkers flashing on either side that declared Virginia Dare Trail closed by sand and surf. The reporter was now saying that Kill Devil's Hill and surrounding areas would get the worst of the storm.

They passed a miniature golf course and Jonathan noticed a small pirate ship bobbing up and down in the little pond, its small Jolly Roger flag whipping in the wind. The sight sent a shiver down his spine as he suddenly remembered.

The flag on the ghost ship he had seen—it had also been flying the skull and crossbones, along with another flag. A flag that showed a heart with two sabers crossed over it. He hadn't thought of it until that moment. *The mysterious voyager with the sad face and beautiful red hair was onboard a pirate ship.* He glanced in his rearview mirror, hoping for another quick look at the little toy boat.

He saw it again—but there was only a small American flag waving from its mast.

"What the hell?" he breathed. Now what? Was he was imagining things? From somewhere in the distance, a dog howled—or maybe it was the wind.

And they were there. Mattie pulled to the side in the driveway of the new place so Jonathan could park, and then she pulled in close behind him. The moment he stopped his car, he felt a prickling of his skin, lightly dancing up his arms, over his shoulders and down his spine—and that wasn't all. He felt a distinct presence in the car with him, as if the pale woman who'd been haunting him was sitting right beside him. The air was heavy with her spirit, and had been since he'd seen the ghost ship.

Or maybe it was just the storm, he told himself, dismissing the ghostly nonsense that was creeping into his mind. Rain was coming down rapidly in thick, heavy sheets. He wondered if Mattie had an umbrella in her car. She did, and they huddled close together beneath it as they hurried up the wooden steps to the front door. Pulling a flashlight out of her oversized purse, Mattie gave it to Jonathan to hold while she removed the lockbox.

"Congratulations, Yankee," she said, handing him the house key and standing back so he could use it. "It's all yours."

"Thanks," he answered and unlocked the door.

The place was already furnished, thanks to the previous owners and their vacation tenants who'd also left behind dishes, cookware, towels and bed linens. Just moments after Mattie switched on the lights, the power went out.

"No worries," she said, and led him out to the kitchen. She pulled a couple of candles and some matches out of a drawer and then they went down to the mud room and dug around until they found a couple of battery-operated lanterns and a good supply of batteries.

Switching on one of the lanterns, Mattie grabbed Jonathan's hand and led him back up the stairs to the living room. Thunder boomed and a crackle of lightning lit up the sky as they hurried in, breathless and laughing. That's when he saw the bottle of Veuve Clicquot champagne chilling in an ice bucket on the coffee table, as well as a welcome basket full of fruit, cheeses, crackers and pastries.

"Mattie," he said quietly. "You never cease to amaze me."

She shot him the quick little grin he was coming to love. "I'm just gettin' started, Yankee," she said softly.

Lightning flashed again and in the quick pulse of radiance, he saw the pale face of the woman on the spectral ship superimposed, for a moment, over Mattie's. Holding his breath, he stared at her.

There was another streak of lightning and she was Mattie once again. Jonathan felt his heart skip a beat or two, his old arrhythmia resurfacing for a moment to remind him of his own mortality. He was losing his mind—he must be. To stay that thought he did the first thing that occurred to him.

He pulled Mattie into his arms and kissed her.

To his surprise she responded to him more heatedly than his wife ever had, returning his kiss and moving closer, pressing her firm, beautiful body against him. He moved his hands down her back, past her waist to her hips. Also, to his surprise, he responded to Mattie as he never had to Patrice—at least, not since her affair.

It was the kind of arousal he had not felt in a long, long time, and it threatened to consume him. Breathless with the passion invoked by Mattie's curves and her response to his own need, he backed her up against the wall next to the big picture window.

She hitched up her miniskirt and wrapped her long legs around him, pressing closer still, and the feel of her moving against him doubled his desire. His kisses trailed down her neck and along her shoulders and then down to her breasts. She pulled her tee shirt off over her head and tossed it aside, and he unhooked her bra and drew it off her, taking a moment to appreciate the sight of her. Another blaze of lightning drew his attention to the window, and out beyond, to the beach, and then the churning ocean waves.

And he saw it again.

The ghost ship, rocking on the raging sea, and that same strange, ethereal face staring out into the bleak darkness of night.

Staring at him.

His hands dropped to his sides and he moved away from Mattie.

"Yankee?" she asked. "Are you all right?"

"Yeah—I'm good," he said and took a deep breath. "It's just—I haven't been in a hurricane in a long time. Not since I was a little kid. I . . . I guess I'm a little nervous."

"Oh, you'll get used to it, livin' down here," she assured

him, studying him a moment. "Maybe I'd better go." She pulled her skirt down and put her shirt back on. Then she stuffed her bra into her purse.

Thunder boomed again and the rain came down harder. The wind outside was blowing wildly, howling like a tortured creature.

"No," he said. "Don't be silly. You can't go out in this. Stay here. I—I'm sorry about before. I don't know what came over me. But I promise to be a gentleman."

She looked up at him speculatively. "Yeah, well," she said. "That would be fine if I wanted to be a lady." He opened his mouth to try and explain but she went on, "Okay. I get it. You still haven't quite left your wife, not really. And maybe you're not so sure you want to. But I knew that goin' in, Jonathan. You didn't do anything wrong, not with the signals I was throwin' at you. Forget it. No harm, no foul."

He grinned. "Not likely I'll forget," he said. "So you will stay, right? I can't let you go out into a hurricane."

"I'll stay," she said. "We'll ride it out together. And Jonathan?"

"Yeah?"

"When you decide what you're going to do about your wife, let me know, okay?"

He laughed. "You got it."

As they gazed into each other's eyes, frozen in time for that one moment, the power suddenly came back on. He smiled and moved away, awkward. Mattie showed him how to close the motorized storm shutters with the touch of a button, but he asked her to leave the one at the big picture window open a little while longer.

Late Spring, 1717
The Open Ocean

The captain's door clicked open and I woke with a start. It had taken Sir David so long to return that somehow, I had dozed off. I thought it must have been the wine he'd insisted I drink. I couldn't tell how much time had passed but the candles on the table had burned down considerably and I could see through his quarter gallery that it was dark outside.

Sitting up slowly, I glanced at the wine bottle, waiting behind his dressing screen where I had placed it. At the same time I slipped my hand beneath the pillow to feel for the letter opener. It was still there.

My captor stepped into the cabin, then and closed the door behind him. Closed and locked it and returned the key to the pocket of his coat.

"Please do not get up," he said, his eyes raking me lasciviously from head to toe. "You look positively fetching there on my bed, waiting for me."

I rose quickly and went to stand before him. "I had no choice but to wait for you, Sir David," I reminded him. "Locked in as I am."

He took off his jacket and threw it over the chair, next removing his cravat, after which he pulled his fine linen shirt off over his head. In the rising moonlight, I could see his eyes still upon me. His chest was broad and his arms muscular and I knew it would be difficult to fight him off if he was determined to have me. But, I silently resolved, I would die trying.

"As we discussed, there is no need for you to be locked in," he said. "I have promised you a pleasant voyage if only you will cooperate."

I crossed my arms to protect my person from his lecherous gaze. "If *cooperate* means what you seem to imply, sir, I am afraid I cannot," I told him. Soon it would be dark and I knew I would have a better chance of putting my plan into action under cover of night.

A hungry smile spread across his features. "I was hoping that would be your choice," he said. "I rather like a challenge." He untied the lacings of his trousers. "Remove your clothing," he ordered. "All of it. Now."

"No."

With one swift motion he reached out and grasped the lace trimming at the neck of my gown, pulling me closer as he ripped the garment from my body.

"Get on the bed," he told me.

"No."

I was standing between him and the screen where the wine bottle was hidden. If I moved quickly, I might be able to reach it—but I knew better than to act in haste.

"Very well," he said, grabbing my arm roughly and dragging me to his bunk. "Lie down."

"No."

Suddenly his hand was at my throat, his fingers squeezing, cutting off my air, before he pushed me backwards, onto his mattress. Before I realized what he was about, he pulled a chain and manacle from a compartment beneath his bunk and secured my ankle to the wall.

"Please," I begged. "Do not chain me—"

"Never fear, little strumpet—I'll leave your hands free. You will need them to aid me in my pursuit of pleasure."

He dropped his breeches to the floor and stepped out of them, leaving his silk stockings on in his haste to get to me. It was a comical sight and it was all I could do not to giggle—but now was not the time for laughing. I searched my mind for a way to distract him. Then I remembered what he'd said when he'd boarded the Royal Thomas.

"Wait!" I cried. "I . . . I will cooperate. But first give me news of my father."

"Who?" he queried.

"My father. Steadman Russell."

He laughed, and seemed genuinely amused. "If he is your father."

"Please. You said he might be losing favor with the crown. What does that mean?"

"That, I believe, is a ploy, Miss Bonny—designed to postpone your fate and my satisfaction," he replied. "Very well, then, if it will ensure your compliance. The gossips at court say that Captain Russell has pushed his privateering too far. The king is tired of this growing pirate menace. Any sanction his majesty has given to privateers in the past may soon be falling by the wayside."

"Indeed?" I glanced out the starboard window, into the inky blackness of night.

"And furthermore, all pirates—including the likes of you, Miss Bonny—will be captured and hanged on the spot. I can save you from that fate, if you will oblige me. Do so now, my girl. Remove the remainder of your clothes—or perhaps you would like me to remove them for you."

With that, he joined me on the bed. None too gently, he tore at the laces of my corset as he tried to kiss me. His breath smelled of cognac and I wanted to push him away but I had to lure him into my trap. Pretending to succumb, I opened my lips to his and pressed closer to him. He pulled the corset away from my body and threw it on the floor, leaving me clad only in my shift and pantalets. Roughly, he moved his hand beneath my shift and found my tender breast. Terrified, I drew in my breath.

"Oh, you like that, do you?" he said, mistaking my reaction. "Then, my dear, I am certain you are no lady." With that, he used both hands to pull my legs apart as he fell on top of me. "And you like that as well, do you not?"

"Indeed I do, sir," I lied softly, trailing my hands across his shoulders and down his back before sliding one of them beneath his pillow. As his unrelenting manhood pressed against me, my fingers touched the letter opener I had hidden.

Before he could carry out his intent, I pulled it out and thrust it with all my might into his shoulder. Howling with pain, he leapt up. Losing not even a moment, I rolled off the bed and onto the floor. I had to get to the wine bottle before he could get to me.

"You bloody little whore!" he yelled, pulling the blade from his flesh and throwing it at me. I was already crawling on my stomach to the dressing screen, where the bottle lay on the floor. The chain around my ankle gave me just enough length to reach it but as my fingertips grazed its smooth surface, he was upon me again. He fell on me just as I managed to grasp the neck of the bottle.

"You will pay for this," he swore. "By all that is holy you will pay. I'll have you and when I'm done I'll throw you to my men. You'll never see London—"

Before he could finish the warning I swung the empty bottle at his head with all my strength. With a grunt, he went down, unconscious. I pushed him off me and crawled as quickly as I could to where he'd carelessly tossed his coat. Retrieving two keys from his pocket I went about setting myself free. My hands shaking, I tried to insert the first key into the manacle lock but it was not a fit.

I took a steadying breath. It was the key to the door. I went for the other one and in an instant I was free. My captor was still unconscious. Spying the silk robe on the bed next to him, I used the sash to tie his hands, and then I hurried to the closet, retrieved my masculine disguise and put it on. Next I took my logbook and papers from his desk and thrust them into the vest pocket of my pea coat. Slipping as quietly as I could out of Sir David's cabin, I made my way up to the deck and hid myself among the rowboats and stacks of canvas. There were only two sailors keeping watch on this part of the ship.

Then I heard the unmistakable sound of someone singing a

bawdy song.

Fournier. And he was drunk!

I withdrew further into my hiding place and waited, listening. The song ended abruptly.

"Ahoy, mates!" Fournier called out.

The two sailors on watch hurried to the railing and, as they were distracted, I risked a peek over the side. It was indeed Fournier, in a rowboat, along with a stack of kegs.

"Who goes there?" one of the watchmen called out.

"Girard Fournier," he replied. "Cap'n of the fastest—I beg your pardon—*one* of the fastest ships in all the world. Which I am now sadly without. Permission to come aboard, if you please."

"An' why should we take the likes of you aboard one of his majesty's ships?" the other sailor asked.

"I have the price of passage," Fournier argued. He held up one of the kegs and pointed at it. "Rum," he said. "The best to be had. Won it all in a game of cribbage."

The two sailors looked at each other and, in unison, licked their lips. "Let's get 'im aboard," said the first sailor.

"What about the captain?" asked the other. "Hadn't we better report this?"

"And we will," said his companion. "After we get him—and the rum—aboard." He added in a low whisper, "And afore it all gets counted we can tuck away a keg for ourselves."

There was quick agreement, and they went about hauling in their catch. "All right, Fournier," the first sailor said. "Secure the rowboat to the capstans there. We'll hoist it up and you with it."

I held my breath, hoping Fournier wasn't too inebriated to accomplish the task. If only he were sober, I thought, he might aid in my escape. As it was he would be an encumbrance.

"There—'tis done!" he called up to the sailors. "Heave away, lads!"

Twice, as they lifted him, he almost fell out of the rowboat. Once they had the rum aboard, the sailors turned to him.

"We have to make a report to the captain," one of them said. "How'd 'e come to be out here in the ocean, in a rowboat?"

"Do you have time for a funny story?" Fournier asked, swaying unsteadily on his feet.

"No," the two sailors said in unison.

"Then suffice it to say, after the card game I was taking this bounty to secure it in a secret place. I must have fallen asleep."

Fallen drunk, you mean, I thought.

"At any rate," Fournier went on, "I must've drifted. But my good fortune—when I woke up, I spotted your ship and I knew I was saved. Now, if you please, take me to your captain and I shall make my request for safe passage to him."

"We ain't disturbin' the cap'n afore morning," the first sailor told him.

Fournier stopped weaving and stood at his full height. "I mush protest," he said. "I mush insist you . . . take . . . me . . ."

But before he could finish, he fell unconscious—almost at my feet. One of the sailors started to go to him but the other held him back.

"Leave 'im be. Let 'im sleep it off afore we takes 'im to the captain—and after we hide ourselves a taste o' rum."

But the commotion had awakened other sailors who gathered round to see what it was all about. When they spied the rum, a joyful shout went up and soon every cask was open and the men were passing them around, drinking freely. Soon they would be as drunk as Fournier, which would be to my benefit—if I could make it to his rowboat, now secured on deck.

An exasperated sigh escaped my lips. "What am I

supposed to do with you?" I whispered to the inebriated Frenchman. "Perhaps I should leave you to your fate."

"I sincerely hope you do not, mademoiselle," he replied, opening his eyes and winking at me. Now I could see he was not at all intoxicated.

"What are you doing here?" I demanded.

"I have come to rescue you," he proclaimed, still whispering—although we needn't have worried. Sir David's men were too occupied with the kegs Fournier had brought to pay any mind to us.

Although I was happy to see him I wouldn't give him the satisfaction of knowing it. "I am perfectly capable of rescuing myself," I snapped.

"I can see that, Kate," he said. "But as long as I am here, perhaps you will think of some way I can help."

Chapter Eleven

"What you can do, sir, is get me that rowboat you just handed over to my enemy!" I whispered harshly. "And what makes you think I need rescuing?"

Fournier grinned. "Steady, Kate," he murmured in my ear. "I knew you would need help when your crew came back and I learned you had sailed with Chatham. I know his reputation. You wouldn't be his first female prisoner never to make it to trial. Where is he now?"

I couldn't hold back my smile as I answered proudly, "In his cabin. I tied him up—after I knocked him out with a wine bottle."

Fournier chuckled at that, but he kept his voice low and told me to stay in hiding until the Dragon's crew had fully enjoyed the spirits he'd brought, and then we could make our escape.

"The Royal Thomas is standing by, just over the starboard bow," he said. "There is a fog off the water tonight, which helps to conceal it. Your crew is very close. With luck we'll be away from here before anyone knows we're gone."

But it was not to be so. At that moment there was a great commotion among the sailors as their captain burst through the door of his cabin and stumbled out onto the deck, a cutlass in one hand and fury in his eyes.

"Where is the prisoner?" Sir David demanded, stopping short when he saw the condition of his crew. "And what in Hell's blazes is this?" A trickle of blood seeped from his shoulder, where I had stabbed him.

One of the two sailors who had helped Fournier offload

the rum stepped forward. "We took on a passenger, Captain Chatham, sir," he said, his speech slurring drunkenly. "And he's got a great store o' rum, what with to pay 'is passage."

"Indeed?" Sir David shot back. "And you took it upon yourselves to imbibe without restraint what is now the property of the British crown?"

As the sailor shifted uneasily from one foot to the other, Fournier got up and walked, weaving and swaying, to where Sir David was standing.

"In their defense, Captain," he said with a little hiccup. "Some of the kegs had come open. Would have been a shame to let it go to waste."

"You! You are like a bad penny, Fournier, turning up where least expected and when certainly not needed. As much as you have won from me at the tables, I should throw you over the side and be done with you."

"Come now, sir. Surely you will not let a few bad hands condemn me," Fournier returned. The sailor looked at him gratefully. Sir David scrutinized the crowd on deck, studying each face. I shrank back further into the shadows.

"Where is she, Fournier?" he asked suspiciously. "I saw how you watched her, back at Proud's tavern." He raised his sword and cried out to his crew, "She's aboard this ship somewhere, mates! A gold sovereign for the one that finds her—and he'll be first man in line to take his pleasure of her!"

A cheer went up from his men just as the canvas sheet on Fournier's rowboat flew back, pushed aside by many pairs of hands. Out came Marcus, Oliver, One-Eye, Hans and Jamie— with two other gigantic sailors, all of them armed with swords, daggers, muskets and pistols.

"Now!" cried Fournier and we stepped out of our canvas hideaway.

"Look lively, Cap'n Kate!" Marcus called, tossing me my sword—the one my father had made expressly for my hand.

Catching it easily I turned, and without hesitation I entered the fray. As I wielded my double-edged blade with force and skill, I saw Fournier's mouth fall open in surprise.

Sir David's men, in their drunken state, were no match for us and my small band quickly dispatched those who had not already fallen prey to the rum. As if by a prearranged signal, Marcus fired his musket into the air and Oliver did likewise, and soon the Royal Thomas came to our aid. My men captured the Dragon with grappling hooks and swarmed aboard, easily putting down Sir David's intoxicated crew.

Toward the end of the conflict, I found myself standing back to back with Fournier as we battled fiercely, our blades ringing with each strike, he with Sir David and I with the Dragon's young lieutenant, Mr. Preston.

"Fournier—trade with me!" I shouted. "I want that one for myself!"

The Frenchman's laughter exploded in my ear. "Done!" he returned, and we shifted our bodies until I was facing the man who had tried to violate me.

"I was right," Sir David taunted me as we parried. "You, madam, are no lady. You're a bloody pirate bitch!"

I feinted and he lunged at me, outraged, but I was able to step aside. He was skilled and strong but he was overconfident. After a few moments he made another powerful lunge, so powerful it threw him off balance. As he fell to one knee the tip of my rapier, aimed at his heart, caught him high on his arm near his wounded shoulder, and drew more blood. I moved the point to his throat.

I had not expected him to beg for mercy, so I was as surprised as my men (and those of his that were still upright) when he dropped his sword and put one hand out to me.

"Spare my life," he said. "Take your men and go. Leave me and my ship to continue in the service of the king." His voice shaking, he added a whispered, "Please . . . spare me."

Marcus, Oliver and the others erupted in cheers, and I shot a quick glance at Fournier, who was smiling broadly and looking at me with admiration. How, I wondered, could my betrayed, mistrusting heart give way to an assault of butterflies at his obvious approval? Was I ready to love again? I quickly dismissed the thought.

"Oliver," I ordered. "Take his weapon and bind his hands." To Sir David, I said, "You may take your men—those who wish to go with you—and the rowboats. With luck you will make it back to Nassau or be picked up by another of his majesty's vessels. We are taking your ship, and all the supplies you stole from us—and anything else of value that might be useful."

Another happy shout went up from my crew, but Marcus was frowning. "Are you sure you want to do this, Kate?"

"What other choice do you see before me, Marcus?" I asked, more sharply than I intended. "If I release him with his ship, he will have the royal navy after us inside a week." I looked at Chatham, not bothering to hide my contempt. I turned to Marcus once more. "Seeing him on his knees before me, pleading for his life, I find more satisfactory than killing him—though he deserves killing. But since this will affect the entire crew, I suppose we should ask the men what they think."

A strange light glinted in Marcus's eyes. "Do you mean a vote?" he asked.

"Yes. I believe I do."

He nodded approvingly. "Aye. That's what your father, and his father, would have done." He raised his arms in the air and shouted, "Gather 'round, lads! Cap'n Kate has something she be wantin' to say! Gather 'round!"

"First, throw the prisoners in the hold—" I began, but Sir David interrupted me.

"Surely you would allow me the courtesy of retiring to my cabin instead," he said indignantly.

Staring right into his eyes, I completed my command. "*All* the prisoners—into the hold until we decide what to do with them."

In short order, it was done and my crew circled about me and settled down to hear what I had to say.

"We have a choice to make tonight, lads," I told them. "First let me thank you for coming to my aid. You put your lives before mine and I'll not forget it. Now then, you must tell me what you want to do, from this point on." I took a deep breath and looked at the attentive faces all around me.

"Because of your brave actions today," I went on, "you must know that the crown will put a price on your heads— mine as well—and we'll be hunted down as pirates. It is clear that we cannot continue on to England, and without the funds waiting for me there I cannot pay the balance due your services. We cannot go back to Nassau so we must find a place to settle in and hide for a while, which brings us to another question. I see no need to waste the bounty on Sir David's ship, some of which was ours already. But when our food stores run out, how will we survive? We might as well go pirating."

To my astonishment, a cheer went up from my men and alarmed, I raised my hands to quiet them. "I cannot in good conscience put your lives at risk. You have served me well this night. I'll not ask you to do more."

Marcus spoke up then. "You put yourself in Sir David's charge to spare us trouble," he said. "You risked your life for us. I think I speak for the crew, Kate. We'll follow you anywhere."

They all shouted then, their cries a mixture of, "Aye, aye, Cap'n Kate!" And, "We're yours to command, Kate!"

"There's worse things to be than pirates, Cap'n." Oliver spoke with a grin. "'Tis a good life and we be a hearty crew!"

"Ain't nothin' we ain't done afore," someone else chimed

in.

"All right then," I said. "Since the British already believe me a pirate—or will, after today—I shall become one."

Another cheer rang out and it did my heart good to know that these men were so willing to give me their loyalty. Something else stirred in me as well, something that called to me. Something that promised a life of freedom and independence from the whim of any man—and adventures the like of which I had never hoped to experience. Perhaps pirating was in my blood.

"'Tis settled then," I said. "But what will we do with two ships? It seems a shame to dispatch one so grand as the Royal Dragon to the bottom of the sea."

"If I may speak, Captain Kate?" said Fournier, stepping forward. "I believe I have a solution on two scores."

I risked a glance at him, hoping I would not reveal with a blush my unwelcome fascination for him.

"Indeed, Fournier?" I asked soberly. "And what would that be?"

"Isle Saint Marie, where my crew is waiting for me," he said. "It's off the east coast of Madagascar and there is no government there to interfere with us. We are free to do as we please. 'Tis lush—there's food growing there in abundance and where it's situated, it is protected from storms. But it is a dangerous journey," Fournier warned. "Around Cape L'Agulhas, off the southernmost point of Africa."

I gave a slight shrug. "No more danger, I wager, than we're in where we sit. In any case, it sounds too good to be true."

"Aye—but 'tis true, Cap'n," put in One-Eye. "And I heard tell there's good booty to be had from passing ships along that route."

"With but a few of your men I can sail the Royal Dragon to Casablanca, where I can pick up a crew," Fournier said.

"Then we can sail together to Saint Marie where I can have it refurbished to suit our needs."

"*Our* needs, Fournier?" I questioned.

"Of course," he returned with a disarming smile. "In case you haven't noticed, Kate, I've joined your merry band of miscreants. If you let Sir David go he'll be after my head as well. With his ship, we can outfit two crews and double our profits."

"But you're a merchant captain," I argued. "What do you know about pirating?"

"More than I have revealed, actually," he said. "In some circles, I am known as the Falcon. And the only merchandise I've ever moved I took from those more fortunate than ourselves, and who have been taxing their subjects into the poor house."

While I had never heard of the Falcon, I could tell by the expressions on the faces of Marcus and most of my crew that they had. They were suitably impressed.

"And you are proposing we join forces?" I asked.

Fournier looked me squarely in the eyes and my heart dropped to my feet. "I am," he said quietly. "And further, I claim the Royal Dragon as my prize for aiding in your rescue."

"Let's put it to a vote, Cap'n," said Marcus eagerly.

"All right then," I agreed. "Who among you is in favor of going pirating?" A chorus of 'ayes' rang out. "And who be in favor of the Falcon's proposal to join forces and go to Isle Saint Marie for a time?"

Another chorus of consent filled the air and it was done. Marcus pulled me aside. "Let's cut the prisoners free, Kate," he said. "If that's what you still want to do."

"It is," I assured him. "I find it difficult to kill a man who is cowering in fear before me."

"Then let's be done with it. And afterwards, I request a bit of a parley with you, in private. I must explain the pirate code to you and . . ." He hesitated for a moment. "And there's somethin' else we must discuss."

"Of course." I looked at him curiously for a moment before I called Oliver to my side. "Bring the prisoners on deck and put them in the rowboats, except any who wish to join us," I told him, then turned to the Frenchman. "Congratulations, Fournier. I trust you will supervise securing the Dragon, in preparation for sailing."

He smiled down at me and the sudden recollection of his heated embrace, in my room at Mr. Proud's tavern, assaulted my senses. "Aye, aye, Captain," he said softly and took his leave.

"Come, Marcus," I said to my quartermaster. "Join me in Captain Chatham's former stateroom and you shall have your parley."

Jamie had found some bread, cheese, ale and rum for us in the Dragon's galley, and he brought it to us in what were to be Fournier's quarters as the Frenchman and my crew prepared both vessels to get under sail. When Jamie left, I told Marcus to sit with me at the table.

"First, the pirate's code," I said. "My father told me a bit of it long ago but I don't remember much."

"Ah, but your instincts be right," Marcus replied. "I knew that when you called for a vote. Here, lass—it's like this. First, you must know that we all share in the spoils, and in the decisions that govern the crew. You be the captain, for sure— but every man gets a vote on where to go and when to strike. So you took the first step right and proper already."

"Good. What else?"

He slugged down some of his ale and went on. "Most pirates live under the code, though it differs a little from ship to ship and can be adjusted as befits ours. When booty is captured, the captain is to have two full shares, the quartermaster one share and a half, the mate, gunner, boatswain and doctor—if there be one—all get a share and a quarter. The rest is divided among the men."

"And the crew will agree to that?" I asked.

He nodded. "It's the traditional way," he explained. "Now as regards behavior on board ship—you must grow a tough hide, Kate, for these animals must be controlled. A man can get stir crazy on a long voyage, and get up to all kinds of mischief."

"All right. Go on."

"Any infractions are punished according to the captain's pronouncement. Any of the lads be guilty of cowardice at time of engagements shall suffer what punishment the captain and the majority see fit. If a man holds back any gold, silver, jewels and such, and do not deliver it to the quartermaster to be divided as spoils, he will also suffer what punishment the captain and majority see fit. If a man is found guilty of cheating at cards or dice or any kind of wager, or defrauding another of the crew in any way, he shall be punished the same, as well as him that be guilty of drunkenness at time of battle."

"I had no idea pirates could keep to such good behavior."

"There are some benefits, too," Marcus explained. "If a man have the misfortune to lose a limb during engagement, he shall have six hundred pieces of eight, and remain aboard as long as he himself think fit. Good quarters must be given to all the men, and he that sees a sail first shall have the best pistol or small arm discovered aboard her."

"It's a good code to live by," I observed. "I suppose we must keep order, especially with a woman for captain."

Marcus cleared his throat. "That be another subject, captain—again, if I may speak plainly?"

"Of course, Marcus. I could not do without your advice. Please say whatever you are thinking."

He began slowly, and I thought he was uncomfortable with the subject. "Kate, you must know that your beauty is unequaled to any these men have ever seen on land or sea.

Given your skill with the sword, 'tis unlikely most men would take the risk of makin' overtures to you . . . if you get my meaning."

"I understand," I said. "Please go on, Marcus."

He drained his mug and then rose and began pacing. "So most men wouldn't approach you for fear of bein' turned away with scorn. But some would take the risk. And . . . and some wouldn't be willing to take no for an answer."

"I see." I admit I was surprised. I had never thought of this particular complication. "What do you suggest?"

"Well, for one thing, you must never look one of 'em in the eye, should you find yourself alone with him. He'd think it an invitation. Most pirates know your grandfather's reputation in that regard and—beggin' your pardon, even your father's reputation—and they'll think you be like your ancestors. In that regard," he repeated, and I knew he was speaking of amorous activities.

I couldn't help smiling. "So, you are concerned for my virtue, Marcus?"

"Indeed I am, captain," he assured me. "But it wouldn't be a problem if . . . I mean, there's a way to avoid all that trouble."

"Then I am eager to hear of it," I replied and I truly thought I was. But I was not at all prepared for what he said next.

"Take Fournier as your lover," he blurted.

What he made of my sharp intake of breath I shall never know, but the shock in my eyes made him hurry on.

"I've seen how you look at each other, Kate," he said. "'Tis clear to me you are aware of each other . . . in that regard. Make him your lover—or get him to pretend he is. Then let it be known to all—these men aboard ship with us, and in any of the ports where we drop anchor. If they think you be the Falcon's woman, no one will interfere with you. You will be safe from all the others who would . . . you know."

I thanked Marcus for his advice, telling him I saw the wisdom in his plan and promising to take it under consideration. At that moment, there was a knock on the cabin door and Fournier entered.

"The Dragon is secure, Captain Kate," he said. "Ready to set sail?"

"Yes," I said. "What about the prisoners?"

"Drifting away from us, as we speak," he replied. "All his crew, save the officers, have chosen to cast their lots with us. If we can pick up a dozen more men in Casablanca, I can manage the Dragon with that."

"Shall we get underway, captain?" asked Marcus.

"I must speak with Fournier first, in private."

"Now?" Marcus asked. "I mean—so soon? It were just a suggestion, Kate. Maybe you want to think on it a while?"

"Indeed, I have already thought about it. There is no time like the present."

Remembering how close I came to having Sir David force himself on me, or handing me over to his men for their pleasure, I decided I would control my own destiny. Instead of suffering the attentions of any man who wanted me, I would choose a man I wanted.

And there was no doubt in my mind. I wanted Girard Fournier.

Furthermore, something strange had happened to me during my sword play on deck with Sir David. My blood rose so within my veins that I felt invigorated—more alive than I had ever felt. Afterward, there was a need in me I couldn't explain. A need for release that was compelling. Somehow— although I didn't know exactly how it worked—I believed Fournier could provide that release.

When Marcus left, I locked the door behind him. Then I went to stand close to the Frenchman.

"What is this about?" he enquired, his eyes glinting with amusement.

I decided to be frank. "Marcus has advised me to take you as my lover," I said. Fournier exploded with laughter. I frowned and demanded, "What exactly do you find so amusing?"

"Nothing!" he exclaimed. "'Tis only that you have surprised me yet again, Kate. First, how you handle a sword, and now . . . this most intriguing proposition."

"Do you not desire me?" I asked. "That would present no problem. In that case, I would ask you only to pretend, until we reach safe harbor."

His voice lowered enticingly as he answered. "You know I want you, Kate. As much as you want me. And there will be no pretending. But why did Marcus advise it?"

I explained my quartermaster's concern and then asked, "Do you have a wife—or a lover—in Saint Marie?"

He shook his head. "No, but—"

"Then why do you hesitate?" I asked before I lost my courage. The way he was looking at me sent an unexpected warmth rushing through me.

He moved closer to me and gazed down into my eyes. "Is that the only reason you want me, Kate?" he asked. "For protection?"

"I think I have shown you, Fournier, that I can take care of myself," I whispered.

"Then say it. Tell me what you want, not what Marcus advises. Say it, Kate."

At that, my gaze met his and I said brazenly, "Very well, Falcon. I desire you. I want you to make love to me because *I want you*. Because I *choose* you, and for no other reason."

He gathered me in his arms and drew me against his long, lean body. As I felt him hard against me, another thrill shot through me. After he kissed me, long and slow and sweet, he picked me up and carried me to the bunk. Laying me gently down, he settled beside me.

"If you are very sure, Kate," he said. "Only if you are sure."

"I am," I responded softly, melting into him. "Very sure."

Chapter Twelve

Late Summer, 2015
Outer Banks, NC

Jonathan woke with a start. It took him a moment to remember where he was. Glancing out the window all he saw was a mass of enormous, black thunderheads rising over the ocean. He looked at his watch and was surprised to see that it was almost eleven. He'd put away more liquor the night before than he had in months, and again he marveled at Mattie's capacity for drink. For life.

Mattie.

They'd fallen asleep together on the sofa a little before dawn, just as the Weather Channel reported that the storm was turning away and heading back out into the Atlantic. Jonathan wondered where she'd gone and then he caught the aroma of fresh-made coffee. He found her in the kitchen drying the champagne glasses they'd used the night before.

"'Mornin', Yankee," she said as she put them away. "Or should I say afternoon?"

"Hi," said Jonathan. He felt a little sheepish that they'd slept together without actually—well, sleeping together. "There's coffee?"

"Yep." She gave him a big smile. "It was in the gift basket. Looks like we dodged the bullet this time. We'll have some wind and rain but the worst of it's over."

There were two cups sitting on the counter—the one

with the Royal Thomas emblazoned on the side, that Mattie had given him, and a yellow mug. Instinctively, as if she'd known he didn't want anyone else using it, she filled the Royal Thomas cup and handed it to him.

"I hope you take it hot and black," she went on. "'Cause you got no milk in this house. Or eggs or bacon or anything else."

He grinned. "Sorry—I wasn't expecting a guest for breakfast on the morning after my first night here."

"How 'bout I run to the store and pick up a few things? I'll make you a good, old-fashioned southern breakfast—grits and all."

"Sure," he said. "I'd like that. Want me to come with?"

She shook her head. "Nah—I'm a big girl. You want anything special?"

"Surprise me," he told her. Not that she wasn't already surprising him. She swigged down the rest of her coffee, put her cup in the sink, gave him a quick peck on the cheek and took off.

She was amazing—willing, pliant, available—and making it clear that she needed no strings attached. He might have to do something about that, he considered, when he was ready. He'd thought he was the night before, when she'd responded so heatedly to his kiss—and then he'd seen the ghost ship again.

"And that's not only kind of sad," he said aloud. "It's stupid." Letting something that might not even be real get in the way of grabbing a little satisfaction with a beautiful woman.

Only, it *was* real.

As real as the sound of the phone ringing, pulling him out of his reverie.

"Hello, darling," Patrice greeted him cheerfully when he answered. "Are you decent? We're about two minutes away. Come down and help with our stuff."

A sinking feeling snaked through his gut at the unexpected invasion. "The girls actually came with you?" he asked, trying to hide his annoyance. Neither Christiana nor Elaine had shown much interest in the new house.

"Of course," Patrice replied. "And that marvelous young artist I told you about—Paolo Cortez, the one we're sponsoring. Our beach place would be the perfect spot for him to work, when we can't get down. I couldn't wait to show him."

"Great," said Jonathan, but his voice was a carefully controlled monotone. His wife, he knew, was in her element, playing the benevolent Baltimore socialite, eager to show off her latest acquisitions—both the artist and the beach house.

He swore inwardly. *No way in hell is some long-haired, unwashed artsy-fartsy stranger ever staying in my house*, he thought. He would have to make the new living arrangements clear to Patrice before her surge of generosity went too far.

She was talking again, oblivious to his mood. "We hit the road this morning as soon as we heard the hurricane was moving away," she said. "Beatrice and Franco and their girls—and Daryl, of course—are coming, too. They should be here in a couple of hours. Should we order in or go out for dinner?"

"I don't care," Jonathan said. "Whatever you guys want to do."

"Fabulous! Now come down and help—we're here."

He didn't think to call Mattie and warn her. A couple of minutes after he and the young artist got all the luggage upstairs, she was back, loaded down with bulging grocery bags. Jonathan had no clue how to explain her sudden appearance, but he should have known she wouldn't leave him hanging.

"Ahoy there, mateys!" Mattie sang out, running up the stairs when Patrice buzzed her in. "Here's your official Outer Banks Welcome Wagon with all the breakfast fixin's you'll need on your first day in your new home."

Patrice glanced at Jonathan, her eyebrows slightly arched as if in question, before she spoke. "How lovely, Mattie—but you shouldn't have bothered."

"It was no trouble at all," Mattie assured her. "I'm off to show some houses, and you folks are on my way."

Patrice introduced her to the girls and the artist and asked, "You'll stay for breakfast, won't you, Mattie?"

"Oh—no thanks. I've got to run. Maybe another time."

"Then how about tonight?" Patrice persisted. "My sister and her family will be here. Just a small gathering." She turned to Jonathan. "Darling, I do think we should order in. Perhaps Mattie knows a good place that can pull together something nice by this evening."

"Sure," Mattie said. "Jonathan, I'll text you some phone numbers."

"You're such a help," Patrice gushed. "Do come—say around eight? And feel free to bring someone."

"I wouldn't miss it for anything," Mattie said.

With a dismissive smile, Patrice turned her attention back to her protégé. "Come on, Paolo," she said. "You too, girls. I'll give you the grand tour."

Mattie grabbed the opportunity to flash Jonathan a big smile and a quick wink as he walked her to the door.

"I hope you will come tonight," he said.

She laughed. "Wouldn't miss it," she replied, and she was gone.

Jonathan picked up the grocery bags and took them into the kitchen. Mattie had thought of everything, he saw as he unloaded it all—bacon, sausage, eggs, bagels, butter, jam, even cinnamon rolls—and yes, a king-sized box of grits.

Patrice came in. "The girls have picked out their rooms and I've shown Paolo the guest room," she said. "We can put Franco and Bea in the den, Angelina and Stephanie with the girls, and Daryl can go in with Paolo or sleep on the couch."

"That's fine," Jonathan said noncommittally. Daryl was married to Angelina, Bea and Franco's firstborn. He was actually a pretty nice kid.

"Well, this is quite a spread! Mattie is a treasure, isn't she?" Patrice said brightly when she saw all the food Mattie had brought, but Jonathan caught the edge in her voice. She got busy making breakfast, and Elaine and Christiana invited Paolo to go exploring on the beach with them. "Be back in half an hour," Patrice told them. "Or everything will get cold. If the rain starts again, or you see any lightning, come right back."

Jonathan switched on the small TV on the kitchen counter and turned it to the Weather Channel. "I wish you'd called to let me know you were inviting the entire Morman Tabernacle Choir for the weekend," he said.

"We discussed this, Jonathan," she returned patiently. "Or at least, I did." She let out a martyred, put-upon sigh. "You weren't listening, as usual."

"It's just . . . I brought a lot of work with me. I have blueprints due for a client on Friday."

She turned to stare coldly at him. "So what are you telling me, Jonathan? You're planning to stay here all week?"

"No," he lied, snapping off the TV. "That's not what I'm saying. But now—I mean, if I'm not able to finish what I brought with me, I may have to stay a couple of extra days."

"Well, after breakfast you'll have the whole afternoon to work," she said dourly, lining a frying pan with slices of bacon.

"Right—until Franco gets here."

"Oh, don't start on Franco." She took the carton of eggs and the sausage from Jonathan before he could put them in the refrigerator. "He makes my sister happy," she added, rummaging in the cabinet for a bowl.

Yeah, Jonathan thought but didn't say, *and the weed he*

brings you every time he visits makes you *happy.* Which was the main reason Patrice was always glad to see her brother-in-law. She would never have bought it for herself—she would have been too worried that her Women's Club or Junior League friends would find out—but since Franco had a prescription, she saw nothing wrong with sharing his. She claimed she needed it for her headaches.

Still, Jonathan had to admit that Patrice had a point. Bea and Franco *were* happy—and they seemed happier with each passing year. It was too bad he and Patrice had never found the kind of glassy-eyed contentment her sister and brother-in-law enjoyed.

And once Franco arrived, he would want to monopolize Jonathan's time with discussions of his off-the-wall politics and Jonathan's business, about which he had no clue.

"I think I'd better get to work now," he told Patrice. "While I still can."

Since he hadn't had a chance to set up his office, the only place for Jonathan to put his laptop and printer, and spread out his blueprints, was on the dining table. But instead of diving into the new design project, he went online, to Google, and typed in the search bar: *HMS Royal Thomas.* He was stunned at the vast number of entries that popped up, and he quickly found what he was looking for. A man named Steadman Russell had inherited the ship from his father, who was proclaimed one of the most dangerous pirates to ever sail the seas, but for some reason, Steadman had deeded the ship to his daughter, Katherine, in 1717. Further research revealed that Cap'n Kate, as she quickly came to be called, became a pirate shortly after she took command. She disappeared a couple of years later.

He found a few sketches of the Royal Thomas online, including a diagram showing every corner of the vessel and a crew list. Then he found a portrait of Captain Kate Russell, done by an unknown artist in Isle Saint Marie, in early 1717. She was standing on deck dressed in men's clothing, one hand on the wheel as she looked out on the ocean. Her long red hair, topped by a colorful scarf, was blowing wild and free around her lovely face, and she was smiling.

"Kate," Jonathan whispered.

It was the woman he'd seen on the ghost ship.

"Who are you?"

And what do you want from me?

"Jonathan? Didn't you hear me?"

He looked up and found his wife staring at him curiously. "What?" he asked absently, surprised. "No . . . what is it?"

"Breakfast—or lunch, I guess—anyway, it's ready. Why are you in here talking to yourself?" She didn't give him time to answer. "Come on—we're waiting and we're ravenous. I swear, if I spend too much time down here, the sea air will ruin my diet."

As they joined the others at the table in the kitchen Elaine, his youngest and a junior in high school, shot Jonathan a big grin.

"This place is awesome, Dad! Can I have some friends down for a sleepover to celebrate summer vacation? Mom says it's okay with her of it's okay with you—in about two weeks?"

"Sure," he said. He felt his gut twisting into a knot at the thought of half a dozen giggling teenage girls taking over his house. *His house.* That was the moment he realized he was going to do it. He was really going to leave Patrice. But now was not the time and none of it was his daughter's fault. "Okay—why not?" he finished affably.

"Great! We'll want to stock up on sodas and chips—"

"As long as you're okay with me for a chaperone," Jonathan interrupted.

"Dad!" she protested. "We're not *children!*"

He shrugged and glanced at Patrice, who was nodding in

agreement. "That's the deal, Lanie," she said. "Only with a chaperone."

"Take it or leave it," Jonathan told his daughter.

"Fine," she gave in with a sigh, and then her spirits quickly lifted. "It's going to be all sleeping and eating and working on our tans during the day. And at night—we have to find out where all the cool people hang."

"You mean all the cute boys," Christiana teased her good-naturedly.

Another band of rain swept in, accompanied by strong winds, ominous thunder and intermittent flashes of lightning. Jonathan's eyes kept wandering to the window, enthralled by such a display of nature. Patrice was not comfortable with it.

"You think it's coming back?" she asked.

"Let's find out," Jonathan said and started to get up.

"I'll do it," Christiana offered, and went to the little countertop TV. "Weather Channel or local news?"

"Both," Jonathan said. "Weather Channel first."

Christiana returned to her seat with the remote. "Okay," she said as she pointed it at the TV. "Let's see if we're going to be washed out to sea."

A pert, cheery reporter was saying that several homes in Kitty Hawk had suffered minor to moderate damage, mostly from flooding, before Hurricane Charlotte turned and went back out into the Atlantic for the second time. She added that it had been the most unusual track any storm in those parts had ever taken. The weather gurus didn't know what to make of it.

"Expect more flooding later today in coastal areas," she warned. "For the moment this storm is not going anywhere. She's stalled just off the Carolinas. Coastal areas, especially the Outer Banks, will experience intermittent, heavy bands of rain until Charlotte decides which path she's going to take. Our latest cone of concern shows . . ."

Patrice's apprehension instantly abated. "As soon as Bea

and Franco get here, why don't we go sight-seeing?" she said. "Let's go out and see what the storm blew down!"

How like her, Jonathan realized—and not for the first time—to find entertainment in the misfortunes of others. But, he supposed, it would be better than being cooped up all afternoon with Franco cornering him and insisting that he try a toke—just one toke.

"All right," Jonathan agreed, reaching for the platter of eggs. He finished breakfast quickly, rinsed his Royal Thomas cup and filled it with orange juice and took it back into the living room.

Kate, he thought, gazing out through the big picture window at the rain and flashes of lightning. It was like she was in the storm, or maybe she *was* the storm. Or maybe he really was losing it. With a sigh, he turned away from the window and went back to the kitchen for more juice.

Patrice was laughing on the phone with her sister, who had called to say they were lost. After a brief, one-sided conversation Patrice decided they would all meet somewhere so Bea and Franco could follow them back to the house.

"I'm going to give you our realtor's number," Patrice was telling Bea. "She's a lovely woman who's been helping us get settled in here. She'll know a place and its better if she gives you directions." Patrice turned to Jonathan and asked him for Mattie's number. "You must have it on your cell," she said pointedly.

He pulled his phone out of his pocket and read Mattie's number off to his wife, who repeated it to Bea. Next, Patrice called Mattie and told her Bea would be calling. Mattie recommended they all meet at a place called Shucker's Pub. She told them it was a local hangout, a place to enjoy dancing, playing pool and telling (or debunking) tall tales.

‡‡

Daryl, Bea's son-in-law, guzzled down his first beer in record time. "Hey, Uncle Jonathan," he said. "What you been up to—designing any more of those award-winning high-rises?"

"Oh, you know," said Jonathan, glancing at the pool table nearby. "Keeping busy."

"Hey, Jonathan," Franco put in. "Up for some eight-ball? Or should I say, up for getting your ass kicked?"

"Be careful what you wish for," Jonathan returned, signaling the waitress and pointing to Daryl. "How about a refill for him?" he asked her. "For me—you have any brew from Baltimore?"

"Sorry," she replied pleasantly. "But we've got Pabst Blue Ribbon, Miller Lite, Bud Lite and Corona. What'll it be?"

"Corona with a lime," he told her. "Make it a round for all of us."

Franco and Daryl were already moving to the pool table. Reluctantly, Jonathan went to join them. He wanted, instead, to sit by himself at the window and watch for the ghost ship.

"How's the new place?" asked Franco, racking up the balls. Daryl wanted to break but he missed the cue ball on his first try.

"Oh, man," Daryl complained. "Every freakin' time!" He gulped down his second beer.

"Hey, kid," Jonathan scolded good-naturedly. "Slow down and savor it."

Daryl grinned at him. "Hard to do when it's so good and I'm so thirsty."

"Jonathan?" It was Franco. "You in?"

"I think I'll just watch," Jonathan said. "Go for it."

"Okay, Daryl," said Franco. "Watch me end your misery. Corner pocket, right now." He applied chalk to his stick and then pulled back for his shot. He hit the cue ball too hard and his ball missed the corner pocket.

Then he looked up and let out a low whistle. Jonathan followed his gaze to the door. It was Mattie. With her was a muscular young stud who, Jonathan thought, looked like a cross between a lifeguard and one of those Calvin Klein underwear models that end up on billboards overlooking Times Square.

As Mattie waved and walked over to join them, Franco said, "Now that is one *fine*-looking woman." Bea ignored him.

"Hey, thanks," Jonathan said as Mattie approached. "I hope we didn't take you away from anything important."

"You didn't," Mattie said. "I was headed here anyway." Then flashing a smile at Patrice, she added. "I'm glad you hooked up with your guests okay."

Jonathan started to introduce Mattie to everyone, but Patrice took over, finishing with a glowing mini-bio of Paolo Cortez, her young artist. Jonathan could see that Franco, like every man in the place, was momentarily awed by Mattie's beauty. Franco missed his next shot.

"My luck's returning!" Daryl sang out. "Now watch me hit the next one back a couple of centuries." Then he took a long, hard look at the pool table. There was only shot he could make and it looked impossible.

"Go ahead," Jonathan couldn't resist putting a little pressure on him. "Let her rip."

"Okay," Daryl replied. "Whatever you say." He pulled back his stick and hit the ball so hard that it took off like a rocket. It bounced off the bumper and slammed into Jonathan's forehead.

Jonathan heard the crack inside his skull as the ball hit him, and then his mind, enveloped by a thickening fog, went into a slow-motion tailspin. As it started to clear, he realized he was lying on the floor with someone bending over him. Someone dressed like a pirate from hundreds of years ago—

and she was beautiful. The sight of her took away all his worries, as if there were no tomorrow and no yesterday, as if there was nothing important in his life before the first time he'd seen her.

Kate.

"Hello?" he said tentatively.

"Jonathan—are you all right?" It was another voice, a familiar voice that was not entirely welcome.

"Patrice?" he asked. And the fog lifted. His wife was kneeling next to him on one side, and Mattie on the other.

"Are you okay?" This time it was Daryl. "Uncle Jonathan—I'm so sorry."

"He's fine, Daryl," said Franco, helping Jonathan to his feet. "But you still suck at pool."

Bea looked worried—more worried than Patrice, Jonathan thought. "Maybe you should see a doctor," Bea said. "We should go the hospital and get you checked out."

"No—it's okay, really," Jonathan told her. His mind was clearing. Looking around at the small group of people encircling him, he saw that none of them were Kate. "Just give me a minute. Maybe if I take some aspirin or Tylenol or something . . ." he said absently.

Patrice and Bea searched through their purses. Neither of them had anything but Mattie did. "I've got Tylenol," she said.

"Of course you do," Patrice returned sweetly. "Aren't you just a *godsend*, Mattie? What would we do without you?"

"Glad I can help," Mattie replied softly and Jonathan wondered if she was finding it difficult to control her temper in the face of his wife's baiting. "If you want to go to the emergency room, Jonathan, I can take you."

"No," he said. "Really. I just need a few minutes to myself." *What he needed was to get away from these people to whom he no longer seemed connected. What he needed was to peer out into the storm for a glimpse of the ghost ship and its lovely captain.*

He swallowed the pills and took his beer over to a table by the window. Patrice looked after him a moment and then went to sit between Franco and Paolo. The pool game over, Daryl joined Jonathan's daughters and their cousins at another table. Glancing at Jonathan, Patrice leaned toward Paolo, whispered something to him and laughed softly. Jonathan knew it was designed to make him jealous or angry or insecure, but he felt none of those things. He felt nothing, and the realization gave him relief. His marriage was over, and he was okay with that.

Jonathan turned back to look out the window again but in his peripheral vision, he saw Mattie watching him. After a moment, as if sensing that Jonathan wanted to be alone, she took her date's hand and led him over to the bar to join Patrice and the others.

The storm was intensifying. Absorbed by the view outside, Jonathan could see the sea getting rougher and the waves cresting higher. Rain came in intermittent bands and then let up a bit, but wind gusts were more powerful, rattling the windows of the restaurant. He peered into the churning waves for a few more minutes but there was no sign of the ship, or of Kate.

"Hey, Patrice," he heard Franco say behind him, as if from a distance. "Come out to the car with me. Got something to show you."

"In this storm?" she said.

"Come on," he urged. "There's a break in the rain and I'm parked close to the entrance. You won't be sorry. It's primo."

She got it then and glanced quickly at her daughters. They were watching the two young men who'd taken over the pool table. Satisfied that they were paying no attention to her, Patrice hopped off the barstool, waving happily at Jonathan as she followed her brother-in-law outside.

"She always like that?" asked a voice beside him. He

glanced around. It was Mattie.

"What's this?" He couldn't help smiling. "Some kind of sneak attack?"

"That's how I roll." She smiled back at him. "Your wife," she observed. "She seems . . . quite the party girl. Now I see where you're coming from."

"Oh. No, it's not like that," Jonathan told her. "At least not with Franco. They're just going out to smoke pot."

"You don't?"

Jonathan shook his head. "Tried it in college. Didn't like it."

"And . . . what do you mean, 'at least not with Franco'?"

He sighed. "That sort of slipped out." He didn't know why, but he was still reluctant to talk about it. "We . . . had a rough spot a while back. She says it only happened a couple of times and it's over."

"That is rough." Mattie sounded genuinely sympathetic. "But she says it's over. Maybe it is."

"Maybe. Probably. I don't think I care anymore."

He didn't—and it felt like a two-ton slab of concrete siding had been lifted off his back. He turned to look out the window again. Thunder boomed and lightning flashed.

The giant-sized television was on satellite so reception was intermittent. It came back on just long enough for the patrons at Shucker's to hear that Hurricane Charlotte was no longer stalled off the coast.

She had turned around and was now heading back to the Carolinas—and straight for the Outer Banks.

Chapter Thirteen

"Jonathan—what should we do?" Patrice demanded nervously. She and Franco, breathless, laughing and slightly damp from the latest downpour, had come back in time to hear the weather update.

"Evacuate?" Paolo suggested hopefully. "Go back to Baltimore?" Patrice waved the girls and other assorted relatives over.

"Better not try it," Mattie advised. "You don't want to get caught out on the road in a hurricane. You're safer in your house. Make sure you've got plenty of flashlights and candles and hunker down. It'll be over before you know it."

Their waitress, holding a tray full of dirty dishes and empty beer bottles, stopped by the table to announce last call for take-out. "The kitchen's closing in twenty minutes so *we* can get home," she told them. "Can I get you anything?"

Patrice looked at Mattie. "We were going to order in for dinner," she said.

"I doubt anyone will be delivering anything until after the storm passes," Mattie told her. "You might want to get something now, in case the power goes out for a while."

"Good thinking," Patrice admitted. Then she asked the waitress, "What's fastest?"

"We got the grill loaded down with burgers and the fryer full of fries, and we've got sides like salad and coleslaw ready to go."

"That sounds good," Patrice said. "Doubles for

everybody. I'll get the order, Jonathan. You and Franco go and bring the cars around to the entrance so we don't all get soaked."

"All right," he agreed, glad of the chance to say goodnight to Mattie with a little more privacy. "Get as much beer and sodas as they'll let you have," he added.

Also seeing the opportunity, Mattie tossed her keys to her date. "Do you mind?" she said sweetly. "I mean, these *are* new shoes . . ."

He looked appreciatively at her spike-heel sandals. "We wouldn't want anything to happen to those little beauties," he said with a lazy smile. Jonathan didn't like the suggestion in his tone. He lingered with Mattie a moment in the doorway, after Daryl, Franco and her date went to get the cars.

"Sorry about all this," Jonathan said, standing a little closer to her than necessary. "I didn't expect the hordes to arrive."

"Don't worry about it, Yankee," she said, smiling up at him. "I know the timing's off—but I'm a very patient woman."

"Good to know," he replied, returning her smile. It was odd, he thought. With so much unspoken between them, they seemed to understand each other perfectly.

"Looks like your wife's little dinner party will have to wait," she said. "Got my own hatches to batten down." She opened her purse, took out the bottle of Tylenol and gave it to him. "Call me when you know you'll be down this way again."

"I'm not sure I'm leaving."

She tilted her head and studied him a moment, as if trying to figure something out. "Like I said—timing," she told him. "Okay, then—the First Flight Ball is coming up soon. If you're here, I'd like to introduce you to some of the local movers and shakers. Patrice, too, of course."

"First Flight—what's that?" asked Jonathan.

"Celebration of the first airplane flight at Kitty Hawk— you know, Wilbur and Orville. It's a big deal. Your wife will love it."

"Yeah, that would be great." He decided on the spot not to tell Patrice about it. If she found out anyway and insisted on going, he would not go. There would be no more social-obligation appearances with his wife, he promised himself. There was no point. It was over and he would no longer perpetuate the myth of a perfect, happy marriage.

The first thing Franco did when they got back to the beach house was roll a joint. Jonathan saw him pulling all the paraphernalia out of his pocket as he followed Patrice and Paolo into the guest room. Bea helped Jonathan set the table and put out the burgers, fries and salads. The rain had stopped for the moment and the kids headed out onto the balcony. In passing them, he'd heard Christiana cheerfully observe, "We're staring into the face of death."

Jonathan's experience with hurricanes was limited. He'd been through only one, when he was a child living for a time with his mother in Florida. His girls had never seen one up close and they seemed fascinated with the wonders of nature. Patrice continued to be uneasy. Before ducking into the guest room with her brother-in-law, she'd told Jonathan she just needed a couple of hits to steady her nerves. Paolo came strolling out, on his way to the balcony, and Jonathan caught a whiff of the pungent smoke wafting around him.

"She really thinks the girls don't know," he said, and Bea looked at him, puzzled. "Patrice," he explained. "She thinks they don't know she smokes that stuff. I mean, with one going off to college in the fall and the other one a junior in high school—she thinks they don't have a clue."

Bea laughed. "They can probably get better weed than Franco," she said, and then she caught Jonathan's look. "I mean, if they're into that sort of thing. Are they?"

"I don't think so. I hope not." Suddenly hungry, he grabbed one of the burgers off the stack and sat down at the table. "You don't partake, Bea. So how do you put up with Franco? I don't get it."

She didn't speak for a moment, as if she was thinking it over, then: "Jonathan, all I can tell you is . . . we've had our problems through the years, believe me. But he can still make me laugh. I can't think of anyone else who could keep me laughing through our troubles. I mean, deep, gut-level belly laughs. That's important in a marriage. I can live without a lot of *stuff*. I couldn't live without the laughter."

"I envy you," he said, and he was sincere. "I still think you're way too good for him—but I envy you."

Thunder boomed loudly and a flash of lightning split the sky. The kids came scurrying back in, laughing and pushing each other, and Franco and Patrice came out of the guest room, their eyes red and glassy. They all gathered around the table and ate with gusto, as if it was their last meal.

As they finished, the power went off for a couple of minutes, leaving everyone frozen in their chairs before it came back on. Intermittent television weather reports warned everyone to shelter in place, saying it was too late to get out of the path of the storm. Evacuation was no longer an option.

After dinner, the young people went out to the den to play some board games they found in the closet and the old married couples, as Bea called them, took their coffee into the living room to watch the Weather Channel and wait out the storm. Patrice insisted Paolo join them and she went out of her way to flirt with him, refilling his beer mug and serving him more salad, all while bestowing lingering glances or whispering little private jokes. Jonathan ignored her.

It wasn't as if he did it on purpose, and it wasn't as if what she was doing didn't register with him. He saw every move she made on the young artist, whose discomfort was obvious to everyone except Patrice—but he felt removed from the situation, as if he had no connection to her at all.

As if he had no connection to any of them.

He turned his gaze out the window again, out to the rain and churning waves. Eventually Patrice got bored with Paolo. She strolled arm-in-arm with him out to the den, and she came back alone. Jonathan wondered if she had even noticed Paolo's obvious interest in Christiana.

"What the hell is wrong with you?" she demanded as she went to stand beside Jonathan.

Before he could answer, Bea grabbed Franco's arm and led him out of harm's way. "Come on," she told him. "Let's go do the dishes."

"What do you mean?" Jonathan asked his wife.

"You know very well what I mean. You've been distant and cold from the moment I got here. What's going on?"

He wanted to say it then. He wanted to tell her, *"I'm leaving you, Patrice. I can't bear living under the same roof with you anymore. I can hardly stand being in the same room with you. I thought I would get past it—the anger and disappointment and hurt and betrayal—but I never will. I no longer trust you. I no longer love you. So I'm leaving."*

But he didn't. This wasn't the right way to do it, in the middle of a hurricane with the family all around. It would have to wait a few more days.

So he said only, "I've got a lot on my mind. I need to work and it's clear that won't happen this weekend. Oh—and I have a slight headache, thanks to Daryl—and thanks for asking."

She sighed—her put-upon, frustrated sigh. "You *said* you were okay. You insisted you were all right when *I* wanted to take you to the hospital. *Now* you tell me you have a headache, in the middle of a hurricane?"

"Forget it," he said. "I'm okay."

"Fine!" she snapped, heading back out to the kitchen and passing Franco on his way back into the living room.

"What's got her panties in a twist?" he asked as he took the easy chair across from Jonathan, who was sitting on the couch, still looking out the big picture window.

"Storm's got her nervous, I guess." Jonathan wasn't about to discuss his relationship with his wife with Franco.

"You want a toke?" Franco offered. "We could step out onto the balcony or go to the guest room."

"No thanks. How many times do I have to tell you that's not for me?"

"Take it easy, man," Franco said. "I hear you. But . . . it's medicinal, for my bad back."

Jonathan chuckled. "Sure it is."

Franco laughed. "You worry too much, Jonathan. You need to relax for a change and try to have some fun. It's legal—I got my scrip."

Jonathan was about to remind him that wasn't the point, when the power went out again and stayed out. They all gathered in the living room with flashlights and candles. Jonathan insisted on leaving the shutters open so he could look out the big picture window, which made Patrice even more nervous. He didn't care.

If the ghost ship was going to make another appearance, it would be in the storm. Somehow he knew that. He didn't know how he knew, but he did—and he had to keep watch.

Daryl found a battery-operated radio in the kitchen pantry so they were able to keep up with what was happening outside. The rain and winds raged for two more hours before the eye was over them. They took advantage of the calm to go outside for a few minutes and look around before the winds picked up

and it was on them again. They all ran back in, laughing, but
Jonathan realized they looked more frightened than entertained.
Sadly, he realized they had missed the point—which was the
power, the majesty, of the storm. The more intense it became,
the more Patrice drank, and the more she drank the more her
interest in Paolo grew.

Mattie had been right, Jonathan thought. The house
was sturdy, strong enough to withstand the beating rain and
howling, raging winds. He kept watch alone, at the window,
while the others huddled together, Patrice and Bea on the
sofa with Franco and Elaine, Daryl and Stephanie on the two
recliners, and the rest of them sprawled on the carpet.

On the downward side, as Hurricane Charlotte moved
away, traveling further inland and weakening as she went,
Patrice began to relax. At two a.m. the power came back on
for good. When the radio announcer assured listeners that the
Outer Banks was out of the danger zone, she found Jonathan
still staring out the big picture window.

"What could you *possibly* be looking at?" she asked, not
bothering to hide her annoyance.

"Nothing. Just the weather."

"Okay, that's it," she said. "I give up. Why do I even try?
I'm going to bed."

"Good night," he said indifferently. He wanted to go out
and walk along the shoreline but the wind was still howling
and his head was hurting worse. He was exhausted and he
knew he should go to bed. Instead he grabbed a beer from the
fridge and taking up his post at the window again, he looked
out at the crashing waves, waiting until he could be sure Patrice
was asleep.

When at last he went to their bedroom (*theirs for now*, he
thought), his wife was breathing deeply, lightly snoring. He
took two more of the Tylenol Mattie had left him, opened a
window and crawled into bed beside the woman who was now

a stranger to him.

The moonlight cast a shadow on the opposite wall and it caught Jonathan's attention. It looked like a person—a woman whose garments moved with the ocean breeze coming in. He found it oddly comforting. She seemed to be motioning to him, as if bidding him to follow her. He reached one hand out to the lonely figure, half expecting her to grasp it in her own. He fell asleep thinking of her. Of Kate.

And then he was in a rowboat—one that looked like it belonged on one of those big old sailing ships he'd seen online. Only they didn't call them lifeboats back then, he knew. They were rowboats, and this was a big one, and Jonathan was rowing as if his life depended on it.

Or Kate's . . .

He had the sense, in his dream, that he was going to her, and that made him row harder. Lightning crackled overhead and thunder rolled like giant bowling balls across the sky, and he realized he was out on the open ocean, in a storm.

That's when he saw it—a flicker of light on the horizon, shrouded in a light mist, and somehow he knew it was coming from the captain's quarters, on board the Royal Thomas.

Kate.

She was close . . . so close. Then someone came up behind him, grabbed his shoulder and shook him roughly.

"Jonathan!" The voice was harsh, and petulant. "Wake up! Jonathan!"

He sat up—bolted up as if a ghost was after him—and came fully awake. "Patrice?"

"Sorry to disappoint you," she said, switching on the bedside lamp. "Who the hell is Kate?"

"What?"

"Kate—you were saying her name in your sleep. Who is she?"

"No one," he said, propping himself against the

headboard. "I was dreaming."

She looked at him dubiously, clearly not believing him. "What about?" she persisted. "We don't know anyone named Kate. Or is that code for Mattie?"

"Don't be ridiculous." He got out of bed, drew on his jeans and grabbed his sneakers.

"Where are you going?" Patrice demanded. She turned the digital clock on the bedside table toward him so he could see the time. It was a few minutes after four a.m. "Is she waiting for you somewhere?"

"Who?" He sat down on the edge of the bed to put his shoes on. He didn't bother with socks.

"Kate—or Mattie. Jonathan, I'm not stupid."

"No," he agreed. "You're just wrong."

"Not about this," she said. "This Kate—whoever she is— the way you were calling out to her, she means something to you. I want to know what."

By now he was standing, pulling on his tee shirt, ready to walk out the door, but he could see she wasn't going to let it go. "It's a name that came up in some research I was doing— and there was a picture, a painting. I don't know why I was dreaming about her."

Patrice looked puzzled. He couldn't blame her when he didn't understand it himself.

She looked unconvinced. "You mean . . . research for the blueprint thing you're working on?"

He shook his head. "Something else." Suddenly, a gust of wind blew the curtains at the balcony door, blew them almost all the way up to the ceiling before they settled back into place. "Okay, look," he went on, hesitant. He didn't want to tell her but he didn't want to fight with her either. He was tired of fighting. "Kate . . . she was a pirate back in the early seventeen hundreds." He shook his head again as if trying to clear it.

"If you're going to lie to me, Jonathan, you should at least try to make it convincing—"

"All right, damn it!" he exclaimed a little louder than he intended. "Stop this! I'm not you. I'm not seeing anyone on the side, or making an ass of myself flirting with someone closer to my daughter's age. I haven't broken my vows and—"

"Are you going to start that again?" she interjected, getting out of bed and stomping over to the dresser to rummage in her purse. "Ancient history, Jonathan—let it go. Now what the hell has gotten you so interested in pirates, of all things?"

He sighed. He certainly didn't want to dredge up what she called ancient history. He didn't want to talk about it or think about it.

"Okay," he said. "Just . . . try to keep an open mind." He told her about the ghost ship sighting, and how it had haunted him since the fishing trip. "I know I didn't imagine it," he finished. "Mike and Tim saw it too." It had weighed so heavily on his mind, he explained, that he was trying to find out more about it, especially since the guys had told him long-lost treasures and pieces of old ships often wash ashore in the Outer Banks.

Even as he spoke, he could see her irritation growing. She thought he was lying. "You know that is the most ridiculous, *preposterous* story you could ever come up with, don't you?"

He shrugged. "It's true."

She was silent for a long moment, searching through her purse until she found what she was looking for. As she pulled out the plastic vial of sleeping pills, she said, "Maybe you *should* go to the ER. Maybe that cue ball gave you a concussion or something. You can't possibly believe what you're saying."

"Except . . . I do."

"Do you know how crazy you sound? I'm going to take a pill and go to sleep. You know I get dark circles under my eyes if I don't get enough sleep. If you're still babbling about pirates and lost treasures when I wake up, we need to get you to a doctor."

He didn't bother to respond to her tirade, but he had no intention of seeing a doctor. A doctor would have no cure for what was ailing him.

Haunting him.

It was dark, but he wanted to walk along the beach. He *needed* to walk along the beach. Storm-tossed waves still crashed violently against the shore, whispering across the sand as they rushed back into the ocean. Whispering as if they were calling to him. As if Kate wanted him there, close to her.

The clouds were quickly breaking up. With the moon shining through them he could see that the sand had shifted dramatically. Long stretches of beach were completely lost to the churning water. Kate was near. He could feel her. It was surreal to sense her presence so close.

With his shoes in one hand, he continued walking, wading in the surf. He had no idea how long he walked, or what time it was, until he saw the rosy glow of dawn coming up in the east. He turned around and headed back to the beach house.

He was almost there when a wave that seemed to come from nowhere crested at his knees, almost pulling him down into the water. His foot caught on something and he tripped. His imagination went into overdrive, convincing his mind that a giant squid had found its way into the shallows, that it had wrapped a tentacle around his ankle and would carry him out to sea. As the waves ran out, away from shore, he recovered his balance and calmed himself. Looking around, he saw something protruding from the sand, and he realized that's what had tripped him. Slogging through the receding tide, he went back to it.

The part he could see looked like a corner of something— maybe a crate or an old chest—and it glinted slightly with the moonlight reflecting off it. Could it be something the sea had buried for centuries and the ravaging forces of the current had now brought close to shore?

There was a baby shark trapped in a shallow tide pool between him and the chest. The urge to get to the box was overwhelming but Jonathan couldn't let the shark die. He reached for its tail and pulled it back into the surf, taking a moment to enjoy the sight of it swimming away as the retreating waves carried the creature back home.

With the tide coming in, the box was now barely visible. He hurried toward it—or, he tried to hurry—but he sank deeper in the wet sand. Struggling against the current, he lurched toward the object. The water covered it now and when he reached for it, he felt a sting as the barnacles encrusting it cut into his flesh. With a low curse, he drew his hand back. It was bleeding slightly. The laceration didn't look deep.

Jonathan debated for a moment. Should he risk being swept into the sea attempting to dig the thing out, or should he wait until later? But it might not be there later, he knew. This might be his only chance.

The surf pounded into him again and he felt the jerky strength of the riptide pulling at him as he tried to get a grip on the box. With every wave, the object moved. Jonathan knew he'd have to get it soon or it would be gone forever. Looking back on the beach, he spotted a big piece of driftwood and went to retrieve it. He'd use it as a lever to pry the chest from the sand. Now soaking wet, he struggled back. The box was now barely visible. Pushing the driftwood deep into the mud beneath it, he moved it back and forth until at last he felt it rising.

"Yes!" he yelled triumphantly. "Yes!"

He had finally dislodged it. The surf moved under it and Jonathan used all his body weight to force the driftwood even deeper into the wet sand. Suddenly buoyant, the chest bobbed up to the surface. Then he slipped and almost lost it.

Still struggling, he managed to regain control of it. He moved towards the shoreline, pushing it along in front of him with the driftwood, until he got it safely out of the unpredictable surf. Exhausted and sopping wet, he collapsed on the beach, wondering why he had risked his life for an empty old chest.

He turned it onto its side to examine it more closely and noticed, in the few places it wasn't encrusted with barnacles and coral, that it was covered with black tar, as if someone had applied pitch in an effort to make it watertight. There was also some kind of bronze-colored metal strapping holding it together, probably for centuries. Barely visible on the surface of the metal were the ridges of what appeared to be a family crest, embossed with two letters—an R and a T.

The Royal Thomas. He knew it. As impossible as it was—the chest was from Kate's ship.

And the sea had delivered it into his hands.

He had to get it home and open it. No—he had to get it home and hide it, he thought. He would open it later, when the family and their guests had gone away.

"Uncle Jonathan!" It was Daryl, walking toward him and waving. "What are you doing out here? Bea sent me to find you. She's got breakfast almost ready."

"Great. I'm coming."

"What you got there?"

"Nothing—just an old piece of driftwood, covered in barnacles. Thought I'd try to make something out of it."

"It looks nasty but—whatever. Franco wants to get going but the radio says all the roads are closed. Looks like you're going to be stuck with us a few more hours."

Terrific, Jonathan thought. *Just terrific.* But, he knew, the roads would open up soon and they would all be gone. And then he would find a way to open the chest.

Chapter Fourteen

Jonathan let Daryl go ahead of him, into the house, before he ducked into the mud room. He hid the chest on the top shelf of a cabinet, behind some cleaning supplies the previous owner or some vacationer had left behind. Satisfied it was safe there, at least for the time being, he went upstairs to join the others.

Bea had gone all out preparing a feast with what was left of the food Mattie had brought and the leftovers from Shucker's Pub. She'd even chopped up the leftover French fries and made hash browns with them.

"There's two kinds of omelets," she said to Jonathan as he took a seat across the table from Franco. "One with onions and the other without. I know you don't like onions in your eggs."

"Thanks, Bea," he said. "Patrice still sleeping?"

"Sure is," Bea returned cheerfully.

What else is new? Jonathan wanted to say, but didn't. He didn't know if it was some kind of verbal contract between the two sisters or if it was an understood but unspoken agreement. During family visits, whether at his and Patrice's home or Bea's and Franco's, when there was work to be done, it was usually Bea who did it. And she never complained.

That was the payback Patrice would expect, for all the little extras she and Jonathan had provided for her sister's family over the years. Lavish gifts at Christmas, vacations at the beach or in the country—and even twice to Orlando for Disneyworld—things Bea and Franco couldn't possibly afford. Bea, being Bea, would have insisted on finding a way to pay it back, Jonathan knew, and his wife would have been more than willing to let her. With Patrice, there was no such thing as giving something and getting nothing in return.

"The roads are closed," Franco mumbled and Jonathan could see he was in a foul mood. "We're heading out as soon as they're clear."

A year before—even a month before—Jonathan would have asked Franco, "What's wrong—your stash run out?"

Not anymore, he thought, and he felt a new sense of peace. Franco was no longer part of his life. Divorcing Patrice meant he didn't have to put up with Franco anymore, so Jonathan got no more satisfaction out of needling him.

Daryl poured himself a cup of coffee and joined them at the table. "Uncle Jonathan found something on the beach," he said. "Something that washed up in the storm."

"Oh, yeah?" Franco's eyes lit with greedy interest. "What?"

"Just some driftwood," said Jonathan.

"Looked like some kind of chest or box," said Daryl.

"Think it's worth anything?" Franco persisted.

"No," said Jonathan, keeping his tone even. "Really—it's just a piece of old driftwood. Thought I'd clean it up and see what I can make out of it."

Patrice came in then, yawning as she went to the coffee pot. She took a cup, sat down and poured a few drops of milk into it. "I've had quite enough of the Outer Banks for a while," she said. "I want to start home as soon as the girls wake up and we can get packed."

"Roads are closed," offered Franco. Bea put a plate of poached eggs and dry toast in front of Patrice and finally sat down to eat her own breakfast.

"Well, as soon as the road is open, then," Patrice said with exaggerated patience.

"I'm staying," said Jonathan. Patrice looked sharply at him.

"Why?" she asked acidly, not caring that the others were

there to hear it all. "Plans with Mattie—or Kate?"

"Think whatever you like, Patrice," he replied wearily. Taking his Royal Thomas cup, he poured himself more coffee and headed for the living room. Behind him he heard them discussing him and he didn't care.

"Who's Kate?" asked Franco.

"He's crazy," said Patrice. "Or that cue ball scrambled his brain. He says she's some pirate he dreamed about. Oh—and he thinks he saw her on her ghost ship, out in the ocean."

The last thing Jonathan heard was Bea: "That can't be good. Don't you think he should go to the ER and get checked out?"

By then Jonathan had gone out onto the balcony and couldn't hear his wife's response. Sipping his coffee, he gazed out at the sea and, like some kind of miracle, he felt every tension, every pressure, evaporate.

A layer of sand about an inch deep and wet with ocean spray covered the deck on the ground floor level. He drew comfort in knowing that when everyone left, he could go down to the mud room and find a shovel and clear it all away. In the distance a flock of gulls flew over the water, their wings spread in perfect symmetry. It was suddenly clear to him, and he knew it as he knew his own soul: only God could provide such a delicate balance of nature. This miracle—this earth and all that's in it—was no accident.

Sandpipers, completely unaffected by the hurricane, now scurried along the beach, digging for sand crabs and moving in time with the motion of the surf as the sea rushed in and retreated, again and again.

Jonathan felt good, complete somehow, and he wondered if Captain Kate had once looked out on this very beach. It was amazing, he thought, how time seemed to stand still for him, here in the barrier islands. He could go on forever this way, he knew. Just sitting on the balcony looking out at the sea. He had always loved the ocean but now it was taking over his life, pulling him in, like he belonged to it.

To her.

And he welcomed it. He thought about the chest again, and the inscription on it . . . an R and a T. He was anxious to get back to it but he knew it would have to wait. Whatever was inside the chest, he didn't want to share it with anyone else. Not yet.

He had no idea how long he sat there. He thought maybe an hour had passed when Patrice came out wearing a cool summer dress and matching espadrilles, her hair and makeup perfect, the strap of her Louis Vuitton purse draped over one shoulder.

"The girls and I are packed," she said. "Paolo is anxious to get back to the city. We're driving behind Bea and Franco, just in case. They're worried about their tires."

"The roads open again?"

"Yes—they just said, on the local news." She paused for a moment, following his gaze out to the horizon. "Are you determined to stay?"

"I told you. I have work to do. This weekend was a washout. I'll be here a few more days. Nigel can run things for a week or so."

"And this . . . Kate person. You're going to stick to that ridiculous story about some woman on a ghost ship?"

It didn't escape his notice that she hadn't asked about his head. Not that he cared anymore, and not that he would have told her it was throbbing so badly he could hardly put two thoughts together. He didn't want to waste time going to the hospital. He wanted to get at Kate's chest. He knew it was hers, and he had to open it. He had to see what was inside.

"I don't want to talk about it," he said.

"Fine. Then come down and help with the bags. And there's a fallen branch blocking the driveway. Daryl can help you with that. Paolo has to be careful with his hands."

Jonathan let that go. He was eager to be rid of them, eager to be alone with his lost treasure. He didn't want to start an argument about his wife's latest, worthless protégé, or anything else that would delay their departure. Gulping down the last of his coffee, he rose and followed Patrice down to the car. Silently, still deep in thought, he hugged Christiana and Elaine and put their bags into the trunk along with Patrice's.

As he straightened up to close the trunk, a darkness swept toward him, descending on him until it enveloped him completely. His mind seemed to separate from his body. The last thing he remembered was the rubbery sensation of his knees giving way as he crumpled to the ground.

When he woke up in the ambulance it felt like someone was hitting him with a sledgehammer, from inside his head. A technician was checking his vitals, with Patrice looking anxiously over the paramedic's shoulder.

"Do you know your name, sir?" the paramedic asked.

"Yes . . . Jonathan," he said and heard his voice as if from far away. "Is Kate here?"

The young technician turned to Patrice. "He wants you, ma'am," he told her. "I'll be out of the way in a second and you can—"

"No," Patrice interrupted. "He doesn't want *me*. I'm not Kate." And she finished bitterly, "I'm just his *wife*."

Consciousness slipped away from Jonathan again. He next awoke to the antiseptic smells of a hospital. Groggy, his head still pounding, he tried to sit up. He was in a hospital bed in the emergency room. Patrice was standing beside the bed, with Franco, Daryl and Bea crowded together beside her in the small space. For a moment Jonathan felt claustrophobic.

"He's *ba-aack*," Franco sang in a creepy voice, imitating some line from a movie Jonathan couldn't place.

"I'm back, too," a nurse said cheerfully, pulling the curtain open. She was carrying a tray holding a couple of tweezers-like implements, some gauze and a bottle full of green liquid. Jonathan figured was some kind of antiseptic. "Doctor's signing your release papers," the nurse told him. "Meanwhile, I'm going to get that little piece of glass or whatever it is out of the cut on your hand."

He drew in his breath at the sudden sting when she swabbed the cut with the antiseptic. Quickly, she removed the little sliver of red stone with the tweezers. "See, look at this," she said, putting it on a piece of gauze and showing him. "Looks like glass or a piece of gemstone. It sure didn't come from a cue ball." She started out with her tray but Jonathan stopped her.

"Wait—can I keep it?" he asked. The nurse shrugged and gave him the chip of red glass. He tucked it into his shirt pocket.

"We were so worried," said Bea. "How do you feel?"

"Head hurts," Jonathan said. "What happened?"

Patrice, who had been pointedly silent—silent and fuming, he could see—took control of the conversation.

"You passed out in the driveway," she explained. "It seems you have a concussion. The doctor has scolded us all soundly for not getting you here sooner, thank you very much. He said you'll be fine—you just need to rest for a day or two. And now that I know you're going to live, we can get the hell out of here."

"Don't you think we should wait and take him back to the beach house?" suggested Bea.

Agitated, Franco sighed. "Come on, Bea. We need to get on the road."

"But maybe we should stay with him a while," Bea protested.

"Oh, don't kid yourself," snapped Patrice. "He can't wait to get rid of us."

"That's true," attested Franco. "All he's done since we got here is stare out the window like he's wishing we weren't here."

"But how will he get home?" Bea argued. "He has a concussion, Patrice. Someone ought to be with him."

Patrice cut her off again. "He can find a ride. I'm sure *Kate* will be glad to come and get him and nurse him back to health—or maybe Mattie. Let's go."

She headed out the door and Franco followed. Only Bea stayed behind a moment. "You gonna be okay?" she asked. "If you want us to stay I can talk to them."

"No—thanks. I'll be all right," he assured her. She was no match for her sister or her husband, Jonathan knew, and he wouldn't let her go up against them on his behalf. Anyway, for once Franco was right. Jonathan couldn't wait to get rid of them.

After they left, the nurse gave him something for pain and he dozed until she came back with a young doctor and Jonathan's release and after-care instructions.

"Is there someone you can call?" the doctor asked. "You can't drive on this medication."

Jonathan nodded. "Sure. Or I'll get a cab."

The doctor, whose name he couldn't remember, wrote something on the paper on his clipboard, then looked at Jonathan seriously. "Your wife seems to think you've been hallucinating," he said. "Seeing ghosts or something?"

"A ship," Jonathan said. "As I understand it, I'm not the only person to have seen a ghost ship off the coast of the Outer Banks."

"No—that's true." The doctor smiled. "There are sightings from time to time. Probably just a distortion of light and shadow, but people seem to enjoy the idea of it. Anyway, your wife is concerned. She says you're under a lot of pressure at work."

"Have been for years," Jonathan replied, wondering why he felt defensive. "That's nothing new."

"Well," the doctor said. "Maybe having an encounter with a ghost is your way of dealing with the stress. I'm giving you the name of someone you can talk to, if you feel the need. Perhaps it would help."

"Right," Jonathan returned. "Thanks." He knew better than to argue. He just wanted to get out of there.

Mattie answered on the third ring. "Jonathan?"

"Hey," he said. "You get through the storm okay?"

"What's wrong?" she demanded sweetly. "You sound weird."

"Not weird," he told her. "Drugged. Can you give me a ride home from the hospital?" He explained about the concussion and she didn't waste time asking questions.

"Be right there," she said. She took him back to the beach house and got him settled. "You shouldn't be alone, Jonathan," she told him.

"No—it's okay. I'm ready to get some sleep. That's what I want most right now," he said. "After two days with the masses, all I want is some alone time."

"Well . . . okay," she answered. "I can give you that— for a while. But only because I need to go and get your prescription filled. Then I'm coming back to stay with you." He told her he didn't think that was necessary but she wouldn't hear any argument. "Jonathan, you have a concussion. You shouldn't be alone, not for the first twenty-four hours. You might slip into a coma or something."

So he agreed. The doctor had prescribed something for pain. His head was no longer hurting but her errand of mercy would give him a little extra time with the box he'd found. *Kate's box.* As soon as Mattie drove away, he retrieved it from its hiding place.

It was a small seaman's chest—he'd seen sketches of them in his research into the Royal Thomas. This one was heavy with the coral that had accumulated around it. That would be his first challenge. To remove the encrustations without damaging the chest.

He felt a small surge of guilt. The chest had to be a couple of centuries old, and it was intact, and maybe there were unimaginable treasures inside. Such a rare find, he knew, should be consigned to a museum, not hoarded greedily and hidden from the world.

But there was no way he could part with it. And if he was right—if this was indeed a gift from the woman he'd seen on the ghost ship—then it, and whatever it contained, was meant for him.

He found a small hammer in the same cabinet and he carefully chipped away the barnacles on the bottom of the chest, removing enough so it could sit upright. On its base he noticed copper clamps, almost like an antique toolbox. With his forefinger he swiped away sand from the letters engraved on the metal band encircling the chest. First he uncovered the R . . . and then the T.

The Royal Thomas.

The urge to open the box was overwhelming. He looked around for something that would help. The screwdriver in the second drawer he opened was too big. He needed smaller tools designed for more delicate work. The chest was so old he was afraid it would crumble. He knew he had to be careful with it.

Hearing Mattie's car pulling into the driveway, he quickly put the hammer and screwdriver in the drawer, returned the chest to its hiding place and went back to the living room, and the sofa where Mattie had left him. He closed his eyes, intending to feign sleep but he didn't have to pretend. When he woke up again, it was dark outside. He'd slept all afternoon and Mattie was still there.

"How ya feelin', Yankee?" she asked brightly when she saw that his eyes were open and he was staring at her curiously. He got up and stretched.

"Actually—I feel good," he said. "Headache's gone. You

don't have to babysit me anymore. You must have something better to do than watch me sleep."

"Not really," she said. "I'm glad you're okay."

They stood there a moment, looking at each other, and then he held out his arms. He wanted her there, would welcome her there with every fiber of his being, but he didn't know what he could give her in return. If she was still willing, and still did not need any kind of promise for tomorrow. . .

"Hey, Yankee," she said softly, looking up into his eyes. "You sure about this? 'Cause if you are, I'm ready. I know all it is for now is a moment's comfort. I'm okay with that. But if you're not, I can wait."

"I'm okay with it," he said. She stared at him another moment, her eyes glistening with some kind of unreadable emotion. "But I don't want you to feel I'm using you."

She laughed softly. "Ah, Yankee . . . how do you know I'm not using you? There's nothing wrong with it if we're both honest and don't make promises we can't keep. Don't get me wrong. I'm happy with the life I've got. I'm not looking for anything. But I wouldn't mind a moment's comfort now and then, you know?"

"Yeah . . . I know."

She went into his arms then and he drew her close and kissed her with all the longing he felt for . . . for Kate. He closed his eyes and saw Kate's face as it had looked on the ghost ship, pale and pensive in the moonlight, her hair falling in auburn waves about her shoulders.

He opened his eyes and looked down at Mattie, suddenly worried that his wife was right. Maybe he *was* losing it. How could he be thinking about some pirate ghost girl he couldn't be sure even existed when he had an amazing woman like Mattie in his arms? *That* was crazy.

He clung to Mattie more tightly, kissed her more desperately. She responded, her passion matching his. Before he quite knew how it happened, they were lying on the sofa together, in front of the big picture window, the moonlight shining through it onto their naked bodies. And they were making love.

Chapter Fifteen

By morning, Jonathan was fully recovered. He had fallen into a deep sleep with Mattie curled against his side, comforted by the feel of her body next to his. When he awoke, his head was clear and his appetite had returned. Mattie was nowhere in sight. He knew she was still in the beach house, though. Her clothes and shoes were there, in a pile with his—right where they'd tossed them in their eagerness to have each other at last.

Maggie came in then, from the kitchen, holding a near-empty jug of orange juice. She was wearing his shirt and her spike-heel sandals. Her shapely legs were wonderfully long and beautifully tanned. Her blond, sun-streaked hair, tousled and begging to be touched, fell about her shoulders. At the sight of her, he was even more aroused than he'd been the night before. She took one of the last two swigs of juice and then handed him the bottle.

"You have to do some *serious* grocery shopping, Yankee," she said, her voice a lazy southern drawl.

"Yeah," he said. "Maybe you could help me with that." He took the last gulp of juice and smiled up at her. "First we should grab something to eat."

"Stack'em High is on the way to the market," she told him. "Best pancakes in the Outer Banks. Just give me a couple of minutes to get dressed—"

"I was thinking more about getting you undressed," he said, rising from the sofa to take her hand. Still naked, he led her into the bedroom, to the bed he would never again share with his wife. His adulterous, disloyal, selfish wife. The sense of liberation he felt was electric. Slowly unbuttoning his shirt, he drew it off Mattie and let it fall to the floor before he lowered her gently to the bed.

"What about the shoes?" she asked.

He laughed. "The shoes stay on," he said. "I love the shoes."

‡‡

Breakfast was amazing. They feasted on pancakes, bacon, eggs and sausage. Jonathan realized with a small shock that it had been a couple of hours since he'd given a thought to the ghost ship, its lonely passenger and the treasure he'd found in the shallows near the beach house.

Sitting across the table from Mattie in the pancake house felt so normal. The bright, airy room was crowded with tourists and locals, and the atmosphere was cheery and upbeat with lively chatter and clinking dishes. He considered that maybe Kate wasn't real after all. Maybe the young ER doctor had a point. Maybe Jonathan had been so stressed and so lonely he'd fabricated her out of his own need. He felt refreshed, renewed, just being with Mattie. She was good for him. As good for him as Patrice was toxic.

"So you haven't told me," she said.

"Told you what?"

"How was it?" Mattie wanted to know. "Being stuck in the house with the people you were trying to get away from?"

He laughed. He'd laughed more with her in one day than he'd laughed in the last year. "Gruesome," he said. "I won't bore you with stories about my stoned-out brother-in-law or pull out pictures of my kids and insist you look at them. But I will tell you this—it was a revelation."

"How so?"

Jonathan thought about it for a moment before he

answered. He wanted to say it right. "I realized . . . I was distinctly out of place," he said. "No, wait—I've got it backwards. They were out of place. They didn't belong there, in my house on the beach. They didn't belong to me anymore. And . . . I don't belong to them."

"Not even your daughters?" Mattie asked.

"Not really," he admitted. "I love them—that will never change. But Christiana will be going off to college in the fall and Elaine's just two years behind her. They're starting their own great adventure. They don't need me like they did when they were little. And that's how it should be. When I get back to Baltimore, I'm talking to my wife about a divorce, and then I'm seeing a lawyer. It's time." They were both silent for a moment before he added, "Now you can tell me something."

"Okay, Yankee. What do you want to know?"

"Why do people call you Pirate Girl? I mean—I know you said it's because you like to do your own thing and live for the moment and all that. Is there more to it?" He didn't think there was. He was just trying to be charming and entertaining, which felt good. He hadn't made an effort to impress a girl in years, and even that was liberating.

"Yep," she said. "There's more, which I really don't like to go into—but for you I'll make an exception. I was teased about it for years, growin' up. The locals who've been in these parts as far back as my family—they know all about it."

"Are you keeping me in suspense on purpose?" he teased.

She grinned and looked, he thought, a little embarrassed. "Okay. As hokey as it sounds—my ancestors were pirates." She slugged back the rest of her rum and Diet Coke. "Real eye-patch wearin', sword carryin', swaggering, grog-swilling pirates. So beware, Yankee. Pirate blood flows through my veins."

She went on talking, but Jonathan didn't hear anything else. As she spoke, he saw Kate's features slowly superimposed over Mattie's. As suddenly as it had left him earlier, his yearning, his need to be close to the beautiful woman he'd seen on the ghost ship was back, stronger than ever. Dizzy, he wavered in his chair. He felt his shoulders slump and his eyes droop, as if he hadn't slept in weeks.

"What's wrong?" Mattie asked. She sounded truly concerned. "You all right?"

"I'm fine," he said. But he didn't feel fine. "Maybe . . . I'm overdoing it. I need to get home."

"Okay," she told him. "Come on. Let's settle up here and I'll drop you off."

"Yeah. Thanks."

"Don't worry about the groceries. I'll pick up some stuff and stop by tomorrow. But you promise to call me if you feel worse, or if you need anything."

He agreed, signaled the waitress and gave her his credit card. He hardly remembered signing, or much about the drive back to the beach house. His anxiety at being away from it, and his eagerness to get back to Kate's sea chest, were making it difficult for him to breathe. When they pulled up in his driveway, he thanked Mattie for the ride—for everything—and gave her a quick kiss on the cheek.

"So . . . I'll see you tomorrow?" she offered. He looked at her blankly. "When I bring the groceries," she reminded him.

"Yeah," he said, and thanked her again before he bailed out of her car, almost in a panic to make sure the sea chest was still there, where he'd hidden it. To make sure he'd actually found it—that he hadn't imagined the whole thing.

As soon as Mattie drove away, he went to the mud room and opened the cabinet door. When he saw the coral-encrusted box where he'd left it, undisturbed, a wave of relief swept over him, so strong his knees almost buckled. Cradling the box against his heart, he bolted up the stairs.

He placed it on the dining table next to his laptop and then stood back and stared at it a moment. He had to get it open and he had to do it without destroying it—and he needed to find out how to do that. He opened his computer, went online and Googled, "Marine Archeology Expert." He found one in the Maritime Studies department at East North Carolina University.

Even though it was too late to call, he pulled out his cell phone and punched in the number. It went straight to voice mail. He left a message.

"Hello. My name is Jonathan West. I need some advice on an artifact I found on the beach in Kill Devil's Hill. It looks pretty old and I—anyway, if you could call me back I'd appreciate it."

Frustrated, knowing there was no possibility of a response before morning, he started reviewing all the web sites he'd bookmarked that mentioned the Royal Thomas. Then he Googled Kate's name—Katherine Russell—and found only a few brief mentions. He printed all those pages out and then Googled images with her name. That search turned up one more portrait, a miniature oil on canvas, also by an unknown artist. She couldn't have been more than fourteen or fifteen when it was done. He printed that one too, along with the one he'd found earlier, and taped them up on the wall so they would be right in front of him when he sat at his computer. Then he turned his attention back to the sea chest.

Turning it this way and that, he examined it from every angle, looking for a seam in the part of the box he could see, or any kind of opening in the coral that covered it. He tried prodding it gently with a few knives of various sizes he found in the kitchen. Nothing worked. It would have to wait until the next day, when he could go to a hardware store and get more appropriate tools for such delicate work.

Maybe, just maybe, he thought, someone from the university would get back to him by then. His cell phone woke him a little after eight the next morning with the insistent refrain:

Fifteen men on the dead man's chest,
Yo-ho-ho, and a bottle of rum!
Drink and the devil and done for the rest!
Yo-ho-ho and a bottle of rum!

He had fallen asleep at the dining table, his head resting next to his laptop. His body was stiff, protesting a little as he reached into his pocket and grabbed his phone. It was Dr. Roger Barclay, director of maritime studies at the university.

"Sorry to call so early," he said. "I've got a class starting in about twenty minutes but your message intrigues me. Exactly what is it you've found?"

Jonathan was almost reluctant to describe it. Somehow, revealing its existence felt like a betrayal but he couldn't just attack it with a hammer. He had to know what he was doing. But somehow, it felt too intimate, too personal to share. He knew the box was Kate's. He also knew it hadn't come to him by coincidence. He had to find out what was inside.

"It's some kind of sea chest," he said. "And it's covered with coral."

After asking where, exactly, Jonathan had found it, Dr. Barclay said, "Can you see any markings on it?"

"I . . . uh, I think so. But they're not distinct," Jonathan lied. He had no intention of telling anyone from any university or museum about the R and the T, for fear they would try to take it from him. "There are two metallic-looking bands running around it, as far as I can tell."

"Where is the object now?"

When Jonathan told him it was sitting on the dining table in his house in the Outer Banks, Dr. Barclay was silent for a moment. Then he asked, "For how long?"

"Couple of days. Why?"

"Well, it's always best to keep the item submerged in water—in your case, salt water—while you transport it to a laboratory. If you bring it here, we could x-ray it for you and see what we're dealing with."

Jonathan hesitated. He was tempted but he wasn't ready to share it with anyone yet. "I don't think I'll be able to do that," he said. "I just need to know how I can remove the coral and get it open with the least amount of damage."

"Ideally, it should be done in a lab," the archeologist said. "But—how long did you say it's been since you found it?"

"Couple of days."

"All right then. You can take some of the coral off with a hammer—but tap *gently*. Your best bet is to get your hands on some Dremel tools. Try Home Depot—look for a kit that has very precise and abrasive points. You'll need a hammer, grinding tool and a pick. Be careful—you may find small artifacts inside the encrustations. Go easy. Take your time and you should be okay."

"Thanks," Jonathan said, preparing to hang up.

"I'd love to see it," Dr. Barclay said. "We can help you date it and maybe even find out who it belonged to, or at least where it's from. Keep in touch."

"I'll do that," Jonathan promised.

As soon as he hung up, he went online to Super Pages, searched for hardware stores in his zip code and found a Home Depot. He washed his face, brushed his teeth and grabbed his keys. No matter how long it took, he would get that box open. The Dremel kit he selected had an assortment of wrenches, grinders and grinding stones. It also had a pneumatic hammer and a few chisel bits. He paid quickly and headed out to his car.

Pulling out of the parking lot, he took a wrong turn and drove away from his house. He'd gone for several blocks before he realized his mistake. Turning up a side street, intending to circle around and go back, he spotted a second-hand store. Big letters on the sign above the window identified it as *Mr. Barnacle's Thrift Shop.* In the window was a huge model ship. All Jonathan could see from that distance was that it was an old sailing vessel. And then he saw *her*, waiting on the corner for the light to change.

Kate.

Her long red hair went mid-way down her back, and she was taller than he thought she'd be. In spite of the baggy pants and bulky sweater she wore, he could tell she was slender. When the light changed, she stepped off the curb and glided gracefully, effortlessly, across the intersection, almost like she was floating an inch or so above the ground. Holding his breath, afraid that if he moved she would disappear, Jonathan watched as she went into the shop.

Behind him a car horn blared impatiently. He drove through the light and made a U turn so he could grab the only parking space in front of Mr. Barnacle's. He paused for a moment to look at the old model ship in the window. As soon as he entered the place the piquant smell of old leather shoes, sweaty feet, stale tobacco mingled with some kind of air freshener, and an undercurrent of mouse droppings assaulted his nostrils.

The aisles were narrow and the counters, shelves and clothing racks were crowded with cast-offs, some that looked contemporary and some that looked like antiques. Jonathan searched for her, walking slowly, looking up and down each aisle. He was beginning to think he had imagined her when he saw her standing at a table at the rear of the store, talking with an old man, probably the proprietor.

"Kate?" He'd intended to call out to her but his voice came out in a whisper. There was no response, except from the old man who looked at him curiously. Jonathan said it again, louder this time. "Kate?"

She turned around.

"Jonathan?" It was Mattie. "What are you doing here?"

He couldn't believe it. He'd been so sure it was Kate. "Your . . . your hair," he managed at last. "What happened to it? I mean, it's . . . it's red." His words faded away as she broke into a radiant smile.

"You like it? I felt like a change. Did it myself, last night."

"It's pretty drastic," he said.

She laughed softly. "Not really. This is actually my natural color. Been doin' it blond since I was about fifteen. I thought my daddy was gonna kill me, first time he saw it."

"But—why now?"

She shrugged. "Got bored, I guess. So what are you doin' here?" she asked again. "The last place I'd expect to see you is in a second-hand store."

His shock dissipated a little, leaving only a dull sense of disappointment. He'd been so sure it was Kate. He groped for an explanation. "Oh . . . well, I . . . the old model ship caught my eye. The one in the window out front. I was at Home Depot and I saw it, driving by."

"Sorry—you're too late," she told him. "It's sold." She looked at the proprietor of the thrift shop. "We had a deal, Mr. Callahan. Now don't you go sellin' it out from under me. It's over half paid for and I'll be able to take it home in a couple of weeks. So even if this fine gentleman offers you more money—"

Jonathan grabbed her hand. "Relax," he said softly. "I'm not going to outbid you, Mattie. Really. Why is it so important to you?"

"Excuse me," Mr. Callahan interjected. "I've got some stuff in the back room to unpack while you two sort this out."

Mattie looked up at Jonathan. "It's a birthday present

for my granny," she said. "She's turning eighty in a couple of weeks. She collects 'em—model ships. Has for years."

"She has good taste," he replied. "I'd like to meet your granny."

"Good," she said. "She'll be at the First Flight Ball, so you'll get your chance."

"How much more do you owe on it?" Jonathan asked. When she told him the balance due on the model ship was a little over a hundred bucks, he said, "Will you let me get it for you? I'd really like to. Consider it a thank-you for helping me find the perfect house."

"For real?" she said, surprised and pleased. He loved that there seemed to be no subterfuge in her, that she didn't try to hide whatever she was feeling at the moment.

"For real," he assured her. Mr. Callahan, Jonathan thought, must have been eavesdropping. He came out of the back room and offered to write it up and wrap it up, right away. He led them up front, to the cash register.

That's when Jonathan spotted an old coastline map of North Carolina in a big frame, hanging behind the counter. There were small markings on it, designating hundreds of shipwreck sites in the Outer Banks, many not far from his beach house. It was labeled *Graveyard of the Atlantic* and it was hand-drawn. It looked authentic. The date in the lower right-hand corner was 1720. Jonathan's gaze traveled over the shipwreck designations and he found what he was looking for—the Royal Thomas. It had sunk in 1719, not too far from his beach house. If the map was genuine, Jonathan thought, it was valuable—too valuable to be hanging in a thrift shop. It belonged in a museum, like Kate's little sea chest—but like the chest, Jonathan knew he would never part with it.

"The map—is it for sale?" he asked.

Mr. Callahan scratched his head, turned and looked up at the map and then scratched his head again. "Well," he said slowly. "I was thinkin' about contacting a museum or antique dealer to see if I can find out what it's worth . . ."

"What do you want for it?" Jonathan asked.

"I don't think I could part with it for less than . . . oh, I don't know. Maybe I should hang on to it."

"How does five hundred sound?"

"Mister, you got yourself a deal!"

The old man wrote up the charges for both the ship and the map, and started wrapping them up in big sheets of brown paper.

"You have breakfast yet?" Mattie asked Jonathan.

He told her he had, and that he was anxious to get home and get some work done. "But call me later," he said. "Maybe we can have dinner."

"You got it," she said softly. She seemed happy with the plan. When Callahan gave her the model ship, she reached up and brushed Jonathan's lips lightly with her own. "See you later, Yankee," she said and held up her package. "And thanks for this."

"Anything else I can show you?" Callahan asked Jonathan after Mattie took off. "If you're interested in artifacts, I've got some old spoons and coins that washed up around these parts."

"Yeah, maybe," said Jonathan. "But not today."

On the way to his car, he saw her again—the red-haired woman he'd seen before. She was standing on the same corner, as if she'd been waiting for him to come out of the store.

His cell phone rang then. He looked at the caller i.d. and saw it was his home phone. He groaned. Patrice was the last person he wanted to talk to at the moment. When he looked up again, the red-haired woman was gone. He swiped the answer icon with his thumb.

"Hey, Patrice," he said not caring if there was resentment in his tone. "What's up?"

"Well, don't sound so happy to hear from me," she said. "Sorry to bother you but I seem to have lost my cell phone. Maybe I left it there. I've been calling it for over an hour. Any chance you heard it ringing?"

"No, I went out for breakfast. When I get back I'll take a look around."

"Never mind," she said. "I've already bought a new one. When I come down again I'll look for it."

"If you're sure," he responded. "I'll let you know when I get back and you could try calling it again."

"No—it's probably out of juice anyway. How's your project coming?"

"What?" For a second he didn't know what she was talking about, and then he remembered the blueprints he was supposed to be working on. "Oh—yeah. I . . . I'm kind of stuck. But I'll work it out."

"So you have no idea when you'll be home?" she asked, her voice tight.

"A week, maybe. Probably."

For a moment there was silence at the other end of the line. Jonathan looked again toward the spot where the mysterious red-haired woman had been standing. She had not reappeared.

"All right then," Patrice said. "How's your headache?"

"My what?"

"Jonathan!" She sounded exasperated. "Your concussion, remember? How are you feeling?"

"Oh. I'm okay. Headache's gone. Look, I've got to go," he said, starting the car. "I want to get back to work."

"You need to get home and see a doctor."

"Yeah—soon," he told her and hung up.

All the way back to the beach house, he slowed down at every intersection, looking for her. *For Kate.* It was a fluke— Mattie with red hair. He knew it wasn't Mattie he'd seen, standing there and waiting for the light to change.

Of course it wasn't.

He felt like his heart dropped into his stomach, as he

remembered, and it hit him hard. The clothes had been different. Mattie was wearing her typical mini-skirt and spike heels. The other woman—Kate—had been dressed in baggy men's trousers, a rough woolen sweater and some kind of old-fashioned boots.

It was Kate. She *had* been there.

He drove fast then, eager to get back to her sea chest, now that he had the proper tools. He didn't care that he broke the speed limit.

Chapter Sixteen

Working carefully, trying various Dremel attachments, Jonathan was able to remove some of the encrustation covering the sea chest. Twice, in the beginning, his hands were shaking so badly he had to stop.

Stop, take a deep, calming breath, and start again.

As he gained more confidence in the new tools, he relaxed. He was able to pick up the fractal pattern in the coral, the Fibonacci-like repeating design of growth, and follow it. The encrustation gradually fell away as he retraced the pattern in reverse.

It was slow and tedious, but also enthralling. Kate had personally delivered this lost treasure to him, and he was desperate to see what was inside. Whatever it was, he knew she wanted him to have it.

He was working in the dining room, on the table, his laptop on and online in case he wanted to research whatever he found. Somewhere in the back of his mind he'd thought about setting up his office in the guest room, but the thought evaporated as he became engrossed in grinding the coral away. He was unmindful of the mess he was making, except a brief satisfaction in knowing it would drive Patrice crazy. That thought drifted away, too; she was no longer part of his reality. The only concession Jonathan had made—and mostly to protect the sea chest and any other artifacts that might be hiding in its casing—was to grab a thick towel from the hallway linen closet and spread it out on the table.

Time seemed to halt in place for him. He heard his cell phone sing out the pirate ditty, and he glanced at the caller i.d.

It was Nigel, and Jonathan knew he should pick up. He made a mental note to email Nigel later. After a while (he really didn't know how long) Patrice called, but he ignored the ring. He picked up for the third caller. It was Mattie.

"I'm pulling into your driveway," she said. "I've got your groceries. How you feelin'?"

"Good," he said. Annoyed at the interruption but trying not to show it, he kept his voice even. "Sorry—I've kinda gotten involved here. That project I've been putting off."

By then he was hanging up the phone and opening the door for her. She smiled up at him. "Hi," she said softly.

"Hi," he said, taking the three Tom's Market bags from her. "Looks like I'll have to take a rain check for dinner. I'm way behind on this project. I'd better keep going while I'm in the zone."

"Sure. I understand," she said, but he could tell she was surprised and maybe a little disappointed—and that surprised him.

"How much do I owe you?" he asked. "For all this?" He held up the bags.

"Oh no, Yankee," she said with a big smile. "You're not getting off that easy. I'll take dinner—soon—at the most expensive restaurant in the Outer Banks."

"You got it," he promised.

Briefly, she touched her cheek to his and left; then he took the groceries into the kitchen. He unloaded only items that had to go into the refrigerator and left everything else in the bags, on the counter, and went back to his task.

With no idea how long he'd been at it, he let his thoughts continue drifting as he slowly, patiently, loosened the barnacles on the sea chest and then gently tapped them off with the hammer. Every now and then he glanced up at the two pictures of Kate he'd found online. At last, his efforts revealed a seam that went all the way around the box. A spiky cluster of coral had grown over the spot where the lock should be.

He was almost there.

Glancing up, through the doorway into the hall and on into the living room and the big picture window, he was surprised to see a glorious sunset splashed across the sky in gold, pink and lavender, and he realized he was hungry. He went out to the kitchen, found some paper plates and devoured what Mattie had brought—cold cuts, cheese, cole slaw, chips and orange juice—without really tasting anything. Then he went back to work on the box.

When he tapped off the knot of barnacles, the lock stayed embedded in the biggest one—but the seam was now clear of any impediment. Now he could open the chest.

Holding his breath, Jonathan probed the seam with the thinnest blade of his pocket knife until it loosened and popped up about a quarter of an inch. He let out his breath in a great sigh. He couldn't move.

The moment of truth had come, and he froze.

What would he would find inside? He wasn't expecting some kind of priceless treasure. All he wanted to find—what he *needed* to find—was Kate.

Slowly, he raised the lid. The briny smell of the sea, mixed with old leather, wafted up and into his nostrils. The interior of the box was surprisingly dry, and there were five small bundles nestled there. They were each wrapped in some kind of oilcloth—to protect them from the sea, he supposed— and tied with leather strips. He opened the smallest, lumpiest bundle first, and his eyes widened when he saw what it contained.

It was a necklace and a jeweled hair comb—and he thought they must be worth a fortune. Rubies, diamonds and emeralds were set in gold around the centerpiece of the necklace—a large ruby cut in the shape of a heart, with two tiny gold sabers crossing over it. It was the most beautiful piece of jewelry he had ever seen. Setting it carefully aside, he reached for one of the other little packages, which was rectangular shaped, like some kind of book. The leather strip securing the oilcloth covering it came apart in his hands. He folded the oilcloth back to reveal a ship's log. Carefully, he opened it. Across the tittle page, *The Royal Thomas* was written in old English script. The oilcloth had done an amazing job of keeping the volume dry, and he thought the coral might have acted like insulation. Browsing through a few pages, Jonathan realized Kate herself had made the later entries and a chill snaked up his spine.

There was another little square-shaped package. He unwrapped that one next. It was a miniature portrait of a family—a man, a woman and a little girl who looked to be about three years old. There was no doubt about it—with her auburn curls and emerald green eyes, the child could be none other than Kate. The man had to be Steadman Russell, her father, who had given her the Royal Thomas. The woman, Kate's mother, was wearing the necklace.

Gently, Jonathan placed the portrait on the towel. He looked at the necklace again, trying to take it in.

Obviously, it had been Kate's mother's, and then— obviously—Kate's. He stared at it in awe. To think that she had held it, touched it, worn it against her heart made his mind spin.

The next bundle—the largest one—contained only an old leather vest with some intricate designs burned into it and a couple of gemstones embedded in the leather. He reached for the last bundle and was dismayed to feel dampness on the bottom. Using even more caution than he had with the other packages, he slowly peeled away the oilcloth. It was also a book, and tears sprang to his eyes when he opened it and saw it was Kate's journal. For a few minutes, all he could do was sit and stare at it.

He felt faint, weak in every bone and muscle, like he was coming down with the flu or something. It was almost like being in a dream, but gazing at the artifacts on the table in front of him, he knew it was real.

She was real.

These were her things. Her necklace, a jeweled comb she had worn in her hair, the miniature portrait she must have cherished, the ship's log, and a journal in which she had recorded her life.

And she had brought them all to him. Had laid them at his very doorstep.

The thought steadied him. He went back to the kitchen, made himself a cup of coffee and returned to his work table with renewed purpose.

Sitting down, he opened the ship's log again and scanned the pages, gradually adjusting to Kate's graceful, flowing hand and the old-world expressions and phrases in use before texting had reduced the English language to a garbled form of shorthand. Her concise log entries about the state of the ship, her crew and their travels were different than the passionate writing in her diary, and it gave him a glimpse into her mind. She had been educated. The little family portrait and the necklace attested to her father's wealth. Although she had lived in harsh colonial times, she had clearly grown up in comfort, privileged and entitled. Why had she become a pirate?

And what did she want from him?

Examining the journal more closely, he saw that the last few pages were wet. He wouldn't be able to read that part of it until he gave it time to dry. But he could begin.

Carefully turning the pages, he started reading. Her words spooled out before him like the tide rolling out to sea, taking him to another place, another time.

He read about the dreams of an innocent maiden in love

for the first time, and how her sweetheart had betrayed her, how she'd killed him and how she'd had to leave the home she loved so much. He made another cup of coffee and went back to the journal, entranced by Kate's daring and bravery on escaping Blackbeard and his crew.

Suddenly, Jonathan remembered the framed map he'd found at the thrift store, still in the back of his car. He went down and got it and hung it on the wall next to Kate's pictures and the drawings of the Royal Thomas. With a fingertip, he retraced her journey from Queen Anne's Creek to Charles Town, and then to Nassau.

Taking his place at the table again, he read of Kate's encounter with Girard Fournier and then with the corrupt British captain who had tried to ravish her. He read of her growing attraction to the Frenchman and felt a stab of jealousy, especially when he got to the part where she told Fournier she intended to take him as her lover.

And there, Jonathan's journey came to an abrupt end. The remainder of the pages were too wet to turn. Frustrated, he went online and researched how to dry an old book without damaging it. Following the most logical instruction he found, he stood the book on its spine with three other books supporting it (books left behind by some time-share tenant, no doubt). Then he found a lamp, set it on the table next to the journal, plugged it in and switched it on. He glanced out the window and was surprised to see that it was night. He called Dr. Barclay anyway, and left a message.

"Hi—it's Jonathan West again. I—uh, I found a book inside the chest. It's a journal. I was able to read most of it but the last few pages are wet. I need to know how I can dry it—you know—what's the best way." He left his number and hung up. There was nothing more he could do but wait until morning.

Stepping out on the deck he felt instantly refreshed. There

was a breeze coming off the ocean and it was the perfect time for a walk on the beach. Wisdom pervaded at the last minute and he took a flashlight. He had no idea how long he walked but he was vaguely aware of laughing softly to himself, delighted that he'd been victorious in opening the chest. Then he had to blink away tears as he recalled parts of Kate's story. Why had she delivered it into his hands?

And what did she want from him?

He knew she wanted something—that's why she had come to him. If he could figure it out, maybe he could help her. Then maybe her spirit could to rest.

At last, he returned to the beach house and to his work table, where he leafed through the ship's log once more, reading bits and pieces of it until his eyes grew heavy. Taking the sea chest with him, he set it gently on the bureau in his bedroom, as if he could not bear to be parted from it. He didn't think he would be able to sleep but he stretched out on the bed, on top of the spread, and closed his eyes, trying to envision what life was like for Kate on these barrier strips of land that were just barely protected from the ravages of the sea.

A little while later, something woke him. He glanced at the spot where he'd placed Kate's little trunk. Somehow during the night, it had fallen (or been placed, he thought) onto the floor. It was open and he was stunned to see a bright light coming from it, pouring out of it and streaming upwards, toward the ceiling. Amazed, he sat up slowly, scarcely daring to breathe.

The light, which had a perfect oval shape, was about the size of a full-length mirror. Jonathan got up and went to investigate. As he got closer, he realized it wasn't just a light.

It was a portal—and he could look through it, as if through an open doorway. What he saw within was unbelievable.

Kate was there, in her ship's cabin, fully visible through the shimmering gateway. She was sitting at a desk with candlelight flickering across her lovely features. She was wearing a white linen nightgown and her long auburn hair fell past her shoulders in a waterfall of waves. She was the most beautiful woman he had ever seen.

He watched silently as she wrote in the journal—that same journal he had found—with a quill pen. Tears were streaming down her face and a tiny dog—a Chihuahua—was lying on her bunk, looking at her with concern. As she was about to dip her feathered pen into the inkwell, she beckoned the dog to come to her. Taking it in her arms, she whispered to it.

"There, there, my little Stewie. I know I have you and my dear babe, who is the treasure of my life. But it looks like I am destined to be alone, with no husband nor even a lover to comfort me. But there now—we'll be home soon. I can only hope there is still a home to go to."

Why is she alone? Jonathan wondered. *What happened to Fournier? Did he abandoned her, or betray her as her first love had done?*

Involuntarily, he reached out to her. To his astonishment, his arm went inside the portal and he saw the light from her candle reflecting off his hand. He put his other hand in, and then his head and shoulders. She looked up, surprised, and he could see she'd been crying. Her need drew him to her and he stepped into the oval of light.

And he was in the captain's cabin, aboard the Royal Thomas, with Kate.

Without a word—for words were not necessary—he went to her. She was so petite, and very young—not much more than twenty. She looked up at him with such sorrow he could not bear it. Trying to comfort her, he wrapped his arms around her. Sobbing, she buried her face against his chest and he felt her pain, her loneliness. Holding her close, he lightly stroked her back, inhaling the pure sweetness of her. She looked up at him, puzzled, and then standing on tiptoe, she kissed his cheek. Her innocence, her fragrant body against his—it was a bliss unlike anything Jonathan had ever known, and he would have been happy to stay with her there—wherever *there* was—forever.

A bright, relentless sun blasting through the window woke him the next morning. He was alone in his bed—and there was no light coming out of the open chest, which was back on the bureau where he'd put it.

It had been a dream. He knew that. He knew it was impossible to step through some kind of weird light, three hundred years into the past. Sighing and rubbing his eyes, he came back to reality.

Just a dream. Nothing more.

But when he got out of bed and put his bare feet on the floor, one of them landed on something sharp. Something sharp on one end and soft and feathery on the other. He looked down, puzzled, and logic flew out the window.

It was a quill pen—the pen with which Kate had been writing. It was lying on the floor next to his bed, in his bedroom at the beach house.

Chapter Seventeen

Winter, 1719
Aboard the Royal Thomas
Off the Coast of Nassau

Oliver has become my special protector, now that Fournier is gone. It started with his care of my little dog Stewie, and now that I have the babe, Oliver is like a doting nanny to them both. I am sailing for home at last, and he is determined to get me safely back to Queen Anne's Creek.

Mr. Potts came to my quarters early this morning with my breakfast tray. He found me searching madly through my desk and around my bunk. After asking if I had slept well, he set the tray on my small dining table and poured my tea.

"I did, Mr. Potts," I answered him. "For the first time in weeks. And I had the strangest dream—but comforting in its own way. I want to write it down before I forget it but I cannot, for the life of me, find my writing quill."

"Never mind, lass," he said. "I'll make 'e a new one. I have some goose quills that would do 'e fine."

It was a dream I didn't understand and I must think more on it. I will record it here—and, I realize, there must be an account of all I have experienced in this year since my crew captured HMS, the Royal Dragon. It has been a year since I have made an entry in my journal, for I have been too busy living my life to write about it. It has been a year of heaven, and then a month of hell.

After setting Sir David and his officers adrift, we went first to Tortuga, where we picked up another twenty good men to crew the Royal Dragon, along with those who'd left Sir David's service. They would sail under Fournier.

Fournier, the Falcon, and my lover.

We stayed only one night in port, a night I spent in his arms. When I retired to my cabin with him that evening, aboard the Royal Thomas, a sudden, brief silence fell over my men—and then from their ranks arose a hearty cheer. I had their approval, even as the Falcon had mine. By the time we sailed the next day, Jamie had already changed the name of Fournier's new ship from Royal Dragon to Devil's Revenge, and my sail maker had made him a flag, with a falcon in flight as its crest.

As happy as I was with Fournier, I had a strange dream about a man I seemed to know but could not recognize. In the dream, we were caught in a nor'easter. The clouds were dark above us and a mighty wind swept upon me like none I had ever felt before, putting us at the mercy of the sea. I was headed for certain disaster with no means to deter it.

Suddenly, then, the dream changed, as dreams do, and I was at the desk in my quarters, writing in my journal. As I wiped my tears away a brief glimmer of light caught my eye. I looked up, toward the full-length mirror Fournier had bought for me in Isle Saint Marie, and I saw a mysterious stranger.

He was standing alone atop some kind of wooden deck beside the sea. He was not old but from the look of him, he had passed more seasons than either Jacob or Fournier. And he was gazing in my direction.

Certainly I had no need of another man in my life (I thought, in my dream). My first love ended in tragedy and my last love—ah, my last love was so warm and rich and perfect. I knew I could never find its equal so there was no reason to look. I was fortunate, I thought, to have found so great a love as the Falcon. I did not need another.

But this man, and the way he regarded me, was compelling. When I looked into his eyes, I felt such comfort, such acceptance, such peace. It was as if I had known him my whole life—and in the dream, I thought he could see me as well. And I had a distinct feeling he would somehow be of great help to me—as if, perhaps, he was my guardian angel.

But then, it was only a dream. I awoke in my empty bed, wishing desperately that Fournier was still by my side. I lay there a while, remembering the feel of his lips upon mine— until the rustling sound of my tiny daughter, stirring in the cradle Oliver had made for her, urged me to my feet.

After tending the babe I looked out the quarter gallery, into the starlit night. The clouds moved with the winds, intermittently concealing a full moon in an eerie, luminescent shroud, and casting an ominous shadow of my ship upon the water. It was quite some time before I could get back to sleep. I tried to comfort myself with memories of Fournier, and our voyage to Isle Saint Marie.

Sailing around Cape L'Agulhas, off the southern tip of Africa, was not as difficult as Fournier had warned me it would be. Fortunately, we were in that region in summer, so the sea was not so tempestuous. In winter, he told me, when the cold northern currents mix with the warmer waters of Africa, there are giant waves over a hundred feet high that can overpower even the mightiest ships. Following the Falcon's direction, we stayed well off shore, for the shallows, he explained, extended far out and were fraught with hazards. Many a time my lover and I crossed the distance between our ships in a longboat, so that we could pass the night together.

Our only trouble, as we traveled toward safe haven, did not come from the sea, which was surprisingly cooperative. When we were not together, Fournier and I communicated ship to ship with a system of flags, using a code of his own invention. That day, the Devil's Revenge (under the watchful eye of the Falcon's first mate) caught a hearty gust of wind and got ahead of us by an hour or more. Fournier and I were aboard the Royal Thomas. Just as we rounded Cape Town, Jamie, our lookout, spotted a vessel making for us at top speed.

"Ahoy, Cap'n Kate," he shouted. "It be a forty-gun frigate—an' flyin' a French flag!"

"Best to steer clear of conflict," Fournier advised me. "Have Jamie fly a flag to enquire of their intent. I would not welcome a meeting as there is a price on my head in France."

"And yet you wanted to sail with me as far as London to get there?" I queried.

He flashed his most charming smile. "It was as good excuse as any to be in your company for a few weeks," he said. "I never intended to go on from England. By the end of the voyage I would surely have won you."

I laughed, delighted with his confession. "You are a devil, indeed," I told him. "But likely you are right. It seems I am won already." I looked back to the ship making straight for us. "What do you think they want?"

"We will know soon enough," he replied.

By that time, she was near enough for me, with a spyglass, to read her name—La Sorcière. Fournier said she was a slaver.

"Those poor souls on board," he told me. "Ripped from home and family, taken to some strange land and treated like beasts of the field. It is reprehensible."

"Can we not do something to help them?" I asked.

He studied me a moment before he replied. "Would that we could, but our purpose is to reach Isle Saint Marie safely before our supplies are depleted. Besides—sadly—stopping one ship will not stop the practice. Best to leave it alone."

But I soon saw we were not to be spared. When La Sorcière's crew sent up the flag requesting parley, we sent back a message asking if they had some emergency. They did not respond to that but continued heading straight for us.

"They're after our provisions," said Fournier. "They've a long voyage ahead of them and many mouths to feed."

"All the poor souls will get from their captors is worm-infested porridge an' moldy bread—if that," One-Eye put in. He was standing at the railing with us. "They be crowded in the hold so tight they can barely move. The weak 'uns will not survive the voyage." When Fournier looked at him sharply, he added, "Served on a slaver once—which were one time too many. Swore I'd never do it again."

"How did you come to serve on it in the first place?" I asked.

"I were stuck in Cape Town after the ship I was on were sunk. All I wanted was to get back to England, any way I could. I'll ne'er forget how them poor creatures suffered. Did my best to help 'em, sneaking food out o' the galley when I could—an' almost got caught. But I picked up a little o' their lingo."

"Good," said Fournier. "That may serve us well in this situation."

"Indeed," I responded softly.

We looked into each other's eyes, having the identical thought at the same moment. "If the captain of La Sorcière insists on parley," I said, "let us give him one he will not likely forget."

"I want you out of sight, my love," Fournier responded.

"I'll not hide like some coward," I protested. "I shall fight by your side—"

"Madamoiselle," he ventured. "I would not deny you the pleasure of battle but you, *ma petite*, must be part of the battle plan. Listen closely, for we haven't much time. They are well manned and they can see we have cannons. They have *not* seen that we have a woman aboard. A beautiful woman. Don't you think we should use that surprise to our advantage?"

What he then whispered in my ear was enough to scandalize any lady—but I was no longer a lady, I reminded myself. I was now a pirate—with a King's price upon my head and Blackbeard after me. Laughing, I agreed to his plan. I would stay out of sight until Fournier's signal, and then I would reveal myself—in a way the enemy would never forget.

Hiding behind a stack of rope and canvas, I watched and waited. Fournier had Jamie flag the signal granting the request and inviting La Sorcière's captain to board.

When the grappling hooks and lines were secured and the gangway between vessels was in place, he came on with his first mate and half a dozen well-armed sailors. I could clearly see his quartermaster standing ready on La Sorcière's deck, as if waiting for the signal to fire on us.

After establishing that their business would be conducted in English, as it was the only language commonly understood, the Falcon addressed our adversary.

"I am Girard Mercier," he lied. "Captain of the Royal Thomas." He gave a slight bow, and the slaver's captain nodded.

"Captain Barbazarie, of La Sorciére, at your service, sir."

"What is the nature of your business, captain?" asked Fournier. "What be the purpose of this parley?"

"We need provisions, sir," was the response.

"I am willing to barter," Fournier said. "With certain caveats."

"And what be those?"

"First, I would like to know how you came to leave port without food enough for your voyage. And second, how many crew and passengers have you aboard that you must feed?"

"We have taken on no passengers," returned the captain of the slave ship. "What we got on board is cargo."

I could see Fournier from my hiding place and I was gratified the word seemed to inflame his anger even further.

"Human cargo?" he asked.

"Some might call 'em human," Barbazerie responded insistently. "Whatever your opinion, sir, we need more provisions to feed 'em all!"

Fournier made one more attempt to quell the brewing conflict. "I will give you half the provisions we carry if you release your prisoners to me," he said. "I beg your pardon—your so-called *cargo*."

"I know who you are, Falcon—and I know your reputation as a thief and a trickster," returned Barbazerie. "'Tis your intent to take my cargo and sell it for your own profit. That is the reason for your generosity."

"Provisions we can get," Fournier explained. "Fish from the sea and game from the land, if need be. Your prisoners have but one life and I would not see them live it in chains."

"Fournier!" Jamie shouted down from the crow's nest. "Look lively, captain!"

I peeked further out of my hiding place to see La Sorcière's crew streaming aboard the Royal Thomas, some across the gangplank and others swinging across on ropes—and all wielding swords, daggers and pistols.

"Now!" shouted Fournier, and raised his own sword. By then I had removed my boy clothes, leaving myself clad only in pantalets and a thin linen bodice that left not much of my bosom to the imagination. When I ran out onto the deck, screaming like a banshee and waving my sword, there was a stunned silence among my crew—and the men of La Sorcière. Their shock (and I must say, obvious appreciation of my feminine form) gave us but brief advantage. It was enough.

"We will have no trade with slavers!" Fournier shouted. "Release your prisoners to me at once!"

"Never!" raged Barbazerie.

The conflict was short-lived but most awfully bloody. As we battled La Sorciére's crew, pushing them back over the gangway onto their own ship, Fournier called out to One-Eye.

"Go below!" he shouted. "See if you can communicate with the prisoners. Let them know what is happening. They can fight with us, or they can escape on the longboats."

When La Sorciére's human cargo came scrambling on deck just moments later, I knew One-Eye's efforts had been successful. Some made straight for the longboats, some dove overboard and started swimming for shore. A few cowered in fear as others picked up billy clubs, barrels or whatever was at hand and fought alongside us.

A tall, thin woman was in their midst, her skin the color of fine ebony, and she was as ferocious a warrior as I have ever seen. I looked into her dark, flashing eyes and she returned my gaze for a moment before she raised a jug she'd found somewhere and threw it with expert aim, bringing down one of Barbazerie's men who was coming up behind me. We stood together then, fighting side by side until we had quelled the enemy.

When the battle was done we set Captain Barbazerie and his few surviving crewmen in rowboats and pointed them toward land. Fournier told them they could take their chances among the natives they had tried to imprison. We had then more than two dozen Africans aboard the Royal Thomas. Fournier said he knew of a place a little further down the coast where it would be safe to dock long enough to let them disembark. When we arrived there and One-Eye explained this, the brave woman who had fought by my side refused to go. Shaking her head, she pointed at my belly and made a cradle with her arms as if she held a baby there.

One-Eye spoke a few words to her and she responded adamantly. He turned back to me, smiling, scratching his head and looking a bit sheepish.

"Beggin' yer pardon, Cap'n Kate," he said. "This here woman's says she don't want to go."

"Why not?" I asked. "Does she understand she is free?"

"She understands," he assured me. "She's sayin' you got magic in you, and that babe yer a-carryin' has got some magic, too."

"A babe?" My hand went inadvertently to my abdomen. Could it be—so soon? Fournier put one arm about me as I asked, "Find out how she knows, One-Eye. And ask her name."

They conversed a moment and I gazed up into Fournier's eyes. He was smiling—grinning, in fact, as if he had done something momentous. One-Eye turned back to me.

"Her name's Malaika," he said. "That mean angel, in her lingo. She says yer havin' a girl child and she will stay with you until you . . . you know. She's like a midwife or somethin'."

Again I looked at Fournier. He was still smiling. "She appears to be determined," he said. "I say we let her come with us. She seems to know what she is about."

I walked to Malaika and extended my hand, which she took. With my other hand I patted my chest. "I am Kate," I said. "One-Eye, please tell her that I will agree to her plan as long as she understands she is not a slave, that she will work for pay, and she is free to go whenever she wishes."

That settled, I ordered Marcus and Oliver to check the captain's quarters on La Sorciére, as well as the galley hold for anything valuable. They found a fortune in gold, and weapons enough to arm two more crews.

Having ascertained there were no more prisoners onboard La Sorciére, we pulled in our gangplank and cast off our lines. When we achieved a safe distance, we turned our cannons on the slave ship and blasted it into splinters.

We made it to Isle Saint Marie a few days later. Fournier, happier than I'd ever seen him, sent a man ahead to the Rose D'or Tavern near the landing, to secure a room for us. By the time we arrived, there was a jolly crowd waiting to receive us, and many of them insisted on buying the Falcon a drink. When one of the men gathered there looked at me with a certain raw hunger in his eyes, Fournier glowered at him and drew me closer.

"Give me a moment with them, or we shall have no peace tonight," he whispered in my ear. "Oliver will show you to our room. There is a surprise waiting for you there."

To my astonishment, it was a bath—a fragrant, lovely bath in a copper tub filled with steaming water. Beside it on a small table was an array of perfumed soaps and oils. Malaika helped me to peel off my clothes and I sank gratefully into the tub. This, indeed, was paradise.

She washed my back, rinsed my body with fresh, warm water and held a big, fluffy towel for me when I was ready to step out. She handed me a beautiful nightgown that was hanging in the closet, and when there was a tap on the door and my lover walked in, she retreated to her own quarters in the adjoining room (which Fournier had also arranged). He was wearing loose pantaloons and a robe open to his waist. His hair was damp from his own bath and his chest shone like bronze in the candlelight.

"Your timing is impeccable, Fournier," I observed softly.

"Are you ready for me, then?" he asked.

"I am," I replied and turned the covers back so he could join me.

Late Summer, 2015
Outer Banks, North Carolina

Jonathan put the quill pen into the chest with Kate's logbook, and then took the chest back into the dining room, to his makeshift desk, still trying to wrap his mind around it all.

The pen was the one she'd been using to write in her journal. Somehow it had ended up in his bedroom three hundred years later. That was impossible—yet it had. And the irony was, he couldn't tell anybody about it. No one would believe him. His wife already thought he was crazy.

After breakfast, he got a broom and swept up the pieces of coral that had fallen to the floor. As long as he was at it, he decided, he'd clean up a little. He put away the rest of the groceries Mattie had brought him and washed the dishes he'd used for his haphazard meals. Then he started straightening out the couch cushions, which were still a little askew from the night before, when he and Mattie had made love.

Mattie. She had called a couple of times, he knew, and he really should get back to her. And he would. Soon.

He grabbed the corner of the seat cushion on the sofa and yanked at it, and he heard a soft thud as something fell onto the carpet at his feet. He stared at the object for a moment, unable to think where it could have come from. And then he remembered. Patrice had lost her phone.

Something—some instinct he knew he would regret—made him look at her call history.

A knot twisted in his gut when he saw over a dozen calls to and from Garrett Paulson, all within the past month. There were also several text messages to and from him. One stood out in particular:

"Sorry, love—didn't mean to push. Of course I don't want to see you to walk away with nothing. I'll wait as long as I have to."

Jonathan didn't take time to think about it. Acting on pent-up rage, he grabbed his keys, locked up his house and jumped into his car. It was already past rush hour and traffic through Norfolk was light. Driving at top speed, he made it back to Baltimore in five hours.

He pulled into the driveway, slamming the car door and setting the neighbor's dog off on a rant. Alex always recognized the familiar sound of Jonathan's car and was at the door, wagging his tail when Jonathan walked in. He let out a happy, welcoming yelp.

Patrice, in her nightgown, came out of their bedroom at the top of the stairs. "What is all this racket—" she stopped abruptly when she saw Jonathan. "Oh—well. This is a surprise," she said, walking slowly down to join him.

"I hope I didn't interrupt anything."

"What the hell are you talking about?" she asked irritably.

"The girls asleep?"

"They've gone out—to a party. Now, why did you decide to grace us with your presence at last?" With each word she uttered, sarcasm crept into her tone.

"I found your phone," he said, reaching into his pocket for it and holding it out to her.

She took it. After a moment, she replied, "And?"

"You said it was over with Garrett."

"It is!" she snapped. "So I called him a few times. What do you expect, Jonathan? With you never home, working so many hours for months on end, and now, down at the beach house doing who knows what with Lord knows who. I had to have *someone* to talk to."

"Seriously? That's all it is?"

At that she softened a little. "I promise you, there is nothing going on," she said. She actually smirked before she added, "Although it is kind of nice to know that you can still get jealous."

"I'm not jealous," he assured her. "I don't care about that anymore."

"Good," she said. He stared at her as she continued, her voice taking on a plaintive tone. It no longer gained his sympathy. "Garrett has been a good friend to me these last few weeks, when I've been so *worried* about you, how hard you were working and—"

"Stop right there." He held up one hand. "First, I don't buy it so you can cut the crap.

He was surprised at how calm he was. "Second, even if I did believe you, I don't care. What I care about is that I wasted so much time thinking we could work it out."

Tension stretched between them like a tightrope about to snap. "We could," she retorted, sweetly sarcastic. "If you'd let go of that one little thing. How many times do I have to tell you? Garrett and I—it meant nothing."

"Somehow that makes it worse." He sucked in a breath and let it out in a deep, cleansing sigh. Then he added, "I'm done, Patrice. I'm packing some clothes and things I need at the beach house. You're welcome to this one. For the sake of the girls, I won't embarrass you by naming Garrett as co-respondent. See a lawyer this week and get it started. Do you want to use Sheldon or shall I?" Sheldon Adams was a family friend and had been their attorney for years.

"Jonathan, I think you need to calm down. This is ridiculous—"

Impatient to get back on the road, he broke in. "You can file for—I don't know—irreconcilable differences or something. Unless you'd rather I do it."

"You can't live all the way down there in the Outer Banks," she said. "What about the business?"

"The lawyers will figure it out," he said. "I can run it from down there, or we can sell it. I don't care. I can start over in North Carolina. In the meantime, Nigel can keep everything going smoothly here."

"Oh, Jonathan! Will you please get a grip!" she exclaimed. "We were doing so well until you insisted on buying that place. You need to keep your butt home and see a doctor. A shrink—because you are losing it."

"You're missing the point," he said, frustrated. "Did you hear what I said? I want a divorce, Patrice. I'm done with all this."

"Well, I *don't* want a divorce."

"Garrett seems to believe otherwise."

She didn't acknowledge that. "Should I name Kate as co-respondent?" she asked bitterly.

"If you do, you'll look pretty foolish," he shot back. "Kate has been dead for three hundred years."

She moved a little closer to him. "And yet you insist you've seen her. Do you hear how you sound? You're delusional, Jonathan. Thinking you see ghosts!"

"She's not a ghost. Not exactly."

"No? Then what is she?"

Triumph flickered briefly in Patrice's eyes but Jonathan didn't take the bait. He refused to discuss Kate with her. With anyone.

"Tell you what," Patrice said, when he remained silent. "If you'll see a doctor—a psychiatrist—I'll see a lawyer."

"Look, Patrice," he answered patiently, surprised that he was more relieved than angry. "One way or the other, we're done. Do whatever you like about the divorce. I'm not coming back." He moved past her and started up the stairs.

"What about the girls? What do you want me to tell your daughters?"

He stopped, turned around and looked at her. "Tell them the truth. Tell them I've finally come to my senses. They're grown now, or almost. I'll provide for them. And you, of course. We'll work out all the finances through the attorneys— but one way or the other, I am done."

"I guess this means Lanie can't have her party at the beach house, then."

"I guess," he said. "I'll work it out with her. Maybe an end-of-summer party instead."

He headed upstairs to pack as many of his belongings as

he could fit into his car. By the time he'd loaded everything and said goodbye to Alex, Patrice was nowhere in sight. She'd probably gone to bed, he thought, or she was calling Garrett Paulson, in the privacy of her bedroom, to give him an update. When Jonathan turned out of the driveway of the house he would never live in again, he grabbed his cell phone and hit the button for Nigel.

"Hey, Jonathan—what's up?"

"Nigel—good. You're still awake. Can you meet me at the Green Arbor site? I've got to talk to you about something."

"Now? I mean—sure. But can't we do it tomorrow, now that you're back?"

"I'm not staying," Jonathan told him. "That's why I need to see you. I'm heading back to the Outer Banks tonight. Figured as long as I'm here I'd do a quick check on how the restaurant is coming along."

"Great so far," Nigel said. "You solved the staircase problem. The artsy-fartsy stained glass window works great. The clients love it. We're on time and under budget so no worries there. But yeah—okay. I can meet you in, say, twenty minutes?"

The old restaurant was now gutted and in full restoration mode. Jonathan had been right. With the implementation of the window, Nigel and his team had been able to put in the bannisters. Jonathan powered up the emergency generator, also the temporary lighting source, and in its dull glow he could see dust motes drifting up around him as he did a walk-through. Overhead he saw a dangling wire, looped up and out of the way in a slip knot. It cast a shadow that made him think of a hangman's noose.

Nigel had kept the crew busy. They had already done extensive work on the interior walls and the new lighting fixtures were all in place. Quick footsteps on the bamboo floors caught Jonathan's attention. He turned to see Nigel striding in.

"Well?" he greeted Jonathan. "What do you think?"

Jonathan looked around and nodded. "Good," he said. "You're doing a great job here."

"Thanks—but it needs the master's touch. When will you be back for real?"

"That's the thing," Jonathan said. "You've got to run the office and deal with the clients a little while longer."

"Can you tell me why?"

It was a legitimate question and Jonathan thought he deserved an answer. "You know I just bought a house down there, in North Carolina? I'll be living there. You can reach me anytime by phone or email if you need me."

"Okay . . ." Nigel said slowly. "What's going on?"

"Patrice and I are calling it quits. We're getting a divorce."

"No way, man! You guys have been married for—well, forever."

"Yeah," Jonathan agreed. "Maybe that's the problem. And the National Aquarium project. I'm going to have to let you finish the blueprints for that."

"Sure, if you think that's best. But—I mean—you *are* coming back, right?"

Jonathan was silent for a moment. He didn't want to return to Baltimore, or to his office—ever. It was like some kind of secret door had opened in his head and suddenly he could see a whole new life before him. Still, he knew, that could change. Once he figured out how to help Kate, maybe she could rest and he would have some peace. Then he might be eager to get back to work.

"You sure about this, Jonathan?" Nigel prodded.

"I don't think I'm sure of anything anymore," he said. "Except the divorce. It's been a long time coming."

Nigel cleared his throat, obviously not comfortable asking

the next question. "What about the business? What's going to happen to the company?"

"The lawyers will work it all out. One way or the other, it'll stay afloat. None of you will be out of work."

"What if they tell you to sell and split the profits with Patrice?"

"Don't worry," Jonathan said, trying to sound reassuring. "I'll make it a condition of sale—that the staff stays in place. Just keep this close to the vest, Nigel. We don't want to cause a panic."

"Sure," Nigel said. "You know I'll do my best for you. But I'll want to get your final approval on every step of any project."

"No problem," Jonathan said. "Emails every day."

"So . . . what are you doing down there anyway? I mean, you could always get a room or something around here if things are so bad—I mean, if you can't stay at home."

"No, it's not that," Jonathan said quickly. "I'm working on something. Some research." When Nigel continued to stare at him, clearly puzzled and waiting for more, Jonathan added, "It's—I've rediscovered an old interest in marine archeology," he lied. "I took some classes back in college. Anyway, I found something down there on the beach that I want to look into."

"Cool. What?"

For a split second Jonathan considered telling him. Instead he said, "Nothing important—not to anyone but me, anyway. Just . . . really interesting. I guess it's helping take my mind off the divorce."

Nigel seemed to buy that. "Yeah. That must be rough. You can count on me, Jonathan. But you gotta stay in touch, okay?"

The drive home was much more relaxing than the drive up.

Home.

Jonathan smiled to himself as he turned into his drive in Kill Devil Hills. That's how he thought of the beach house now—as home. And it brought him a simple, pure kind of peace.

He hadn't rushed back to the Outer Banks. Finally speaking to Patrice about the divorce had given him an unexpected release, a sudden sense of liberation, until exhaustion crept in. He'd pulled over at a rest stop to grab a quick power nap.

When he drifted off, he dreamed about Kate. He woke abruptly and before encroaching consciousness could steal it away, he went over every aspect of the dream. She was still on the ship—the Royal Thomas—and it was bouncing around in a stormy sea. Holding some kind of bundle in her arms, she was giving orders to her crew as thunder rolled and lightning flashed.

"Avast, you laggards!" she shouted. "We are almost there! I *will* make it home if it is the last thing I do!"

And suddenly, Jonathan understood. *She wanted to go home.* She'd been on her way there when the storm hit. That must have been when the Royal Thomas sank, he thought, right off the coast of the Outer Banks. Close to where he was living now.

Now he understood. The ghost ship he'd seen on the fishing trip with Mike and Tim was the Royal Thomas, and Kate's spirit was restless because her remains were still on board. If he could find the ship and retrieve Kate's bones, he thought, he could bury them on her father's land. Then maybe she would be at peace. When he learned, by digging into North Carolina history, that Steadman Russell had owned a plantation in Queen Anne's Creek, now called Edenton, he was convinced his instinct was right.

That's what she wanted—he was sure of it. That's what he had to do. The first step would be finding the Royal Thomas.

Chapter Eighteen

"I'll take it," Jonathan told the boat dealer Mattie had recommended. It was a twenty-one-foot Carolina skiff—used but sturdy and seaworthy—and he'd be able to handle it by himself, if necessary. Then he asked the dealer to refer him to the best place to get diving equipment.

"Oh?" the dealer said. "You goin' treasure huntin', son?"

"Something like that."

"Long as you know where to look," said the dealer.

Jonathan smiled. "That won't be a problem."

Dr. Barclay, from the university, had called him shortly after he returned from Baltimore, to let him know that he had a vacuum freeze-dry machine that would dry Kate's journal.

"First we freeze the wet pages," Dr. Barclay explained. "Then we draw the air out of the chamber and add a heat source. The ice crystals vaporize without melting, so most of the time we can preserve the material."

Jonathan was leery about trusting anyone else with the journal. "Look," he said. "I know this is something that may belong in a museum—and someday, that may be a possibility. But first I want to learn as much about it as I can."

"Of course," Barclay said. He seemed to understand Jonathan's reluctance. "Mr. West, it's perfectly legal for you to keep whatever you find washed up on the beach. My only interest is historical, I assure you."

It was hard to let go of the journal, even for a few days, but Jonathan couldn't take the chance of damaging it. And he had to know the rest of Kate's story. He had to read those last few pages, so he took it to the university and entrusted it to the archeologist's care. It would take a few days, Dr. Barclay told him. Jonathan intended to pass the time getting acquainted with his new boat.

She was a beauty but he knew he had to take it slow. He had to learn every inch of her before he took her out any great distance—and certainly before he started diving. He knew he should have someone on board with him for those excursions and he thought about asking Mike or Tim. They'd seen the ghost ship too, even if they hadn't seen Kate. Maybe he'd call them. Or maybe he'd ask Mattie. Living here as she had all her life, she probably knew a thing or two about boats and diving. She might even believe in the possibility of a ghost ship. He thought again he might tell her about his sighting, and then decided against it.

When Jonathan wasn't on his boat, he was on the beach looking for artifacts that might have washed up. To aid in his search he went back to Home Depot and bought a metal detector. He walked along the shore line every morning, and whatever he found, he took back to the beach house and added to what he thought of as Kate's wall, hanging some and stacking what he couldn't hang on the floor. Driftwood that had once been part of some old ship, a couple of gold coins from the early eighteen hundreds, pieces of broken china, old bottles, shark teeth, a few buttons. He also found a gold ring with an oval of ivory set in the place a stone should be—and carved into the ivory was the image of a falcon. When he found in his shirt pocket the piece of red glass the ER nurse had removed from his hand after he'd found the chest, he taped that to the wall too.

In the afternoons if the weather was fair, Jonathan did practice dives with his new equipment. If it was storming, he stared out his window at the churning sea, looking for the ghost ship for hours on end, or he went online looking for information about Kate and the Royal Thomas.

When he learned that the original of the miniature portrait he'd found and printed out was now in a museum in England, he gently peeled his version from the wall and took it to Prints Plus where he had it enlarged into a poster. He made it the centerpiece of his growing tribute to Kate.

Jonathan lost all track of time, for time had lost all meaning for him. He saw Kate everywhere, with that same sad, beseeching look in her eyes—staring at him from inside the post office when he passed by, at Wink's when he was restocking his food supplies, or at Walmart, when he was buying new sneakers. He slept only fitfully, ate little and subsisted on coffee, beer, potato chips and sandwiches. Once, when he had run out to get food, he caught a glimpse of his reflection in a store window. He paused for a moment, surprised at the stark, anxious look in his eyes and the growth of beard on his face. For an instant—a brief flash—he caught a glimpse of Kate standing behind him. He turned quickly, only to find her gone.

The phone was a minor distraction and eventually he stopped answering it altogether. For a while, Patrice called two or three times a day and then, apparently, gave up. He didn't care. He had no more need to talk to her. He supposed he would be getting a letter from her attorney soon, and that was fine with him. Whenever Nigel called, Jonathan shot off a quick email to see what he wanted. A couple of times—once when Jonathan returned from wandering the beach and again, when he'd come back from a practice diving session—he had looked at his phone and seen message alerts from Beatrice. He figured Patrice had ordered her sister to talk some sense into him.

He didn't even answer the phone for Mattie, although she was often on his mind. When he wasn't thinking about Kate, he was remembering how soft Mattie's skin was, or how sweet her kisses tasted. More than once he reminded himself to call her, and just as quickly forgot.

He was making a sandwich late one afternoon (he wasn't sure what day it was) when he heard the doorbell. Trying to ignore it, he cut his ham-and-cheese in half and grabbed a beer out of the fridge. Whoever it was leaned on the bell, more insistent. He sighed and put down the beer. Whoever it was had no intention of going away.

"Well, hello stranger," Mattie said when he opened the door. "You mad at me or somethin'?"

Stunned for a moment, simply because he'd forgotten how beautiful she was, he didn't say anything. When he caught the shock in her eyes he looked away.

"Whatever I did—and I must have done something," she said. "I guess I owe you an apology. Sure would be nice to know what for, though."

After another moment, he said, "No. You didn't. I mean, I'm not. Mad at you." His words seemed disjointed, as if he had become too accustomed to silence. He moved aside. "Come in. Sorry. Been kind of busy, you know?"

"No—I don't know. That's why I came by. Don't want to bother you, though. I just wanted to make sure you're still alive."

"Yeah—thanks. Look, Mattie—a lot's been going on. Come on out to the kitchen with me. I was just having a snack and a beer. You want one?"

"A beer would be nice," she replied, walking in and closing the door. Following him to the kitchen she added, "Jonathan—you okay? You look awful."

"I'm fine," he said, smiling as he opened the refrigerator. "You want a glass?"

"No, I'm good. So what the hell is going on?"

He handed her a beer. As she popped the top and took

a swig, he said. "I went to Baltimore. I told Patrice to see a lawyer and start divorce proceedings."

Mattie looked deep into his eyes before she said, "That's good, I guess. But that's not it, Yankee. Somethin' else is goin' on with you."

"No," he told her. "Just busy."

"Finishing those blueprints you mentioned?" she asked.

"Well—yeah. And some other things."

She picked up his plate from the counter and headed into the dining room. "Good," she said. "Okay, then. Come on in here to the table. While you eat you can tell me all about 'em—" She stopped abruptly when she saw Kate's wall, and she turned to face him. A sudden flash of fury, like a lightning bolt, streaked across her face. "What is all this?" she demanded.

"Just . . . something I'm working on," he said. He couldn't understand why she would be angry.

Slowly regaining control of whatever she was feeling, Mattie looked deep into his eyes. "Jonathan—you listen to me. Whatever you've heard about some old legend and a stupid lost treasure, don't believe it," she said. "That tired old story has caused more trouble for some people than you can imagine."

"I haven't heard about any treasure or legend," he said.

She glanced at Kate's picture on the wall. "Then how do you know about *her*?" she demanded resentfully.

"I saw something," he said, and then added slowly, "I saw her ship."

"Okay," she said. "Maybe you *think* you did, but I have to tell you. Lots of people think they see something, which always turns out to be nothing. Don't tell me you're falling for all those stories about ghost ships and sunken treasure."

He considered carefully before he answered. This was his moment of truth. He could tell Mattie about Kate and ask her to help him look for the Royal Thomas. Or he could buy time. At last he said, "Yeah. Maybe I am. I bought a boat from that place you recommended. Maybe we could go diving sometime."

He couldn't tell her yet. He wasn't ready to share Kate with anyone, not even Mattie.

She studied him, skeptical. "You look like you haven't slept in a week, and you've lost weight. Have you seen a doctor since you had that concussion thing?"

"No need," he said, a little more sharply than he intended, surprised at the sudden threat of tears that hit him. Blinking them back, he nodded at Kate's wall and added, his voice falsely cheerful, "This is just some stuff I stumbled across on the Internet. I like history and I got interested. Hey, thanks for checking on me, Mattie, but I'm fine. Love to chat some more but I've got to get back to work."

"Okay then," she said doubtfully. She gave her beer back to him and headed out. He didn't like the look of concern on her face but he quickly dismissed it, as if it had nothing to do with him. Online earlier, he'd uncovered a treasure trove of information about Isle Saint Marie and he wanted to get back to it while he waited for Kate's journal to go through the freeze-drying process.

Hours passed as he got lost in a world long gone when piracy reigned the seas, fascinated that Kate had been part of it all. Sometime toward morning he fell into a restless sleep on the sofa in the living room, the framed map of old shipwrecks in the Outer Banks propped against the coffee table in front of him. A loud, rapid knocking on the door awakened him to bright sunshine streaming through the window. Rubbing his eyes, he stumbled to the door and opened it. It was Patrice. The girls were standing behind her. With them was a tall, bespectacled man Jonathan didn't know.

"Since you won't see a doctor," Patrice said, storming past him. "I've brought one to you."

"What time is it?" he asked as his daughters and the stranger followed Patrice in.

"Almost noon," she said. "You look dreadful. Mattie was right."

"Mattie?" Instantly, he was more alert.

"She called me last night, after she stopped by here," Patrice told him. "She said you were in real trouble and—let's see. What were her exact words in that sweet, southern drawl of hers? Oh, yes—she said, 'Someone really needs to *git* down *heah* and see about him.'"

"Mom—come on," said Cristiana. "Not now, okay?"

Jonathan followed Patrice as she rushed into the dining room. She stopped short as soon as she caught sight of Kate's wall. The girls were also speechless, staring at all the images and trinkets Jonathan had collected.

"Mrs. West, if I may?" the tall man said.

"Who the hell are you?" Jonathan asked him as Patrice stepped aside.

"This is Dr. Warren Nelson," Patrice explained. "He's a psychiatrist, from somewhere around here. Sheldon referred us, which is the only reason he agreed to make a house call."

"Patrice, what is this?" Jonathan asked wearily.

"Talk to him," said Patrice. "You owe me that much. You owe it to our marriage. We'll give you some privacy. Come on, girls. Let's go find a nice place to have lunch."

"Take him with you," Jonathan said. "Because you're right. I have no intention of talking to him."

"Dad!" Elaine protested, and Jonathan was surprised at the fear he saw in her eyes. "Have you looked in a mirror lately?" she asked. "There's something wrong with you."

"Yeah, Dad," said Cristiana. "Just do it. Just talk to him."

"Please," Elaine added, her voice breaking a little.

Jonathan turned to his wife. "That's a low blow," he said. "Getting the kids to do your dirty work."

"Jonathan, you need to listen to me," Patrice said. "Talk to the doctor. If he says you're okay, then I'll let it go."

"What are you trying to do?" he asked. "You think if you can get me committed you can take everything? I've already told you I don't want it—any of it. I just want this house and I want to be left alone."

"Oh, for godsakes!" she exclaimed, turning to the doctor. "Do you hear him? Now he's paranoid."

"Mrs. West, if you wouldn't mind," said Dr. Nelson. "Why don't you go ahead to lunch with your daughters? We'll be fine here, in the meantime. What do you say, Jonathan?"

Jonathan turned to Patrice. "Don't leave," he said. "This won't take long." He turned back to the shrink. "If I talk to you, then you'll go and leave me in peace?"

"Absolutely," the doctor assured him. "If, by then, that's what you want. Now—where can we sit and be comfortable while we talk?"

Patrice and the girls settled in the living room as Jonathan led Dr. Nelson into the dining room. They sat on opposite sides of the table, with Jonathan's back against Kate's wall. "Okay," he said. "What do you want to know?"

"Why don't you tell me what's been going on with you," suggested the doctor. "You might start with this . . . *ghost* your wife says you've been seeing."

"Mike and Tim saw it too." Jonathan hated that he sounded so defensive about something he was sure of. "The ship, anyway."

"And did they see her? The ghost?"

"Maybe. They didn't say."

"I see." The psychiatrist hesitated and Jonathan knew the man was waiting for him to go on. Jonathan remained silent. "Your wife says that recently, out of the blue, you asked her for a divorce."

"That's what she said?"

The shrink nodded. "She said it came out of nowhere. Took her completely by surprise."

"Did she tell you she had an affair with one of my best friends?"

"Yes, actually—she did," the doctor said. "And she told me you'd both gotten past it and moved on."

"The evidence would say otherwise," Jonathan informed him quietly. "But that's not why I'm leaving her. Not really."

"Then why? May I know the reason?"

"Sure," Jonathan said sullenly. "The reason is, doctor, I'm *done*. I don't want—whatever it is our marriage has become—I don't want it anymore."

"And you have no interest in saving your marriage?"

"There's nothing to save," Jonathan declared. "There has to be something better, for both of us. Even if there's not, I'm just . . . done."

Again, unexpectedly, tears sprang to Jonathan's eyes. Angrily, he palmed them away and sternly composed himself. The doctor spoke again.

"Your wife says this all started about the time you bought this house."

"Right," Jonathan said. "Which was right after I saw the ghost ship."

"And, exactly what did you see?" the doctor probed.

Jonathan told him everything—the fishing trip, the dinner and drinks and camaraderie of the men gathered at the place that night, going out on the deck with Mike and Tim and seeing Kate and the Royal Thomas. It was a relief to finally unload it all. He finished with, "That's why I bought this place. So I could see it again. See *her* again."

The shrink was silent for a moment. Then he smiled benevolently. Jonathan found that somehow amusing. "Do you want to know what I think?" asked Dr. Nelson. "Shall I give you my . . . oh, let's say, my ten-minute, Psych 101 textbook diagnosis—which, more often than not, turns out to be the case?"

"Sure," Jonathan said. "Why not?" Anything to get the man out of there, he thought. To get it over with so he could get back to Kate.

"This delusion you're experiencing—I don't think it's serious. I think it will pass—"

"It's not a delusion," Jonathan broke in. "I'm not imagining it."

"I know it seems that way for now," the doctor said soothingly. "What we have here—what's *happening* here is quite simple."

"Really?" Jonathan tried to quell the sarcastic edge in his tone.

"Mr. West, you're a middle-aged man trying to come to terms with a midlife crisis. Now that can actually turn out to be useful for you, believe it or not. We all go through it, in some form or another. Yours just happens to coincide—or perhaps was triggered by—a trauma."

"Yeah? What trauma is that?"

"Your failed marriage, for one thing," explained the doctor. "Fading youth. Reaching the age where you start to evaluate your life—you know, make an accounting. Confronting your unrealized professional goals, perhaps. That's why you've created this fantasy of a woman on some kind of ghost ship. It is an effort to replace all you feel yourself losing."

Jonathan considered for a moment. Then he said calmly, "Well, doctor—I've gotta tell you. That's the biggest pile of steaming crap I've ever heard."

The shrink looked at him, stunned. "I beg your pardon."

"First of all, I've achieved every one of my professional goals, and then some," Jonathan told him. "My marriage failed because my wife cheated on me. As for middle age—I was born that way. I wouldn't know any other way to be. Kate is not a delusion, doctor. She's real. You see this wall behind me? She's real."

"Perhaps she *was* real," the doctor said gently. "Even if some person named Kate, who resembles your delusion, really lived three hundred years ago, she is dead now. You cannot possibly have seen her. Or her ship."

"What about Mike and Tim—my fishing buddies? They saw it too. How do you explain that?"

The doctor shrugged. "Most likely a trick of light and shadow and your suggestive states of mind."

"What do you mean?"

"It was after dinner. You were relaxing with your friends after a day on the water. You'd had a few drinks. You said it was raining. And what had you all been talking about? Shipwrecks in the Outer Banks . . . the sea giving up her dead. It was a trick of shadow and light, Mr. West. Nothing more."

"Even though we all saw the same thing?" Jonathan asked.

"It happens," the doctor said. "Suggestive minds. Would you be willing to explore this idea a little further?"

Jonathan knew better than to turn him down right away. Instinctively, he knew that would only make the man more determined to psychoanalyze him. "I'll think about it."

"Good," the doctor said, reaching into his pocket. He handed Jonathan his card and then took out his prescription pad. "Call my office tomorrow and make an appointment. In the meantime, I'll prescribe something that will help you sleep."

"Fine," Jonathan said. "Thanks." He folded the prescription around the card and led the doctor out to the living room.

"Good news, Mrs. West," Dr. Nelson announced. "Your husband has agreed to start therapy with me."

"Thank you, doctor. That's wonderful," Patrice replied

crisply, as if they were discussing a recalcitrant child. "Would you mind waiting in the car with the girls while I have a word with Jonathan?" When they'd gone, she turned to her husband. "I'll ask this only once," she said. "I want you to come home and see a doctor in Baltimore before it's too late for us."

"It's already too late, Patrice. I'm sorry."

For a moment she didn't say anything, and then: "Will you at least agree to wait on the divorce until you've had a few sessions with Dr. Nelson?"

"Sure," he said. "Why not?" She seemed satisfied with that answer—at least satisfied enough to leave. He didn't really care about a divorce. Any ties between him and Patrice were already severed; a divorce, at the moment, would be just a piece of paper. He'd be damned, however, if he'd be psychoanalyzed by some quack his wife had found. Maybe he'd take the pills the doctor had prescribed, though. He could do with a little sleep.

But first, he wanted to touch base with Mike and Tim. He wanted to put them on standby so they could tell the doctor, and his wife and maybe his daughters, that he was not out of his mind, that they had also seen the ghost ship and its lonely passenger.

"Mike—hey, Mike!" Jonathan almost shouted with joy when Mike picked up on the first ring. He hadn't been so lucky with Tim. "I need to see you guys—you and Tim. I tried to call him but his phone keeps dumping me into voicemail."

"Oh. You don't know," Mike's voice was hoarse, as if he'd been crying.

"Know what?" A knot of dread curled in Jonathan's gut.

"Timmy's . . . he's gone, man."

"Gone? What do you mean?" But Jonathan already knew.

"We were trying to call you. Me and some of the guys. Timmy's dead, Jonathan. That little Cessna that took a nose dive, a few days ago? He was on it, man. He and some other guys leased it. They were on their way to the NASCAR races in Tennessee."

There was a moment of silence as Jonathan tried to take it in. "Oh . . ." he said slowly. "No . . . I didn't know. I haven't seen the news lately."

Tim was dead. By comparison, what Jonathan was going through seemed trivial.

"The funeral was today," said Mike.

"Oh . . . I'd have been there if I'd known," said Jonathan.

"I know, buddy," Mike said. "I'm sure Tim knows it too, wherever he is."

"Yeah."

"So . . . what's going on with you, anyway?" Mike asked. "Why aren't you answering your phone? And you never seem to be at your office."

Jonathan mumbled something about Patrice and the divorce. "Things are kind of in turmoil at the moment," he said, anxious to get off the phone.

Mike, in the way of men, mumbled some awkward commiseration.

"So," Jonathan ended it, equally awkward. "Sympathies to the family. Thanks for letting me know, Mike."

Chapter Nineteen

Onboard the Royal Thomas
Early Winter, 1719

Shortly after our arrival in Isle Saint Marie, Fournier had me installed in a house some distance from town. As he'd pointed out that day, there was not much in the way of law and order in the bustling port city. He had joked he would be too busy preventing some other pirate from stealing all he had (including me, as if that were possible) to do much to increase our holdings. Convinced of Malaika's diagnosis that I was with child (as my own body soon confirmed), he insisted I stay safe at home while he looked for ways to increase our fortunes.

"I do not take orders from any man," I told him with a scowl. I had no intention of playing the invalid while waiting for our child to be born.

"Have no fear, Kate. I'll do no more than cause trouble for any slavers I see, and perhaps relieve a few Mecca-bound pilgrims of their purses. You won't miss much."

No matter how I protested, Fournier would have it no other way. I was left to keep house with Malaika and make tiny garments while waiting for the babe to come, and for my Falcon to return to me. And he always did return.

After every excursion we would talk about our plans for the future. "One more trip and I'll have enough put by that we can retire from this life," he'd say. "We can go anywhere, Kate. To the New World, perhaps. To New York or Boston.

I could run a respectable business there. Or maybe we could carve a great plantation out of the wilderness. We can go where no one can find us unless we allow it."

"And you would be happy with so quiet a life?" I asked him.

"Indeed I would," he always assured me. "Pirating is for younger men. We have the little one to think about now. I want my child to grow up in a house, not a ship, with the honor and pride that a loving father can instill in a son."

"Or a daughter," I said.

He drew my hand to his lips and kissed the tips of my fingers. "Or a daughter," he agreed tenderly. "Gossip in port is that the kings of both our countries are losing patience with the likes of us. In time they will put rout to us all."

At that, I was alarmed. "Are we not safe here, then?"

"For a while—perhaps a year or two. But we shall be well away before then."

Marcus did not remain long with us, after we arrived in Isle Saint Marie. Now that he'd seen me to safe haven, he told me, he was leaving.

"My duty be to your father now," he said. "I must make my way back to Queen Anne's Creek and let him know how you fare, and that you're bein' looked after. You are happy, lass? Truly happy?"

"Indeed I am, Marcus," I assured him. I gave him a big smile and a letter to take with him, to give to my father. "Tell Papa how much I miss him."

Watching Marcus walk away, I was homesick for a moment. *Maybe someday*, I thought, *I will be able to go back and see Papa again, and my dear Bertha*. I would not allow such poignant memories to linger, however, for I was determined not to let anything spoil my happiness. Fournier was at home that day and sensing my mood as he often did, he swept me into his arms and held me close, comforting me as no other could.

Some of my crew signed on with Fournier, to sail with him aboard Devil's Revenge. Others were content to gamble, drink, fish and enjoy more amorous pursuits with the many congenial women they found in our new domicile. Still others stayed aboard the Royal Thomas and did all necessary repairs, making sure she would be sea worthy as soon as I was able to sail. All had assured me that when the day came, they would be ready to serve with me again.

Malaika quickly mastered enough English to take full charge of my life and she and I learned to communicate. The little garden we planted thrived in the tropical climate and she saw I had plenty of fresh food and exercise every day, disappearing like a wraith if Fournier was about, or offering me cheerful companionship if he was away.

When Fournier was in port, we led merry lives indeed, doing nothing in particular but everything together. Every day in his company and every night in his arms was time spent in heaven.

He insisted on providing me with every luxury and comfort he thought I needed. He even had my portrait painted by an artist he met in the pub, showing me in my sailor's clothing with a scarf about my head, posted at the helm of my ship.

My lover had many acquaintances and a few friends in that society of brigands on Isle Saint Marie. Among his closest associates were Olivier Levasseur (La Bouche, which means, the Buzzard) and Bartholomew Rodgers (Black Bart), and they knew him as the Falcon. Both of them, although rumored to be deadly, showed him respect—and me, as well, as the Falcon's wife. For that is what I was, in every sense of the word, in those brief, joyful days.

Occasionally we entertained Fournier's friends over dinner in our home, after which the men enjoyed a game or two of cards. Fournier was quite adept, and he taught me how to hold my own at cribbage. It wasn't long before I talked the men into letting me play. I managed to win a good amount of gold and jewels for myself, which seemed to amuse them all no end.

When my Falcon was not at sea he was always at home. He did not linger in town even long enough to have a draft of ale with his crew when they returned from a voyage. Fournier was with me when I went into labor, and Malaika took charge completely, even shooing him out of the room when he got in her way. The birthing went easily—as easily as such things can go, I'm told. It was primarily, I think, due to this amazing woman. The tea she made with roots and herbs she found in the jungle eased my pain and seemed to speed things along.

My daughter arrived in good health, loudly announcing her entry into the world—which delighted her proud papa. We named her Islamorada, calling her Mora for short, and she was but two months old when the news reached us that Blackbeard was dead. Captain William Maynard of the British Royal Navy had caught up with him in Ocracoke Inlet. The evil Mr. Teach suffered two dozen wounds to his person before one of Maynard's crew slit his throat—and then placed his severed head on the ship's bowsprit for the voyage to Virginia.

There was a big celebration in Isle Saint Marie. Many a sailor wanted to drink a toast to one of the greatest pirates of all time. Others, myself among them, were relieved at the unexpected stay of execution. A sudden burst of freedom swept across my soul as I rejoiced at the news. Tending our babe, Malaika sat on the shore and watched as my lover and I frolicked in the ocean like children.

It was about that time, also, that Marcus returned to Isle Saint Marie with news of my father, informing me that Papa had lost favor with King George.

"The king has rescinded his permission for Captain Russell to be a privateer," he told me.

"What does that mean?" I asked. "I doubt my father has any need to continue that endeavor. Nor has he, for some time."

Marcus frowned. "It means, lass, the crown can have him hanged for a pirate any time it wants. Don't really matter if he's through with the life or not," he said. "Perhaps now, with Teach done for, it'd be safe—and wise—for you to venture home."

"But what about Sir David? He's out there somewhere. I wager he would be eager for retribution if we crossed paths."

"'Tis rumored he be haunting the coast of France, lookin' for the Falcon—and word is he's too busy chasing pirates to bother with the colonies," Marcus said. He paused for a moment before adding, "I think your father needs you, lass."

"Of course," I agreed. Fournier and I made plans to go immediately but he insisted on making one more run with the Devil's Revenge, in order to supplement our growing reserves. I argued against it. A sudden foreboding came to me, as if I knew some disaster would befall him.

As I stood on the landing with him, holding him tightly, my eyes filled with tears I could not forestall. "You must take every caution," I told him. "The babe and I—we cannot do without you, Fournier."

He laughed at my fears and gathered me in his arms. "I will be careful," he promised. He kissed me with a passion I shall never forget, and then added tenderly, "Have no fear, Kate. I will always find my way back to you."

But Sir David Chatham, in command of his new vessel, HMS Lyme, intercepted Fournier at sea, as my lover was making his way home. There was a bloody battle, according to Jamie and One-Eye, who were among the few survivors. They are the ones who brought the news to me that Fournier had been taken.

"But 'e give us a message for you, Cap'n Kate," said

Jamie. "Yer to make fer Nassau an' wait for 'im there."

"If 'e don't come to you within a fortnight, then you're to head home—to Queen Anne's Creek," One-Eye took it up. "Seems Chatham be headin' fer England so the Falcon can be tried in public, to make an example fer us all."

"There's more," Jamie finished. "He said if that comes to pass, he will find a way to escape and go to you in the New World. An' he will too, knowin' the Falcon."

And so, I headed for home, taking the same route back I had sailed with Fournier. With the goods and gold we liberated from Sir David and what the Falcon had captured since we'd arrived in Isle Saint Marie, we had amassed quite a fortune. Marcus saw to the loading of that, as well as food and livestock for the journey to Nassau.

I was desperately worried about Fournier but having the babe to look after gave me great comfort and hope. When we reached Nassau, I sent two of my men into Old Fort, to make sure there were no British around.

We couldn't have asked for a warmer welcome than the one we got from Mr. Proud and all our old friends at his pub. They toasted the health of the little one and commiserated with me over the Falcon's untimely capture. Mr. Proud installed us in the best rooms in his establishment, and when he learned that Malaika was quite an accomplished cook, he commandeered her services for the kitchen. He paid her handsomely, and she ran the kitchen like the king's best drill sergeant, and within a day or two, the bar and the room registry as well.

I was in agony, waiting for word from Fournier, and when I wasn't worried half out of my mind, I was bored. That is likely why I turned to my grandfather's logbooks. I had heard stories all my life about a treasure he had hidden somewhere. It was supposed to be a king's ransom in gold and jewels but I had never put much store in it. I couldn't see the logic in hiding a treasure to go back for later, instead of taking it directly home.

In reading his logbook, I realized that there was something to those stories after all and I decided I would try to find it. When I told Marcus I wanted to go exploring I could see the concern in his eyes.

"Are you sure, Kate?" he asked. "It could be dangerous to go wandering about wi' the babe."

"Malaika will look after her," I told him. "She will be all right without me, for a few hours." I had already found a wet nurse in the person of Mr. Proud's buxom daughter whose little boy was close to weaning age, and who assured me she had milk enough for two. "Come, Marcus," I wheedled. "We must sojourn here for two weeks, in any case. While we wait for Fournier, I want to follow my grandfather's path—walk in his footsteps. I want to see if I can find any of his markers. If we find his treasure, there will be a share for every man in the crew."

"We'll take One-Eye as well," said Marcus. "And we must be back by nightfall. Best not to linger in the jungle after dark—and wear yer cabin-boy duds, lass."

As I set out with my small party, my spirits lifted a little. I'd been sick with worry about Fournier all the way from Isle Saint Marie to Nassau but returning to the place we'd met seemed to renew my faith in him. He said he would escape and come to me, and so he would. I had to believe that. We had already surmounted nearly impossible odds, and I was convinced we would weather this latest storm as well.

I knew Sir David was no match for the Falcon. Fournier would be watching for any opportunity to get free and I had to believe that somehow, he would. Perhaps it was the optimism of youth that made me eager for exercise and adventure and I looked forward to a foray into the brush. My grandfather's journal had been quite specific. If I could find his markers, I might very well find the legendary treasure he had hidden.

Although hot and humid, there was a strong wind blowing, and I was quite comfortable as we headed away from Mr. Proud's tavern and into the jungle. The tropical breeze did wonders for my soul. Above us, we could hear birds calling out to each other from their nests in the crevices of the rocks.

One-Eye insisted on taking the lead. "I can get you rightly through," he boasted. "I spent many a year in Cartagena pushing through the undergrowth. I know the dangers 'at be lurking in there. Never fear, Cap'n Kate. I'll do 'e well."

"My faith in you is absolute," I assured him and turned my attention to the landscape, looking for the markers. The first one would be a grotto, which I should recognize by the appearance of thick cacti in the underbrush. When I spotted it, I called out, "There! Take care getting through!"

One-Eye and Jamie hacked through the thick brush as Marcus, Oliver and I followed. Taking great care, we made our way into a clearing where we came upon a rock formation so unlike the landscape it seemed completely out of place. At the base of one of the rocks—most of which were bigger than every man in our party—I spotted some marks and stooped to examine them. They looked as if they had been chiseled into the stone, perhaps with a dagger. Brushing dirt and leaves away, I recognized my father's flag, also carved into the stone—the flag that had first been my grandfather's. Beside it, engraved roughly in the rock, was an arrow.

"This is it," I announced, excited at my discovery. "This is the intended course."

My men caught my enthusiasm. We walked in the direction the arrow pointed until we reached the edge of a cliff and found ourselves suddenly at the top of a powerful waterfall. It descended for about three hundred feet.

"We must descend alongside the waterfall," I said, looking around at my men who regarded me hesitantly. I suspected it was due to my fair sex—but I would have none of that. "What are you waiting for?" I demanded. "Drop the lines!"

Oliver scratched his bald head. "Are you sure, Cap'n Kate?" he asked. "It won't be easy. And it ain't been that long since the babe come—"

"I am fully recovered, thank you!" I snapped. "Drop the lines!"

Marcus exploded with laughter. "You heard the captain, ye bilge-suckin' vermin," he ordered. "Cast down the lines and be quick about it!"

They joined in his mirth and got busy. As soon as the lines were secured Oliver started down. When he got to the waterfall's basin, I scampered down like a monkey on a vine. As a child I had often climbed the ropes on Papa's ships so I was not in the least intimidated.

"What now?" asked One-Eye. "Which way, Cap'n?"

"We follow the rocks—this way!"

The spray from the rushing water was cool and refreshing and provided us much relief from the tropic heat. The rocks were wet and slippery, and white, foamy water flowed around them. We managed to keep our footing and walked on, following the line of boulders, which took us up again. Soon we were standing on a cliff on the other side, looking down once more at the waterfall's basin.

"Do you see any other markers, Captain?" asked Oliver.

"There's naught else here," said Jamie. "We've come to the end, I think."

But I could not accept it. The markers we had found were there for a reason. Suddenly I recalled something my father had told me, many years before.

If you don't understand what you are seeing, then close your eyes and imagine what you think you should *see and the truth shall be revealed.*

I closed my eyes and tried to form a picture in my mind. What should I be seeing, I asked myself. What clue had my ancestor left behind? There had to be another marker down there. But where? And what? The first one had contained the emblem on my grandfather's flag.

Then it came to me. I opened my eyes and pointed to the rushing, thundering water pouring down into the basin below.

"There," I said. The men all looked around, clearly puzzled. "Don't you see—down there," I said. "We were standing *within* the next marker. This—the shape of this little grotto, with the waterfall—it's a giant-sized version of my father's insignia, which was also my grandfather's. It's the heart and dagger inscription we see on all his flags!"

"Aye," said One-Eye, cocking his head and squinting his one eye. "I see it now, clear as daylight—and we don't have much of that left. But you be right, Cap'n. That's got to be the place."

"We need get back down there and go through the waterfall," Marcus interjected. "There must be a cave or cavern or some'at back there."

With Marcus leading the way, we all passed through the cold, thundering water. I feared the force of it would sweep us all into the current, but we made it to the other side and found ourselves in a shallow cave. I noticed a narrow opening at the back. At that distance, it appeared too small for us to pass through.

"Look there!" I said. "Mayhap it opens into another cave." I went first, turning sideways. I realized it was much wider than it appeared. "Come through," I called out to the others. "Be careful—the rocks are sharp as razors! Suck in your bellies, boys, or the edges will slice you like a roasted pig."

One-Eye was the last to squirm through the tight space, and indeed, we were standing in another cave, much bigger than the first.

"Light the torches," I ordered. I saw the spark of the flint and then they flared into life. "Make your way slowly, lads," I warned, but One Eye was eager for treasure and moved ahead of me. Suddenly he dropped out of sight, disappearing completely.

"One-Eye?" called Oliver. "Where the blazes did ye go, man?"

"Down here!" came his cry below us. He had fallen into a hole. We followed the sound of his voice, careful lest the same fate come to the rest of us.

"Are you well?" I asked. "Any bones broken, mate?"

"A little bump on me head," he said. "Other than that, I be blind as a bat down 'ere wi' no light. Pass me down a torch, if you please, Cap'n!"

Oliver lit another torch and dropped it down, illuminating the cavern enough to reveal a line of wooden torches affixed to the wall.

"What do you see?" I called.

"Better come down an' ave a look for yerself," he replied soberly.

Oliver and Jamie passed another line down and as soon as I reached One-Eye he raised the torch high. Turning slowly, I looked around.

"What is it, Kate?" asked Oliver. "What do ye see?"

"I . . . I'm not sure," I replied, trying to take it in. "It looks like a dozen or so corpses sitting down here around the remains of a campfire. Better come down, Marcus."

"You need me, Cap'n?" asked Oliver. "I could find somethin' to secure the rope and come down."

"No," I said. "No need. Stay where you are so you can pull us up." Marcus scaled the rope and landed with a soft thud at my feet. One-Eye was walking around the circle of skeletons.

"What do you think?" I asked Marcus. "Who could it be?"

"It is your grandfather," he replied thoughtfully. "An' as far as I can see, these be some of 'is crew."

"Oh . . ." I could hardly believe it. I lowered my head, reverently, but for only a moment.

"Don't look as if it were a violent passing," he went on. He took the torch from One-Eye and held it closer to the remains. "Looks to me like they were making their own grog. That be my guess. Or perhaps your grandfather poisoned the rum, to do away with any witnesses to where his treasure is stashed. They let it boil a bit too long and the fumes got to him, too."

"Which one is he?" I asked, moving closer. "And how do you know it's my grandfather?"

He pointed to the one lying on a slab of stone. He was fully dressed and still had a sword in one hand. Plumes of feathers streamed from in his hat, now interwoven with cobwebs and spider eggs, his voice silenced for all eternity in this peculiar tomb of pirate brotherhood.

"This one here," said Marcus. "He's wearing that vest of his—I'd know it anywhere. The one he would never remove. That's him, lass. I'd swear me life on it. That vest is one of a kind."

"He never took it off?" I asked. "I wonder why. Draw closer with the torch." In its flickering light I could see the vest was made of a hard leather and engraved with the compass headings my ancestor had burned into it. "Look," I pointed out. "It links the islands together like . . . like a map! I think these are the coordinates we need to follow. It's a code, for where he hid everything! That's where the treasure is!"

"Indeed, lass," said Marcus. "You could be right."

"Let's get it off him," I ordered.

As One-Eye removed the vest, I saw the glint of something shiny within the bony grasp of the skeletal hand. Marcus pried it open to reveal the twin of the necklace my father gave to me when I left Queen Anne's Creek.

Indeed, the necklace was almost identical to the one my father had given my mother, and then to me. Only the small gold sabers that crossed the ruby were slightly different. The hilts of the swords had red gold stripes running through them.

"It *is* him," I said, my voice tight with unspent emotion. "My grandfather."

"And he's left 'e a legacy, it seems," said Oliver.

We were all quiet for a moment before I continued, "Marcus, promise me that should anything happen to me before we reach home, this necklace and all my ship's logs will be passed on to my child."

Marcus looked square into my eyes. "Aye, aye, captain! That I'll make sure of, if I am still breathing and walking in me boots. Now, we'd best be gettin' back. Nightfall will soon be upon us an' the little one will be crying for her mama. What say you, Cap'n Kate?"

I nodded. We all climbed the rope and left the cavern, gathering brush to stack around the entrance to conceal the site of the tomb. Once back at Mr. Proud's, I gathered my baby in my arms and bade Marcus follow me. We took the vest to my room for further examination, and Malaika brought us something to eat. Then Marcus waited patiently, smoking a pipe in the kitchen with her, while I fed little Mora. When she was full and content and once more asleep, I asked Marcus to join me again, in Mr. Proud's parlor. There I spread the vest out on the table. Beside it, I opened my maps.

"We must discover what this means," I said. "The symbols on the vest must have meaning or he would not have taken so much trouble."

"Aye," Marcus admitted. "I do see the reason in that,"

Something else on the vest caught my eye. "Marcus, look—this spot appears to be burned twice over. Mayhap he changed his mind and tried to make it obscure." I thought for a moment and then it occurred to me. "If I lay this spot directly in line with the compass facing south instead of north, the arc it forms aligns with the Leeward Isles."

He studied the vest and the map for a moment. "You be right, lass. I see it as well."

As Marcus moved the lantern closer to the map, I ran my hand over it. My right thumb caught on something sharp and instantly the vest was stained with my blood.

"You've cut yourself, lass," said Marcus.

I sucked the small wound for a moment and leaned closer, along with Marcus, to see what had caused it. The vest had been constructed of two layers, both leather. Something glistened from a small perforation in the outer layer— something I had not seen before. With my dagger I removed the object and held it up for Marcus to see.

"This was placed intentionally," I said. "It's an emerald, like the ones in my necklace, with the same cut and color."

Oliver observed more closely where the stone had been. "Captain—look," he said. "He placed it on the map as our heading. I think he be speakin' to us from his grave. Think you that's where we must go?"

"I am sure of it," I said. "That's where he hid his treasure. When you sailed with him, Marcus—was it ever to the Leeward Isles?" Marcus nodded and I went on, "Was there a place he favored, to drop anchor?"

"Aye captain," Oliver said. "There was indeed."

"How long do you think it will take us to get there?" I asked.

"That be three days from here, without any bad weather— maybe longer if the winds be not in our favor."

We waited another week but there was still no word from the Falcon. It was time to go home. I asked Malaika if she wanted to make the voyage with us to look for the treasure, and then all the way to the new world, but she chose to stay with

Mr. Proud, who had become quite fond of her. Word came to us that the British navy was also moving toward the Leeward Isles, so I decided we would make straight for the colonies. It was sad, I thought. I couldn't go and look for the treasure, but little Mora's welfare was uppermost in my mind.

As we left Old Fort, I shouted orders to my crew. "Raise the main sails! Keep the moon to the stern, winds to your backs and the devil in the seat of your pants. Let's make quick time getting out of this harbor! We're goin' home, boys—we're goin' home!"

Chapter Twenty

Mid Summer, 2015
Outer Banks, NC

Jonathan got the prescription filled but he didn't call Dr. Nelson's office to make an appointment. He Googled the drug and seeing that it was harmless enough, he took two pills that night, washed them down with beer and watched some innocuous sit-com rerun on TV until he went unconscious. It was a relief to finally get some sleep. To have a brief respite from Kate and her sad, imploring eyes. And from trying to figure out what the hell was going on.

When he allowed logic to creep in, he knew he couldn't have traveled back in time, through some mysterious light coming out of Kate's sea chest. He hadn't really been with Kate on her ship, in her cabin, holding her in his arms. He couldn't have been.

But he was.

He also knew, logically, that he couldn't be seeing her almost everywhere he went, dogging his every step. But he was tired of arguing with logic. The pills, at first, gave him a little relief. Sleep, sweet sleep with no haunting dreams to startle him awake, refreshed him. But after a week of not dreaming about Kate (in fact, not dreaming at all) he realized he missed her. He threw the pills away.

Desperate to feel her presence again, he lifted the lid of the sea chest, hoping in vain that the oval of light would open for him. He took the necklace out and peered into the large ruby, centered in its frame of emeralds, as if he would find answers there. He studied the leather vest engraved with carvings that held secret the location of Kate's treasure. Unable to wait any longer he called Roger Barclay to see if the special vacuum dryer at the university had performed its miracle.

"Hey, Jonathan," Dr. Barclay greeted him. "It's done. Those few pages you haven't been able to read—they're pretty clear now. There are only two more entries. When can you get over here?"

"Now." Impatient, Jonathan drove as fast as the limit would allow. As anxious as he was to see Kate's words again, spooling across the page in her bold hand, he didn't want to share the moment with anyone. He thanked Barclay and promised to call him if he found anything else. He waited until he was home to open the journal.

☦☦

At sea, onboard the Royal Thomas
Early Winter, 1719

Once we left Nassau, our journey across the ocean to the colonies was without incident, except for my discovery of my grandfather's secret journal.

It was a glorious day and we were midway through the voyage. I had just changed the wee one's nappy and got her all cozy and comfortable when a sudden lurching of the ship made me reach out to steady myself. My cabin wall seemed to give way beneath my hand and I looked to see that at my touch, a secret compartment had sprung loose. Eagerly I pulled it open and inside found a small sea chest. Within that, I found my grandfather's journal. Excited, I leafed through it quickly. It contains a full accounting of his pirating days, including an

*inventory of the treasure he had hidden—which was a king's
ransom. I determined then and there that someday I would go
back and retrieve it. It would secure my family's future for
many generations.*

The other entry Kate made a few days later:

*At sea, onboard the Royal Thomas
Early Winter, 1719*

*The nor'easter approaches us rapidly. I have never
encountered such ferocious weather in all my life. I fear for the
fate of my crew, my vessel, my child and myself, as the waves
are now coming over the decks and filling the bilges. I have
lost most of my sails and I fear the main mast will crack under
the pressure of the winds. If that should happen, I will have
only the forward spinnaker left with which to navigate.*

*We are very close to home now, but not far enough north
to make entry into the bay where we can gain safe harbor, and
the storm continues to drive us off course. I know from my
father's stories (and now his father's log) that I must keep a
distance from the shoals as I approach the Carolina coast, else
we shall end up a pile of wrecked timbers. Some instinct has
compelled me to wrap a few items in oilcloth—my necklace,
a portrait of myself and my parents, the leather vest that is
really a map—and place them in the sea chest. I had One-Eye
coat the outside with tar so that if the storm prevails, these few
things, so dear to me, might survive and lead Fournier to my
grandfather's treasure, and to the watery grave I will share
with our child.*

*Oliver has just come down. He scooped up my little
dog Stewie and stowed him inside his shirt, which he tucked
securely into his trousers. Then he told me I'd best lash the
babe to my side, as the weather is deteriorating rapidly. That*

done, I will take my place at the helm of the Royal Thomas and pray that she is—that we all are—strong enough to bear the storm."

And that was all. Her entry came to an abrupt end. The last few pages in her journal were blank.

Little by little, as the days wore on and the grogginess from the pills wore off, Jonathan felt Kate drawing near again, and again he was catching brief glimpses of her. She was so beautiful, with long red hair and eyes that reached down into his soul. He wanted her as he'd never wanted another woman, never mind that actually having her was impossible. From the moment he'd seen her on the ghost ship and their eyes met, he was connected to her.

So, he thought, logic be damned. Something deeper, more compelling than logic told him it was no coincidence that her ship had gone down somewhere along the coast, near the house he'd bought in order to be close to her. He might never know what their connection was, but he knew she wanted something from him. And he had to help her. It was all tied to the Royal Thomas, he knew, which had to be very close. If he could find it—find her—he would know what to do.

As anxious as he was to get on with his search, he realized it was crazy to take the boat out alone. In the end, he asked Dave, the first mate on Captain Harv's fishing boat, to help him out. Dave wasn't nosy. He didn't care about Jonathan's agenda and wasn't likely to ask questions, and he was happy— or at least less grumpy than usual—about getting the extra work.

On a couple of dives, as Dave steered them out to sea, Jonathan spotted a ship on the horizon—an old, three-masted schooner—only to blink and find it gone. Occasionally he had moments of rational thought when he considered that maybe (probably) there was something *really* wrong with him. What had been a chance sighting on a stormy night while hanging with his fishing buddies had now become a full-blown obsession, and it had taken over his life. Then reason would retreat into his subconscious and Kate would move in. At those times, she was as real to him as Patrice. Or Mattie.

He didn't mention the ship, or Kate, to Dave. Sensible, down-to-earth Dave would try to get him to check into the loony bin for sure.

Jonathan plotted a course to the Outer Banks from Kate's last known location, according to her own logbook. He was focusing on a length of the North Carolina coastline as the most likely place her ship would have gone under. Although it covered hundreds of miles, some instinct told him to start with the shoals just off Corolla. On his dives with Dave, he looked for clues, mainly a grouping of ballast stones in the shape of a ship. Even if the Royal Thomas had decayed around them, he knew, they would mark the spot where she had sunk.

He'd found them on his last dive, and that morning he was in the living room on his laptop—the dining room could no longer contain all his notes and maps and artifacts—zeroing in on the new location and mapping out a new grid when the television suddenly clicked on.

Strange, he thought, since he didn't remember setting the timer—and since the channel abruptly changed, by itself, to a shopping channel Jonathan never watched. As he looked around for the remote, the channels started changing again, faster and faster, before stopping at a local station where a news bulletin was scrolling across the bottom of the screen:

Happening Now: Ghost Ship Sighting on Our Shores.

Jonathan found the remote and turned the volume up. Tongue in cheek, as if she were poking fun at a UFO sighting, the reporter admitted that more than one caller had seen it— the ghostly apparition of an old three-masted ship. It had appeared just off the coast (she went on more seriously), in a fog bank after the recent stormy weather. Then she got even more serious, saying a viewer had captured a few seconds of it on his phone. Jonathan recognized it immediately. Silvered translucent, shrouded in fog and backlit by moonlight, it had triple high-def detail. It was the Royal Thomas.

Kate was sending a message directly to him. She was close. He called Dave and set up a dive for that afternoon.

It was fair when they headed out and Jonathan's mood was lighter, more hopeful than it had been in a while. In what seemed an instant, however, the weather turned and a squall came out of nowhere. Jonathan had already made two dives and wanted to do one more but Dave insisted they go back. Waves were swelling almost level to the deck and the wind gusted around them.

"Looks like we're headin' into somethin' real bad," Dave shouted above the storm. "We need to go back."

"Yeah, okay," Jonathan shouted. And then he saw it.

The Royal Thomas, coming out of a ghostly mist, was heading straight for them. He glanced at Dave, wondering if he was seeing the same thing. Like Jonathan, he was looking right at it—but he turned his face away.

"Did you see it?" Jonathan demanded. "Did you see the ship?"

"I didn't see nothin'!" Dave yelled over the wind. "Come on, Jonathan! Let's head 'er back!"

A large wave crested at the bow, pouring over the deck and knocking Dave down. Jonathan grabbed him and lifted him. Somehow they managed to stay upright.

"We're goin' back," Dave said sharply when the water receded. "Now!"

"No!" Jonathan protested, pointing at the Royal Thomas. "It's coming—don't you see it? We have to wait!"

But Dave was already bringing the boat about. Jonathan kept his eyes on the ghost ship. Its phantom sails were billowing, spreading like the wings of a giant demon—and it was bearing down on them.

"Dave!" Jonathan yelled. "You're looking right at it! Don't tell me you can't see that!"

"Told you, Yankee—I don't see nothin'! We're goin' back!"

Jonathan couldn't go back. Not yet. Not when Kate was so close. The ghost ship was right there, in front of them, whether Dave would admit it or not. He'd never have another chance like this. He couldn't bear to lose her—not when he was so close to finding an answer. He jumped into the water without oxygen tank or face mask. He went deep, very deep . . . deeper than his jump should have taken him . . .

It was the first time in his life he had ever been truly terrified. His lungs were burning, bursting, begging for air. Struggling, fighting, reaching out for release, he knew there was nothing he could do. He was completely helpless. The ocean would decide his fate . . . or the ghost ship . . . or Kate.

What had he been thinking, to jump into the sea in a storm? The knowledge that he was going to die came to him with sudden clarity. It calmed him for a moment—long enough for him to be certain he wanted to live. He fought against the current, trying to swim in the direction he thought was up, toward the surface.

Time seemed to slow down. Gradually, he became aware of a presence next to him. He glanced around and saw it was Kate, smiling at him as long auburn tendrils of her hair floated weightless in the water around her, caressing her face.

And then some force was pushing him up . . . up . . . until his head was out of the water and he was gasping big gulps of wonderful, blessed air. The ghost ship was still with him, just a few yards away in the fog bank, and it looked surprisingly solid. The water around it was eerily calm. Swimming slowly over, he found a line trailing in the water beside the hull and was able to climb aboard, at the stern. Once on deck, he saw clearly who was at the helm.

Kate.

As he walked toward her, the ship lurched and rocked as if trying to shake him off. Somehow he held on. Reaching her at last, he grabbed the wheel to steady himself and his hand covered hers. He was shocked to feel warm, real flesh beneath his own—not the skeletal hand of some spectral wraith. As they drifted deeper into the mist, her face turned up to his and he was able to look into her eyes.

⸷⸷

One Week Later
Outer Banks, NC

Staring into the full-length mirror in his bedroom, Jonathan could hardly believe the transformation. His gaze shifted momentarily to the newspapers scattered on the bed, and on the floor beside it. The photograph on the front page showed him in a shallow pool of water on the beach, lying unconscious on what looked like a very big piece of driftwood. The back end of it—and one of Jonathan's feet—were buried in sand.

What was left of the Royal Thomas.

It had washed ashore on a huge wave, along with sand, shells and debris, with Jonathan clinging to it as if it was his last hope.

As soon as Jonathan went overboard, Dave had alerted the Coast Guard and the police, and they had all been out there looking for him for hours. By the time he made his miraculous appearance on the beach, the press was already waiting for rescuers to bring in his body. Newspaper and TV reporters crowded around him shoving microphones in his face.

All the photos from that day showed Jonathan as he had

been, before, with his hair and beard grown out long enough to rival that of any self-respecting pirate. Now his hair was neatly styled and he had shaved for the first time in weeks. In his tuxedo, he thought, he looked reasonably presentable, especially after almost drowning.

He didn't remember much when he came to, at least not in the first few moments. He didn't know what to make of all the reporters and the crowd of sightseers standing around him pointing to the wreckage he was lying on, and then he realized he was clutching it with all his strength. He sat up, dazed, not understanding how the glorious ship where he'd stood on deck with Kate was now just a piece of old driftwood.

Dave had been the first to reach Jonathan. After pulling him up and grabbing him in a big bear hug, Dave motioned to the EMT guys who were standing by, their ambulance at the ready. They wanted to take Jonathan to the hospital for observation and he almost went—until he heard one of the reporters say there were some marine archeologists from the university on their way to investigate the artifact. He let the paramedics check him out but he refused to budge from the scene. He was still arguing with them when Mattie showed up, pushing her way through the crowd.

"Jonathan—are you all right?" she asked as she reached him. Then turning to Dave she demanded, "What the hell, Uncle Dave? Why did you take him out in the middle of a storm?"

"Calm down, sugar baby," Dave told her. "It wasn't stormin' when we went out. You know me better'n that."

"I take it you two are acquainted," Jonathan ventured.

"He's my mama's sister's husband—never mind," Mattie answered. "What's going on? What happened to you out there?"

"You don't want to know."

"Seriously?" she asked. "More of that pirate treasure

nonsense?" He nodded and she gazed at him for a moment with something like exasperation. "Okay then," she gave in. "We can talk about that later. For now you need to get over to the hospital and get checked out."

"No," he said. "I'm fine. I want to talk to the archeologists."

Before he could say more, a TV news guy set up shop right in front of him and started his report: "An old sailing vessel—a ghost ship some viewers claim to have sighted recently—has now surfaced," he said, looking earnestly into the camera. "It happened during this afternoon's inclement weather. When the artifact washed ashore after the storm, noted architect Jonathan West was clinging to it. What makes this story so unusual is that some of our viewers have called in, claiming they've seen the ghost ship in this area, along the shores of the Outer Banks, near Kill Devil Hills." The reporter turned to Jonathan. "Mr. West, one of the paramedics says you mentioned also seeing the ghost ship while you were out there. Can you tell us what happened?"

"I don't really know," Jonathan said vaguely. "We went out diving. A storm came up and . . . somehow I went overboard. I remember . . . I spotted a ship. I managed to get on it, which is probably what saved my life. But it didn't look like a ghost ship or . . . or an artifact. It seemed real enough to me. That's all I remember."

The reporter went on to say that Dr. Roger Barclay of East North Carolina University and his team of archeologists and student interns were on their way to investigate the long-lost treasure. They would work with rescue crews to salvage the remains of what appeared to be an ancient shipwreck.

"This rare treasure is thought to be the oldest shipwreck ever found in this part of North Carolina, and may date back as much as three centuries," the reporter went on. "A significant find experts will want to study for many years to come."

There was another flurry of activity as Dr. Barclay and his team arrived and reporters rushed to them, firing questions from every direction.

"Dr. Barclay, how is it that even this much—just the hull—could survive the elements for three centuries?"

"Well," the archeologist replied slowly. "My guess is that the sand that covered it for much of that time protected it from the elements."

"What is your biggest concern for the artifact, in its current state?" asked another reporter.

"What's left of the vessel will deteriorate, now that it's exposed to the air," Barclay said. "We must act quickly. In the interest of preserving history, I'm asking the public to refrain from sightseeing or trying to take souvenirs. When we've finished with our work, the artifact will be on display at the university or in a museum in a protected environment. Everyone can get a closer look then."

His interns were already setting up yellow tape barriers to try and keep the crowd from doing any damage to the hull. The professor ambled over to Jonathan.

"Mr. West, is it true what they're saying?" he asked as he shook Jonathan's hand. "It was on the radio—and we watched it on YouTube on the way here. They're saying you were clinging to the artifact when it washed ashore?"

Jonathan nodded. "That's what they tell me. I guess I was. It's coming back to me little by little. Only—" he hesitated. He knew how it would sound.

"Go ahead, Jonathan. Talk to me."

Jonathan sighed and looked warily into Barclay's eyes but he remained silent.

"I've been privileged to work on many ancient sites," the professor went on. "I have seen things that could not be easily explained. I'll believe you."

Jonathan hesitated. He wanted to say, *maybe. Maybe*

when I know you better, when I trust you more, but that didn't ring true. Somehow he already knew he could trust this man. He actually felt more comfortable talking to him than the shrink Patrice had forced on him. But he still wasn't ready, especially with reporters and tourists looking on. He said, "No—sorry. I'm still a little foggy. That's all I remember."

Dr. Barclay nodded. "All right. Can you tell me—how did you find it? What made you pick that specific location?"

Jonathan explained his grid-mapping process and then added, "I found some ballast stones."

"Can you take me there?"

"Sure," Jonathan said. "But I want to be in on it. I want to help with the excavation or whatever you call it."

"What are you looking for, Jonathan? What has compelled you so far? Is it treasure you're after?"

"No," Jonathan said. "That isn't what—as you say—compels me. I need to find—" he stopped himself before he blurted out *her*. Instead he said, "I want to see if there are any remains. You know—of the crew, and the captain."

"The remains of whatever crew went down with the ship—it's likely the currents, or storms and shifting tides have washed them away. We might find something among the ballast stones but I wouldn't count on it."

"I'd still like to be part of your team," Jonathan told him.

"Of course."

"What's going to happen to the . . . the artifact?" Jonathan asked.

"After we've done our part, it will go to the Maritime Museum in Hatteras."

A firefighter approached Dr. Barclay then. "Any way we can help out with this one, Doc?" he asked. "We can get a backhoe in here and dig her out, if you like."

"No backhoe. No machines," said Dr. Barclay. "It's in the water at high tide, so we work at low tide. You guys can blast the sand away, from underneath the ribs—but slowly. And gently. That's where we'll put the inflatable bags."

Small waves lapped over the archeologist's rubber boots as he stood next to the eroded hull. It was his task to document the three-hundred-year-old wreck and preserve what he could before it disappeared completely. Jonathan could tell he was eager to begin.

Barclay took a deep breath before he went on quietly to the fireman, "We'll remove the sand with a teaspoon if we have to. When we have it out of the water, we'll load it onto our flatbed and take it over to the lab at the museum. We don't need a backhoe."

"Dr. Barclay?" Jonathan spoke softly as the fireman strode away. The archeologist turned and smiled at him. "Do you think it's the Royal Thomas?"

Barclay shrugged. "It could be. The wood appears to be live oak, so it could have come from the colonies. Wooden pegs held it together—not iron spikes. So far, it has all the markers. Come and have a look. It's at least as old as Blackbeard's ship—Queen Anne's Revenge."

‡ ‡

The next day, Jonathan took Roger Barclay and his team to the site where he had found the ballast stones, and Barclay let him dive with them. They found some china—almost a complete tea set—a few spoons and some gold coins among what was left of the wreckage. There was nothing else. No treasure chest and no human or animal remains of any kind.

Then, on the beach, Jonathan stuck with the team through the excavation of the artifact, even going with them to deliver it safely to the museum. That done, he went home and read through Kate's journal again. When he came upon the passage where she described losing her quill pen, he felt hot and cold and exhilarated, all at the same time. He didn't even try to hold back his emotion. He sobbed like a little child.

He realized he might never know what happened to Kate or the Royal Thomas, or whether she'd survived the shipwreck or what she'd wanted from him. Even though he still felt a strong bond between them, she was no longer haunting him. He hadn't had a glimpse of her or felt her presence since he'd washed ashore. Maybe because she knew he had tried to help her. Maybe that was enough to let her rest. And he was strangely at peace.

The doorbell chimed, and he went to answer. He'd told Mattie he could drive himself but she had insisted on picking him up, as if she'd known he would cancel at the last minute. She breezed in, some exotic, tantalizing scent wafting around her, looking even better than she smelled, resplendent in some kind of glittery designer evening dress. The only thing Jonathan knew about fashionable gowns was what he'd overheard of conversations between his wife and daughters. The only thing that registered with this one was that it had a seductive, nearly thigh-high slit up the side that showed off just enough leg.

"Wow," he said. "You look amazing."

"Thanks, Yankee," she shot back with a grin. "You clean up pretty good yourself."

"I don't suppose there's any way we could skip this ordeal? We could order some pizza and—"

"Sorry," she broke in. "Granny wants to meet you. She insists on it, in fact. It's the last time she'll be able to host the First Flight Ball—and this year it's at her place. And she wants to see your map."

"My map?" Jonathan was puzzled for a moment.

"That old map you bought at Mr. Barnacle's. And she wants to show you something. After your big adventure, I guess you need to see it."

"I don't have the slightest idea what you're talking about," he said. "What's going on?"

Mattie let out a huge sigh before she answered him. "Look, I don't believe in it—any of it—not for a minute. I've heard those tall tales all my life. Pirate treasure is one thing, Jonathan. But a ghost ship?"

"Then you explain it," he said.

"I can't," she replied. "But I'm willing to listen . . . I guess."

She had waited patiently the day Jonathan had washed ashore, and when he could finally bring himself to leave, she drove him home. He'd tried to tell her what had happened to him out there, in the ocean on the ghost ship. She had refused to listen, distracting him instead by removing her clothes, and then his. She'd wanted to make love to him and he had let her—and he'd reciprocated—and he hadn't dreamed of Kate that night. Now he needed Mattie to hear him.

"Where was I all that time?" he asked. "And how did I survive? Dave radioed the Coast Guard for help and they looked for me as long as they could before the weather got so bad they had to come in. How, after being lost in a storm, could I wash up on the beach clinging to the decaying hull of a three-hundred-year-old ship?"

He stopped, but only to pause for breath. For some reason he didn't understand, he needed to make her believe him.

"When I was on it, Mattie, it was a whole, beautiful ship— like new. A three-masted, twenty-gun, *whole* ship. Not just a hull—a *full-fledged* ship. I stood on the deck. I touched the wheel. I saw the sails filling with wind. And she was at the helm." It struck him again how much Mattie looked like Kate. "She was wearing her sailor's clothes, with a baby strapped to her side."

"Jonathan—I know you believe that's what you saw and trust me, I'm trying to get my head around it."

"It was real, Mattie. *She* was real. At first she didn't say anything, just pointed in the direction she was steering the ship. She looked at me with that same haunting, pleading . . ."

He had to stop and take another deep breath before he could go on. "Finally, she spoke. And she said one word, Mattie. She said, '*Home* . . .' How do you explain that?"

"I told you—I can't," Mattie admitted. "Only . . . you almost died, Jonathan. Maybe you were hallucinating."

"You don't believe that any more than I do."

Before she responded she looked directly into his eyes, intense and searching. "What I believe is that you believe it, and that's good enough for me. But this is all new to you, Yankee. I've been living with it all my life."

"Living with what? Why don't you just tell me what you're talking about?"

"Yeah, I will," she said. "But first there's something you need to see. Come on—we'd better not keep Granny waiting."

‡‡

When Mattie had first mentioned her granny to Jonathan he'd pictured an old woman living in a little cottage in the woods somewhere. He never imagined her home was one of the oldest, grandest mansions in Edenton.

As they pulled up and Mattie surrendered her car to the valet, Jonathan said, "That's your granny's place? Definitely not what I was expecting."

"It's beautiful, isn't it? It's over two hundred years old. You can't tell, with all the flowers and festive lights she has strategically placed, but it's in danger of falling down around her ears."

"A great place to have a party, though."

She nodded. "Usually the First Flight Ball is held in Kitty Hawk, but since Granny won't have the house much longer, the committee agreed to have it here." By then they were walking

up the stairs to the huge front door and Jonathan offered Mattie
his arm. "Thanks," she said. "Don't know if I'd make it in
these new spike heels."

"Why is she losing the house?"

"Oh, you know—our family fortunes are not what they
used to be," Mattie explained. "I don't want to sound like most
of the rednecks around here who claim they were all quality
folk before the Civil War came along. In our case, it happens
to be true. Only, we were already quality folk before that, and
pretty wealthy long after the Civil War. As the years dwindled
down, so did the money. By the time my mama was born, most
of it was gone. Granny sold off some of the land, tryin' to save
the house—even took out a mortgage on the place. Now it's
about to go into foreclosure."

A uniformed servant opened the door and welcomed them
inside. Mattie had been right about the lights and flowers.
Hundreds of silver and gold balloons floating around and
clustered in every corner took care of any faults the abundance
of summer blossoms didn't hide. In the grand ballroom,
chandeliers sparkled with thousands of lights and beneath
them, guests wearing evening gowns, black tie and early
twentieth-century flight costumes were talking, dancing and
taking advantage of the open bar.

Dave was already there and he hurried over to greet
them. He was wearing a tuxedo and a World War I aviator's
helmet and goggles. After shaking Jonathan's hand, he told
Mattie, "Granny's waitin'. She wants you to bring him into the
library—soon's you get here, she said."

Jonathan didn't know what he thought Mattie's
grandmother would be like—maybe a little old bespectacled
lady, chubby from eating her own home-baked pies and
cookies. She was the exact opposite—tall, thin and elegant—
and she was beautiful, ageless, like her amazing home. She
had all the old world charm of a southern belle with steel for

a backbone. Her flaming auburn hair, shot through with silver streaks, was done in a dramatic upsweep that accented her high cheekbones. Her large, clear eyes were as startlingly green as . . . Kate's.

She was sitting at a huge desk at one end of the library. Hanging on the wall behind her was a large oil painting of Kate at the helm of the Royal Thomas, in her pirate clothes, with the scarf tied about her head, her long hair flowing free in the wind.

Seeing his surprise, she said, "It's not the original, unfortunately. My great grandmother, who was her great-great—well, I don't know how many greats—granddaughter, had this copy done when I was a little girl." She rose from her chair and went to Jonathan. Taking his hand, she added, "I'm so pleased to meet you, Jonathan. Please call me Lenora. Mattie can't say enough good things about you."

"Don't embarrass me, Granny," Mattie warned playfully. "I don't want you givin' away my secrets."

The old woman laughed. "Darlin', why don't you go out there and help your Uncle Dave greet our guests while I have a word with Jonathan. We'll be along directly."

"Sure, Granny." Mattie gave Jonathan a quick kiss. "When I'm done with that," she told him, "I plan to monopolize you for the rest of the evening."

"That would be my pleasure," Jonathan responded, surprised to realize he wouldn't mind if it was for the rest of his life.

When Mattie and Dave had gone, Lenora turned to him. "Well, young man—I can't pick up the paper or turn on the news without seeing your handsome face. The reporters say you were on some kind of ghost ship—even though you haven't admitted any such thing."

"Yeah—well," he said, wondering why he was admitting it to her. "It's true. It happened."

She nodded. "I've seen it, you know. The ghost ship. More than once. I've had a devil of a time getting anyone to believe me."

He looked behind her, at the painting. "Is that who I think it is?" he asked. "Kate Russell, infamous lady pirate?"

"Indeed it is."

"I understand she's quite a legend around these parts. Too bad her ship went down before she could make it back."

"Oh, but she did," Lenora said. "She did make it back."

For a moment, Jonathan felt dizzy. He was having trouble breathing, as if all the air had been sucked out of the room. "How do you know?" he asked at last.

"She wrote about it, in her journals. I have them all here." She went back to her massive desk and opened one of the drawers, from which she took a stack of old books.

Jonathan was stunned. "She survived?"

"She did—along with her child and her little dog and two of her crew. They made it to shore, and she made it home."

That didn't make any sense, Jonathan thought. If she'd made it back home, then why had she been haunting him? What was it she wanted? But Lenora was speaking again, and he made himself pay attention. He didn't want to miss one word.

"She found the fortune her father had hidden away in a cave near here. Steadman left clues for her in a letter, before he was tried and hanged for pirating. It sustained our family through several generations. But in her journals, Kate wrote often of another treasure. One that she'd never had a chance to recover. I can't help thinking what good it would do now, if only we could find it. But the only map to its location sank with the Royal Thomas. It's lost forever, I'm afraid. So I'm hoping, if I can have a look at that old map you found at Mr. Barnacle's—"

"It won't help you," Jonathan broke in. "But I have

something that will." She looked at him, questioning, her eyebrows raised. "I have it," he explained. "The treasure map."

It was her turn to be surprised. "You have it?" she repeated. "Are you sure?"

"It was in an old sea chest I found," he said. "It had washed ashore. I also have Kate's logbook and one of her journals, and an extremely valuable necklace that obviously belongs to you."

Lenora rose from the desk again and went to stand very close to him. "You have her necklace—the ruby heart and saber necklace?" He nodded. "And the map?"

"It's burned into an old leather vest, which I also found inside the chest."

Healthy pink color flooded Lenora's cheeks. "Do you know what this means?"

He thought he knew but he wanted to hear it from her. "You tell me."

"It means—maybe we can use the necklace to finance an expedition," she said. "Maybe we can find the treasure. There would be a stake in it for you, too, Jonathan—if you're game. What do you say? Would you like to go on a treasure hunt? Or do you need some time to think about it?"

Jonathan grinned. He felt reenergized, bursting with new purpose. He didn't have to think about it. He knew exactly what he wanted to do.

It didn't take him long to find Mattie, who was talking to Dave and two other men. They were also dressed in black tie and vintage aviator helmets. Without waiting to be introduced, Jonathan swept Mattie into his arms and out onto the dance floor. Fortunately, it was a slow song.

"I'm about to go on the adventure of a lifetime," he whispered. "Want to come along?"

She looked up into his eyes and smiled. "Hate to admit it, Yankee," she said in her soft southern accent. "But I'm gettin' a real strong feeling I'd follow you 'bout anywhere."

He laughed and as he pulled her closer, he caught a glimpse of another woman, watching them from a corner of the room. She had red hair, with a pirate's scarf tied around her head.

It was Kate, and she was smiling.

‡‡

37114970R00173

Made in the USA
Middletown, DE
19 November 2016